D0412035

THROUGH ROSE-COLOURED GLASSES

By Anne Baker and available from Headline

Like Father, Like Daughter
Paradise Parade
Legacy of Sins
Nobody's Child
Merseyside Girls
Moonlight on the Mersey
A Mersey Duet
Mersey Maids
A Liverpool Lullaby
With a Little Luck
The Price of Love
Liverpool Lies
Echoes Across the Mersey
A Glimpse of the Mersey
Goodbye Liverpool
So Many Children
A Mansion by the Mersey
A Pocketful of Silver
Keep The Home Fires Burning
Let The Bells Ring
Carousel of Secrets
The Wild Child
A Labour of Love
The Best of Fathers
All That Glistens
Through Rose-Coloured Glasses

Through Rose-Coloured Glasses

Anne Baker

headline

First published in 2009
by HEADLINE PUBLISHING GROUP

1

Cataloguing in Publication Data is available from the British Library

ISBN 978 0 7553 5664 5

Typeset in Baskerville by Avon DataSet Ltd,
Bidford on Avon, Warwickshire

Printed in Great Britain by Clays Ltd, St Ives plc

Headline's policy is to use papers that are natural, renewable and
recyclable products and made from wood grown in sustainable forests.
The logging and manufacturing processes are expected to conform
to the environmental regulations of the country of origin.

HEADLINE PUBLISHING GROUP
An Hachette UK Company
338 Euston Road
London NW1 3BH

www.headline.co.uk
www.hachette.co.uk

Through Rose-Coloured Glasses

Chapter One

Grand National Day, Liverpool, March 1934

DINAH RADCLIFFE WAS fizzing with excitement. She'd never been to the races before and the atmosphere at Aintree was electric. It was her first afternoon out in months and she felt on top of the world, even though she and her friend Millie Hunt were pinned against the course rails by a frenzied crowd screaming encouragement to the horses. She could hear the thunder of horses' hoofs coming closer. The spring sunshine blinded her as she strained to pick out Tim Reece riding Pomeroy.

'Let's hope he's in front.' She was yelling to make herself heard above the crowd. 'It would mean so much to Tim.' The ground seemed to shake as the horses hurtled past in a bunch. She caught one glimpse of Tim wearing the owner's silks: white polka dots on a cerise background.

'He's there,' she screamed. 'Did you see him?' The horses were gone in an instant, except for two stragglers. 'Tim's not leading the field but he was well up.' Dinah could hardly get the words out she was so excited.

'Yes, yes.' Millie was jumping up and down and her ginger hair bounced. 'What a shame we can't see the winning post from here.' Those in the crowd who could roared in a tantalising crescendo.

'Has he? Has he?'

'It must have been close.' Millie's cheeks were scarlet with excitement. 'Gosh, my throat's sore with all the screaming.'

The crowd fell silent as they waited for the results board to light up.

Dinah held her breath until it came. 1st Ardwick Beauty, 2nd Pomeroy, 3rd Doubting Dan.

'He was second,' she gasped, as the loudspeaker crackled with the same news.

Dinah felt exhilarated and hot, almost as though she'd run the race herself. 'I hope he's not disappointed with that.' She was afraid he might be.

'I'm glad we backed him each way,' Millie chortled. 'We've won something, haven't we?'

Dinah and Millie were apprentice milliners working at Carlton Hats, a business making the expensive confections that ladies wore at smart weddings and fashionable race meetings. They'd had a good look round before the race started, trying to spot hats they'd helped to make. They'd seen a few, but the free passes Tim had given them didn't allow them into the areas reserved for owners, trainers and the seriously rich, so there could be many more Carlton Hats here than they were likely to see.

Dinah would have loved to see Tim and Pomeroy parade in the winners' enclosure, but their passes did not allow them to go there either.

'That was marvellous.' Millie Hunt was still jumping up and down, but it was only the second race of the afternoon. There were three more to come including the famous Grand National. Tim would be riding Flyswitch in one of them.

'Let's collect our winnings, and then have a cup of tea and a sit down.'

They headed towards the bookies' stalls, but Dinah pulled at her friend's arm. 'Look, there's a long line of punters waiting to collect their winnings. Why don't we have tea first?'

But there were also people waiting for tables in the cafeteria. While Millie queued, Dinah went to the ladies' where she found there was also a line. She could see herself reflected in the big mirrors, her cheeks flushed, her brown eyes sparkling, and her brown felt hat slightly askew. It was meant to perch on top of her head and slant forward over one eye. Beneath it, her curly shoulder-length dark hair was wind-tossed and untidy. She pulled out a comb to set it to rights before repositioning her hat.

She and Millie had spent ages trying to decide what they should wear today. They wanted to look smart. Her best oatmeal tweed coat made her look slim and tall and she'd borrowed the hat from Aunt Enid, who was no relation but her mother's best friend and Tim Reece's mother. The Reeces lived next door but one to them. Like her mother, Aunt Enid had been widowed in the Great War and they'd helped each other out with shopping and childminding ever since.

Dinah knew Tim counted himself lucky to be working for the trainer Llewellyn Digby, who was considered one of the best and owned the Rivington Lodge stable in Birkdale. It had taken Tim a long time to work his way up from stable boy, but when he had completed his apprenticeship he had been thrilled to be kept on as a yard jockey. He was twenty years old now, a year older than Dinah.

The yard had no horse competing in the Grand National this year, but Tim had been given two rides today in the supporting races that made up the meeting: Pomeroy in the two-five in which he'd just come second and Flyswitch in the three-fifteen.

Tim had been given the free entrance tickets and had intended his mother to come with Dinah this afternoon, but she hadn't wanted to.

'Saturday is my busiest day,' she had said. Enid earned her living giving piano lessons to children. 'You go, Dinah, and take a friend. Tim will be glad to have you there to watch, and you could do with a break. All you've done recently is go to work and look after your mother.'

The one blot in an otherwise happy upbringing had been her mother's illness. She'd been fighting breast cancer for the last seven years and was growing noticeably more frail. Dinah was very concerned about her now.

Millie's bright auburn hair made her easy to pick out across the cafeteria but she gave Dinah a wave just in case. She had got a table and had ordered a pot of tea and some fancy cakes.

'Wildly expensive here,' she whispered. 'But what the heck, it's our big day out and Tim's come in second.'

Millie looked unfamiliar in the blue hat she'd bought for her sister's wedding. It suited her; like Aunt Enid's, it was in the latest style. She and Millie not only worked together but spent a lot of their spare time in each other's company. Like several other girls from Carlton Hats they belonged to a cycling club and went on long trips on summer Sundays.

After tea, they went back to where the bookies were paying out. There were fewer people waiting in line now. Heavy cloud was building up and the brisk breeze was getting stronger.

Millie shivered. 'I should have worn an extra cardy under my coat,' she said.

'But we decided looking our best was more important than comfort,' Dinah giggled. 'I wish I'd worn flat heels.'

'We'll know better next time.'

'Why don't we wager our winnings on Tim's next race?' Dinah suggested. 'It's a lot more fun if we have a bet on, isn't it?'

'Yes. To win or each way?' Millie grinned at her.

Standing just in front of them was a broad-shouldered, smartly dressed man with smooth hair the colour of butter. Dinah saw him take what seemed to be a bundle of betting slips from his pocket. He was shuffling through them when one slipped through his fingers and fluttered off across the grass. He looked round and seemed shocked to see it go. Dinah ran after it and anchored it with her foot.

She picked it up as he came over, touching his grey trilby. 'Much obliged,' he said. His eyes were the colour of amber and lingered as they met hers. Then he smiled. 'Thank you. I'm glad that one didn't blow away. I think there's a payout on it. Very grateful.'

When they returned to their places in the line, Millie gripped her wrist and whispered, 'Isn't he handsome? He could be a film star. Don't you think he's like Clark Gable?'

'No, he hasn't got a moustache. He's more like Gary Cooper.'

They watched the bookie pay out on the errant betting slip. He put quite a lot of pound notes into his wallet. It seemed he'd backed the winner.

'This is the place to see the rich and famous. It's a popular pastime for them,' Millie said. 'A different world from ours. Wait till the girls at work hear about this – they're going to be so envious. I wish I could come to the races every week. With a jockey for a boyfriend, you'll often be coming to places like this.'

'He's not a real boyfriend,' Dinah said. 'He's a neighbour who I've more or less grown up with.'

'But you like him? You talk about him a lot.'

'Oh yes, he's good fun.'

Tim Reece won the three-fifteen on Flyswitch, which made Dinah's day. 'Winning is everything for a jockey,' he'd told her, and she was thrilled for him.

'It's everything for me too,' Millie giggled. 'This is wonderful fun.'

Everywhere she looked, Dinah saw a sea of excited and smiling faces. The earlier races were acting as a warm-up for the Grand National. Half the population of Liverpool wanted a bet on that race and Aunt Enid and her mother had each given her a shilling and the name of the horse they favoured to win.

'My family want me to put sixpence each way on Rombola,' Millie said, 'but they don't know anything about racing.'

'Aunt Enid thinks Golden Miller will win and Mum wants her money on Prickly Pear, but Tim reckons it will be Bombero.'

'We must put bets on for ourselves,' Millie said. 'Which horse will you pick?'

'I think I'll go for Bombero,' Dinah said as they made their way towards the bookies' stalls again. 'Tim's best placed to know what the horses can do.'

Millie changed her mind four times and it was almost impossible to move in the crowd. They could only get an occasional glimpse of the horses saddling up and parading in front of the stand while a crackling voice over the loudspeaker announced the name of each one.

'Did you see that piece in the morning paper?' Millie asked. 'It said some of the toffs are complaining about the huge crowds from the back streets of Liverpool who jam themselves into the Aintree course.'

'No, but they'll never stop us.' Dinah laughed. 'Why shouldn't we all come and join in the fun?'

As the starting time for the Grand National drew nearer, she could feel the tension growing. The crowd was going mad, the excitement building up like a wall. This time they couldn't get close to the rail; others had beaten them to the best positions.

When the shout went up, 'They're off,' they were standing on their toes in the crush, craning to get a glimpse as the horses flashed past. They circled the course twice, and there was a commentary so the crowd could follow their progress. In the last moments of the race, the crowd was screaming encouragement to the front runners and Dinah caught the name Golden Miller echoing through the crowd.

Golden Miller won. They heard on the loudspeaker that he had already won the Cheltenham Gold Cup five times.

'Aunt Enid will be delighted,' Dinah chortled. 'I'm glad she's won something – she's awfully good to Mum and me. Hurry up, let's get in line to collect her winnings. There could be a long queue.'

'Nothing for us, though.' Millie pulled a face.

'But we won on Flyswitch, and we've had a smashing day.'

The afternoon was not quite at an end for those who could get into the winners' enclosure. Still to come were the photographs, the congratulations, the applause and the presentation of the prizes. But for the Dinah and Millie and the average racegoer the excitement was over, and the huge crowd was swarming at the bus stops.

Dinah didn't mind that they had a long wait for a bus back to Walton. The queues were reliving the thrills of the afternoon and were in a jolly mood.

'I brought five shillings with me to spend,' she marvelled, 'and I'm going home with fifteen. And we've had a slap-up tea and an ice cream.'

Millie pulled a face. 'Same here, but I wish I'd put my money on Golden Miller. How did your Aunt Enid know which horse was going to win?'

'How does anybody know? She just fancied it.'

They were both tired and windblown but agreed they'd had a wonderful day out. Dinah said goodbye to Millie and got off the bus in County Road to walk the rest of the way home. Picton Street, where she lived, was in a maze of similar streets built in Queen Victoria's day to house the workers needed for Liverpool's burgeoning industries. It was a narrow street with two facing terraces of small, two up two down houses, each with a single bay window to the living room and a front door that opened straight on to the pavement. Number fifteen had been their home for as long as she could remember and she'd found it cosy in winter and sunny in summer.

Her mother smiled her welcome. Once she'd had dark curly hair like Dinah's, but it had thinned and faded. 'We've heard Golden Miller won.' She looked tired and washed-out; only her blue eyes had kept their colour. 'Gladys came round to tell us when she heard it on the wireless. Marvellous that Enid backed the winner.'

'I'm made up,' Aunt Enid said as she went to put the kettle on to make some tea. She was Dinah's mother's age but her hair was thick and a glossy brown. Her back was straight and her features strong. 'You're quite late back. Your mum was getting anxious, but now you're here safe and sound we can't wait to hear how you got on.'

'It was thrilling. I loved it.'

'Even though you didn't win?'

'We backed Tim's horses, so we did. You heard that he'd won?'

'Yes. All the racing results were announced and Gladys listens out for Tim's mounts.'

'He said Bombero would win the National. I thought he was giving me a hot tip.' Dinah handed Enid's winnings over to her.

'Just stable gossip,' his mother scoffed.

'Bombero fell at the first fence, but we had a great time. How d'you feel, Mum?'

Sarah Radcliffe looked frail and ill. 'I'm fine, love. I've slept most of the afternoon.'

'A pity your horse dropped at Becher's Brook.'

'I didn't have any great expectations,' Sarah smiled. Dinah bit her lip. That was poor Mum's lot in life.

'They say the BBC will soon be giving live commentaries on the big races.' Enid brought cups of tea in from the kitchen. She was bubbling over. 'It's been quite a day for me. Not only did I pick the winner but

I'm absolutely delighted for our Tim. First in one race and second in the other.'

'I'm sure he was thrilled to bits, but we couldn't get close enough to say congratulations. Such a crush.'

'They were talking on the wireless about the huge prize money Golden Miller won.'

'Money isn't everything,' her mother said quietly. 'We're rich in other ways.'

'Yes. We're very grateful to you, Aunt Enid,' Dinah said.

That the Reeces lived in the house next door but one meant Enid could look after her mother while Dinah was at work. She'd never asked her to; Enid had just come in and done what was needed for her mother. She was doing more and more these days.

'I only do what's neighbourly,' she said now. 'We're all in the same position, aren't we? We help each other out where we can. You've done your share of that, Sarah, over the years.'

'Well, it's been a good place to live,' Sarah answered, looking round her home.

Dinah knew that now Mum was ill, the house didn't suit them as well as it had. The stairs were steep and narrow and had a sharp turn in them which Sarah was finding hard to cope with. The only lavatory was out in the back yard, and although chamber pots were generally employed in the bedrooms during the night, Mum couldn't easily get down low enough to use one these days.

It had been Aunt Enid who'd told her that a neighbour at number thirty-six had a commode for sale for twenty-five shillings. Mrs Biddolph had bought it second-hand when her father was ill, but sadly she'd buried him the month before. Tim Reece had helped Dinah carry home the heavy, old-fashioned piece of furniture. They'd swung it between them while their younger neighbours laughed and cheered them on. It had come complete with its own large chamber pot, but they'd removed that to make it lighter.

They'd had a fit of giggles as they'd tried to get it up the steep stairs and make room for it in Sarah's room, but eventually they manoeuvred it alongside her bed and it had eased things for her.

Mum needed to lie down during the day, but they had no sofa and getting upstairs took too much out of her. Dinah had looked for a sofa in the shops but could find only three piece suites, and their living room was too small to take that much furniture. It was a local furniture shop that finally matched her up with another customer who wanted only the two easy chairs.

Dinah had gone with the customer to the shop in question to pick out the suite, and fortunately they were able to agree on the red and brown uncut moquette. Mum said the sofa had good springs and was as comfortable for a nap as her bed upstairs. Dinah thought they were still managing well.

Last year, the landlord had modernised the living room by putting in a new grate with a back boiler to give them hot water. They had no bathroom, of course, but they did have a deep sink in the kitchen and once a week they brought in the zinc bath from the back yard and filled it with hot water. At first they had both bathed in it, but poor Mum hadn't been able to do that for a while either. Dinah had to give her bed baths.

Everybody in the street was willing to help. Gladys next door at number thirteen and Flo on the other side in number seventeen were in and out all day, making cups of tea for Sarah. Flo helped with the shopping and Gladys made stews and casseroles for Dinah to heat up when she came home. Mum had plenty of company and was always well up with the local gossip. She encouraged Dinah to go out with her friends, and Dinah did so though nowadays it made her feel, guiltily, that she was neglecting her mother.

Chapter Two

At work three days later, Dinah's team had had a busy stint blocking felt crowns into the latest fashionable shape. It was hot steamy work, and after two hours the next team relieved them, allowing them to return to the main workshop where the hats were decorated and finished.

Dinah looked up to see a man come in with a confident swagger. He took off his hat, revealing hair the colour of butter.

'Could you help me?' he said to the whole workshop. 'I'm looking for Mr McKay. Where will I find his office?'

Dinah happened to be closest to the door and knew immediately that she'd seen him before. His was not a face anyone would forget. She scrambled to her feet to show him the way to her boss's office.

'I'm Richard Haldane.' He pushed a card into her hand. *Richard Cameron Aldgrave Haldane*, she read. 'I made an appointment. Mr McKay is expecting me.'

He had the polish of a man who enjoyed the best of everything; the sort of man who attracted second looks wherever he went, and every girl and woman in the workshop stopped work to watch him. Dinah found him magnetic.

He said, 'Do I know you? Haven't we met somewhere before?'

She smiled. She hadn't forgotten. 'Wasn't it at Aintree racecourse?'

'That's right. On Grand National Day.' His gaze was interested, intense; he seemed to stare right into her. When they reached her boss's office, Dinah found the door open and the room empty.

'He won't be far,' she said and stood chatting, curious to know more about the visitor. By the time Mr McKay returned to his office she felt drawn to and totally dazzled by Richard Haldane.

Back in the workshop, Millie squealed, 'It's him, isn't it?'

The other girls pointed out the smart blue Riley saloon that he'd parked outside. 'Isn't he handsome? Millie says you saw him at the races. I bet he's rich. What could he possibly want from Mr McKay?'

Dinah smiled. 'He told me he owned a business making petersham ribbons like the ones we use to decorate our hats, and that he'd come seeking a order to supply us.'

'I hope he gets it,' Millie said. 'We might see more of him then.'

The girls did not stop talking about him all day. Before they left work that evening, they noticed that his car was outside again. As Dinah came out with Millie, Richard Haldane got out of it and came towards them.

'Hello,' he said, fixing his gaze on Dinah. 'I had to bring back more samples for your Mr McKay. I hoped I might see you.' He drew her to one side. 'I'm sure you're going to think me very forward,' he said, 'but I have to say I've never seen anyone more beautiful. I feel quite bowled over.'

Dinah didn't know what to say.

'I can't rely on meeting you again at the races,' he went on, 'and I'd like to know you better. Would you come and have a meal with me? I know a good restaurant.'

'Heavens!' she said. She couldn't remember ever being taken to a restaurant, but with him it would be wonderful. 'When?'

'Now, this evening.'

Dinah felt a mess in her everyday clothes; she'd been working all day and was tired. She had an attack of cold feet. He looked too much a man of the world for her. And what about her mother?

'Sorry, I can't,' she said. 'I have to go home. My mother's ill. I picked up some new medicine for her in my dinner hour and she needs it now. Thanks all the same.' She was about to walk on to the bus stop.

'What if I drive you home? Give you time to have a wash and brush up first?'

She paused, flattered by his eagerness. 'Please,' he said. 'I won't eat you. Your Mr McKay will tell you I'm quite respectable.'

She smiled. 'His car's gone so it's a little late to ask him now.' But she let him take her arm and settle her into the front seat of his car.

She turned back to look at Millie, whose face was wreathed in smiles of encouragement. 'Good luck,' she mouthed.

Dinah had never ridden in a car before. If her friends and family wanted to go further than they could walk, they travelled by bus. It took them all their time to pay the rent and put food on the table.

Richard Haldane talked on the way about horses and horse racing. 'You enjoy it, don't you?'

She said she did, and he seemed to assume she knew as much about racing as he did. So she told him about Tim and Aunt Enid. Dinah thought they got on well together, and he was pulling up outside her house in what seemed a very short time.

'You'd better come in and say hello to my mother,' she said. They found her drowsing on the sofa. These days Sarah did little else after she'd got dressed and come downstairs.

Dinah introduced them and he said, 'I'm so pleased to meet you, Mrs Radcliffe.'

Her mum looked exhausted but he chatted on quietly and easily about how he'd met Dinah and Millie at Aintree racecourse and how his friend Mr McKay of Carlton Hats had told him how impressed he was with her work.

'He called her his brightest apprentice,' he said. 'Very hardworking and interested in everything. He thinks she'll go far.'

Dinah knew Mum loved hearing things like that about her. Then he added, 'Why don't you let me take you and Dinah out for dinner?'

'Dinner? Oh, no thank you. I don't think I can.'

'You could act as chaperon for your daughter.'

But Sarah's face was twisting with pain. She hadn't been outside for weeks, so there was really no question of her going.

'You take Dinah,' she said. 'She needs to get out more. It can't be easy for her, having me to look after.'

'Mum, I'm very happy to stay at home tonight.'

'I'll be quite all right,' Sarah said. 'Enid will come round later, you know she always does.'

'All right, but I'll pop round and tell her I'm going out anyway.'

Dinah gave her mother a dose of the new medicine and then went upstairs to change, leaving Sarah with Richard. From upstairs she could hear his voice, low and gentle, still chatting to her.

She found him hard to understand. He seemed suave and sophisticated in many ways and yet here he was, almost throwing himself at her feet. She was surprised that her mother seemed to approve of him. Dinah had expected her to make a fuss about her going out with a man she hardly knew, but poor Mum was so sick she probably didn't realise how short the acquaintance was.

Richard had implied that he knew her better than he did and that he was familiar with her boss. Dinah knew she should have corrected him, but she was thrilled to think Richard could be interested in a girl like her. Already she could feel her heart race when he smiled at her.

Having dinner at a restaurant with him was a revelation. The roast beef was delicious but it was the hovering waiters with their silver platters that impressed her. Richard was good company and seemed to enjoy it as much as she did. It was exciting and very different from anything she'd done before. But she knew nothing about him and had to ask.

'I'm a widower with two young children, a boy and a girl.'

Dinah felt a rush of sympathy. 'You've been left with young children to bring up on your own?' She knew how hard that must be for him. Mum and Aunt Enid had made no secret of the problems involved in raising a child alone.

'They've always had a nanny. She takes full charge and is very good with them, so I cope.'

He looked much older than she was and she was curious about his age. 'I'm nineteen,' she added, afraid he'd think her still wet behind the ears.

'And I'm thirty-seven,' he replied gravely, 'But you mustn't let that worry you. I enjoy being with you, and what has age got to do with that?'

Richard drove her home and kissed her when he pulled up outside her front door. She was glad it was dark and the neighbours couldn't see them. They'd have gossiped about her for a month, being brought home by car and then kissed in the street.

He whispered, 'I've lived a lot longer than you and it gives me a history. I hope that doesn't put you off?'

'No, of course not.' Nothing could put her off him now.

His kisses were urgent and pure heaven. They lifted Dinah to unimagined heights of pleasure. He had a way of running the back of his finger down her cheek that thrilled her to the tips of her toes and made her reach out to stroke his yellow hair. He was like a magnet pulling at her senses. In the dim light, she wanted to feast her eyes on him. She was still in an emotional spin when she went to work the next day, and she made a point of asking Mr McKay about him.

'He took you out to dinner?' He was taken aback. 'My goodness! I didn't know he was one for the ladies.'

'No, he isn't,' she said. 'His wife died quite recently, and I think he's lonely.'

'I know. I was quite shocked to hear about Myra. It hasn't taken him long to get over her. Oh, well, you've certainly caught his eye. I hope you aren't boxing above your weight.'

Dinah laughed. 'Course not. Richard can get down to my level; he says he works hard but he needs more orders for his factory.'

'I know. He asked me to give him one.'

'Are you going to?'

'No. Once I used to buy a lot from his factory, and there's nothing the matter with what he makes, but business is slow at the moment. All my suppliers are trying to get me to buy more. Still, if he's struck up a romantic dalliance with you, he won't feel he had a wasted journey yesterday.'

'It's not a romantic dalliance,' Dinah protested with an embarrassed laugh.

Richard had asked if he might take her out again. He brought flowers for her mother and chocolates for her. Millie and the girls kept telling her she was definitely on to a good thing. He was rich, wasn't he, as well as good-looking? And he had a lovely car.

He chatted to her about steeplechasing and flat racing.

'I'm fond of horses,' Dinah told him. 'When Tim became a stable boy at Rivington Lodge, he got me a job there on Sunday mornings, mucking out and grooming the horses. I loved doing it, but I had to give it up so I could spend more time at home. Once Mum became sick, I had to shop for food on Saturday afternoons and do the washing and cleaning on Sundays.'

'I have a couple of racehorses myself.'

Dinah was amazed. 'You mean you own them?' She knew that in Tim's world an owner was an important person. She'd known Richard was rich, but he must be very rich if he owned two racehorses.

'Yes. Ardwick Beauty and Ardwick Prince. I must take you to see them run.'

'I've already seen Ardwick Beauty,' she reminded him. 'I saw her at Aintree the other day.' Dinah remembered only that she'd beaten Tim's mount Pomeroy into second place.

'Yes, I have high hopes for Beauty. High hopes for both of them really. Prince is bigger and stronger and probably better at jumping.'

'Then why didn't you enter him in the Grand National?'

'He'd pulled a tendon in his foreleg. I'd have loved to enter him for the big race.' He gave a wry smile. 'Next year, with a bit of luck.'

'Gosh, is Prince that good?'

'I hope so. His trainer thinks he is.'

'Tim Reece loves going over the jumps. He's very ambitious, you know. He's hoping to win the Grand National one day.'

Richard's expression told her he didn't think that was likely.

'He's winning quite a lot of his races,' she told him proudly. 'Did you see him win on Flyswitch in the three-fifteen? He did it by two lengths.'

'So he did. Well, good luck to him.'

'All he needs is more experience,' Dinah said.

Richard's smile was even more wry. 'Plus the horse that jumps fearlessly and faster than any other horse in the race.'

Soon Richard was asking her out almost every night and giving her frequent gifts. He took her to places she'd never been: theatres and expensive restaurants. It was not long before he asked her if she'd like to go with him to Chester Races to see Ardwick Beauty compete for the Chester Cup.

'I'd love to.' Dinah was thrilled. That Sunday, Tim had a day off and was at home with his mother. He was very impressed when she told him where she was going.

'You'll love it. I'll be there too. I've got six definite rides over the four day meeting, including the Huxley Stakes and the Dee Stakes. I'm down as substitute for the Chester Cup, in case one of the other jockeys drops out.'

'Because they're sick, you mean?'

'It's usually because they don't make the weight.'

'What's that?'

'Well, the weight a horse carries means the jockey and his saddle and stuff, so we jockeys can't afford to weigh much or we'd never get a ride.'

'You don't weigh much, Tim.'

'I'd like to weigh less, we all would. The lighter we are, the greater the possibility of getting rides. But horses that win a lot of races are handicapped by being made to carry more weight, and then making the weight is our big problem.'

Dinah found that being taken to a race meeting by Richard was a very different experience from going with Millie. To be driven to Chester was luxurious compared with going by bus, and as an owner Richard was able to get them seats high in the grandstand. It was Cup day and there was a buzz of excitement in the air.

'It's such a pretty place,' Dinah said, feasting her eyes on the loop of the river and Curzon Park on the far bank. 'And we'll be able to see the whole race from our seats.'

Richard laughed. 'Chester is the only racecourse in the country, if not the world, where you can see top race horses and jockeys for free. The best vantage point is over there on the city walls. You can see people on them now, where the walls parallel the finishing straight of the course.'

Richard bought a racecard for her and she saw that Tim would be riding in the next race as well as a later one in the supporting programme.

'It's the flat racing season now,' Richard told her. 'The next race is run over one mile five furlongs and will be over in the blink of an eye.'

Dinah almost missed seeing Tim to begin with because he was wearing silks of a different colour. 'Why isn't he wearing white spots on a cerise background?'

'Warrington Lad belongs to a different owner. Your friend will take every ride he's offered.'

The horses were lining up at the starting line and were away in seconds. Dinah was thrilled to see Tim leading the field and winning easily.

'Not an important race,' Richard said. 'I've entered Ardwick Beauty in the next race, and Ardwick Prince will be taking on the best horses in the country. I've entered him for the Chester Cup.'

'Who trains your horses?'

'They're with Bob Watchit at his stables near Tarporley in Cheshire. Come on, I'll introduce you. He'll be in the paddock. We'll have time to say hello before the horses start saddling up for the next race.'

Bob Watchit was a burly man with an affable manner. Dinah didn't catch the name of the jockey, though she was introduced to him too.

'How d'you like my silks?' Richard asked. Dinah had heard enough about racing from Tim to know that meant the jockey's green and white outfit. 'I designed it myself.'

'It makes him stand out.'

'That's the idea. Easy to pick out as he runs.'

Ardwick Prince was a large grey colt. He was trying to nuzzle the trainer's neck. Dinah looked round for Tim, but the congratulations were over and he was riding Warrington Lad back to his stall.

'He'll be staying with the horses,' Richard said dismissively. 'He won't have time to come and chat to you.'

Dinah wished she knew more about racehorses. One looked pretty much like another to her, but Richard and his trainer were discussing their finer points, and it seemed Richard rated his horses very highly.

'There's nothing like seeing your own horse run,' he told her, his eyes glowing with enthusiasm. When the horses began coming into the paddock to saddle up for the next race Dinah was photographed between Richard and Ardwick Beauty and then he hurried her back to their seats.

'They're about to start now. Come on – I don't want us to miss this.'

Ardwick Beauty won by a head. Richard was delirious with joy. 'I knew she could do it!' he cried, almost running to the winners' enclosure to congratulate the horse, the jockey and the trainer. They were all laughing with delight, none more so than Richard when he was presented with the prize money.

He bustled Dinah to the owners' bar after that and bought champagne to toast Ardwick Beauty. They watched Tim win again, and then Richard said he was hungry and took her to the owners' restaurant for a plate of smoked salmon and prawns and other lovely things Dinah had never tasted before. Richard seemed to move in a circle that was seriously wealthy. The women round her wore fur coats and lots of jewellery. Dinah had borrowed a different hat from a friend at work, and the coat was her mother's Sunday best. Although it was four years old, Dinah felt very smart in it, though her outfit had not cost any great fortune when new.

It was almost time then for the big race of the day. Dinah could feel the tension tightening its hold and could hardly believe how excited Richard and the other owners and trainers became. As soon as they were off he was shouting himself hoarse trying to spur Ardwick Prince on. It took Dinah's breath away. Her own heart began to pound and she felt strung to fever pitch.

'He's going to win,' she screeched. No, he was being overtaken, no, he could still do it. But over the last furlong other horses swept past him, and Blue Vision won the Chester Cup. Ardwick Prince came in fifth in a field of eighteen.

'No good,' Richard spat the words out and tore up his betting tickets. 'No damn good. Damn, damn, damn. Is his foreleg still bothering him? Perhaps he hasn't quite recovered from that pulled tendon.'

Richard had little to say on the drive home. Dinah was afraid he was disappointed.

'Of course I'm disappointed,' he said. 'But I can't expect my horses to win every race. They bring the best horses over from Newmarket to compete.'

When he pulled up outside Dinah's house, his amber eyes had sparkling depths of gold and they stared into hers while his deep voice whispered endearments. Several of her neighbours were on their doorsteps watching with interest; it wasn't often a smart car came down their street. She was embarrassed. 'I wish it was dark and they couldn't see me.'

She wouldn't let Richard take her in his arms and kiss her. Instead, he held her hand and told her it had been love at first sight for him. Dinah was in no doubt that love had come in the same way for her.

Gladys from next door had come to spend the afternoon with her mother. Usually, Auntie Enid did that, but it was Saturday and she had pupils to teach. When Dinah told them about her afternoon out, Gladys said, 'He must be making a fortune from his ribbons, then, even though the country is in the middle of a depression.'

'He makes buttons too,' Dinah told her proudly.

She couldn't get enough of Richard. She'd found love and couldn't believe her good fortune. She wasn't sleeping properly, she couldn't eat and she found herself thinking of Richard all the time.

Chapter Three

On the following Wednesday, Dinah was coming home from work when a group of passengers on the bus ahead of hers got off at her stop. She recognised Tim immediately: a small slight figure with a long athletic stride bouncing towards Picton Street. His brown hair was unruly and tossed in the wind.

She'd always been very close to Tim. He was the one person in the world with whom she could be entirely herself, and she believed he was completely honest with her. She felt she knew him inside out. He'd heard all her fears for her mother and done his best to help. As Sarah had grown weaker over the years, Dinah had had to take over much of the housework. Tim had come round regularly to help her; he'd laid fires and carried in the coals and even on occasions washed her kitchen floor. They'd cooked meals together, often for four people so that his mother could come round to share them.

In return, Dinah had listened to all his fiery ambitions and self-doubts. She hadn't shared his obsession with horses, but she liked them well enough and had gone with him to beg unsold apples and carrots from the corner shop, then helped him feed them to the horses that hauled the milk floats and coal carts.

When at fifteen he'd gone to work at Rivington Lodge she'd really missed him, and waited impatiently for his day off to come round so she could spend some time with him. To their mothers, they'd always been a pair. They were more than friends; they went out together to the pictures, to dances and to parties. Until recently, she'd expected it to go on, and she knew Tim wanted that too.

Then Richard Haldane had come into her life and offered not only love but romance. He wouldn't share the housework; he'd swept all that away. He'd come between her and Tim and she felt guilty about letting Tim down. But at twenty Tim was still a youth, full of dreams and plans for the future, while Richard was a mature man. And she was head over heels in love with him. A love that blotted out everything else.

She ran to catch Tim up and his face lit when he saw her. 'I was planning to call and see you,' he told her. '*King Kong* is on at the Odeon this week, and everybody says it's a marvellous film. How about it tonight? I'll come round for you about seven, shall I?'

She was stricken. 'Oh, Tim, I'm sorry. I can't.'

'But we've always gone to the pictures on my night off and it's usually Wednesday.'

That was true and it brought another rush of guilt. 'I've arranged to see Richard tonight,' she told him. 'I'm sorry. I wasn't thinking straight.'

She knew Tim would have heard from his mother that she'd taken up with Richard, and was afraid he'd be hurt, but she had to be honest with him.

He pulled a face. 'I suppose I should have expected it. How can the likes of me compete with a man who owns racehorses?'

'Next week, Tim. We'll go next week.'

'He's too old for you,' he told her. 'And he's not a nice man.'

'How can you say that? You don't know him.'

'Perhaps not in the way you mean. He wouldn't deign to speak to a lowly jockey like me, but I see him parading round at race meetings. The lads from the stables that train his horses say he has a terrible temper.'

'That's not fair, Tim. You don't want to like him.'

'You're right there, but don't let's fight about him.'

'No.' They covered two hundred yards without speaking, then Dinah said, 'I saw you win two races at Chester. You're a great jockey.'

'I have to win to stay in the game.'

'Richard was disappointed Ardwick Prince didn't win the Cup.'

'He was a rank outsider. Nobody else thought he had much chance.'

'I wish I knew more about horses. Richard assumes I know more than I do.'

'You know a lot. You used to muck out on Sunday mornings at the stable.'

She laughed. 'I wanted to learn to ride, but in the end I didn't manage more than mucking out and giving them clean bedding and water. But I meant about racing horses.'

'It costs a huge amount to own horses and race them. Richard Haldane must be a millionaire.'

'Really?'

'Yes. Thoroughbred horses are expensive, but it's not just that. The horse has to have the best trainer too. You wouldn't believe how particular a trainer has to be. He takes the horses into his stable and controls everything.'

'Yes, I heard all about it while I worked at Rivington.'

'Then they have to be taken to the racecourses and sometimes stabled there for a few nights, not to mention the fee for entering them in a race.'

'And vets' bills. Richard complains about vets' bills.'

'They can be enormous.'

'But horses can win a lot of prize money for their owners.'

'Sometimes, but there's no guarantee. Llewellyn Digby reckons it's a rich man's hobby and that the owners spend more on getting a racehorse ready to compete than they win.'

Dinah laughed. 'I don't see why they do it, then.'

'They do it for the fun. It's big business for everyone involved.'

'And the jockeys?'

'The owner has to pay his jockey's wages too, and he needs the best rider he can get. We have to understand the horses, and know how to handle them. There are times when you push the horse to the limit and times when you hold him back.'

'For heaven's sake, why would you want to hold them back?'

'It depends on their stamina and strength. Not many horses can run flat out for a mile and a half. We may keep the horse jogging for the first mile, then give him his head. There's a strategy worked out for every horse to give him the best chance of winning. And luck comes into it too. To draw a place on the starting line nearest the rail is marvellous.

Then some horses start well and some trip over themselves and fall. Some are fouled or blocked by other horses in the race and are never able to get through.'

Dinah was thinking of Richard. Tim must be right about his being a millionaire, but she found it hard to believe a millionaire would be interested in her.

'A good trainer can even things out and so can a top jockey, but the best of it is that we all get a share of the fun. It's not like working for a newsagent.'

The following Wednesday, Dinah refused Richard's invitation in order to go to the pictures with Tim, but the evening was not a success. Her thoughts were with Richard and Tim was edgy, so she could not even console herself for displeasing one by feeling she had pleased the other.

When she came home late the following night, she found Enid tidying up in the kitchen.

'Is Mum all right, Aunt Enid?' Usually, when Dinah went out, Enid settled Sarah for the night and then went home.

'Yes. I sat with her and had a little chat. She's been brighter today. It's you I'm worried about. I waited to have a word.'

'I'm fine.' Dinah smiled. Everything was going so well with Richard she'd never been happier. 'No need to worry about me.'

'Well I do. Your mum isn't well enough to see what's happening. She can't take care of you now and I feel somebody should.'

'Why?'

'Dinah, you're a pretty girl and very young. You're vulnerable. This Richard you've taken up with, well, he's much older than you, and a man of the world. Tim reckons he has a reputation for chasing women.'

'How would he know?'

'He says he's seen him with other women at race meetings. One in particular.'

'He's only recently lost his wife. Tim doesn't really know him, just sees him from time to time.'

'Well, all I'm trying to say is, do be careful. We know very little about him, after all. Don't let him land you in trouble.'

'I won't, Aunt Enid.'

As Dinah understood it, there was only one sort of trouble a handsome man could get her into. She knew by the way Richard held her that he was eager for serious lovemaking. She'd told herself it was understandable: he'd been married for a long time.

For herself, she was not only curious about lovemaking but desperate to try it, but even so Enid was right. She must damp down her own feelings and take care not to encourage him. Not yet. All that should wait until they were married.

Richard was always eager to take her in his arms, and as he had a car they had some privacy for kissing and cuddling. A few nights later he started to unbutton her blouse, and when she pushed his hand away he said, 'Sorry, I shouldn't do things like that. Not until I put a ring on your finger.'

That had made Dinah catch her breath. It was only a few weeks since they'd met. He kissed her cheek gently.

'I'm very much in love with you,' he said. 'I want us to be married. Darling, will you?'

That he was ready to make the ultimate commitment so soon was more than she'd dared hope for. For her part, she thought about him in every wakeful moment; she was living in a bubble of ecstatic happiness.

The following day, she popped in to have a word with Aunt Enid. 'Richard isn't going to get me into trouble,' she said happily. 'He's asked me to marry him and I've said yes.'

Aunt Enid was smiling too. 'So his intentions are honourable?'

'Absolutely. Mum's over the moon.'

'So am I, love. I want you to be happy.'

The following evening Richard slid a diamond ring on her finger. 'I hope you like it,' he said, pushing the leather box into her right hand.

She gasped. 'It's absolutely beautiful.' It was a large and handsome stone. None of the girls at work had a ring like this. Richard was very generous. 'Thank you.' It was all happening so quickly she felt quite overcome.

In the next breath he was talking of their wedding and suggesting a date just a month away. Dinah drew back, twisting the diamond on her finger.

'Richard, I can't marry you yet. I'm an apprentice. I need to finish my time.'

He seemed taken aback. 'How long will that take?'

'Another eighteen months.'

'Goodness! We can't wait that long. Do you want to be a milliner that badly?'

'I love hats. Perhaps I could carry on? After we're married, I mean. Though I think there might have been something in the agreement I signed to say I couldn't. I'll ask Mr McKay.'

'No, Dinah! I was hoping you'd come and help me in my business. I really need you there. We'd be parted all day and every day if you carried on with your hat-making. I'd hate that and so would you.'

Richard's calm assumption that she would be willing to change every detail of her life took her breath away.

'If you came to work with me, we'd be able to see much more of each other.'

'Well, it's a big step . . .'

'It is, and I'm afraid you might not find ribbons and buttons as interesting as hats at first. But I enjoy working there and in time you might too.'

'In time, perhaps,' Dinah agreed. Her head was spinning. That he wanted her beside him at work showed how much he loved her. 'But it's not just that. My mother needs me. She can't manage on her own, and I have to think of her. I feel I'm neglecting her now because I spend so much time with you.'

'You spend a lot of time at work too.'

'Yes I do, but I can't marry you next month. No, I can't do that.'

'Yes you can,' he pleaded, holding both her hands in his.

'No.'

'Listen for a moment. We can look after your mother together. What she needs is a nurse to take proper care of her.'

'Mum doesn't want to be bothered with strangers now. There are times when she barely has the energy to talk to me.'

'But a trained nurse to see to her requirements and be with her all the time? Surely that would be the best thing for her.'

'No, Richard. I can't move in with you and leave her at home. Not even with a nurse. She'd want me there. Anyway, I can't just tear myself away from her. I want to be with her too.'

'Of course you do.'

'I mean, I don't know how much longer—'

He said quickly, 'There's no reason why she can't come to my place. I've got two spare bedrooms, one for her and one for the nurse.'

For the first time, Dinah hesitated. 'Are you sure?'

'Darling, of course I'm sure.'

'I don't suppose it'll be for very long,' Dinah said, and a tear rolled down her cheek.

There was nothing she wanted more than to become his wife and share his life. She was very much in love and wanted to be a wife he could be proud of, and the best mother she could be to his children. He was offering her a wonderful future.

Mr McKay was popular with all the girls. He was fair to everybody and went out of his way to teach them their trade. Dinah liked him and enjoyed his teasing.

'Young lady,' he'd said – he addressed all the girls as young lady – 'you could talk the hind leg off a donkey and you let every thought in that pretty head bubble out in an excited rush.' Even Mum told her she talked too much. 'When I bring buyers in here to see what we're making I wish you'd think before you open your little rosebud. You're a great help with sales as long as you like the hat and think it suits you, but you're not very good at hiding your feelings when you don't like something. Unfortunately, we have to make hats to suit everybody, so I need you to look as though you love them all. You're a real tonic for everyone, but be a good girl and watch that tongue.'

Dinah was quite nervous when she knocked on his door to tell him she wanted to leave, and he seemed quite shocked.

'I'm sorry to hear that,' he said. 'You're the last one I thought would leave before you were out of your time. Look, if it's to look after your mother, perhaps we could arrange for you to take time off.'

'No, it's not that. I'm going to be married.'

'What?' He laughed. 'You give out about everything, but I hadn't heard that you had a serious boyfriend.'

'We got engaged last night. You know him: it's Richard Haldane.'

'Oh!' He was taken aback. 'Mr Haldane, eh? Young lady, you only met him a few weeks ago and he's old enough to be your father!'

'He's only thirty-seven.'

'That's nearly twice your age! I hope you've thought about this?'

'Yes, of course.'

'Oh, dear. I had high hopes for you – I expected to turn you into a master milliner. And weren't you planning to take over Miss Eccles's job?'

Miss Eccles was his main saleswoman. She was about forty; old in Dinah's estimation but extremely elegant. She always wore a Carlton Hat and teamed it with an equally smart and expensive suit. She was tall and slim and in the winter she wore a glossy fox fur round her shoulders and carried a leather attaché case with details of their latest designs. Her job was to visit expensive hat shops and hat departments in the big department stores in Lancashire, Yorkshire and Cheshire and get orders for Carlton Hats. She drove herself round in a Morris Eight and talked golf to Mr McKay when she came in. All the apprentices admired Miss Eccles.

'Only after years of experience here,' Dinah said, 'and when you thought I was good enough. But yes, I did fancy her job.'

Her boss sighed. 'But once Richard Haldane offered marriage, all that went out of the window?'

'I suppose it did. I'm sorry, Mr McKay. I've been happy here and I know I'd have loved selling your hats.'

'You might even have been good at it,' he told her. 'You've got the gift of the gab and you can hold forth to anyone. Mr Haldane, eh? Well, I hardly know him.'

He was smiling down at her. 'Take no notice of me, I'm a miserable old curmudgeon. I wish you every happiness. Look, as a leaving present, you can help yourself to whatever materials you need to make a hat. Something smart to wear on your honeymoon.'

'Thank you, Mr McKay.' She leaned over and kissed his cheek. 'I love the new pastel straws we're making for the summer.'

'Only one, mind, not a whole wardrobe full.'

'Of course. I shall be married in it. That's marvellous, Mr McKay. I'm thrilled.' She'd already decided on the pale blue. 'Thank you!'

Dinah was very curious about Richard's life. He didn't say much about it and she wanted to know every detail. She'd asked countless questions about his home and his family and his business, but he seemed more interested in hearing about her. She asked several times about his first wife and discovered that he found it painful to talk about her.

'I do understand,' she told him. 'It's only four months since she died and you're still grieving. But I need to know about her, or I'll never stop wondering. How old was she?'

'Thirty.' Richard wouldn't look at her now.

'That's very young to die. Go on.'

'She hadn't been well for some time. Her mind . . . You're forceful and clear-headed about what you want, but she was never like that. She was troubled and nervous, and always frail.'

'She needed support? From you?'

'Very much so. She needed support from everybody. The doctor . . . Her mind wasn't strong. She couldn't manage things on her own.'

Dinah frowned, 'Are you saying she was mentally ill?'

'I'm afraid I am.'

Dinah put her arms round him. 'That must have been awful. Mum's really ill and that makes life hard, but her mind is clear and we can talk things through. Mental illness would be much harder to cope with. For both of you.'

'The children too.'

'Of course. It must have affected you all. Tell me about them.'

'My daughter's like her mother, timid and nervous.' He hesitated, biting his lip.

'And your son?' He was shaking his head. 'How old are they?'

'Oh, darling . . .' She heard the break in his voice, and wondered what could be making him so upset that he couldn't even tell her how old his children were. She would have liked to know his wife's name. He'd referred to her only as 'my wife'.

She said gently, 'You haven't told me how she died.'

'Suicide,' he choked out. 'She killed herself. Can you imagine how awful it was telling the children?'

Dinah was full of sympathy and love for him. She could see tears on his cheeks.

'I'm sorry,' he said. 'I can't talk about it even now.'

Chapter Four

ONE COLD WET evening, Richard took her out for a special dinner. 'Dress yourself up,' he told her. 'I'm taking you to my favourite restaurant in Southport. Quite a long way to go for a meal, but it's worth it.'

Dinah didn't have much to dress up in, so she borrowed a silky cream-coloured blouse from her mother to team with her brown skirt. She thought the restaurant very smart and enjoyed being pampered after working all day. Richard had said he wanted to discuss details of their wedding, but he was making all the arrangements himself and it turned out he had firm ideas about what they should be.

'I don't want you to be disappointed, but I think it ought to be a low-key affair because your mother's so ill.'

Enid had already told her she thought her mother would like them to have the ceremony in church, but when Dinah asked her about it Sarah said no, she'd be happy with the choice of the bride and groom. Dinah knew her mother was feeling poorly and wouldn't be comfortable sitting through a long church ceremony and formal reception, so she was happy to go along with Richard's wishes. She wanted the state of marriage rather than a lavish ceremony. There was to be no large guest list and no fuss.

Richard had chosen the date. They were to be married on a Friday. 'It's half term then,' he said, 'so the children will be home and can come too. About the honeymoon . . .'

'I can't leave Mum with the neighbours for long,' Dinah said.

'And I don't want to leave my children or my business for long.

Not in these times of economic uncertainty. I want to be home from our honeymoon by Sunday evening.'

Dinah was pleased that at last she'd persuaded Richard to talk about his children. He told her that Nellie had been a difficult baby who'd had health problems, and Mark hadn't settled well at school. They were, he said, missing their mother and were much in need of another.

'It would be better for us all if we don't delay. That's if, Dinah, you're quite sure it's what you want?'

She was absolutely certain it was. 'I want to be your wife, I'm sure of that.' She smiled. 'Mum thinks it's very romantic, the way you're sweeping me to the altar.' So did the girls at work, most of whom were green with envy.

Richard was never out of her thoughts. To see him striding towards her made her heart miss a beat and to feel his lips against hers turned her to putty in his hands. Dinah was in love in a way she'd never been before, and the amazing thing was that right from the moment they'd met, Richard had felt the same way about her. The last two months with him had been a revelation. The world he lived in was very different from and much more exciting than hers.

'Richard,' she said, as they drank their coffee, 'the wedding is only a fortnight off now but I haven't seen your house yet or met your children. Don't you think I should?'

'Of course.' He looked disconcerted. 'What am I thinking of? The children are at school, so that's a bit difficult. Nellie's in North Wales and Mark's near York.'

'Boarding school?' Dinah could hardly believe it. 'How old are they? I thought they were infants. You said they had a nanny.'

'Well, Bunty Sugden was always their nanny and I kept her on long after she was really needed. The children were fond of her and she of them, and with their mother the way she was . . . Well, they needed somebody to look after them.

'As for my house, well, I'm out all day and it has an unlived-in feel to it. I tend to spend less and less time there, but all that is going to change.'

Dinah smiled. 'When we're married.'

'When you'll be mine and living there too. I could take you to see it now. Why don't I?'

'I'd like that.' Dinah was eager. The idea sent a thrill running down her spine. She felt on the brink of a new and altogether more exciting life.

When he pulled up in front of heavy iron gates, she got out to open them and could see in the headlights the name *Ardwick House* engraved on one of the stone pillars. He hadn't told her much about his home, but she'd known it must be grand compared with hers. Millie Hunt and the other girls at work had speculated more than once.

'It'll be a huge mansion. I bet he lives like a lord.'

It certainly seemed a far cry from Picton Street, where the small houses huddled together in a friendly manner. She got back in the car and it climbed slowly up a longish drive. It was getting late and tonight there was no moonlight. The house seemed to stand on a little plateau. She could make out the shape of a high narrow building with a cluster of tall trees to one side.

'It looks a big place,' she said.

'Not really. There's a big garden, though; over two and a half acres.'

'I can't envisage how big that is,' she said. 'I'll have to wait until I can see it in daylight.'

'I've lived here all my life. My parents had it built in 1884 and they left it to me, together with the business.'

The house was in darkness except for one feeble light over the front door, itself as big and strong as that of a bank. He pulled up and switched off his lights. The night crowded close, heavy and black. It seemed thick enough to cut with a knife.

He rang the doorbell and then let them in with his key. 'Bunty should be here, unless she's gone out.'

It was cold inside. Even he shivered. They were in a long narrow hall with stairs at the far end. An elderly woman with thick wavy white hair wearing a nanny's uniform came hurrying down to meet them. 'Mr Haldane, I wasn't expecting you.'

'It's all right, Bunty. I've just brought Dinah to see round the house.

We won't need anything.' He smiled at Dinah. 'Unless you'd like another cup of coffee?'

'Erm . . .' Dinah was about to say she would, not because she really wanted another drink but because she thought it might give her a chance to get to know the nanny and find out more about the children, when Richard answered his own question.

'Better not, perhaps,' he said. 'It's a bit chilly to sit down here and too late to think of lighting fires now.'

'Would you like to come up to see the nursery?' The nanny asked Dinah. She had kindly eyes of faded blue. 'I have a fire there, and it's nice and warm.'

Richard answered for her. 'No thank you, Bunty. We'll just have a quick look round.'

He started throwing open the doors. 'This is the dining room, this is my study. Here is the kitchen and scullery. This is a little sitting room my mother used to use.'

They were mostly big rooms with high ceilings, but his mother's room was somewhat smaller. She'd had a treadle sewing machine and there was a bookcase full of books, but Dinah wasn't given time to look round properly. Another door was opened for her.

'Mother used to call this the drawing room,' he said.

'What do you call it?'

'It's the main sitting room.'

She went and stood in the middle of the room. Compared with what she was used to, it was enormous. The whole ground floor of number fifteen Picton Street would fit in here. The ceiling had a border of ornate plasterwork and a cluster of fruit and flowers in the centre from which hung an electric light. The grate was empty; it was cold here too.

'I knew I'd be out tonight with you,' he told her. 'The fire's never lit unless I'm planning to stay in.'

Dinah looked round, trying to take everything in. The furniture and decor dated from the Victorian era. Everything seemed heavy and old-fashioned.

'I'm afraid I haven't been looking after the house as I should. It needs repainting.' He smiled. 'In fact it probably needs totally redecorating. You could see to that if you wanted to.'

There were racing prints on the walls; she'd noticed some in the hall too.

'Most of the stuff here belonged to my parents, but those I've added. I've got some new pictures of my horses in my study. Come and have a look.'

She followed him back and he took two framed photographs off the wall and put them in her hands. 'Ardwick Beauty and Ardwick Prince.'

She'd seen them race. They were handsome animals. 'I see you named them after your house.'

'Yes. I'm hoping to have a whole string eventually, all called Ardwick something. Perhaps Ardwick Lad or Ardwick Castle next.'

'Goodness, Richard! You sound more ambitious than Tim Reece.'

'But I'm going to realise my ambitions,' he said confidently. 'I'll work at it until I do.'

'Tim works at it,' she said. But he'd had to start lower down in the scheme of things. 'Was your father fond of racing too?'

'Definitely not. He didn't approve of me going near a race course. His only interest was the business.'

'We're all different.'

'Yes. Look, it's getting late. I'd better take you home now. It's a working day tomorrow.'

Dinah wished it was daylight; there was so much more she wanted to see. This had been a flying visit; he hadn't even invited her to take her coat off. She didn't know whether she liked his house or not, but it certainly wasn't the luxurious place she'd expected. Was there something oppressive about it? Whatever the answer, it made her own home seem cosy and bright.

It was only when she was telling Mum about it later that she realised he'd shown more interest in his horses than in his children. He hadn't shown her any photographs of them. It was almost as though he didn't want her to know anything about them, but that was silly. She was going to be their stepmother. How could she have thoughts like that about Richard?

* * *

A few days later Tim stopped Dinah in the road. 'What's this I hear about you getting married? You've only known this Richard for ten minutes.'

'It's true.' She showed him her diamond ring. He clutched at her hand to take a second look. The diamond was flashing with colours.

'Very posh,' he said sarcastically. 'Opulent, in fact. I thought you'd agreed to marry me? You did, you know.'

She almost laughed. 'Tim! We were ten years old then. We didn't know what being married meant.'

'I know now,' he said, 'and I was hoping to keep you to it.'

She hadn't thought about Tim in that way. 'I didn't think you were that interested,' she told him.

'We've always stuck together, you and me, haven't we?' He seemed quite heated. 'But how can I think of getting married now? I don't earn enough to keep myself.'

'Neither do I.'

'It doesn't matter for a girl. It needn't stop you. But I can't contemplate . . .' He looked the picture of misery. 'Well, you know.'

'I'm sorry, Tim.' Dinah struggled for words, hating to see him upset. 'You'll always be a good friend.'

His lips straightened. He looked wounded and she knew she'd hurt him. What else could she have said? Tim didn't send little shivers of ecstasy down her spine as Richard did. His touch couldn't thrill her.

'I'm sorry. Really I am.'

'Are you in love with him?'

When she didn't answer, he said with even more heat, 'Of course you are,' and strode off down the road.

It was Dinah's wedding day; she felt heady and exhilarated at one moment and in a flurry of nerves the next.

She was dressed ready to leave for the register office and had just helped her mother down the steep and awkward stairs when she felt Sarah's lips kiss her cheek.

'This was what I was hoping for, Dinah,' she murmured. 'To see you married and settled before I die.'

Dinah struggled to swallow the sudden lump in her throat. Her mother was only forty-four; she couldn't bear the thought of losing her.

'That's a long time off yet,' she said as brightly as she could, but Mum's face had a greyish tinge against the maroon of her hat, and she'd said it wasn't worth spending money on new clothes for her. It added a bittersweet taste to Dinah's wedding day.

'Enid's here,' Sarah said. They could see her through the little side window. Before she had time to ring, Dinah bounded to the door. She wanted to know whether Tim was with her. He was, looking serious and withdrawn in his new grey flannel suit.

'I'm afraid you haven't got a sunny day,' Enid said.

'Is it drizzling? Come inside for a moment,' Dinah said. 'Richard said he'd pick us up at half past three and it's not quite that yet.'

'Thanks, Dinah. You're looking very pretty – radiant, in fact.' Enid was dressed in her best. She paused in the doorway of their front room. 'I love your hat.'

'I made it myself.'

Dinah turned to assess the effect in the hall mirror. Her brown eyes stared nervously back at her, and her dark naturally wavy hair was curling round her face under the blue straw hat. Richard had given her some money and she'd matched her hat to a fashionable pale blue suit. It was the most expensive outfit she'd ever owned. It fitted well and it suited her, but did she look like a bride? No, not in the least. Their neighbours as well as the girls at work had been shocked to hear she was not getting married in a long white dress and veil.

'Why not?' they'd asked. 'He's rich; he can afford all the trimmings. You should have told him you wanted a big wedding.'

Dinah was listening to the clock on the living room mantelpiece ticking away the minutes. It was gone half past three. The waiting was making her feel jittery. Where was he? They couldn't be late for their wedding!

Her mother had settled back in the rocking chair and closed her eyes, but Dinah could see that both Tim and his mother were growing restive. Tim was standing at the window watching for Richard. From the look on his face he might have been hoping he wouldn't come at all.

Enid said, 'Don't worry, love. It's traditional for the bride to be late.'

'But not the whole wedding party, like this.'

'He'll be here in a few moments.' Tim's mother was comforting her, knowing her own mum was too sick to notice how uncomfortable she was. 'The wedding isn't until four o'clock. There's still plenty of time.'

Dinah nodded, 'I know.' She might have grown up without a father but Auntie Enid had been a second mother to her. She dropped a grateful kiss on her plump cheek. Enid and Tim had always played a big part in the Radcliffes' lives and Dinah was grateful. It was on her conscience that she was moving her mother away from such good friends.

Aunt Enid had taken her aside again only last week and said, 'I'm still worried about you. Don't be rushed into this, Dinah. I know you think he's wonderful and I'm sure you're right, but give yourself time to get to know him. Think it through. He's so much older than you that he may not want to do the things you do. Tastes change as time goes on.'

'He says he wants to look after me, so it's a good thing he's older than me, isn't it?'

'Yes, but you'll be making big changes that will affect the rest of your life. You'll be stepmother to his two little children.'

'I know, but I'll love them because they're his, and they'll be away at school for much of the time. He wants me to help in his business. Aunt Enid, it's what I really want.'

Enid shook her head. 'Don't forget the old proverb. Marry in haste, repent at leisure.'

Dinah laughed. 'What would I have to repent? I'll have no money worries and I'm going to live in a big house in Woolton with a husband I love.'

'That's true. I'm just being silly. I suppose, love, I hoped you and Tim might get together one day. I said that to him this morning and he almost jumped down my throat. He told me to mind my own business, and that a mother has no say in things like that.'

'Here he is. Here's the bridegroom.' Tim turned round from the window with the look of resignation on his face that she'd first seen when she'd asked him to come to her wedding. Then he'd said, 'Dinah, I'd rather not. I don't want to be there.'

'But I want you to come. We've always done everything together. You're my best friend.'

So he'd come, but he didn't look happy. She went to his side and saw Richard bringing his car to a halt at the front door.

'Right, we'd better go.' She took her mother's arm, Tim moved to Sarah's other side, and together they walked her out.

'Hello, darling.' Richard's lips brushed her cheek. 'Sorry I'm late. There was an accident on Queen's Drive, and it held everything up.'

Relief flared through her. There was nothing to worry about. She must shake off these nerves. She was about to be married to the man she loved; she should feel happy. Many of the neighbours had come out to see her go and to wave her off and call their good wishes.

It was Richard who helped her mother settle into the front seat. He towered over Tim, who squashed into the back of the car with Dinah and his mother.

They were actually a little late, and when they walked into the register office they found a group of people waiting for them. Millie Hunt had come with Jenny Brown, another friend of Dinah's from Carlton Hats. She hadn't specifically invited them: they'd come along to witness the ceremony and give their support. Richard didn't seem pleased to see them.

Nobody seemed at ease. A woman Dinah hadn't seen before was ushering two children into the room. The boy was staring at her. Could these be Richard's children? He had said they'd be coming, although earlier he'd told her they were too young to understand what marriage meant and needed time to settle at school.

She watched Richard go up to them and say, 'Hello, you two.' He turned to Dinah. 'I'd like to introduce my children.'

She gasped. They were much older than she'd imagined they'd be. The boy was taller than she was. The girl was hanging on to her brother as though her life depended on it. Dinah had been expecting small children; Richard had given her to understand they were of primary school age. He was smiling. 'This is Fenella, known as Nellie. Say hello to your new mother, my dear.'

She was a frail but pretty girl in a pink coat with bright blonde hair like her father's. She looked scared, and her blue eyes were wary. He bent to kiss her but she was shy and trying to hide behind her brother.

Dinah felt she should offer a kiss too, but the girl shrank back even further and the kiss got lost in the two inches between her cheek and Dinah's lips.

'And this is Mark,' Richard told her, making no effort to show affection for his son. The boy was dark-haired and dark-skinned with no resemblance to the rest of his family. He looked rebellious, defiant almost. Her ready-made family.

'My goodness,' she managed, 'you're almost grown up. Hello.'

'And Mrs Banks my housekeeper,' Richard added. She was a gaunt woman in late middle age, her grey hair drawn back severely under her black hat.

'Good afternoon,' she said. 'Yes, the children are growing up. Mark is fourteen and Nellie has just had her eighth birthday.'

Dinah was shaken, and she knew her mouth had dropped open. That made her only five years older than Richard's son and eleven years older than his daughter! It wasn't so easy to mother children of that age. They would always remember their real mother.

She gave a nervous laugh. 'I was imagining you to be much younger. My goodness, Richard, what made me think that? Did you tell me how old they were?'

He looked embarrassed. 'I thought I had.'

The registrar came up to speak to them. 'If you're ready we can begin. We'll hold the ceremony in our small room. It's more personal when the wedding party isn't too big. This way, please.'

They were ushered into a room panelled in light oak that was bright in the brief sunny spell. There was a large polished desk and bowls of flowers everywhere. Dinah was unable to drag her eyes away from the children. Had Richard deliberately given her the impression they were much younger? She thought he must have done, but why? What point could there possibly be? To meet them like this for the first time moments before her wedding had given her a nasty jolt. It seemed hardly kind either to her or to them.

The ceremony seemed to be over almost before it began. She'd not been concentrating on what was going on. Before she realised it, she was outside on the steps wearing her wedding ring and being photographed. That took quite a long time, as Richard insisted on organising the shots he wanted the professional photographer to take. Then he ushered them back to the car and drove them to the Adelphi Hotel for the wedding breakfast.

Dinah found herself in a small foyer where one waiter was handing round glasses of champagne and another was offering savouries. She could see her mother beginning to sag and asked if a chair could be brought for her. It came within moments.

'It's just like a throne,' said Tim, smiling as he helped Sarah into it. 'All gilt and damask.'

It was only when Dinah was sitting at the sumptuously laid table in a private dining room that she missed her friends from work. She wished she'd suggested to Richard that they join them for dinner. His housekeeper wasn't here either.

The many courses were served with great formality, and the food was excellent, but she noticed that the children were eating hardly anything. Richard gave rather a lengthy speech, in which he promised to take good care of her. There were no high spirits. Tim looked miserable, and she knew her mother wasn't feeling well; only Enid seemed her usual self.

Once it was over, it felt to Dinah as though nothing so momentous as a marriage could have taken place. It might have been a visit to a solicitor's or accountant's office. Certainly, apart from the wedding ring on her finger and her marriage lines in her handbag, nothing seemed to have changed. But from the moment he left the register office, Richard was a different man.

Chapter Five

As Richard paid the bill he asked for a taxi to be called. The woman who'd brought the children was waiting downstairs to take them home. Richard would have dismissed them straight away, but Aunt Enid kept them talking, while Dinah tried to make their leave-taking more friendly. Then Richard drove the rest of the wedding party back to Picton Street. With help from Enid, Dinah took her mother indoors.

'I don't like leaving you,' she said.

'I'll be quite all right,' Sarah insisted. 'Everybody's entitled to a honeymoon, and you're only going for the weekend.'

'We'll look after her,' Enid said. She'd agreed to come and stay with her while Dinah was away in the Lake District. 'Don't you worry about a thing.'

But Dinah couldn't help worrying. She couldn't forget the pain she'd seen in her mother's eyes, and she was increasingly certain that the brave smiles Mum had put on were all for her benefit. And what about Nellie and Mark, whom she'd met for the first time that day?

'Richard,' she said, as they were driving away from Picton Street, 'why didn't you tell me Mark was fourteen? You led me to believe your children were still small.'

'Darling, I'm sorry. That was not my intention. You must have realised they couldn't still be toddlers. Not at boarding school.'

'Perhaps I should have.' Was she being silly? She'd let it upset her and spoil her own wedding. But there was something else. 'You didn't tell me you had a housekeeper.'

He took his eyes from the road for a moment to glance at her. 'With the children, I have to have help.'

'What about Bunty Sugden?'

'They'd long outgrown their nanny. It seemed a good idea to have a competent cook-housekeeper now. I want you to help me with my business, so I can't expect you to do housework as well. We also have Mrs Parr who comes in to do heavy cleaning three mornings a week.'

'It's just that we haven't talked about it.'

'I always have more interesting things to talk about when I'm with you.' He smiled at her. 'But now we'll be together all the time, and you'll soon know everything there is to know. We'll all get along very well, you'll see.'

'I hope so,' Dinah said. She tried to relax as they drove through the outskirts of Liverpool. The streets of shops and houses were giving way to open fields. Perhaps it was just a communication problem.

She told herself she must look at things clearly. Balanced against the sadness about her mother and the bafflement about his attitude to his children and his home was the ecstasy of being Mrs Richard Cameron Aldgrave Haldane. It was what she'd longed for and it promised a new and happy life for both her and Richard.

'We'll stop in the next town for a drink,' he said. 'I'm thirsty.' But he found a lay-by on an isolated country road before they reached the town and pulled into it. Dusk was just deepening to darkness and there was nobody about. Richard's arms came round her, pulling her closer for a long kiss.

Dinah clung to him, full of love. He had only to run the back of his finger down her cheek to make her passion flare. His own passion was never in doubt. She found herself on the back seat, folded in his arms.

'You belong to me now,' he whispered. 'I can't wait a moment longer.'

She'd thought that this was what she'd longed for these last weeks, but now the moment had arrived she found the whole business off-putting, sordid and totally unromantic. What was more, she was shocked that he dared make love to her on a public highway. She'd thought of him as a correct and gentlemanly person until that moment. Other cars' headlights lit up the inside of Richard's, and once an old man walked past with his dog, his boots crunching on the road. She associated such behaviour with reckless youth, and told him so, with a little laugh, as she straightened her clothes.

'Oh, that increases the thrill, doesn't it?' he said, climbing back into the driving seat.

Enid Reece saw Sarah into bed and settled her for the night. Then, needing a few moments to herself before going up to Dinah's room where she was to sleep, she poured herself another cup of tea and sat down by the dying embers of Sarah's fire. What she'd seen at the wedding had raised more questions in her mind about Richard.

She'd had her misgivings about him from the beginning. The romance had raced along too fast and Dinah was too young to rein it in. A wedding was always an emotional occasion, but today Enid had sensed a tumult of feelings not only in Dinah, but also in the children and in Tim. Even Sarah must have felt it: the atmosphere had been thick with it.

Nobody at the wedding could have missed the fact that Dinah and the children were meeting for the first time. Dinah's shock had been unsettling, and it seemed that things were not as either she or the children had imagined. It had made Tim angry and as anxious for Dinah's welfare as she and Sarah were.

In the days before the wedding, Enid had tried to quieten Sarah's growing fears and play down her own. Over the years, the two of them had spent hours chatting, putting the world to rights and imagining how things would work out for their children. It had never crossed their minds that Dinah would marry a rich man. Sarah had been delighted when her daughter had become engaged, but was having second thoughts now. She was afraid Richard was too old for her, and had noticed that he was very dogmatic about having things exactly as he wanted them. She feared Dinah might find him a difficult man to live with.

But then, Enid had never wanted Tim to become a jockey. She'd wanted a better life for him than that. Of course, horses had always fascinated him. He'd never been afraid of them: even as a small child he'd wanted to be lifted up on their backs and to feed them sugar lumps or carrots. At the time, Enid had been quite proud of the fact. She told everybody that Tim took after his father, who'd loved horses too.

It had seemed to bring her dead husband closer, almost close enough to touch. Especially at times like this, in a silent house lit by the dim glow of the fire. Tim had been less than a year old when she heard her husband had been killed at Ypres.

Her husband had been a jockey and quite a successful one, as had his father before him. Tim's grandfather had had a fall at Becher's Brook at Aintree, and broken his leg in two places; despite years of treatment the fracture had never healed. They'd shot his injured horse and he often said that he wished they'd shot him too. He couldn't ride and couldn't walk properly and had ended up as a cobbler, working on shoes for humans not horses.

Enid knew her husband had found the life exciting, but it had always terrified her. She'd watched him race two or three times when they were first married. With all those horses thundering down the track and jostling for the best position, it had looked incredibly dangerous.

'No,' he'd told her, 'not if you know what you're doing. It's fun.'

She was there the day his horse tripped and he was catapulted over its head. She knew he'd fallen under its hooves and the horses behind were piling up on top of them. She'd been so paralysed with terror that she'd sat staring straight ahead, seeing nothing.

The race was over before she jumped to her feet and started pushing through the crowd towards him, and a trolley was being wheeled towards the still figure on the track. She thought he was dead. An ambulance had been called and she went with him to hospital.

The doctor told her the fall had concussed him. His face was covered with cuts and bruises but, incredibly, his only other injury was a dislocated thumb. The joint was put back there and then and she took him home by taxi.

'Just a spill,' he said.

For years afterwards, Enid had nightmares about seeing her husband under that awful pile-up of horses and men. She'd never been near a racecourse since and she was filled with dread whenever she knew Tim was taking part in a race. She'd never been to see him ride. She never would.

* * *

Throughout the year he turned fifteen, Tim Reece kept telling his mother, 'I've got to have a go. Horses are in my blood.'

'You don't understand what a terrible life a jockey has,' she told him. 'I watched your father go through it.'

'Mum, I'm bored out of my mind at that paper shop.'

'You said the Atkinsons were good to you.'

'They are,' he groaned. The couple had no children of their own and since Tim had started work as a delivery boy three years before they'd treated him like an adopted son. 'But that doesn't make selling cigarettes and newspapers exciting. I don't want to do this for the rest of my life.'

'I know, and I've been thinking about it, Bryant and May are offering engineering apprenticeships to sixteen-year-old lads. That would be a good opening for you, wouldn't it? I could help you draft out an application.'

'No, Mum, I can't see myself as an engineer. It sounds too dull. I want a bit of fun and some excitement.'

To distract his mother, Tim switched on their wireless and the room was filled with dance music.

'What band is this?'

'It's Ambrose or Harry Roy. It's good, isn't it?' Enid sighed. 'I thought you were aiming to be a dance band pianist.' She'd taught him to play, and had encouraged that earlier ambition. 'You've got talent there.'

'Mum, you know I tried hard to find a band to take me on.'

'You mustn't get disheartened. You're only fifteen, for heaven's sake, and you look even younger. They want men not boys in a dance band. You have to look the part.'

'Well, of course, if I could get it I'd jump at a job with a band. Particularly a band like this, where I could play late night dance music on the wireless. But you know everyone I wrote to for an audition just ignored me. Anyway, I've decided to try being a jockey instead.'

'You wouldn't believe the number of jockeys who break their legs or get killed. Racing is very dangerous.'

'Give over, Mum.' Tim had heard about the hardships of a jockey's life too often and didn't want to hear it again. He swept her into a slow foxtrot, but there wasn't enough room in their living room and he kept backing her into one piece of furniture or another. When they knocked over a dining chair she broke free from his arms.

'Go to bed,' she laughed, switching off the wireless. 'It's high time. You've got to be at work before six in the morning.'

'Up at five to give me time to have a cup of tea and walk to the shop. Marking up the papers for delivery at a newsagent's isn't all milk and honey either,' he told her. 'And I'm bored out of my mind.'

After Dinah's wedding. Tim caught the train back to Birkdale. He was upset. The last thing he'd expected was that she would put herself beyond his reach so finally and so quickly. He felt she'd deserted him.

He blamed himself, too; he'd been too involved with horses in general and Flyswitch in particular and hadn't given enough attention to anything else.

The only way he could get Dinah out of his mind was to get back to the stables as quickly as he could and take Flyswitch out for a gallop along the beach.

When Tim had been invited for an interview at Rivington Lodge he'd found he was one of six boys hoping to be taken on. All of them were weighed and measured in one of the sheds. He'd always been told he was the right build for a jockey, and he weighed in at six stone nine and measured five feet.

Three lads were told they were already too big and sent straight home. The rest sat on the long benches and were given a form to fill in.

Tim read it through. It seemed the usual thing: name, address and age. The next question brought him up short, and he pointed it out to the boy sitting next to him. 'He wants to know what size shoes we take.'

He was about to write down 7 when the lad said generously, 'I'd be careful what you admit there, mate.'

'Why?'

'If you've got big feet he won't have you.' Tim was surprised. The lad explained, 'It means you'll grow too big to be a jockey so training you would be a waste of time. He's afraid we'll have growth spurts as we get older. Didn't you know? No jockeys in your family?'

'My dad was a jockey, but he died before I was born.' Tim wrote down 6½.

The lad looked over at the name on Tim's form. 'Not Timothy Reece? My dad always said he'd have made the big time if he hadn't gone to fight the Kaiser.'

Another of the boys was sent home as unsuitable. Llewellyn Digly came over. 'That leaves you two, Tim and . . . ?'

'Robbie.' The lad had red hair and was stick-thin.

'You two can start. You'll learn to ride and you'll take the horses out for their daily exercise,' Mr Digby told them. He was a short, heavily built man in middle age, with a craggy facc and a kindly smile. 'And if you're good enough I'll train you to be jockeys. But first you'll start by pulling your weight with the stable work.

'I started out as a stable boy myself. Take heed of what I'm going to tell you now. I ate too much and grew too heavy and that was the end of my dream of becoming a jockey. Horses are handicapped by the amount of weight they have to carry, and I weighed too much. I've seen it happen to countless lads, even successful jockeys who loved racing and were earning a lot of money. And it'll happen to you unless you always watch what you put into your stomachs, unless you're very, very lucky.

'Now, this is Stan. He's been here a while so he can show you the ropes. He'll start by taking you on a tour of the stable.'

Tim was amazed by the size of the place. Digby trained nearly eighty horses that season, and in every direction he saw horses' heads peering out at him over stable doors. He was shown round the tack room, the paddocks, the indoor ring where the horses were schooled in bad weather and the six furlong sand track outside.

'We often exercise the horses along the foreshore too,' Stan told them. 'Mr Digby has put posts in at every furlong so we can measure the distance. That's great on a sunny morning but it's mostly stable work you'll be doing, and that's endless. We have to feed every horse, muck them out and groom them. And then it starts all over again in the evening.'

They were to lodge in the trainer's house, 'So I can keep an eye on you,' he told them. It was a rambling dwelling that had once been a farmhouse. Tim and Robbie were allotted beds in the attic where Stan slept. There were seven other beds in the room. Their meals were served in the enormous kitchen. The food was plain and light and the servings so small that they all got used to getting up from the table still feeling hungry. Nobody asked for a second helping.

Tim thought he knew a good deal about horses, but he soon found that all the other lads had been brought up either on farms or in the racing world. They'd all spent their childhoods on horseback and knew all there was to know about horses. Tim had gained his knowledge from library books and felt his lack of experience put him at a disadvantage.

'There are two basic facts a jockey must never forget,' Mr Digby told them. 'You're in this game to win. You've got to get the prizes; nothing else will do. The more races you win, the more quickly you'll progress and the more money you'll earn.'

Tim and Robbie were starting on what the other boys thought of as an abysmal wage; it was even less than Tim had earned in the paper shop. He didn't mind. He liked the sound of the job and he was going to be taught to ride like his father.

For Tim, the working day started at five o'clock, and for much of the year that was before dawn. He rolled out of bed when the alarm reverberated through the attic and pulled on his clothes. The other boys did the same, but not with any enthusiasm. After a cup of tea in the kitchen it was outside to muck out the stables while the horses let everybody know they were impatient to have their breakfasts. When they'd eaten, they were saddled up for their exercise routine.

All the staff were up by this time, even Mr Digby. He checked over each of the horses and decided with the exercise riders how far each horse should go and at what pace, and whether a horse should be galloped flat out between distance markers, so he could assess their form. He wrote down the amount of food the stable boys must weigh out for each animal. Only the best meadow hay and highest-grade oats would do for them.

Tim found he was the only lad in the stables who couldn't ride. He was started on an old fat gelding, who was said to be quiet and easy to manage. He did little more than plod round the track, but Tim felt it was as much as he could do to cling to his back, and began to doubt he had any aptitude for riding. But he was determined to learn, and after a time he was allowed to try some of the more spirited horses. Some ran away with him, others tossed him over their heads. Others actually teased him: the more he urged them on, the slower they moved, and then just when he was giving up they'd suddenly charge down the course at forty miles an hour and he'd be fighting to pull them up. These occasions usually ended with Tim being tossed out of the saddle, but he was always able to stand up and walk away.

'They know you're a beginner.' Digby laughed. 'They're just showing you who's boss.'

All the stable lads were keen to ride in the way the jockeys did. The trainer had showed Tim and Robbie a racing saddle with the stirrups dangling barely a foot below the seat.

'A jockey doesn't sit on his saddle. These stirrups take all his weight and he crouches over the horse. When a horse is galloping, only the insides of the jockey's ankles and feet touch it,' Llewellyn Digby told them. 'The horse can carry him more easily if he's in that position, but it's a question of balance and that has to be learned. Tip a touch too far back and you'll slide off. Tip a little too far forward and you'll fall over its head.

'This is too advanced for you, Tim. You're to ride with your leathers long and learn to control your mount before you go on to this.'

The first winter, Digby sent him up to Cumbria where a friend of his, Johnny Roscoe, was just starting out as a trainer and had a small stable of eighteen horses. Tim was his only helper. It was a cold wet winter and they were miles from any town. Tim knew nobody in the area and had nothing to do but work. He learned to muck out and groom at twice the speed he used to and every morning he exercised nine horses. They were no better behaved than Digby's horses, but Tim learned fast, and when he returned to Rivington Lodge in the spring he knew how to swing himself up into the saddle and felt at home there. Mr Digby said Roscoe had made a rider of him and now he would train him to be a jockey.

From then on, Tim was allowed to take the stars of the stable out for their morning exercise. There was nothing he enjoyed more on a summer's morning than a good gallop along the foreshore at Birkdale with the breeze off the Irish Sea buffeting him. It felt marvellous.

Chapter Six

It was getting late when Richard and Dinah booked into their country house hotel. Dinah had never stayed in such a place before. It seemed very grand as she followed the night porter up to their room. He insisted on carrying their small cases upstairs for them. The room was sumptuous, the bed under a golden satin bedspread both high and wide.

Richard asked him to bring up a pot of tea for her and a brandy for himself. Dinah felt tired and emotionally drained. She opened her case, intending to hang up the dinner dress Aunt Enid and Tim had bought for her as a wedding present. She felt a little shy of Richard now she was alone with him in this fine room.

He came behind her and started unbuttoning her blouse. 'Again?' he whispered. 'Let's do it again.'

Dinah could see her own face in the wardrobe mirror twisting with denial, but he turned her round to cover her mouth with kisses.

'You enjoyed it in the car, didn't you?' he asked.

Dinah wasn't sure she had. Of course she knew what a husband wanted from his wife. Hazel Stott, who had worked with her at Carlton Hats, had spelled out explicitly what she should expect. But she sensed a big change in Richard now he was no longer courting her. Hadn't he said she belonged to him now? He was no longer trying to please her; he was indulging himself.

She hesitated. 'Well,' she said, 'I'd have preferred more privacy and more romance.'

He laughed. 'Darling, I'm sorry. But we have privacy now.' He slid her blouse off her shoulders and flung it to a chair. 'And you're not a virgin any more. You're my new and very attractive wife and I love you very much.'

His amber eyes, full of adoration, were looking into hers. Wasn't this what she had wanted? She did love him. He unfastened her bra and lifted her on to the bed.

'Be gentle with me,' she whispered.

'Was I rough last time?'

'Yes.' He'd been very rough.

'I'm sorry, darling. I'm sorry. I'll be more careful this time.'

Was he? Yes, perhaps this time he thought less of his own needs. She lay in his arms afterwards, reassured. Everything would be all right; she just needed to get used to being a wife.

She went along to the bathroom in the fluffy dressing gown provided by the hotel and had a long hot bath. The tea tray had arrived when she got back. She spent the night in Richard's arms, being caressed and kissed her and made love to again. At dawn they could stay awake no longer.

At eight o'clock a maid bustled in with the newspaper and another tray of tea. As she drew back the curtains, Dinah forced her eyes open and wished her good morning. When they went down for their egg and bacon breakfast, Richard ate with gusto but Dinah would have been satisfied with just another cup of tea. The rain was driving against the dining room window and the majestic scenery could be seen only dimly.

'What would you like to do today?' Richard asked.

'Climb that hill.' She nodded towards the window. 'But it's hardly climbing weather, is it?'

'It's our honeymoon, so we'll make the most of it.' He smiled at her. This was the Richard she was used to and had grown to love. Dinah could see other women turning to look at her husband in his new Fair Isle pullover. 'I know the countryside round here. I'll take you out in the car – we'll go round the lake and up into the hills, and if the rain stops and the mist lifts I'll show you the glorious views. I'm afraid, darling, it's the only way today.'

Once they left the village behind they didn't see another car. There were small fields on each side of the road to start with, but after that the purple hills rose up with just a few sheep and an occasional isolated farm to be seen. Although the empty landscape was sodden and dripping and the sky remained overcast, the rain eased within the hour.

Richard was intent on driving higher and higher into the mountains and didn't speak much. The warmth of the car was making Dinah feel sleepy, but then Richard braked and said, 'Now then, how's this? A bit misty today. If only it were clearer it would be scenic beauty at its best.'

Dinah pulled herself up in her seat to take a look. One glance was enough to make her heart jolt into her throat. Before her, the rough road was an empty ribbon zigzagging from one side of the mountain to the other as it fell into the valley a thousand feet below. Down there it stretched several miles into the distance to run alongside the dark glimmering waters of a lake.

'Breathtaking, isn't it?' He turned to look at her, his eyes slits, his mouth a straight line. She could see his jaw clenching with terrible intensity.

'What are you going to do?' But she could sense his intention. She was scared.

'Let's have a bit of fun. All the thrills of the fair, but better.'

'No, Richard. No!' She watched with dreadful fascination as he released the handbrake and put the gear in neutral. She felt the car roll forward down the slope and start its downward journey.

His laugh was feverish with excitement. 'We'll have a roller coaster. A real one without the engine.'

A wave of terror shot through her. 'Stop it!' Dinah screamed, gripping both sides of her seat. The car was gathering momentum as it gathered speed down the steep incline. She could see a ditch on each side of the road. 'I don't like this. Stop it.'

His face was working with an emotion Dinah didn't recognise. She could hardly breathe, afraid he was about to lose control and come off the road. 'What if we meet another car coming up?'

'We won't. You saw the road was empty.'

It was little more than a mountain track and falling away at a terrible rate. They shot past a sign saying the slope was one in four, and a hundred yards on they came to the first of the switchback turns.

Richard was crouched over the steering wheel, both hands clenched hard enough to turn the knuckles white. They careered round the bend on two wheels. Now on one side of the road was a sheer drop of scree, while on the other the mountain reared up.

Dinah screamed, 'Richard, for God's sake! Stop!'

He laughed out loud and paid no attention. The only noise was the crunch of the tyres on the road and the rush of the wind in her ears. She couldn't bear to look down that sheer drop. It made her stomach turn over.

'Stop! What's got into you? You're going to kill us both!'

He laughed again. Dinah crouched lower in her seat, holding on tight and pressing the back of her head into the leather. She closed her eyes, feeling sick. She hated the feel of the car heeling over on the steep hairpin bends. Every minute, she expected to feel it spin over, roll down the precipice and crash.

She'd held her breath for so long her lungs were bursting when at last she felt the car begin to slow down. Gingerly, she opened her eyes. They were down by the lake, still rolling at sixty miles an hour but on the level.

Richard braked and pulled in to the side of the road. 'Wasn't that marvellous?' he said.

'It was damn dangerous,' she stormed, angry and not far from tears. 'What were you doing? You scared the living daylights out of me.'

'I didn't mean to. Wasn't it thrilling?'

'No. I was terrified. I thought you were going to kill me.'

'Not you, my pet, not my new bride. I love you.'

'But with the engine off . . .'

'It's more of a challenge like that.'

She was shaking all over and ready to rave at him. She wanted to tell him it was stupid to do a thing like that and risk their lives. But he put his arms round her and pulled her tight against him, covering her mouth with his own so she couldn't speak.

'Don't be angry with me,' he said, kissing her. 'You were perfectly safe, really you were.'

She pulled away. 'The last thing I felt was safe.'

'I was fully in control. I'm good at that sort of thing.' He started the engine. 'A bit of fun hurts nobody.'

'Fun? I wouldn't call that fun! It was dicing with death!'

'Nonsense, darling.' He laughed again. 'Shall we drive into Windermere? We could find a café and have a spot of lunch there, rather than go back to the hotel.'

Dinah felt sick and shaky; the last thing she wanted was food. She hadn't recovered by bedtime and spent another wakeful night. Beside her, Richard was deeply asleep and apparently untroubled.

She couldn't stop thinking about him; he was not the sort of man she'd imagined him to be. She'd seen him as rather staid, perhaps a father figure, and that was the last thing he was. He was a risk-taker, a thrill-seeker. He loved horseracing, and she'd wanted to share the excitement of that, but the roller-coaster ride had been a step too far.

True, she'd thought him a little odd for not telling her more about his children or letting her see more of the house that was to be her home, but today – to hurtle down that mountain with the engine switched off had been plain crazy. Whatever he said, she knew very well it had been extremely dangerous. He'd apologised and said he hadn't meant to scare her.

'Then why did you do it?' she'd demanded.

'For the challenge. To measure my nerve and my driving skills,' he'd said. 'For the thrill of it. Me against the world.'

Wrapping her in his arms at bedtime, he'd petted and kissed her and asked to be forgiven. She couldn't resist him. But the question continued to niggle at her. Would any normal man risk his life and that of his bride of one day for that sort of thrill? She thought not, and it was making her nervous and wary of him.

For the first time she felt a prickle of unease. She hardly knew him, and she didn't understand him. It was going to take her time to settle down.

Sunday morning turned out to be a little brighter. Richard and Dinah took a walk, then had a late lunch and read the Sunday papers. The news from the continent was disquieting. The fascists were increasing their hold in Germany. When they set out for home, the clouds had thickened and it was raining again. Dinah kept a nervous watch on Richard but here on the main roads he seemed a good and careful driver.

He lived in Woolton. Dinah was not familiar with that district of Liverpool and had not seen his house in daylight. When she got out to open the wrought-iron gates she was craning to see all she could. The house was built of smoke-blackened brick in the Victorian Gothic style. It had three storeys and narrow arched windows. Sharply pointed eaves reached up against the black clouds. No light showed inside.

Dinah thought it looked deserted, and shivered. 'I thought the children would be here?'

'They are. Their rooms look out over the back garden.'

Richard rang the bell and then opened the door with his key. His housekeeper was coming down the stairs to meet them. Dinah had thought her rather a cold woman at their wedding. Today there was no smile of welcome.

He said, 'Please take our bags upstairs, Mrs Banks.'

Dinah held on to hers. 'I'd like to freshen up after the journey,' she said.

'Yes, of course. I'll show you.' He turned to the housekeeper. 'Tell the children we're here and they're to come down to the sitting room in ten minutes.'

'Yes, sir.'

It surprised Dinah that they hadn't come running to meet their father. They must have heard him ring the doorbell.

'Thank you. We'll have dinner in fifteen minutes.'

'You said seven thirty, sir.'

'Yes, so I did. As soon as you're ready, then.'

The woman went swiftly upstairs ahead of them.

'Come on up, Dinah. I'll show you our bedroom and bathroom.'

It was a big bedroom hung with heavy dark draperies in the Victorian style.

'Do you like it?'

'It's very nice.'

'The bathroom is right opposite, across the landing.'

There was a vast bath on splayed feet and a lavatory with blue flowers inside the pan. Dinah rinsed her face and ran a comb through her hair without wasting time. She didn't want to keep Richard and the children waiting.

When she came out, Richard said, 'You'll want to see the rooms your mother and the nurse will use. I told Mrs Banks to prepare them.' He threw open the next door along the landing. 'We've always called this the guest room, but I can't remember when anybody last slept here. I thought it would suit your mother.'

It was very similar to the room in which she and Richard would sleep. Dinah wondered for the first time if her mother would be happy here with this strange family.

'Mrs Banks suggested we bring in this day bed, and also that small armchair. She thought it would make the room more comfortable for an invalid.'

'That was thoughtful of her.'

'Your mother could eat her meals at this little table if she doesn't feel like coming down.'

Dinah went to the window and looked out into the garden. She could hear the wind moaning through the large trees and see them swaying against the scudding clouds.

'Mum will be pleased with this,' she told him. But would she?

'We'll fetch her tomorrow morning. The nurse will be starting at nine o'clock.'

He led her down to the sitting room. The heavy velvet curtains were already drawn and a big fire roared in the grate. Tonight, it seemed a warm and comfortable room; there were several framed photographs on the top of the piano. Dinah went to look at them.

'My parents,' Richard told her. 'They worked very hard. The button trade meant everything to them.'

They looked a lot older than her own mother, almost Victorian. 'You were their only child?'

'No, I had two brothers. They both died in the war, fighting in the trenches.'

Dinah shivered again. 'How awful for your mother.'

'It happened to a great many mothers, I'm afraid.'

'I know. My mother lost her husband and two brothers in the war.'

Feeling on tenterhooks, Dinah warmed her hands at the blaze while she waited for the children to come down. It had been on her mind that she'd not started off well with them. She'd not given them enough attention on her wedding day. A moment later, Mark's head came round the sitting room door. He was towing Nellie after him and they both looked agitated.

Richard said, 'Now, you two, come and sit down here on the sofa. I want to talk to you.' With heavy deliberation, he went on, 'You saw Dinah and me married on Friday. That makes her your new mother. I want you to call her Mum and help her settle into the family.'

Mark burst out heatedly, 'Call her Mum! That's a bit rich, isn't it?' His dark eyes were assessing her. Dinah could feel his resentment. 'Why spring it on us like that? Why didn't you warn us you meant to get married again? The first we heard of it was on Friday morning. Why keep it a big secret?'

Nellie was clutching what looked like a ball of ribbons to her and said nothing, but Dinah saw the look of horror on her face before she buried it in the cushions. She felt equally tongue-tied. The poor kids had recently lost their mother. What was Richard thinking of? It would have been kinder both to them and to her if he'd introduced them sooner, and he certainly shouldn't push her forward as a replacement mother like this. She opened her mouth to tell him so, but then realised she shouldn't criticise what he'd done in front of his children.

She managed to say instead, 'Hello, Mark and Nellie. You can call me Dinah if you'd rather. In fact, I think that might be better.'

Mark said with studied insolence, 'Hello, Stepmother.'

Richard said sternly, 'Come along, Nellie, there's no need to be this shy. I want you to be civilised and say hello.'

Slowly, the little girl lifted her head, but she wouldn't look at Dinah. 'Hello, Dinah,' she said obediently.

Dinah saw that the ball of ribbons was some sort of doll. 'How are you getting on at your new school?' she asked. 'Are you enjoying it?'

Nellie's face twisted in sudden fear. 'No, I hate it. I don't want to go back there.'

'Don't be silly,' Richard burst out. 'You've hardly tried it yet. You'll settle down in time.'

'I won't. I don't like it. I want to go back to my old school. I've got friends there.'

'Well, you can't. This school is better.'

Dinah was embarrassed but tried to smile. She put out a hand to the child. That made Nellie look up, but she pulled herself further along the sofa. Her deep blue eyes were full of suspicion.

Making an effort, Dinah said, 'I hope we'll be friends before long, Nellie.'

'Have you nothing to say for yourself, Mark?' Richard snapped.

'It's all so soon. It's only four months since Mum died. Why didn't you warn us?'

Richard was angry. 'Because I knew you'd kick up a fuss like this.'

'What are we supposed to do?' Mark asked rudely. 'Wish you every happiness?'

'Yes, why not? You could at least try being polite to your new mother.'

'I've got a holiday task to do,' he said, leaping to his feet. 'I'll get into trouble at school if it isn't done.'

Richard said, 'Dinner will be ready. I've asked Mrs Banks to give us something special tonight.'

'You enjoy it, Dad. I'm not hungry after this. Come on, Nellie, let's go.'

She shot to her feet and grabbed his arm; she couldn't get out of the door quickly enough. Mark paused on the threshold to look Dinah in the eye. 'I hope you know what you've let yourself in for,' he said before closing the door quietly.

Dinah was horrified. She swallowed hard. This wasn't the happy family she'd looked forward to joining. And again, this wasn't the Richard she'd thought she knew.

She said slowly, 'The children and I should have met sooner, Richard. Been given time to get used to each other. Then we'd have known what to expect.'

He was still angry. 'Mark's an impossible boy. I was afraid you'd be put off.'

'It must have come as a shock to the children. They're grieving for their mother still. You'll have turned them against me.'

Richard's face clamped in a scowl. 'Mark will get over it and Nellie will be all right when she gets used to you.'

There was a knock on the door and Mrs Banks's head came round the edge. 'The pheasants are on the table and ready to carve,' she announced.

Richard stood up, 'Good. Remind the children that dinner is ready and they must come down now. Come on, Dinah.' He strode ahead of her to the dining room.

The table was beautifully laid with white damask, silver and flickering candles, but Dinah didn't feel hungry. When she sat down she couldn't take her eyes from the two places that had been set for the children. 'Would you like a glass of sherry with your soup?' Richard asked.

He poured it without waiting for an answer. When the housekeeper came in, he barked at her, 'Have you told them dinner's ready?'

'Yes, sir, but they haven't come down yet.'

'Then we'll start without them.'

Dinah was shocked again. This wasn't at all what she'd envisaged. The pheasant was excellent but she found it hard to swallow. The children never did come.

When they'd finished eating, Richard was about to take Dinah back to the sitting room fire when Mrs Banks said, 'What shall I do about the children's meal? I'm keeping it warm—'

'Don't bother,' Richard snapped. 'If they can't come to the table at the proper time, they can go to bed hungry.'

Chapter Seven

In the sitting room, Dinah threw herself down on the sofa. 'Richard, should you send the children to bed hungry?'

'They have to be disciplined. They'd grow up wild if I didn't.'

'Not like this.' She'd never been treated with anything but love and kindness, and she knew it was the same in Aunt Enid's house. Goodness knows, Tim had had his wild moments, but he was always polite and took the feelings of others into account. He and she had had happy childhoods, but these two children looked the picture of misery. 'We should have avoided a scene like that.'

He seemed upset too. 'I'm sorry,' he said. 'It's spoiled your first night here.'

Dinah sighed. 'Where are the children now?'

'They'll stay up on the top floor. They use the old day nursery as a living room. Their bedrooms are up on there too.'

'And you use this room?'

'Yes.'

'But that means you hardly see anything of them.'

'We're up and down. They have supper in the dining room with me every evening.'

'You mean they did before they went to boarding school.' Dinah's spirits were sinking. She couldn't forget that on the night he'd brought her to see this house he'd shown more interest in his horses than in his children. 'What about breakfast?'

'I need to get to work in the mornings. They have theirs later.'

'Shouldn't you rethink their routine? From now on, they'll only be here in the school holidays. How am I to get to know them if we hardly meet?'

'Don't fuss, Dinah. You'll find you see more than enough of them.'

She sighed. 'Perhaps I should go up to see them now?'

'They won't expect it.'

'All the more reason.' He ignored that and turned to another page in his newspaper. She stood up. 'I think I should. Why don't you come with me?'

He shook his head. 'No. Mark can be quite aggressive with me; he's always trying to pick a fight. You'll be better on your own.'

'Right.' She must make the effort. She had to get to know them. 'Where is this old nursery?'

'Straight up, on the top floor. It's over our bedroom.'

Dinah left the room. She could hear Mrs Banks clattering saucepans in the kitchen. All was silent and dark upstairs and she had to seek the light switches as she went. She paused on the top floor. Which door? She tried one, but the bedroom it revealed was in darkness. She tried the next and the light was dazzling. Two sets of eyes jerked up in surprise to see who'd come in. Mark was writing in an exercise book; Nellie, who looked as though she'd been crying, had part of a jigsaw puzzle laid out in front of her.

'I'm sorry,' Dinah said. 'We seem to have got off on the wrong foot.' They stared silently back at her. Nellie picked up her beribboned doll and nursed it as though for comfort.

Dinah went on, 'As we're all going to live here together, I'd like it to be in peace. We could be a happy family.'

'Fat chance,' Mark said derisively. 'Anyway, it'll only be in the school holidays.'

Dinah ignored that. She went to sit at the table with them and smiled from one to the other. 'Couldn't we be friends? Wouldn't you like us to go out and do things together as a family? Have a bit of fun?'

Mark kept his distance. 'That's never going to happen.'

'Why not?'

'Dad won't want it. He wouldn't take us out.'

'I think he would if I asked him.'

'Huh! You don't know him. He won't agree to anything he hasn't thought of himself. He reckons he's in charge and he decides on everything. Absolutely everything. He won't do what you want.'

Dinah gasped. Mark's words struck home. Hadn't she told Richard how much she loved her work and that she wanted to carry on at Carlton Hats? He'd brushed her wishes aside. But no, that wasn't fair. He was bending over backwards to help her mother.

'Have you ever tried him? Asked him for anything?'

'I asked him not to send me to boarding school.' Nellie's eyes were flooding with tears. 'I told him I didn't want to go. I'd been picked for the school choir at my old school, but he'd already decided we were going. He took us straight out to buy the uniforms and packed us off the very next day.'

'I didn't want to go either. What's more, term had already started,' Mark said bitterly. 'I don't know why he was in such a hurry.'

Dinah shivered. She was afraid it was because of her. But this was a large house and even as a newly married man he'd have all the privacy he needed while his children were living on the top floor. In any case, was privacy important to Richard? When she thought of how he'd behaved in the car on the way to the honeymoon hotel, she didn't think it was.

'And we asked him not to sack Bunty,' Mark went on. 'We pleaded with him not to. We wanted her to stay with us. And anyway, she had nowhere else to go. She'd been with us since Nellie was born. She's always looked after her – and me, of course.'

'And your dad sacked her? When was this?'

'Last week. Mrs Banks came in her place.'

'Mrs Banks has only been here since last week?'

'Yes. She says she started last Wednesday.'

Dinah was shocked. 'Good Lord! Why would your father do that?' Richard was doing some very odd things. But why? There must be some reason. 'I'll talk to him about it.'

'Fat lot of good that'll do.'

'Mark, the only way to understand is to ask your father about it.'

Mark straightened his lips and dipped his pen in the ink bottle. Dinah said, 'You upset him by not coming down for your supper.'

There was another frosty silence. Mark glared at his books. Nellie hugged her doll tighter.

'Aren't you hungry? Shall I ask Mrs Banks to make something for you?'

'No!' Mark burst out. 'Leave us alone, can't you? If you carry on like this, you'll have Dad storming up to start another row.'

Nellie was cringing back. It occurred to Dinah that they were scared of Richard.

'Do you put yourselves to bed?'

'Of course. Just leave us.'

She didn't know what else to do. 'Good night, then.'

Dinah went slowly back to the sitting room. Richard looked up from his newspaper. 'Has Mark calmed down yet?'

'Not entirely.'

'Still bristling for a fight? I was afraid he would be. He can be very difficult.'

'Richard, he said you'd sacked their nanny and hired a complete stranger only last week.' She saw the storm clouds gathering on Richard's handsome face.

'Yes,' he said, 'and did he tell you why?' He didn't wait for her answer. 'They aren't babies. They shouldn't need nannying any more. At fourteen and eight they're way too old, and as they're at boarding school they wouldn't see much of her if she was here. There will be three more people living in this house from now on, you, your mother and her nurse. We need a proper cook-general who can cater for a large house and more people, not a nanny to take care of absent adolescent children who can do no better than turn her hand to an occasional meal.'

Dinah hesitated. 'I can see the logic of that, but did you explain it to them? They say you whisked them off to boarding school with hardly any warning. They didn't even know we were getting married until our wedding day.'

She knew he was angry but she couldn't stop. 'They see only that you want them out of the way and the one person they knew and trusted has been sent packing. You can't expect them to be happy that there's a stranger in her place. Two strangers, if you count me as well.'

'Things change. They can't expect everything to remain the same, not in this world.'

'But they lost their mother a few months ago and now they've lost the nanny who's looked after them since Mark was six. What I'm trying to say is that sudden changes like that upset children. They'd upset anybody. I want them to accept me, but all these other things make it difficult for them to adjust to me.'

Richard's face was screwing. 'Now, Dinah, you listen to me. They're my children and I know what's best for them and I'll not have you interfering. Now you're my wife, I'll decide what's best for you too.'

'What?' Dinah was beside herself. 'You're not telling me I have no choice in—'

'You chose to marry me, didn't you? The law expects me to support you from now on. The choice of how it will be done is mine. I don't think we should quarrel about this. It won't get you anywhere.'

'I was brought up to make my own decisions. Everybody should have a say in what happens to them. When you suggested Mum should come to live here, I discussed it with her more than once.'

'She's too ill to care. She just wants to be close to you.'

'Yes, but —'

'So other people take the responsibility for her and decide on what would be best.'

'I know I did that.' But it made Dinah feel guilty. It was what she'd wanted, not necessarily what was best for her mother.

'And as your husband I support your decision. But now you are my wife the responsibility for her welfare is mine too. Just as your welfare is my responsibility and it's not up to you to question it.'

Dinah frowned. 'I'm not sure I agree with that.'

She could see that Richard was losing his temper. His handsome face had twisted and grown ugly. He put it down on a level with hers and said heatedly, 'It doesn't matter whether you agree or not. I am your husband: I will take care of you from now on.' He got to his feet and stamped out of the room, slamming the door behind him.

Dinah fell back among the cushions on the sofa, tears burning her eyes. Richard was cross because she'd disagreed with the way he was treating his children, she understood that much. She also understood that she'd given up everything she knew in order to come here and share his life.

The tears began to fall; she couldn't stop them. She got out her handkerchief. Why hadn't they talked things like this through before they were married? He certainly had some very strange ideas.

But she'd been head over heels in love with him and Richard had told her he loved her. Upsets like this made it harder to feel love for him, but she was surely not so shallow as to say she no longer did? Last week she loved him enough to welcome marriage; three days of it could not change that. Of course she still loved him. Yet here they were, already arguing. Getting married brought all the emotions up to the surface, but crying here by herself would solve nothing. She needed to make it up. She couldn't bear to be at loggerheads with him.

Dinah knew she had to pull herself together. She dried her eyes and went to look for him. She could see the light on in his study further down the hall and knew he'd be there. But she felt a tear-stained mess and decided to go to the bathroom to bathe her eyes in cold water first. She ran a comb through her hair, which made her feel a bit better, but she still looked miserable in the mirror. She went downstairs to find Richard.

'Dinah!' He leaped to his feet as soon as he saw her and threw his arms round her. 'I'm so sorry. I hate to think I've upset you.'

'Why did we fall out like that? An argument so soon!'

'Just a slight tiff. Darling, I can't bear to see you looking so sad. Forgive me.'

Dinah felt reassured. He did love her. All they needed was time to adjust to each other. 'Being married is going to take me a bit of getting used to. You'll have to be patient with me.'

'Yes, it means big changes in your life.'

'I don't think I thought it through. Big changes for you too.'

'I've been married for most of my adult life. I didn't like being on my own. So perhaps for me the changes aren't so big.'

He'd been sitting at his desk. It looked as though he spent a lot of his time in this room. There were papers all over his desk, no doubt relating to his business. She hadn't yet been to see his factory, though she knew he wanted her to work there. Her eye caught a photograph in a silver frame on the mantelpiece. She leaned over the popping gas fire to pick it up. A younger, even more handsome Richard was smiling out at her.

'Oh, you served in the war too.' He was resplendent in full army dress uniform. 'A captain?'

'Yes.' She could hear the pride in his voice. 'I managed to survive the war, though my two older brothers were killed.'

'You fought in the trenches?'

'Yes. On the Somme and through Arras.'

'All through the war?'

'It was 1916 when I was sent out.'

'All the same, that's two years.'

'The best part of three, actually.'

'To have survived that long is almost miraculous.'

'I was very careful to make the right decisions, both for myself and my men. I didn't want to lead them into trouble.'

'Careful? Richard, that's the last thing you are. You're a big risk-taker.'

His smile had gone. 'Only when I'm quite sure it's safe to do it.'

Dinah hesitated. That sounded arrogant. She knew he didn't always make the right decisions. 'Were you not injured?'

'Oh, several times, but never seriously. I always managed to recover and go back to fight again.'

'Gosh! That makes you a hero. Your parents must have been proud of you.'

He sighed, 'Well, I think they might have preferred my brothers to have survived instead.'

'What?' She shivered. What sort of son would think that of his parents? For the first time it occurred to Dinah that he was a very unhappy man.

'Both Rufus and Gerald were being trained to work in the business, and when they were killed it left Father with a gap in his plans. He said I'd have to do it.'

'Didn't you want to?' She was amazed. Most of the lads in Picton Street would envy him. He'd had a thriving business handed to him on a plate.

'I wanted to work with horses. I thought perhaps I could keep a few and give riding lessons, hire them out for hacking, that sort of thing. Dad was against it. He said for those who kept horses, it was usually a matter of spending out on them. But I'd have made a living and enjoyed doing it.'

'Not such a good living as the family business provides.'

'I've hated buttons all my life. My parents lived for that small factory. They decided I should train as an accountant to better understand things like profit and loss. I hated that too. Figures. I envy your friend Tim. He's doing what I'd have loved to. do.'

'You could have gone as a stable boy too.'

'Mucking out stables wasn't exactly where I wanted to start, and I'd have had to run away from school. My father was a powerful man who always got his own way. I had to do what he wanted even though I knew it was the wrong decision for me.'

'Richard!' She couldn't believe his business didn't satisfy him. 'Now you have a free hand and you're running it yourself, surely you enjoy it?'

'I suppose being in charge does make things better.'

'It's given you a good life. You're able to indulge yourself, you own race horses. It's given you everything you could possibly want: a big house, marriage.' She smiled. 'A second marriage even.'

'Yes, and I love you very much, Dinah. I couldn't wait to bring you here to live with me. I've now got exactly the wife I want.'

Dinah sighed. She was afraid that wasn't strictly true. She was not exactly what he wanted: he wanted a second wife who didn't question his decisions, who fell in with his every whim. Perhaps a second wife more like his first?

She'd been curious about his first wife from the moment she'd met him, and now she asked, 'Was your first wife happy to let you organise every little detail in her life?'

His lips straightened into a hard line. She'd known he wouldn't want to talk about her. 'I wish you'd tell me about her. Why not?'

His cheeks were flushed. 'Don't pry. Many second wives develop an unhealthy obsession about the first. They want to know whether she was prettier, whether she was good with children or not. Whether she managed the house or garden better, whether she could cook . . . I don't want you to bother your head about Myra. As far as I'm concerned all that is over and done with. You're a different person.'

Dinah let her breath out very slowly. The message was clear: Richard didn't want her to know anything about his earlier life.

Chapter Eight

The next morning, Dinah and Richard were finishing breakfast when Mrs Banks showed the nurse Richard had hired to look after Sarah into the dining room. Dinah welcomed her, putting out her hand.

The girl took it. 'Joan Allen,' she said. She was young and chatty, and looked cheerful. Dinah thought her mother would take to her.

Shortly afterwards, she and Richard set out for Picton Street. Sarah was ready and waiting in the living room. Enid had helped her dress and packed two bags to go with her. Richard carried them out to his car.

Sarah looked ill and exhausted. 'Dinah, I don't think this is a good idea. Wouldn't it be better if I stayed here?'

Dinah's heart sank. Her mother didn't want to come. Dinah felt guilty. She was moving Sarah to suit herself, and she too had doubts about whether she'd be happy at Ardwick House.

Enid said, 'Sarah, we've talked this through, haven't we? You decided you should go, that you'd be fine once you'd settled in with Dinah.'

Sarah sighed heavily. 'I did, didn't I?'

'Poor Mum,' Dinah said. 'I want you to come. We have to be together so I can look after you.'

'Perhaps Enid will look after me. She always does. She's very good.'

'I'd be happy to look after you, Sarah,' Enid assured her. 'But I think it would be better for both of you if you went to live with Dinah. You'll see more of each other that way.'

She retreated to the hall, pulling Dinah with her, and lowered her voice to say softly, 'It's just that she has no energy. All she wants is to be left alone. She'll be all right once she settles in.'

Richard was back. 'We'll get her into bed right away,' he said, 'so she can rest. The nurse is there to take care of her.'

'Goodbye, Sarah.' Enid gave her a parting hug.

Sarah clung to her. 'I don't like leaving you. You will come and see me?'

'Yes, of course. Don't you fret. You'll be very comfortable in your new home.'

Enid was giving Dinah a farewell hug when Richard announced, 'I've given notice to the estate agent that we're ending the tenancy of this house at the end of the month.'

Dinah was astounded. It took her breath away. He'd said nothing to her about this.

'We'll come back in a day or two,' he went on to Enid, 'to sort out what Sarah and Dinah want to keep, and then I'll arrange for a house clearance firm to get rid of the rest of the stuff.'

Dinah felt ready to explode. How could he be so unfeeling as to say this in front of her mother? Surely he could see she was upset at leaving her friend and her home of many years? She managed to keep quiet, but only because if she snapped at her husband of less than a week it would upset her mother more.

She got into the back seat of the car feeling shocked and upset. Sarah, in the front, laid her head back and closed her eyes, some strands of thin and greying hair falling over the back of her seat. Dinah fingered them and felt like crying. She shouldn't be moving her mother when she was so ill. Sarah would be happier staying in her own home.

When Richard pulled up at his front door, they had to wake Sarah up. She was past noticing her surroundings, but the nurse was attentive and seemed kind. Together they helped Sarah to the guest room.

'Would you like to rest on the day bed for a while, Mrs Radcliffe?' Joan asked. 'I'll make you a hot drink. Milk perhaps, or tea?'

'Good.' Richard was rubbing his hands. 'We can go to work now, Dinah. I want to show you my business. We mustn't neglect that.'

She swallowed back an angry retort and pulled a chair closer to the day bed.

'I'd like to stay here with Mum until she settles,' she said as calmly as she could.

'As you wish,' he said coldly. He strode to the door shutting it behind him with some force.

Dinah sat beside her talking softly about Windermere and the Lakes. She learned for the first time that her mother had spent her honeymoon in Torquay. She would not leave until Sarah fell asleep.

Richard was not in a good mood when Dinah finally said she was ready to go.

'It's so late it's hardly worth going at all,' he said. 'Still, I suppose we might as well. I do hope you'll be able to tear yourself away from your mother a little earlier tomorrow.'

Dinah was determined not to let him rile her, nor to give him any reason to fly into a rage. 'Yes, of course. But today is Mum's first morning here and we haven't seen each other for a few days.'

'From the way you carry on, it could have been a few months.'

Dinah was tense and anxious because married life was proving to be more difficult than she'd expected, and sarcasm from Richard was more than she could stand.

'Richard, I want us to be happy, not keep on having these arguments, disagreements, whatever you want to call them.'

He was forcing his words out through straight lips, keeping his eyes on the road. 'It's you who's arguing. I've done my best for your mother. She has a nurse to see to her needs. Now I want you to give some thought to me and my needs.'

'What about me and my needs?' she blazed back at him. 'You had no right to interfere with the tenancy of our home. I wanted to keep that on for a little while in case Mum wants to go back.' And she had begun to see it as a bolt hole for herself if she found she couldn't live with him.

He sneered. 'Don't be silly. She can't go back. It would be a waste of money to keep it on.'

'A waste of money?' That shocked her too. 'With your racehorses, and the champagne and fancy meals we've been enjoying, I can't believe twelve and six a week to rent a two up two down would matter to you.'

'Any expense matters if there's no point to it.'

'No point? It's my mother's home. My home! It has nothing to do with you.'

He pulled up in front of an old rambling building with few windows, turned, and took both her hands in his. 'Dinah love, it has everything to do with me. You belong to me now.'

She snatched her hands away in fury. 'I'm not another of your chattels.'

'I'm your husband and the responsibility for looking after you is mine.'

'I can look after myself. I neither need nor want that sort of help.'

He ignored her. 'I'll look after your mother too. You must leave these things to me.'

'For heaven's sake! I need a say in matters that affect me and Mum. Why not? This is the twentieth century, Richard. You sound like someone from Queen Victoria's time.'

His arms went round her. 'Please don't carry on like this, Dinah. It churns me up. I want us to be happy as much as you do. I've brought you to see my business and I don't want my staff to see us scrapping like this. What will they think?'

Dinah could feel tears scalding her eyes.

'We'll go to a café I know round the corner first,' he said, making the car glide forward. 'You need a few moments to pull yourself together. I can't take my bride in there with tears running down her face. I want you to learn about the business and become involved. I want them to respect you.'

Fifteen minutes and a cup of tea later, Dinah had her tears under control. Or she had as long as she didn't think about how much Richard had changed since she'd married him. But perhaps he hadn't changed? Perhaps he'd been like this all the time? He'd told her little about himself, and nothing at all about the life he led, so how could she tell?

He wanted to control everything: her, her mother, his children, his home. Being in love had made her take leave of her senses. She'd been looking at him through rose-tinted spectacles.

Aunt Enid had warned her not to rush into marriage. Dinah knew now she'd been too impatient to become Mrs Richard Cameron Aldgrave Haldane to think through what she was doing. What had Enid said? Marry in haste and repent at leisure. In her case she was repenting in haste too. It was only four days since their wedding.

They walked the hundred yards back to his factory in order to give her what he called 'a little air'. It was in a run-down area of the city near the docks. Like his house, it was bigger than she'd expected, but in a drab and smoke-blackened building.

He reached the door. 'You're all right now?'

'Yes.'

'I do love you, Dinah. I do so want our marriage to be a success. I want the people who work for me to like you and admire you. Come on, smile for them.'

She tried as she followed him inside and down a passage into a big open workroom, noisy with the clatter of machines stamping out buttons. It was dusty too, and the only natural light came through dirty skylights. Electric lights swung on long cords from the ceiling.

She was awestruck. This was Richard's business, where he earned the sort of profit that enabled him to buy racehorses. It was a lot bigger than Carlton Hats and there were more workers. Dinah sensed that at the sight of her and Richard they suddenly snapped to attention and gave all their attention to the job in hand. Richard ignored them all and started explaining things to her.

'These are shirt buttons for the Liverpool Shirt Company.' He had to raise his voice against the noise. Tiny mother-of-pearl buttons were being collected and packed in boxes by girls in dark green overalls, their hair covered with turbans of the same cloth. They were curious about her and kept glancing up at her from under lowered lashes, but there was a heavy atmosphere too, and on this first visit she couldn't have said what it was. She guessed immediately that Richard was not a popular boss.

She smiled back at the girls and murmured hello when they caught her eye, but she knew they'd never hear her in this clatter. Richard took no notice.

'Buttons for women's dresses,' these were big and deep red in colour. He was waving towards one machine and then another. 'Rubber buttons, for the Supreme Underwear Company. They use them on liberty bodices. They won't break when they're put through the mangle.' Dinah recognised them from her childhood. Grey buttons were coming from yet another machine. 'These are for Mersey Tailoring: men's suits, coats, that sort of thing.'

'What about the petersham ribbon?' Dinah had to repeat the question, and the noise was hurting her ears. He took her back through the passage and ushered her into an empty room with several filing cabinets ranged along one wall. With the door closed the noise was reduced to a dull background rumble.

'The ribbons are made in a different room. Our core business is buttons. We produce them to order for clothes manufacturers, and also stitched on cards to be sold retail. You've probably seen them in haberdashery shops and department stores.'

Dinah looked up as an elderly man came in with some ledgers. He was wearing a khaki drill coat. 'This is my foreman Gilbert Hopper,' Richard said. He indicated her. 'My wife.'

She put out her hand. 'Dinah.'

He looked nervously at Richard before taking it. 'How d'you do?'

'I want my wife to understand my business, so explain what you do and tell the others to do the same.' The phone rang at that moment and Richard went towards it.

Dinah asked, 'Shall I ask Mr Hopper to show me the room where the ribbons are made?'

Richard ignored her. He was speaking to the caller.

She smiled at the foreman. 'We might as well make a start.'

He set off down the passage and Dinah followed. A woman came towards them carrying a tray.

'This is Gertie Jones, who takes care of the cleaning and the tea-making.'

The woman's rotund figure was wrapped in what had once been a white overall but was now somewhat stained. 'Just taking in Mr Haldane's tea.' The tray was elegantly set for two and included a plate of biscuits.

Mr Hopper was hovering. 'Do you want to go back for that?'

She smiled. 'I'd like to see the ribbon room first.'

He threw open another door. 'This is it.' All was silent and in semi-darkness. He switched on the lights. 'We haven't any work for these machines now. They're out of use.'

'Oh!' Dinah was taken aback. 'No work at all? Since when?'

'It's declined over the years, but we haven't had a contract for ribbons for some time, not since Mrs Haldane . . .' The foreman looked embarrassed. 'I'm sorry, I mean the other Mrs Haldane.'

Dinah felt that to clear the air she needed to speak directly about her predecessor. 'My husband's first wife?'

'Yes. She looked after the ribbons business.'

That surprised Dinah. Now she was more curious than ever.

'She was Myra Copthorne before she married. Daughter of the owner of Arthur Copthorne Limited.' Mr Hopper was looking edgy, clearly uncomfortable with the conversation.

'Copthorne?' The name seemed familiar.

'Copthorne Ribbons. They had a big place further along the Dock Road.'

'Oh, yes! Of course! I used to work at Carlton Hats. I remember seeing the name printed on some of the reels of petersham ribbon we used there.'

'That's right. We still used the Copthorne name and we supplied Carlton's.'

Dinah hesitated. 'What happened? I mean, why did you stop supplying them?'

The foreman wouldn't look at her now. 'I don't know. I never get to hear things like that.'

Dinah knew that less than three months ago Richard had asked Mr McKay for an order to supply them again. She also knew that Carlton's had always worked full time and hadn't laid staff off. No reason why they should: they made gorgeous hats. But that meant they still needed petersham ribbon, so why had Richard been turned away empty-handed?

'What happened to the original Copthorne Ribbons business?'

'Myra's brother was killed in the war, and when her father died the firm went under.'

'What d'you mean, went under? It went bankrupt?'

'No, not that. Mr Haldane took it over. He wanted to run it in with his business and he brought these machines and some of the staff here. Stands to reason, doesn't it? The expense of running it would be less.'

Dinah was burning with curiosity. 'When was this?'

'Oh, we were still in the old factory for a year or so after he married Myra. It's a decade or so now since he closed it down. Things got hard for everybody in the twenties and now, with the Depression, there's less ribbon needed and work is harder to find. Trade is slack.'

'But not for buttons?'

Mr Hopper hesitated. She could see he didn't want to answer questions. He said, 'Mr Haldane finds the button trade more to his taste. It's what he grew up with.'

She walked further down the passage and opened another door. 'Is this another workroom?' She switched on the lights and saw that it wasn't being used either. 'Are these machines to make ribbons too?'

'No, buttons. As I said, trade is slack. We aren't all that busy with buttons either at the moment.'

The room seemed vast. 'Only half the button machines are in use?'

'Mr Haldane's closed this room up. He's had to lay off staff.'

Richard came down the passage. 'There you are, Dinah. I've been looking for you.'

'Mr Hopper's been showing me round.' She guessed she'd learned more from him than she would have done from Richard.

'Yes, thank you, Hopper. But there's a good deal I need to explain before you'll understand our set-up.'

Dinah tried to smile. 'He's been telling me about . . .' She almost said Copthorne Ribbons, but Hopper's face stopped her. He looked almost scared. Richard wouldn't be pleased to hear they'd been talking about his first wife. Instead she said, 'About petersham ribbon. I used to use that on the hats I made.'

'Yes, thank you, Mr Hopper. Dinah, why don't you come and see my office?' he said dropping his voice as they went down the corridor. 'I want to tell you about the staff and the pay scales I use. Perhaps you'd like to help me make up the wages every week? It's impossible to let a paid employee know what all the others earn. It would only cause trouble, wouldn't it?'

Dinah paused to think. Would it? Perhaps, but she'd liked Gilbert Hopper: he'd seemed a reasonable and responsible person. 'I suppose you'd have to trust them.'

Richard's office was reached through a small room presided over by Miss O'Marney, a buxom middle-aged lady with heavy spectacles whom he introduced as his secretary. She leaped to her feet and offered Dinah a podgy hand.

'Very pleased to meet you, Mrs Haldane,' she said, then sank back at a large desk furnished with a telephone and a typewriter.

'I thought you would like to work in this room too.' Richard showed Dinah a more modest desk jammed against the stationery cupboard. 'I want you to know all about my business so you can really help me.'

He led her through to the adjoining office, which was large and airy and had his name on a wooden plaque on the door. He began handing ledgers over to her, explaining what the entries were and what he wanted her to do.

For the rest of the afternoon, Dinah struggled to master his pay scales and method of bookkeeping. She'd never done work like this before and wasn't sure she could do it to his satisfaction. Her predecessor in the job had been meticulous: the ledgers had been very neatly kept.

She turned to Miss O'Marney. 'Who's been keeping these books up to now?'

'Recently, it's been me.' The secretary kept her voice at whisper level as though afraid Richard might overhear what she said.

Dinah was puzzled. Miss O'Marney was clearly capable of doing the work, so why did Richard want her here? Surely a wife's place was in the home, especially a newly married wife. In the car going home that evening, she put it to him.

'Darling, everything's running smoothly at home. It's with the business that I need help. I thought you'd want to do that.'

'Of course I want to help all I can.'

'You're used to going out to work, and we can see more of each other this way. I've been looking forward to having you at my side, teaching you how to run the business.'

'Do you think I could?'

'I'm sure you could.'

After that, Dinah went with him to the office every day, though she found it a struggle to grasp what it was he wanted her to do. She asked him many questions but rarely seemed to get a clear answer.

At home, everything was running smoothly; he was right about that. Joan Allen and Mrs Banks seemed to have taken to each other. They both fussed around her mother and Sarah seemed content with the arrangement. Meals appeared on the table on time, and the days passed without disruption. In the office, however, things were not so harmonious. Richard had said he meant to teach her how to run his business, but that was not what he was doing. Dinah soon found out there were some things she was allowed to know and some he wanted to keep hidden. She was expected to enter daily figures in some ledgers, but she saw him working on others that he kept locked away in his safe.

If she asked questions, there was always some reason why he couldn't sit down with her at that moment. When she asked for explanations in the car and didn't get them, she began to think he was fobbing her off.

She still had little idea of how the business was run, but she could see they weren't getting enough orders.

She really couldn't understand how Richard could afford the champagne lifestyle he'd been drawing her into. He had his children to support, a live-in housekeeper and now a nurse too. He owned two racehorses and was paying to have them trained, as well as for stabling and feed. Tim had told her that keeping a racehorse cost a fortune. And she couldn't help remembering how Mr McKay had often called out,

'Young lady, when you leave an empty storeroom, please put the light out. I'm not made of money.' Yet Carlton Hats was bustling compared to this.

She took one of the ledgers into Richard's office and closed the door behind her so that Miss O'Marney wouldn't hear what they were saying. Then she looked him in the eye and asked, 'Does this business make a lot of money?'

His voice was harsh. 'No need to concern yourself with things like that, Dinah.'

'You said you wanted me to learn all about your business. Surely what it earns is very important?'

'It's not making quite as much profit as it used to. Things have tailed off a bit because of the Depression. It'll pick up again when the economy improves.'

'I see.' She looked him in the eye again. 'Are you going to pay me for working here?'

He laughed. 'You'll share in everything I have. You'll hardly need money.'

Was he expecting her to work for nothing? Dinah swallowed hard. 'Oh, but I will. I'm used to juggling the pennies,' she said as firmly as she could. 'There'll be the housekeeping, clothes, bus fares and such like. I'll have to have money.'

'I don't want you to worry about household affairs. I've always taken care of things like that. I'll drive you here and home again every day. For your clothes and personal needs, I'll open an account for you at Bunney's. You can buy things for the children there, get your hair cut, all that sort of thing.'

Dinah knew she sounded suspicious. 'A personal allowance, you mean? How much a month will that be?'

'No need to be mercenary, darling. You're my wife; I'll settle your bills, whatever you charge to your account.' He shrugged his shoulders. 'Is that all right?'

'I'd prefer you to put a figure on it.' She had no idea how much he'd feel was reasonable. 'In fact, I'd prefer to be paid a wage like everyone else.'

'Darling, as my wife you'd be working at salary level, but with an account you can spend as much as you like, so you'll be better off, won't you?'

'I suppose so.'

'You can have the account at Bon Marché or Lewis's if you prefer. Or why not more than one shop? Are you fussy about the cut and style of your clothes?'

Dinah laughed. 'I haven't been able to be too fussy up till now.'

'There you are then. I can give you a better standard of living than you've been used to, and you can have all the clothes and knick-knacks you want. I'm not ungenerous.'

She couldn't quibble with that. 'You're very generous,' she said. 'But I'd like a few shillings to rattle in my pocket. I'd feel bereft with nothing.'

'Of course.' He dug into his pocket and handed her a pound or two in change. 'In case you feel like an ice cream sometime. Let me know when you need more.'

'Thanks, I will.'

'I have to go out. I've got an appointment in town.' He picked up his hat and umbrella.

'What time will you be back?'

But he'd gone, slamming first the door of his office and then the outer door.

Dinah hardly knew what to make of it. Richard was generous, yes, and the money he'd given her was far more than she'd had to spend on herself before she was married, but all the same it was a very odd way of doing things.

She sank down on the chair behind his large mahogany partners' desk. Spread out before her were expensive implements denoting wealth and power. A silver lighter and matching cigarette box. When she lifted the lid, she saw it was filled with Black Russian cigarettes. A cut-glass ashtray, a cut-glass and silver ink stand, expensive pens.

What Mark had told her was right. It was clear Richard meant to control everything. But surely every married woman ran her own household, decided what should be bought and what meals would be put on the table? This wasn't at all the sort of marriage she'd expected to have.

He'd made no secret about wanting to control her. He'd said, 'You're mine now,' and he'd used her for his own ends.

Dinah asked herself yet again why Richard had wanted to marry her. He'd said he loved her and she'd taken him at his word, but to treat her the way he had on their honeymoon made her think he saw her as some sort of sexual toy, a plaything. He'd actually enjoyed the blue terror on her face during that downhill helter-skelter: she'd seen him smiling. Was that love? He was telling her one thing but showing her something quite different, and that made her shudder every time she thought of it.

Dinah stretched out on his office chair and tried to think. It was leather, of course, and comfortable enough to doze in. He had an impressive office, carpeted, with pictures on the wall.

Richard's way of controlling her was to isolate her from her friends and sap her confidence by belittling everything she did. He didn't want her to spend all day with her mother, so he brought her here. He said it was to work in the business, but there was little work for her to do. He was taking important decisions for her without consulting her. Was that how he'd taken over Myra's fortune?

Dinah pulled herself upright. She would have to fight to keep her friends and control her own life. To survive, she must change her habit of a lifetime. She must learn to hold her tongue, to think before she spoke. Richard must continue to believe she loved him, and that she accepted his bad moods as normal.

She must be very careful. If he were to suspect how she really felt and what she was doing, he could turn against her.

CHAPTER NINE

DINAH DIDN'T FIND settling into her new life easy. For her mother, things seemed even harder. She didn't always know where she was, and because they'd moved across town the doctor she'd come to trust could no longer visit her. Richard asked his own doctor to call and make himself known to her. Dinah insisted on staying home that morning to meet him.

Dr Jones was over sixty and rather stooped, but he seemed to exude energy. His bald head shone through thin strands of mouse-brown hair, and his manner to her mother was kind and soothing. She seemed to like him and Dinah thought she could trust him.

The children were making it plain they didn't want to know her. She introduced them to her mother and Joan, and both asked them to pop in again to see them, but they didn't do it. They kept out of Dinah's way, and when she went up to their old nursery for a chat they were non-committal and tried to look engrossed in their own affairs.

Dinah attempted to focus on her husband. She realised now that he had a more complicated personality than she'd first thought.

'You're always asking questions,' he said to her tetchily, though he must surely understand that a new wife would want to know every detail about his family and his past life. She asked about his school days, his parents and his brothers, but he wouldn't talk about personal matters unless he was in the right mood.

In the evenings, she liked to spend as much time as she could with her mother, until Joan wanted to settle her for the night and she came downstairs again.

Late in the evening, Richard had a habit of disappearing either to the garage or to his study. Feeling at a loose end Dinah would drift round the house, trying to familiarise herself with her new home. One night she decided to take another look at the small sitting room Richard had said his mother had used.

She must have enjoyed sewing, Dinah thought, eyeing the fine Singer sewing machine. Dinah's mother had made clothes for them both but had never owned a good machine like this. If only she were well enough now, she'd love to use it.

Dinah opened the drawers in a small chest. It was full of cotton reels, needles and pins and other sewing aids. In another chest, all neatly folded, she found offcuts and leftover bits of material from garments his mother must have made.

Dinah crossed the room to the bookcase and saw immediately the calf-leather covers of what must be a photograph album. Her heart quickened as she opened it. Here was Richard, a child of about three, wearing a sunbonnet. Or was it one of his brothers? There were several little boys pictured here and all were very good-looking children. It was only when she saw them photographed together that she could reliably pick Richard out, and then only because he was the youngest.

There were pictures of his mother wearing blouses buttoned high up her neck and her hair piled on top on her head. His father was an upright confident figure in a heavy worsted suit with a gold watch chain across his waistcoat. They looked solid, hard-working, Victorian citizens, and now she was able to visualise the family in her mind's eye. They were her in-laws, and she was glad to know what they'd looked like.

In the background, the house and garden looked more attractive than they did now. Somebody in Richard's family had been a keen photographer. She went to return the album to its place on the shelf and found it had been hiding another one with white leather covers that was being held flat against the back of the bookcase. Dinah wondered if it had been deliberately hidden.

It looked like an album of wedding photographs. She lifted it out and had it open on the table in moments.

She heard her own gasp of surprise when she realised it held the pictures of Richard's first wedding day. This had been a dream wedding. The bride wore white satin with a filmy veil and carried an immense trailing bouquet of flowers. Dinah's fingers shook as she turned the pages. She studied Myra's face eagerly. The Copthorne heiress was a smiling and happy girl of about her own age and she'd been very pretty.

Her heart turned over to see a younger even more handsome Richard wearing morning dress with a carnation in his buttonhole. Myra was smiling up at her groom with love in her eyes.

Dinah felt a shaft of guilt and half closed the album to listen for footsteps. Richard would not like her seeing this, but what were photographs taken for if not to be looked at?

There were pictures of them riding away from the church in a carriage pulled by two high-stepping greys, and of their four-tier wedding cake. It had been a summer wedding. The guests were wearing filmy dresses as they smiled into the camera and the reception had been held in a garden with a larger house than this in the background. Myra had come from a very comfortable middle-class family.

When the half term holiday was over, Richard told Nellie that he'd drive her back to school.

'Please, Daddy, I don't want to go back.' Dinah had never seen Nellie as defiant as this. 'I hate the place.'

'It's no good fussing, Nellie. You're going. It's a good school and I've decided it's the best thing for you. I don't want to hear another word about this.'

The child dissolved into tears. Mark put an arm round her shoulder and said, 'Please, Dad, let her stay at home and go back to her old school. It's what she really wants.'

'How many times do I have to tell you? When I say no, I mean no.'

'Dad, Nellie's unhappy there. She's being bullied.'

'Bullied?' He bent to put his angry face close to his daughter's.

'Yes,' she whispered.

'Show some guts, child. Don't let them get away with that sort of thing. Kick back at them. Let them know you won't stand for it.'

Mark stood his ground. 'Dad. She can't.'

'Can't? Of course you can, Nellie. You've got to learn to stand up to people.'

Nellie dried her eyes. 'I won't be any trouble to you if you let me stay at home,' she gulped.

'I keep telling you, no.'

'Richard.' Dinah had meant to hold her tongue, because she knew Richard would resent her joining in, but she couldn't keep quiet any longer. 'It sounds as though the bullying has gone too far. Don't you think—'

He turned on her. 'Don't you start putting your oar in. The children are not your responsibility.'

'Perhaps not, but Nellie's upset. I don't think you should just take her back to somewhere she hates.'

'Whether Nellie likes it or not,' he said, 'that's what's going to happen. Just accept it, Nellie, can't you?' The girl burst into tears again.

'Shall I come with you?' Dinah suggested. 'Perhaps if we had a word with the headmistress?'

Richard looked at her and said slowly, 'No.'

Dinah felt Nellie needed her support. 'I'd like to see the school—'

'Absolutely not,' Richard barked. 'You will stay here where you're needed. Those girls in the workshop won't do a thing unless somebody keeps them at it.'

Dinah was learning that if Richard had decided on a course of action, nothing she or anyone else said would change his mind. Her voice shook. 'Have it your way, but at the very least I think you should have a word with the headmistress.' She couldn't believe how much Richard seemed to have changed since their wedding.

On the morning he was taking Nellie back to school, he dropped Dinah off in Picton Street with some large boxes in which to pack what she wanted to keep.

'When you've done your packing you can go down to the factory on the bus, and we'll collect the stuff on the way home from work this evening.'

It was only a fortnight since she'd left home but now it seemed cramped and shabby. It made her sad to see it, because she and Mum had been happy here. She set about sorting through the clothes she'd left behind, picking out a few things she thought she might still wear. She was glad to see her comfortable old work shoes, and packed those too.

She'd hadn't been in the house ten minutes before the neighbours started looking in to ask how she and her mother were getting on. Gladys and Flo were very helpful, suggesting items Sarah might like to keep.

'I remember her embroidering that tea cosy and that tray cloth years ago. She won't want to part with them.'

Dinah took the clock from the living room mantelpiece and a picture of highland cattle near a stream that spelled home to her.

'Mum might like them,' she said. 'They'll surely remind her of the happy times we spent here.' Gladys started wrapping them for her.

She heard Aunt Enid calling her. 'Dinah? Are you there? I've just come home from the shops and saw your front door open.'

She kissed Dinah's cheek and asked after her mother. 'You've come to collect your things?' She pointed out her mother's best tea service. 'Sarah was proud of those cups,' she said. 'She'll want them. I'm sure she told me they were a wedding present. You'll have to take them, love.' She provided old newspaper and together they wrapped them up.

Dinah looked in her mother's wardrobe and decided she didn't need her old coats and aprons. If she hadn't enough clothes with her, Dinah would buy her more. She had another look round her old home. 'I don't think there's anything else I want to take. If there's anything left you can use, I want you to have it.'

'You really mean that?' Gladys asked. 'You could sell some of this.'

'No. Richard was talking of getting a house clearance man in, but they pay hardly anything. I'd rather you took it. Is there anything you want, Aunt Enid?'

'I'd love to have Sarah's sofa. I've always admired that.'

'Could I have your hearthrug?' Gladys asked.

'I'd like these curtains,' Flo added.

'Take it all. You're welcome to everything,' Dinah insisted. 'Mum would want you to have it. You've been very good to us since she became ill. We're both missing you.'

They were full of thanks. Gladys's son Jimmy had just got married and had virtually nothing to make a home. He and his bride would be glad of anything here. 'I'll get him and his dad to come round and move it tonight.'

'What about Mum's old clothes? I've taken anything worth keeping. Could you get the rag and bone man to call?'

'This stuff is far too good for the rag and bone man.' Flo was indignant. 'He'd only give a jam jar with a couple of goldfish in it for all this. Old Mrs Bassett further down the street is very much in need of a good warm coat, and she's pretty much your mum's size. She'll give you a bob or two for it. Shall I fetch her if she's in?'

'Yes, but I don't want anything from her,' Dinah said. 'Her husband used to sweep the chimney for us and help us decorate.'

Flo brought Mrs Bassett back with her, still wearing her bedroom slippers. She looked pleased. 'It's my lucky day,' she told Dinah. 'This mac too?'

'Everything, if you want it.'

'Oh, yes, love, that I do. You thank Sarah for me. I'll think of her every time I wear her coat.'

'That's it then.' Dinah eyed the packed boxes now stacked ready to go and felt sad to be leaving.

'Come and have a bite to eat at my place,' Flo invited. 'All of you. I made a big pan of soup this morning from bones the butcher gave me. It'll only be that and a slice of toast but it'll fill a hole.'

It was very tasty. Dinah felt she was leaving good friends.

'Remember us to Sarah,' they said when she was leaving. 'Tell her we're very grateful.'

Gladys gave her four freshly baked scones to take to her mother. Dinah felt quite homesick as she took the bus into town.

Nurse Allen was in the habit of getting up early to eat her breakfast in the dining room with Dinah and Richard before her patient woke up. One morning the following week, Mrs Banks came back to the dining room when they were all having a second cup of tea.

'Please, sir,' she said to Richard, 'George Weeks is in the kitchen. He says Arthur Phelps looks pretty bad this morning. He's not eating or washing himself.'

'George Weeks is my gardener, and Arthur Phelps lives in the flat over the garage,' Richard explained. 'He's worked for my family all his life as a gardener and handyman and must be in his mid-eighties by now. Would you go over later on, when you've got time, Nurse Allen, and see what ails him? If he's ill, call out Dr Jones.'

'Yes, Mr Haldane.'

'Tell George we'll see to him, Mrs Banks. Come on, Dinah. It's time we went to work.'

When they came home that evening Richard asked Joan if she'd been to see the old man.

'Yes, but I didn't call out the doctor, because I don't think he's ill, just not looking after himself. I think it's just his age – he's given up keeping himself and the flat clean. He had no food in the kitchen; he said he doesn't go out much any more. I think he finds the outside steps up to his flat difficult.

'I helped him wash and Mrs Banks found him some clean clothes and helped me change his bed. Then she sent Mrs Parr over with some food and got her to tidy up the place a bit.'

'Good, but you all have enough to do looking after us. Mrs Radcliffe needs you here.'

'I think the time has come when Mr Phelps needs to be in a home.'

'Do you know of a suitable one nearby that would take him?'

'Only the workhouse.'

Dinah saw Richard wince. 'No, not for Arthur Phelps,' he said. 'He gave my family good service all his life. Next time the doctor comes, ask him if he knows a place where Arthur might settle down. I want him to be happy in his declining years. I'll be glad to pay for a home for him.'

'That's very good of you,' Joan said. 'Dr Jones said he'd call and see Mrs Radcliffe tomorrow, and I'll ask him then.'

Two days later, Richard told Dinah that the doctor had been to see Arthur Phelps but that he'd refused to go into a home. He wanted to end his days in the flat over the garage where he'd lived for most of his life.

'I've told Mrs Parr to spend one morning each week cleaning up his flat and doing his washing. And Mrs Banks is going to take a hot meal over to him every day.'

Dinah could see her mother was being well looked after by Joan Allen, but she seemed to be growing more frail. Enid came to see her quite often in the afternoons while Dinah and Richard were at work. Dinah spent several hours with her every evening, and she always found time to go into her room to see how she was in the mornings before she went to work.

One day she came home and found her mother dozing on her day bed. 'Hello, Mum. How are you feeling?' she asked, kissing her cheek.

Sarah opened her eyes. 'Am I in hospital?' she asked.

'No, Mum. What makes you think that?'

Sarah looked confused. 'I'm not at home, and the nurse . . .'

'You're at my house. Mine and Richard's. Don't you remember, I brought you here when I got married?'

'Yes, love, of course you did. Aren't I silly?'

'No, no.' Dinah didn't know what to say. Her mother had always had a very clear head. This wasn't like her.

'I was looking at this lavender. Enid brought it, and said it was from home. From that tub in our back yard.'

'Yes. Don't you remember?' Dinah was struggling to hold back her tears. Poor Mum, thinking she was in hospital. However well Joan was looking after her, she was a stranger. Mum would have been happier at home with Enid whom she'd known and loved for most of her life.

She left quickly for her own bedroom before Mum saw that she was upset. Richard came in shortly afterwards and as he seemed more sympathetic than usual she told him what had happened and had a little weep on his shoulder.

'Why don't I bring a bottle of sherry and some glasses to the guest room? It might cheer your mother up if we had a drink with her and Joan before dinner.'

At home, they'd never been able to afford the luxury of sherry, but Dinah had noticed that Sarah seemed to relish it, and enjoyed having them all round her bed. She had never found the strength to go downstairs, so Joan took both their meals up to her room and ate with her.

As she got into bed that night, Dinah reflected that Richard could still be very charming when he chose to be. He was being so pleasant and helpful towards them all again that she wondered whether his conscience had troubled him. But she hadn't got over how he'd terminated Mum's tenancy without first mentioning it to either of them.

In the days that followed, Dinah got to know the girls working in the button room, as well as Gertie who did the cleaning and made the tea. They were all very much in awe of Richard and were tongue-tied and careful about what they said to Dinah. The heavy atmosphere she'd felt on her first day she now recognised as tension. They were all wound up as tight as drums and were scared stiff they'd lose their jobs. While Richard was on the premises, fear wafted through the works in great clouds.

Dinah did her best to get his employees to talk about him. She wanted to know more about her husband, his family, his history and his business, but most of them wouldn't say anything. However, she soon came to understand that they disliked him. They were always glad to see him go out and leave them to get on with the work.

Several mentioned that Myra, her predecessor, had been in day to day charge. Dinah couldn't understand that, because Richard had indicated to her that he made all the decisions. She decided that Mr Hopper was the most likely member of staff to tell her what she wanted to know, but even he was too nervous to speak to her while Richard was about. He only relaxed when Richard went out.

'The girls are a good team,' he told her.

'They seem frightened of Richard and wary of me. As though they're afraid I'll eat them.'

'It's not you personally,' he said. 'Mr Haldane makes them nervous and they're scared of what you might tell him.'

'About them? I'd never say anything that might get them into trouble.'

'Mr Haldane can be a very charming man,' Mr Hopper said, 'but his temper can blow up to hurricane strength in moments. They've seen it happen. He's a very strict boss, strict with everyone. If one of the girls displeased him he'd sack her on the spot, so they're all careful when he's around. It's hard to get another job these days.'

Sack her? Yes, Dinah could believe that. Hadn't he sacked the nanny his children loved? It was what Dinah had supposed: the Liverpool Button Company was not a happy place to work. Not for the first time, she thought how lucky she'd been in her place at Carlton Hats.

'And what about you?' she said. 'Aren't you afraid of getting the sack?'

He gave her a wry smile. 'I'm past retirement age already, but I'm kept on because I'm the only one left now who knows how to keep the place running.'

'Apart from the boss?'

'Well, that's just it. I'm not sure Mr Haldane takes all that much interest in making buttons. He blusters and shouts, "You do this, and you take care of that," but half the time it isn't what's needed. And should the tide turn in the market for ribbons, I'm the only one left who knows anything about making them. His wife virtually ran this business over the last few years.'

'That surprises me. He strikes me as the sort of person who wants to manage everything himself.'

Mr Hopper's face twisted into another wry smile. 'He's quick to delegate the jobs he doesn't want to do.'

She couldn't help reflecting that while Richard was insisting she came into work every day and was giving her jobs to do here, at home he was refusing to let her take over the housekeeping. Was that why he'd been in such a hurry to marry her? Did he need a replacement for Myra here as well as in his bed? He was making no secret of wanting help to run this business. For a wealthy man, that was surely an unusual way to treat a new bride. Especially when she had a sick mother at home she wanted to look after.

'I'd like to know more about making ribbons,' Dinah told Mr Hopper. 'Will you teach me?'

'Of course, if that's what you want. I'll dig out the old records. But as it's only buttons we make now, wouldn't it be better to start with them? Mr Haldane said he wants you to learn about everything here.'

'We'll start with them then, but I want to know all about ribbons too.'

Ribbons interested her more because she'd used them on the hats she'd made, but also she wanted to know more about Myra Copthorne. If she got Mr Hopper to talk about ribbon-making, perhaps she could get him to talk about her.

CHAPTER TEN

ONE SUNDAY AFTERNOON, Dinah was reading out bits from the Sunday papers to her mother when Mrs Banks showed Enid and Tim in. She was delighted to see them, and her mother too brightened up. It was a happy reunion with some noisy light-hearted chatter, until Richard appeared.

'You're very noisy in here, Dinah,' he said, his face stern, 'considering this is a sickroom. I do worry for the patient.'

Her mother had been smiling up to that point. As though Richard had burst a bubble, the chatter suddenly dried up.

'Mum's enjoying her visitors,' Dinah told him. 'It does her good to see her friends.'

Enid tried to gloss over it. 'I've been here several times but I've never seen sight nor sound of your children – Dinah's stepchildren now. Are they well?'

'Yes, thank you.' His manner was cold. 'I'm afraid you won't see them now either. They're away at school.'

'Boarding school,' Dinah said. 'Didn't I tell you?'

'Yes, sorry. I'd forgotten.'

Tim tried to fill the silence that followed with a stilted sentence or two about racing.

Richard turned to Dinah. 'I think I'll go over to Tarporley to see how Beauty and Prince are getting on. I take it you'd rather stay here with your friends?'

'Yes, this time,' she said, trying not to feel relieved that he didn't demand she go with him. She understood now that Richard didn't like visitors coming to his house but she didn't want him to be unpleasant to

Enid. Nothing must put her off coming to visit her mother.

Once the door closed behind him they all relaxed. 'It's a big house you've got here,' Enid said.

'It feels a bit creepy, though, doesn't it?' Tim was walking round the room examining everything.

'No,' she said hotly, though that was exactly what she'd felt when she'd first come here.

'It's an old house,' Enid said. 'That's all.'

'This is . . . a feather bed,' Sarah gasped. 'Very comfortable.'

'Richard says the house is full of memories for him.' Dinah didn't want them to think badly of him. 'His family built it back in the 1880s and have lived here ever since. He doesn't want anything changed or brought up to date.'

Tim shivered. 'I think the ghosts of his family are still here.'

'Don't be silly,' Enid told him tartly. 'I expect they've modernised some things. What about the kitchen and the bathroom?'

'No, it's exactly as it was built.'

'You'd think he'd want to, with all his money.' Tim frowned.

'Well, there is one thing. Richard's father had the old stables turned into a garage. Why don't I show you round? Tim first. I'll ask Mrs Banks to bring up a tray of tea for you and Mum, Aunt Enid, and I'll take you on the tour later.'

Dinah showed Tim round the ground floor of the house and he marvelled at its size. Then she took him through the kitchen where Mrs Banks was making salad for their light Sunday supper. He was amazed at the two large sinks for washing clothes and the special room for the airing and ironing, not to mention the storerooms and larder. She led him out to the garden through the back door and gave a little giggle when she saw, for the first time, a flight of stone stairs going down from the back step.

'I didn't even know there were cellars here,' she said.

'Big cellars,' Tim said. The steps went down to a passage. 'I can see a door and three windows down there. Let's take a look.'

There was moss growing on the stone steps and they were slippery. Dinah was glad to have Tim with her, but the heavy door was locked, and they couldn't go any further.

'They won't get much light through these windows, will they?' They were only a few feet from the eight-foot brick wall that was holding back the garden soil, and so grimy that Dinah couldn't see inside. She decided she'd look for the key and if she could find it she'd have a good look round later.

'I think the servants must have lived down there when this house was first built,' she said.

'Where do they live now?'

'There's only Mrs Banks living in and she has the nanny's old room up on the top floor. Come and see the garage.'

'What a lovely garden you've got. And it's huge! Nearly as long as Picton Street.'

Dinah laughed. 'It's over two and a half acres, but it's long and narrow and slopes all the way down to the front gate.'

'Wow! Not that narrow by my standards. Didn't I see a mass of roses as we came into the drive?'

'That's known as the rose garden.'

'Then there's that little wood.'

'There's a walled vegetable garden over that way, and cages for gooseberries and blackcurrants so the birds don't get them. There used to be three gardeners here, but now there's only one. The garage is up here. It used to be the stables and there's a flat on top that was originally meant for the groom. The old head gardener lives there now.'

Tim whistled through his teeth when she opened up the doors. 'I see Richard is keen on cars as well as horses. He's got three?'

'Four. He's gone out in the Riley. He mostly drives that. It's the newest.' They were all polished and sparkling. 'This Lagonda is quite old.' Dinah looked more closely at the lovely open-topped car. 'I think I've seen it in a photograph.' Could it have belonged to Myra's family?

'Does he maintain them himself? Yes, he must do – he's got a lot of tools here. Even a pit, so he can get underneath them.'

'He spends a lot of time here.'

'So would I, if I had a set-up like this. I wish I could drive. Why don't you ask him to teach you?'

Dinah looked at him warily. 'D'you think I'd be able to learn?'

'Course you would, why not? And then you could teach me.'

Dinah smiled. 'That might be some time off.'

'Have you heard that you're going to have to pass a test soon before you're allowed to drive?'

'Yes. We've left it too late to avoid that.'

On their way back upstairs to her mother's room, Tim asked, 'Are you happy, Dinah?'

'Yes,' she said as brightly as she could, though she still felt more at home in Tim's company than she did in Richard's. With Richard there was always some thought she needed to hide, some response she ought to bite back because he was touchy and might blow up. But she couldn't bear to admit to her old friend that everything in her new life wasn't marvellous.

'What new bride isn't happy?' she asked lightly.

Tim was glad to have seen where Dinah was living, so that he could now picture her in her new house. But it left a bittersweet taste in his mouth to think of her being out of his reach for ever now she was Richard Haldane's wife.

Sarah had brightened up in the Reeces' company and said she felt better. The sun had come out and was shining full into her room, and she was hot.

'I'd love to go out in the garden,' she said, 'and get some fresh air. It looks a lovely day.'

So Dinah and Enid took her down and had Tim set the wickerwork armchairs out under the trees. The Reeces didn't leave until Richard returned from Tarporley, and on the bus home Enid was nursing the large bunch of roses that Dinah had cut for her in the rose garden.

'Sarah seems very settled now,' she said. 'She has every comfort there. And Dinah has too, I suppose.'

Tim was troubled. Ever since Dinah's wedding day, he'd been unable to blank her out of his thoughts. He kept wondering how she was getting on as the wife of a millionaire owner of racehorses.

'I'm not sure that I like Richard,' he said.

'You were never going to.'

'Do you like him?'

'You can't blame her for marrying him. It's lifted her out of poverty for good. Few girls in her position get a chance like that.'

'He's arrogant.' Tim had felt the tension between them, and he knew Dinah well enough to know she wasn't happy whatever she said. He felt uneasy about her and thought his mother was too. 'And they look more like father and daughter than a married couple.'

His mother laughed, but Tim wasn't amused. He was having his own problems. He was having a late spurt of growth and knew his weight was increasing. He was glad to be growing taller, but if he got too heavy nobody would want to employ him as a jockey. He'd have to find another way to earn his living. It was all the more galling because he loved the life and in every other way he was making a success of it.

'Don't rush back tonight,' Enid said, breaking into his thoughts. 'Stay and have tea with me. There's enough beef left to have with a bit of salad.'

'Thanks, Mum, but I won't. I've told Robbie I'll be back in time to go out with him.'

Tim had come home the night before to spend his day off with his mother. He'd taken her to the Rialto to see *Chu-Chin-Chow* and she'd loved it, but she thought he wasn't eating enough.

'You'll make yourself ill, Tim, if you starve yourself,' she said now.

'Don't you worry, I don't starve myself.' He smiled at her. 'You gave me a lovely Sunday dinner, not to mention a good breakfast.' He didn't tell her that Robbie, too, ate very little. A night out for them was half a pint of mild and they made it last.

Tim and Robbie counted themselves lucky that when they had completed their apprenticeship Mr Digby had kept them on as yard jockeys. It meant they were now regularly racing horses of different abilities and getting wider experience.

A few years before, Horace Bellamy, who already owned Pomeroy and Saucy Sue, had bought a pair of yearlings from the same sire. Their breeding was top notch and they could count several successful racehorses as forebears, but while Dido was a handsome filly, Flyswitch, her half-brother, did not have her sleek lean lines. He'd been put in Tim's charge.

The first thing he and the stable boys had to do was break the new horses in. Dido was excitable and gave her riders plenty of trouble, but Flyswitch was relaxed and seemed to enjoy having Tim on his back.

He'd grown into a big gangling horse with a coat the colour of Mersey mud. No amount of grooming would make it shine, though Dido had a shimmering chestnut coat. Mr Digby provided linseed oil for Tim to add to Flyswitch's feeds but it didn't help.

Dido had a white flash down the centre of her face, but Flyswitch had two round patches of greyish-white hairs intermixed with black down the left side of his face, one above the eye and one below. It looked for all the world as if he'd been splashed by seagull droppings.

The first time Mr Digby rode Flyswitch to assess his ability, the horse tripped over himself and flung him over his head. Tim following on Pomeroy, saw it happen and dismounted quickly to go to Mr Digby's aid, but the trainer got to his feet without help.

'I'm all right, except for jarring my shoulder. Damn that animal.' Mr Digby normally patient and gentle with the horses in his care, but the fall had shaken him. Flyswitch had galloped on a bit and come to a standstill a couple of hundred yards away, and was now surveying the turmoil he'd caused.

'You take Pomeroy, sir,' Tim said, handing him the reins. 'I'll get Flyswitch and bring him back.'

He expected the horse to be difficult to catch, since he knew such accidents upset the mounts as much as the riders and often made them more than usually nervous. But Flyswitch allowed Tim to walk right up to him and take hold of his bridle. His eyes were pools of black misery and his ears were flat against his head. He was trembling.

Tim felt sorry for him. 'Not to worry too much, old chap,' he told him. 'We're all allowed one mistake here.' He patted his neck. 'Come on, cheer up.' The horse rubbed his face against his shoulder as though in apology. 'You couldn't help it, could you? It wasn't intentional.'

Tim always kept a sugar lump or two in his pocket for treats. He gave one to Flyswitch and then swung himself up on his back.

'It's those big front feet of yours,' he told him. 'You need to take more care, particularly with the boss. It won't pay you to toss him off again.'

Since then Tim had taken a special interest in Flyswitch. He took to taking him carrots and sugar lumps from the kitchen and it pleased him to have the horse nuzzle at his pockets for them. Flyswitch was fond of his food, and if nothing better was forthcoming he'd nibble all evening at his bedding of best oat straw.

Soon his speed and stamina were surprising everyone. He outpaced Dido and the other horses in the stable, and Digby began to enter him in the juvenile stakes with Tim as his jockey. They started to win. 'Keep this up,' Tim told him, patting his neck, 'and we'll soon be running important races.'

Flyswitch was the most intelligent horse Tim had ever come across. He understood that the most important thing about a race was to win it, and he put his heart and soul into doing so. He loved the glory of being the winner.

He was a sprinter and soon was rarely beaten over ten furlongs, but when Mr Digby told Tim to start schooling him over the hurdles in the yard it turned out the horse loved to jump and was better than average at that too. He was game for everything. Both owner and trainer thought he was showing exceptional promise.

'We'll have him going over the sticks this winter,' Digby had chortled to Tim. As a three year old Flyswitch earned good prize money and became the star of the stable.

But best of all, if Flyswitch was entered in a race, Tim always got the ride. No other jockey understood the horse as well as he did. Once, Tim heard Mr Digby saying to Mr Bellamy, 'Tim can always get Flyswitch to make that extra effort to win.' His status went up with each success and he was delighted with the way his career was shaping up.

Over supper that night Dinah said to Richard, 'I was looking round the garden this afternoon and went into your garage.' He'd never offered to take her to see it, just mentioned from time to time that he had some job he wanted to do there. 'I didn't know you had four cars.'

He was frowning. 'I suppose you were showing that lad round?'

'Yes. There's no harm in that, is there?'

He glowered silently at his Melton Mowbray pie and salad. 'Richard, would you teach me to drive?'

That brought his head up with a jerk. 'You?'

'Why not?'

'No, I couldn't. I'm not a good enough driver myself.'

'Richard, you're an expert driver.' Dinah had no doubt about that.

'I'd be worried you'd get things wrong. Have an accident.'

'I was reading in the paper that they're setting up driving schools. They'd teach people properly at places like that. I'd like to do it.'

'It wouldn't be safe.'

'If it's safe for you, why wouldn't it be safe for me? There are cars sitting idle in your garage while I'm waiting around for buses. I quite fancy driving myself.'

'No, Dinah.'

She felt a flush of irritation run up her cheeks. 'This is the nineteen thirties, not Queen Victoria's day. Lots of women drive now.'

'Those cars are quite old. They aren't easy to manage.'

'But I could try, couldn't I?'

'I've already told you, no. I'd be afraid you'd have an accident and kill yourself.'

She was exasperated. 'Why would I be more likely to kill myself than anybody else?'

'Darling, no. I don't want you to learn to drive. My relatives and friends have had some bad accidents and I couldn't bear it if it happened to you.'

She remembered the mad way he'd driven down that hill in the Lake District. 'I wouldn't take risks – it's not in my nature. I'd be slow and safe. Probably safer than you.'

'I've driven a lot. I understand cars and how to manage them.'

Dinah sighed. 'Which of your relatives was killed in a car crash?' He didn't answer, didn't look at her. 'Why won't you tell me?'

'Please, darling, don't.'

She suddenly noticed he looked upset. She would have said he wasn't far from tears, and she didn't want to cause another argument that would upset her more than it did him. Instead of pursuing the point she said, 'People have been known to get hurt in bus crashes.'

'It's just that I don't want any harm to come to you,' he said.

It was a very definite no. As his children had told her, Richard decided everything in this household, and nothing she could say would persuade him to change his mind. As he wasn't paying her a wage, and she had no ready cash, she'd have to accept there'd be no driving lessons for her. She consoled herself with the thought that, even if she hadn't married Richard, she wouldn't have been able to learn.

When they'd finished eating, Richard said abruptly, 'I'm going out to the garage for an hour. I have some jobs I want to do there. I'll have coffee later.'

Dinah followed him outside. She'd started walking round the garden at this hour on fine evenings because Richard usually wanted to be on his own, and also because he'd told her she might see Arthur Phelps pottering round.

Since Richard had shown such kindness to the old gardener who lived in the flat over the garage, it had been obvious to Dinah that if she wanted to know more about the Haldane family Arthur Phelps would be a good person to ask. He'd be bound to know a good deal about Richard too, and perhaps he'd be so full of nostalgia for the old days that he'd open up to her.

Tonight, however, the flat above the garage had the curtains drawn in two of the windows. It looked as though the old gardener had gone to bed early, and Dinah didn't feel she should knock on his door.

The garage doors were wide open and she could see a figure wearing the all-in-one overalls of a mechanic under the bonnet of the Riley. She hardly recognised her husband. She had never seen what was under the bonnet of a car before, and, curious, she went to stand next to Richard. 'It looks terribly complicated,' she said.

'It is, and not the sort of thing women take much interest in.'

'What's the matter with it?'

He was not taking much notice of her; clearly he was concentrating on the engine. 'The timing isn't quite right.'

She asked what that meant, and he seemed to enjoy showing off his knowledge. He was not so pleased when she turned her attention to the three other cars.

'Did they belong to your parents?' she asked.

His civility was gone. 'You're distracting me, Dinah. Would you mind giving me a few moments on my own?'

'Sorry.' She went out, and strolled down to the rose garden where the blooms were at their best, their scent carried on the evening air. To her delight, she saw Arthur Phelps smoking his pipe and deheading the odd bloom that needed it.

'Good evening,' she said. 'I'm Dinah Haldane, Richard's new wife.'

His bleary eyes studied her. 'I know you are,' he grunted.

'You must be Arthur Phelps?'

He shot a suspicious glance at her. 'I am that.'

'This is a lovely garden. I believe you were in charge of it once?'

He took his pipe out of his mouth. 'Yeah, I was.'

Dinah was finding it hard going. 'I suppose you had more than one gardener under you in the old days?'

'Yeah. We had two, and an extra boy in the summer.'

'I expect the garden was even better then.'

'Yeah, it was. Old Mr Haldane was very fond of his roses.'

'He was fond of cars too, I believe?'

His pipe had gone out, and he was trying to relight it. 'That he was.'

'He drove himself and serviced them himself?'

'Yeah, except the under-gardener had to wash and polish them. Heat of the day has gone now; I think I'll go in. Good night, Mrs Haldane.'

Dinah was cross with herself. Here was a man who could tell her what she wanted to know, and she'd not been able to draw him out.

Chapter Eleven

Dinah was getting used to working in the button factory, but found she hadn't enough to do, and nobody else seemed busy either. She asked herself if she was needed there at all. She was, she thought, doing jobs that Miss O'Marney would have had plenty of time to do, and was puzzled as to why Richard wanted her there.

She thought Mr Hopper was right: Richard took little interest in his factory and didn't seem in control. He gave the impression it was beneath him to concern himself with the button trade. The business lacked the buzz of activity and the enthusiasm she'd grown used to at Carlton Hats. If Dinah wanted to know some detail about the job she was doing, she found the other workers more capable of answering her questions than he was.

When the big classic race meetings were being held, Richard would send Gertie out to buy several newspapers and do little but read the racing news. At home he rushed to the wireless in his study to find out which horses had won.

When Ascot week came round, Dinah asked, 'Are your horses going to race there?'

'I'd go if they were.' Richard's eyes shone with enthusiasm. 'I'd love to be at Royal Ascot, wouldn't you? It's the pinnacle of the racing season.'

'Aren't your horses good enough to run there? I notice you don't put them into the top races.'

'Their trainer makes the decisions.' He frowned. 'They haven't got the form this year.' That seemed to be the closest he could get to saying no.

'Will they have the form next year?'

'They're improving. I very much hope so, but we'll have to wait and see.'

'The top races give the most prize money, don't they?'

'Naturally,' he said drily and she knew he'd lost patience with her.

Because she had too much free time at work, Dinah was in the habit of walking round the workroom, chatting first to one girl and then to another. She was beginning to feel more at ease with them, and with Miss O'Marney. Working on the account books gave her satisfaction, too. She was pleased to find she understood what the figures meant, but she was growing more curious about the amount the business was earning.

Richard had pointed out the ledgers he wanted her to keep up to date. He kept them stacked on a shelf behind his desk. Each day, she entered the amounts paid out for raw materials and wages, and the amounts coming in by cheque for the work they'd completed. At the and of the month her totals would be entered by Richard into the books showing the overall state of the business, and these were kept locked in his safe.

Having entered yesterday's figures, Dinah took the books back to their shelf.

'Richard,' she said. 'How much profit does this business earn?'

He didn't look up from what he was doing. 'It varies from month to month.'

'I mean in a year. About how much?'

'As I said, it varies. Would you believe the weather has an effect on sales?' He looked up at her then and smiled. 'In a hot spell more summer clothes are sold and more buttons have to be ordered.'

She could see now that he was skilled at glossing over things he didn't want to tell her. If she didn't listen out for the answer, he could do it almost without her noticing. She'd guessed he wouldn't tell her about his profit because he guarded the ledgers in which the figures were set down.

Dinah didn't know what to make of him. He'd said he wanted her in the business so they could be together all day, but he frequently went out alone without saying anything to her or anybody else. Nobody could fail to notice his duties didn't keep him busy either. He often disappeared before lunch time and stayed away for several hours.

Today, he hadn't come in until after four o'clock and she could smell alcohol on his breath. Dinah asked, 'Where did you get to this afternoon?'

'I was trying to get more orders for the business,' he said shortly. 'I've got to keep the machines running or sack some of the girls.'

'Did you succeed?'

'No.'

Dinah was thinking of her old boss at Carlton Hats. She'd always got on well with him. 'Perhaps if I asked, Mr McKay would give me an order to supply petersham ribbons for his hats.'

'Don't be silly,' Richard told her disdainfully, his tone implying that if he couldn't get the business, she certainly would not.

'I'm serious. I'd like to know how much ribbon you provided for Carlton Hats and for other companies like them. How much you charged —'

'Dinah,' he thundered. 'Leave it. I don't want you meddling. You don't understand business.'

'No, I don't understand, but only because you won't explain. It's no good saying you're looking for more business and then telling me not to meddle. Does it matter who gets the orders, as long as somebody does?'

To Dinah, it seemed obvious that Richard's factory was crying out for more work. Mr McKay had pointed out to his apprentices that, to thrive, every business had to manufacture its finished product and then sell it. He'd impressed on them that every girl he employed was there to work, and that the time spent by experienced staff on teaching the apprentices was time when they weren't producing hats. The apprentices must realise that it was the hat sales that paid for their tuition, as well as giving him his profit.

Dinah knew she needed to know more about the button business and that Richard, for some reason, was hiding the business records from her as well as from everybody else. She went to find Mr Hopper.

'I'd like to know where the old ledgers are stored. The figures for orders fulfilled and materials bought in. That sort of thing.'

'Mr Haldane keeps everything like that in his office. You'd better ask him.'

'This business has been running since the 1880s,' she said. 'They must have kept records, and there isn't room in his office for all of them. Do you know where the rest are kept?'

He shook his head. 'They might have been destroyed after all this time.'

'Some of them, yes, but not the most recent. They'd be kept for a few years.'

'There's some old cupboards in the cellar stuffed with papers. They might be there.'

'Show me,' she said.

The stone steps went down from a corner of a small storeroom. Mr Hopper flicked a switch and in the dim light Dinah could see they were extremely steep and narrow. A rope had been attached to one wall to provide a handhold. She followed Hopper down and found herself in a big room with a low ceiling that seemed to be in use as another storeroom. It was airless and smelled of damp and decay.

Dinah didn't like the place. 'Are there a lot of cellars here?' There seemed to be other rooms leading off the first but in the heavy gloom she could see little.

'I think they stretch under the whole building, but I've never been further than this. You'd need a torch; only this room was ever wired for electricity.'

'Where're the cupboards you spoke of?'

They stretched across the whole wall and had three sets of doors. Dinah tried them and was disappointed to find they were all locked. 'Do you know where the keys are kept?'

As she'd expected, he didn't. She decided to look in Richard's office. Miss O'Marney was typing hard when she went back.

'Keys for the cellar? It's a horrible place – we all avoid it.' Her snub nose wrinkled in distaste. 'I don't know. Mr Haldane keeps a lot of the keys himself, but there's a key board behind his door; you might find them there. If he's not back by closing time, Mr Hopper has to lock up.'

Dinah went to look. Miss O'Marney called after her. 'I think there's one he calls a master key, but it won't open everything.'

It was labelled and she took it. She found two more keys labelled *Cellar cupboards*. She took those too and sped back, pausing only to fill her lungs with good air before going down.

She thought at first she wasn't going to get the cupboard open. She tried all three keys, but it was the lock that was stiff and she managed it eventually. The shelves were divided into sections and each was stuffed tight with office files. Her spirits soared. Surely the information she sought would be here, but exactly where?

She brought out one dusty file after another. They were years old and all related to the buttons business. Here were the files that would tell her how much the business earned, if only she knew where to look. Some figures related to stock and others to wages, but nowhere could she see the word profit. Anyway, the file she was looking at related to 1910; she'd need more recent figures than this. She put it back and continued to search. The button business didn't add up to what Richard wanted her to believe, but nothing about Richard ever did. Why wouldn't he answer her questions about it? If he really wanted her to learn all about his business why exclude certain information? What was he hiding?

She sorted through every file in that cupboard and put them in date order. The file for 1918 was the most recent. Richard had been fighting in France then, so his father would have been running the company. Richard was keeping his own records somewhere else. Dinah decided to keep the last file out so she could look at it more carefully and perhaps learn something.

She needed to get back upstairs where she could breathe. The cellar smelled horrible. She headed for the kitchen and found Gertie up to the elbows in sudsy water washing teacups.

'Am I too late for tea?' she asked. 'I've been down in the cellar for ages and I'm parched.'

Gertie switched on the urn in an instant. 'That cellar's a terrible place for filling your mouth with dust. Everybody says so.'

'Is it used much?' Dinah sat down at the scrubbed table. 'I got the feeling it had been shut up for years.'

'You're right there. It was never used all that much even in the old days, just for storing things. Nobody liked going down. Mr Richard locked it up, saying the stairs were dangerous and he'd find a better place to store the files.'

'Did he? Do you know where they are?'

'Glory be, no. You'll have to ask him about things like that.' A cup of tea slid on to the table in front of Dinah.

'Thank you, Gertie. It sounds as though you've worked here for a long time.'

'That I have. I was here in old Mr Haldane's time. He was a lovely man. He'd talk to any of us, ask after our families. A real gentleman.'

'And his two older sons, Rufus and Gerald?'

'They were lovely too, not moody like Mr Richard. This was a happier place in the old days.'

Dinah sipped her tea and smiled. 'Tell me about the old days,' she invited, but Gertie wouldn't or couldn't, except to say the place had been busier then.

She went back to her office and replaced the keys on Richard's key board. Some of the hooks had two keys on them and some only one. After a moment's thought she slid the key that had opened the cupboard back in her pocket. She'd need to return the file she'd brought up before long. She opened it on her desk and tried to fathom out what the figures for 1918 had meant for the company.

'Do you know anything about accounting?' she asked Miss O'Marney.

'I learned a bit of bookkeeping at commercial college and I used to fill in those ledgers before you came. It's mostly been shorthand and typing in the jobs I've had.'

She pulled her chair over to Dinah's desk and did her best to help. She was able to point out the difference between gross profit and net profit, and that in 1918 the latter had been a handsome one. Dinah learned a few other things, such as the cost of raw materials and labour in that year, but that was that.

She showed the file to Mr Hopper, but he could tell her nothing more. He didn't know much about business accounting. She kept the file in her desk for a few days while she tried to fathom out more. Eventually, because she knew of no one else, she took the file in to Richard and opened it on his desk.

'I'd like to understand what these figures mean,' she said. 'Will you explain them to me?'

'No need for you to bother your head with those.' His tone was dismissive.

'It isn't a bother. I want to know.'

He checked the date at the front of the file before flicking through the pages, but he repeated only the few obvious facts she'd picked up from Miss O'Marney.

'Where did you get these from?' he wanted to know.

'The cupboards in the cellar. They're full of old records.'

'Stay out of there,' he ordered. 'It's an unhealthy place and the stairs aren't safe.'

Shortly afterwards she heard him rattling the keys on his key board and he left his office. She thought he went down to the cellar. After he'd gone out she checked, and found everything locked up and the other two keys gone.

Dinah told herself she'd been a fool to say anything to him until she'd had time to look through all that was there. Luckily she'd put one of the keys in her pocket. She'd seen a big torch in Mr Hopper's store cupboard. She'd check that its battery worked and one day soon she'd take a closer look round the cellars.

Later that afternoon she had reason to go into the store cupboard. The torch was there, and beside it were two batteries. She put them in and switched it on, and was pleased to see it gave a good bright beam. She took it back to her desk and shut it in one of the drawers. Richard might be back any time now and she didn't want him to catch her down there. She'd wait until tomorrow morning when he went out again.

Dinah spent a wakeful night thinking about exploring the cellar. She would have liked Mr Hopper's company, but she mustn't involve him or anyone else. She felt guilty about going behind Richard's back, but he had problems and she had to know what they were before she could help him.

At work the next morning, she waited for Richard to go out. Shortly afterwards his phone rang and Miss O'Marney went into his office to answer it. Dinah took the torch out of the drawer and headed down to the cellar. It was airless and the smell was suffocating, and the further she advanced into the dark passages the worse it got, but she wasn't going to let that put her off.

It was clear that over the years the cellars had become a dumping ground for everything outdated, broken or no longer in use upstairs. She found disintegrating machines, broken tools, damaged chairs and desks, all damp and covered with dust and mildew. There were passages with rooms leading off in all directions and some walls were dripping with moisture. Dinah's resolve faltered. If she wasn't careful, she could get lost down here. She ran back.

In the storeroom upstairs she'd seen a box of chalk, and she took a piece out. After a cup of tea with Miss O'Marney she went back down to the cellar to explore some more, drawing arrows on the walls to mark her way back. In one room she found a bed with soggy bedding and even some old clothes. The beam of the torch caught a stone hot water bottle, a hurricane lamp and a pair of pyjamas that had once been brightly striped, but were now dark with mildew. There was a huge spider's web with the spider in the middle, and grime and disintegration everywhere. Who would want to spend a night down here? The thought of trying to sleep here appalled her. But it certainly looked as though someone might have done a long time ago. She ran back upstairs, replaced the torch and the chalk, and felt it had been a wasted effort. She'd learned nothing that helped.

It continued to niggle at the back of Dinah's mind that Richard might be hiding something dreadful from her. There could be no other reason for him to be so secretive. He didn't want her to know anything about his earlier life, or the business in bygone times. He was very reluctant to talk about his family, but surely a son should be proud of his father's success in building up a company like this? She kept racking her brain to think of some other way she could find out more.

She decided that if there was anything in the house to give her a clue, the most likely place to find it would be in the little sitting room where his mother had done so much sewing. She went there after supper that evening when Richard disappeared into his study.

The photograph albums drew Dinah like a magnet. She came across more pictures taken at another family celebration, but didn't know what it was until she took one of the photographs out of the album and turned it over. *8 July 1913*, she read. *Rufus's 21st birthday and coming of age.*

The family of that era were shown under the trees in the Ardwick House garden, clustered round a table laid with a luxurious buffet meal. Standing behind the table ready to carve the ham and serve portions of the whole dressed salmon was a young woman in a cook's apron and cap. Also in the picture was a young girl in a housemaid's uniform of black dress and frilly white apron, holding out a tray of filled glasses.

Loose at the back of that album was another wedding photograph, but not of a family member. It took her a moment to match up the pictures and decide it must be the cook.

Dinah paused to think. A servant who lived in would be bound to know a great deal about the family, but both these women had gone, and probably a long time ago. She sighed. Richard had even sacked the nanny just before she'd come, so there was nobody working here now who might have known them then. But yes there was. Arthur Phelps had been here. The trouble was, she'd already tried to talk to him and had got nowhere. There was Mrs Parr the cleaner who came in the mornings, too, and she thought she'd been working here for some time, but she'd seen her only once.

What about the present gardener? She went to the window and saw George Weeks weeding the borders in the front garden.

She didn't want Richard to catch her with the album and ask what she was doing with it, so she took out the photograph of the lavish buffet table at Rufus's twenty-first birthday party showing the two servants and slid it under her cardigan. Then she let herself quietly out into the garden, meeting no one on the way. The gardener was getting on in years and had grey stubble on his chin.

'George,' she said, 'this photograph was taken in 1913. Were you working here then?'

He straightened up, and a dirty fist encrusted with soil clamped on to the picture. 'Yes, Mr Rufus's twenty-first, this was. A high old time we all had that night.'

'I was wondering if you could tell me who these two girls are.' Dinah pointed out them out. 'Do you remember them?'

'Why, yes. This one was the cook.' He stabbed the photograph with a grimy finger. I remember her well. I used to live in then. She married Ernie Cummins, one of the gardeners. There were three of us working in the garden then. Now there's just me.'

'That must keep you busy.'

'It does that. Arthur Phelps was head gardener in those days. Always very close to Mr Richard was Arthur, and it's paid off. He's well looked after now.'

She said, 'Tell me about the cook.'

'Ivy, her name was. She was a very good cook, used to win prizes for her cakes. Ivy Brown.'

'And this girl?'

'Ruby Wilkes, the housemaid.'

'Do you know where they are now?'

George shook his head. 'No. Ivy and Ernie left at the same time. I think they had a row with Mr Richard.'

'I suppose they must have found other jobs?'

'I heard Ernie got a job with the council, but whether he's still there . . .'

'But you didn't ever have an address for him?'

'No, this was all ages ago. Nothing's the same now.'

'Well, thanks anyway.' Dinah dusted off the photograph and returned it to the album. She was afraid she'd reached another dead end.

It was the following evening that she found Eliza Haldane's household account books. The bills from the grocer, butcher, baker and fishmonger. The income she must have had! Richard might want to manage these things now, but it was certainly his mother who'd run the household in her day.

Dinah was fascinated by what the accounts revealed about the household then. The wages Eliza had paid her staff! How much lower they had been in those years. Dinah felt she had more in common with people who'd worked as housemaids than with the people who employed them. Housemaid Ruby Wilkes was being paid three pounds three shillings a month in 1919; and here was Ivy Brown, cook. Her wages had been four pounds five shillings.

Dinah flicked through the pages. It seemed Ivy was married in 1928 because that was when her name changed to Ivy Cummins. Both she and Ruby had been working here up to 1930, so they'd been here for a long time. Living in, they'd know most of what had been going on.

Then amongst the odds and ends at the bottom of the drawer she found a folded cutting from a local newspaper and opened it up. It was dated September 1932 and headed *ST HUGH'S CHURCH FETE*. She read on.

Mr Ernest Cummins, Head Gardener of the Council's Parks and Gardens Department, judged the entries in the flower section and gave the prize for the best roses to Mrs Pole of Langden Avenue.

There was a list of other prize winners and at the bottom of the page she read that Mrs Ivy Cummins of Aldgrove Street won first prize for the best Victoria sponge cake.

Dinah studied her picture again. It was rather grainy and yellowing at the edges by this time but it was certainly Ivy Cummins. Another look at the account book showed that Ernest Cummins had worked here up to 1930 too. Something must have happened then for all three to leave at the same time. Eliza Haldane's household account had revealed a lot about how the family lived but nothing about Richard's boyhood. But it was possible Ruby Wilkes or Ivy Cummins could.

Chapter Twelve

THAT NIGHT, DINAH had a bath before going to bed and lay back in the hot water pondering on what she'd discovered in her mother-in-law's account book. She knew where St Hugh's Church and Aldgrove Street were; they were both quite close to where she used to live. But Aldgrove Street was a long one and no house number had been given in the newspaper. Was there any way she could find out which was the Cumminses'? Had Aunt Enid said years ago that it was possible get facts like that from the electoral roll at the library? Or perhaps she could get it through the church? She definitely meant to follow it up.

As soon as she reached the bedroom Richard's arms went round her, helping her off with her dressing gown and fondling her through her satin nightdress. He had that off soon too, just as she'd known he would.

'I do love you, Dinah. You're so beautiful,' he whispered. 'I think about you all the time.' She looked up into his eyes and ran her fingers through his butter-coloured hair and was lost. He knew how to make her forgive and forget his earlier outrageous behaviour, his moodiness and sins. He was her husband and she couldn't resist him. He knew how to make her feel his love until she was wrapped up in it.

Afterwards, he was soon asleep, but Dinah lay beside him with her conscience pricking. She was planning to go behind his back to find out what he was hiding from her and it was making her feel like a traitor. She'd accepted his love, told him she loved him; how could she do this? Why couldn't she trust him? She decided she'd do nothing about trying to trace Ivy Cummins. No self-respecting wife would.

They were eating their breakfast the next morning, Joan was telling Dinah what sort of night Sarah had had, when suddenly Richard was all scowls and berating Mrs Banks because his bacon was salty.

'Send it back to the shop,' he said. 'I'm not paying for inferior food.'

To Dinah the bacon tasted as good as it always did. 'Is yours all right?' she asked Joan.

'It's very nice.' The nurse was frowning. 'Done to a crisp, just as I like it.'

Richard blew up at them. 'Don't contradict me. The bacon is salty this morning.'

Dinah could feel her heart pounding. He was going to antagonise Joan if she didn't stop this.

'It was all cut from the same flitch, sir.' Mrs Banks was indignant. 'And there's nothing to send back; you've eaten it all. You had some yesterday and you said nothing about it being salty then.'

Dinah hurriedly drained her teacup and stood up. 'Come on, Richard, let's go to work. We don't want to be late.' Joan was looking aghast; Dinah felt she had to get her husband out to the car as quickly as she could.

Mrs Banks would never have answered him back a few weeks ago. Dinah was afraid he'd give her the sack. Fortunately, the purr of the car's engine seemed to soothe him.

'Why are you so moody this morning?' Dinah asked gently. 'You seemed happy enough last night when you kissed me good night.'

'I'm not moody,' he insisted. 'The bacon was too salty.'

She wondered whether he had felt left out because she and Joan were discussing her mother, and decided she would, after all, try to find Ivy Cummins. She needed to know more about him. Something must have made him this way: almost impossible to like, let alone love. All her wariness and suspicion of him had returned.

As soon as Richard left his office that morning, Dinah took a bus up to St Hugh's church. She'd never been inside it and wondered if there would be anybody about she could ask. As soon as she pushed open the main door she heard women's voices, and was pleased to find two women busy with brooms and dusters.

'Would you be able to help me?' she asked. 'I'm looking for a Mrs Ivy Cummins. I know she attends this church and lives in Aldgrove Street, but I don't know which number.'

'You're in luck, love. She's here now, doing the flowers. Hang on, I'll give her a shout. Ivy? Ivy? There's a girl here asking for you.'

Dinah had the sweet feeling of success and couldn't suppress a smile as Ivy Cummins came bustling out of a door at the back, half hidden behind an arrangement of flowers she was carrying. She put the enormous vase down on one side of the altar and turned to face her.

She was middle-aged and built like a battleship: taller than Dinah and rotund in shape, a cook who'd always enjoyed her own food. Her dark hair was cropped in a severe, mannish style.

'Hello, Mrs Cummins. I'm Dinah Haldane.' She went forward to meet her. 'You don't know me, but I think you might be —'

'Haldane, you said?' she snapped. Dinah met her gaze. It was hot and intense; her eyes were so dark they seemed almost black.

'I'm Richard Haldane's second wife. You used to work for him, I believe?'

'Yes. What d'you want?'

Dinah swallowed hard, only too aware that the cleaning had stopped and the other women were openly listening. Her request must sound strange. 'I'm trying to find out about something. I'd like you to tell me about your time at Ardwick House. Why you left.'

Ivy's face was stiffening, and she was drawing herself upright. Dinah rushed on, 'You worked there for several years.'

'Twenty years.' She sounded angry.

Could she get her to talk? But not here. 'Could we go outside and sit in the sun? I believe it's one of those days when it's warmer outside than in.' The woman was following. 'Twenty years is a very long time.'

Dinah sat down on a sun-warmed stone bench. When Ivy joined her, she said slowly, 'It was a good place to work while his mother was alive. It was like a second home to me. I went straight there from school, and old Mrs Haldane treated us well.'

'When did she die?'

'It was the year after the war. She and her husband both died then.' Her face was working, and she looked upset.

Dinah said gently, 'In a road accident, Richard says.'

Ivy was on her feet again, restless and agitated. She burst out, 'It was no accident. He tampered with the brakes.'

Dinah couldn't get her breath. The woman ranted on. 'He's evil, is Richard Haldane. What made you marry him? Is he ill-treating you? Is that why you're asking?'

She whispered, 'Yes.' She was tingling with shock and horror but she mustn't stop this woman. Wasn't this what she wanted? Somebody who'd pour out all the things Richard kept buried. She needed to understand him.

'Me and Ernie are very glad not to be working for him now. Sacked us both he did, at a moment's notice, and bundled me out of the house. D'you know why? Because he found me sympathising with his wife . . . Pardon me, his first wife. Myra was a poor little thing.' Anger was spilling out of her. Dinah could see she was bristling for revenge.

'But Richard can't hurt her now and he can't hurt us either. Ernie worked for his father first. Always gave satisfaction, but he knew too much about what had gone on at Ardwick House. Ernie's got a job with the council, so he's safe now and he'll get a pension this time. He'd understood from old Mr Haldane that he'd get one from him, but when he got the sack he was given just one week's wages. When he asked for the pension he'd been promised, Richard Haldane told him to whistle for it.'

Dinah felt as though she'd disturbed a viper's nest. She looked across the old churchyard, full of grey slanting gravestones, which had been a peaceful backwater for centuries, while beside her Ivy Cummins was fulminating with malice and spite.

'What was Richard like as a boy?' Dinah asked. That was what she really wanted to know.

'Difficult. He never fitted in and was always in trouble of one sort or another. His parents gave him everything but it was never enough. He had two brothers, lovely boys who were learning to run the family business. Richard said he didn't want anything to do with buttons; he was going to follow a profession and do much better for himself.'

Her black eyes were flashing with hate. 'To please him, his father articled him to an accountant, but after six months he walked out because he didn't like it. He didn't seem to like anything or anybody, and he didn't get on with his brothers.'

She turned to grimace at Dinah. 'Nobody liked him.' Dinah waited for her to go on. 'Everything else was going well for the Haldanes. Richard was their only problem, but the war changed all that.'

'It changed things for a lot of people,' Dinah agreed. 'Millions died.'

'Richard's two brothers, Rufus and Gerald, both volunteered. They were officers and heroes, but they were both killed within eighteen months,' Ivy said. 'Rufus was given a medal.'

Dinah felt she had to say, 'Richard was an officer and fought in the war too.'

The woman gave a mirthless laugh. 'No he didn't. Bless me, no. Richard waited until he was called up, and then he was a private in the pay corps and never left England.'

'No . . .'

Ivy seemed to be in her element. It was as if there was nothing she wanted more than to blacken Richard's name. She couldn't be stopped.

'But he didn't like the army either, and after a few weeks he just walked out. They said he was a deserter. Soldiers came to the house looking for him. We all knew he'd gone missing but not where he was. His parents were out of their minds with worry. They were ashamed of him.'

Dinah sat up straighter. She'd sensed that Richard had something to hide, but surely it couldn't be this bad. She couldn't believe it.

'It's true enough,' Ivy insisted.

'Where did he hide?'

'He came home, but nobody knew he had at the time. Arthur Phelps looked after him. He was head groom and gardener then, Ernie's boss. He and his wife Esther lived in the flat over the stables – that's the garage as it is now.'

Somehow this detail drove home the truth of what Ivy was telling her.

'They took him in and hid him for the rest of the war. He couldn't stay at home openly because the police were keeping a watch for deserters.'

'This is awful.' The hair on the back of Dinah's neck stood up with horror. 'And the family didn't know?'

'We none of us knew, although we heard noises in the night. Food went missing from time to time and the gardener's boy was blamed, though like the rest of us he was fed as well as possible in wartime. All of us in the kitchen were convinced the place was haunted.'

'It's still a bit creepy. But Richard would have had to stay hidden indoors for months on end.'

'It was years.'

'But everybody knew him. How did he manage?'

'Arthur Phelps had taught Richard to ride when he was young, and Richard could always get Arthur to do what he wanted. He bought him food and newspapers, that sort of thing. I believe there are cellars under the works, and when he got fed up with one place he moved to the other.'

'He did go out and about, then?'

'Yes. When his brothers were killed, all their belongings were sent home, including their uniforms. Gerald's was covered in blood from the wound that killed him. Old Mr Haldane got Ernie to bury it in the garden before his mother saw it. You wouldn't think they'd send things like that back to their relatives, would you?'

'I wouldn't have thought they'd send their uniforms home at all.'

'Officers had to kit themselves out at their own expense, so they owned them. Anyway, Rufus was a captain and Richard commandeered his dress uniform. Ernie saw him strutting round town in it one day. He couldn't believe his eyes.'

'What a risk,' Dinah breathed. 'If he'd been caught . . .'

'He thought he could get away with anything, and he did. Esther Phelps was no better than she should be, either. She cooked him meals, washed his clothes and went to bed with him.'

'What?'

'Oh, yes. As I said, he could talk people into doing anything for him, and it wasn't just once or twice. He took over Arthur's wife on a more or less permanent basis. Would you believe that? A married woman of nearly forty, with a son of Richard's age in the trenches?'

Dinah felt sick. Yes, she could believe it. Richard had a huge appetite for lovemaking. But was it love he felt? She was beginning to doubt it.

'She had his baby.'

That took Dinah's breath away. 'Richard's baby?'

'Yes. He was very handsome as a young man. With a silver tongue that could bewitch people. Charm his way into their good books.'

Oh, God. Dinah was hugging herself. Hadn't he done that to her?

'Give him his due,' Ivy went on. 'Esther Phelps had TB and was dead within the year. He promised her he'd take care of the baby, and he has.'

Dinah felt she could no longer think straight. 'Where's the baby now?'

'That's Mark,' Ivy said.

Dinah couldn't take in any more of these shocking details. 'But I thought Mark was Nellie's brother. That Myra . . .'

Ivy looked at her pityingly. 'He meant you to think that.'

Dinah closed her eyes and tried to make sense of what she was being told. Was this all a fairy story? Just make-believe? It was too far fetched to be the truth. Ivy was bristling with rage, and obviously trying to get her own back on Richard for sacking her and Ernie. She was out for revenge. Should she be believed? Dinah felt ill, but she had to know more.

'At the end of the war, when there was no further need to hide, what did Richard do?'

Ivy tossed her head. 'He pretended to his parents that the army had just released him and he'd come straight home.'

That was going too far. 'And they believed him?'

Ivy drew back her massive shoulders. 'No, even he couldn't convince them of that. There was an under-gardener here then called Tom Baxter. He'd seen Richard too and decided the time had come to tell his parents what he knew.'

Dinah's mouth was dry. 'He told them what you've just told me?'

'He thought they ought to know.'

'What happened then?'

'They had a row. It went on all night. There was no bed for any of us until the early hours. In the kitchen, we were all ears, of course, but we couldn't help but hear. His father was shouting that he didn't want him living with them any longer. Richard was pleading to be forgiven, and his poor mother was crying. In the end, his father relented. "All right," he said. "I'll give you one last chance. You'll have to learn to run the business and settle to it, or get out. If you refuse, I'll cut you off without a penny."'

Dinah couldn't get her breath. It was an appalling way to treat his parents. It had never occurred to her that Richard was like that. She swallowed hard. 'So he settled down,' she asked, 'went to work every day and all was well?'

'Oh no, quite the opposite. He killed his parents.'

Dinah felt the gooseflesh come out on her arms. 'Go on,' she whispered. 'Tell me about it.'

'Before the Great War, there were more horses than cars on the roads. Old Mr Haldane continued to keep a horse and governess cart here, but he made a hobby of driving and owned two cars as well. There were very few garages to maintain them or sell petrol then and the old master knew as much about tuning and repairing cars as any mechanic. He had the stables turned into a garage and fitted up to a higher standard than many commercial ones.'

Ivy's face was set with determination to bring to light every last sin Richard had committed. 'Richard was keen on cars too, and while he was in hiding he'd amused himself by reading his father's manuals and tinkering around inside the engines of his cars.'

Dinah groaned. It could be true.

'We think he decided to rid himself of his parents.' Ivy's voice was bitter. 'Ernie and me, we think he half cut through the brake cable on one of the cars so the next time his father drove it the brakes failed. His wife was with him when it happened. They were driving down Exchange Street.'

'They were both killed?' Dinah's voice was a horrified whisper.

'His father was killed. His mother died of her injuries in hospital a week later.'

'Oh, my God!' Dinah could no longer think straight. 'But surely . . . The brakes . . . wasn't it noticed that they'd been tampered with?'

'Not as far as we know. In the papers it was reported as an accident. We don't think there was any suggestion of foul play.'

'But didn't you or Ernie tell the police what you knew?'

'What good would that have done? They wouldn't have believed us, and we had no proof. It was just a gut feeling, and Richard certainly had reason to do it.'

'What was that?'

'His parents were laying down rules for him; telling him he had to knuckle down and behave, or get out and leave with nothing. Once his parents were dead, Richard inherited their house and business. With one stroke, he'd escaped from their control and everything they'd worked for was his. It gave him a comfortable life.'

'Well . . . Perhaps . . .'

'You don't believe me, do you?'

'Surely nobody could be so brutally vicious?' Not Richard! She'd thought him kind and gentle; she'd fallen in love with him.

'He's evil, I tell you. We kept all the newspaper cuttings,' Ivy said. 'I'll show them to you, if you want to come home with me.'

Dinah could feel herself trembling. She wanted to be on her own, where she could think quietly about Ivy's story. She needed time to make up her own mind. 'What did it say? In the cuttings?'

Ivy shrugged her powerful shoulders again. 'Just how it happened. That it was raining heavily, he lost control of his luxury car and it ran into a horse-drawn dray heading for the docks. Twenty tons of salt was spilt over the road. The dray driver was injured and one pedestrian died. One of the horses pulling the dray had to be shot because of its injuries, and the other was lamed for life.'

'And Richard's parents both died.' Even all these years later, Dinah felt the horror of the tragedy. She said, 'But it could have been a pure accident, couldn't it? Why are you so sure the brakes of the car had been tampered with?'

Ivy's lips twisted with hate. 'Well, very much the same thing happened to Myra's parents when they refused permission for Myra to marry him. That was when we got suspicious.'

With a lump the size of an egg in her throat, Dinah said, 'You mean her parents died in a car accident too?'

'That's what I'm telling you.'

'But what about the police? Weren't they suspicious this time?'

'No, I don't think so. The Copthornes lived on top of a hill and the brakes failed as Mr Copthorne drove it down. He rarely drove himself, he had a chauffeur, but it was a new car bought only two days before. It was assumed he wanted to try it out, but couldn't control it.'

'Oh, my Lord! But if the brakes had been tampered with, surely the police would have noticed?'

'This was in 1920. With the war and that, there weren't many cars about. This one had been brought over from America. Nobody had ever seen anything half as grand. Neither the police nor the local garages knew much about how it worked.'

Dinah squinted into the sun, asking herself if it was possible for her husband to have murdered four people without even being suspected of it? No, absolutely not. How could it be true? Her head felt full of fog as she tried to consider the facts, but Ivy was still holding forth. It was a struggle to take in what she was saying.

'You want to look after yourself, love,' the bitter voice advised. 'He ill-treated his first wife, but she was a timid little thing; she stayed and let him kill her. You've got to get away while you still can or he'll do the same to you.'

Dinah flinched; she had to get away from Ivy. She couldn't stand any more of this.

'Thank you, Mrs Cummins. I have to go. I'm in a hurry.' She got to her feet and had to force herself not to break into a run until she left the church grounds.

She was heaving with doubt. Yes, Richard had the knowledge needed to tamper with car brakes, but he'd have had to have a heart of ice to do that to his parents. And then do the same thing to Myra's parents?

Perhaps Ivy Cummins had been too ready to blacken his name. She'd been full of hate and she'd let it burst out in vindictive rage. Although she'd been telling her of things that had happened fourteen years ago, it all seemed very clear in Ivy's mind. Too clear. It couldn't be right. It was too far-fetched. Dinah couldn't believe it.

She was breathless and shaking when she reached the park and was back in familiar surroundings. She strode rapidly round the perimeter twice and when she'd exhausted her energy she sank down on an empty bench to rest in the sun.

Dinah couldn't drag her mind away from what Ivy had told her. There was no way she could believe Richard had hidden in Arthur's flat for years while the war was on. Well, she knew that was a lie. He'd been an officer like his brothers, because he'd shown her the photograph of himself in uniform that he kept on the mantelpiece in his study.

And if Ivy was lying about that, how could Dinah possibly believe that Mark was the result of an affair with Arthur's wife before he'd married Myra? Or that he'd killed four people and got away with it? It was like something out of a film. But even so, she couldn't be sure. There was a ring of truth about what Ivy had said.

It was another hour before she felt able to take the bus back to the factory, where sooner or later she'd come face to face with Richard. She tried all afternoon to push what Ivy had told her out of her mind. It had given her the fright of her life, and that she couldn't make up her mind about whether it was true or not was making her feel worse.

It was almost time to go home when Richard returned. She tried to greet him in her usual manner but his face was like thunder, his mouth clamped in a straight line. Clearly, he'd had an afternoon as bad as hers and he didn't want to talk about it. He looked severe enough to be guilty of all Ivy accused him of, but she knew it could just be that he'd tried to get more orders for the factory and failed.

For most of the evening Dinah sat talking to her mother, burning with frustration and indecision. If there was one grain of truth in what Ivy had told her, she ought to get away from here and take Sarah with her. But that was impossible now that their house had gone.

Guilt was a greater burden then because she'd brought Mum here. Eventually, she decided they had to stay with Richard. What she'd done could not be changed, but she'd had a warning. She would be much more wary of him in future.

Chapter Thirteen

WHILE HE WAS at the factory, Richard spent most of the time in his own office with the door shut. One day when Miss O'Marney had been in with him taking dictation, she had come out to get something from her desk and left the connecting door open.

Dinah heard the phone ring and Richard answer it. He sounded calm and businesslike to start with, but suddenly erupted.

'What d'you mean, she's missing?' In the moment's silence that followed Dinah wondered whether it was Nellie who was missing and felt a shaft of anxiety.

'Headmistress,' he bellowed, 'you must inform the police. What? You have already? Good. I want her found immediately. I hold you responsible. Yes, yes. If you found her bed empty at seven o'clock this morning, what have you been doing since? It's nearly eleven. She could be anywhere by now. No, I have no idea where she might have gone. She certainly isn't here. Ring my home number and ask my housekeeper if she's turned up there. But I doubt she has; I'd expect Mrs Banks to let me know.'

Miss O'Marney tiptoed to his door and closed it quietly so they could hear no more. When she turned round Dinah saw that her mouth had dropped open. She whispered, 'It sounds as though Nellie has run away from school.'

Moments later, Richard wrenched his office door savagely open again. 'Dinah,' he bellowed, his face flushed. 'Come in here.' He was choking with anger and could hardly get his words out. 'Nellie, the naughty child . . .'

'I heard, Richard.'

'You'd think a school like that would be able to control its pupils. What are they thinking about?'

'I'll ring Mrs Banks,' Dinah said, 'and see if Nellie's at the house. She'll be coming home, won't she?'

'How would I know? Tell the woman to keep a look-out for her, and let me know instantly if she turns up.'

As Dinah had feared, Nellie was not at home. She said slowly, 'I'm worried. I suppose we could have half expected this to happen.' She was careful to say *we* rather than *you*. 'Nellie made it clear she didn't want to go back. Did you tell her headmistress she'd said she was being bullied?'

Richard exploded. 'For heaven's sake, stop it. I might have known you'd bring that up and blame me.'

Dinah sighed. How could she not blame him? 'I know how anxious you must be,' she said, 'not knowing where she is. I'll ask Gertie to make you a cup of tea.'

'Anxious? Nellie isn't a baby any more: she's eight years old. She should be capable of getting on a train or a bus and finding her way home. She needs a good hiding for this, causing trouble for us all. Her mother was too soft with her. The staff at that school should take good care the children can't run away. Surely they provide some supervision?' He was pacing round his office. 'This has put everything out of my mind. I can't think straight. I'm going out, Dinah.'

'Out? But if there is any news, this is where you'll hear.'

'How can I concentrate on work after this?'

Dinah asked, 'Well – where can I get hold of you if there is any news?' But he swept past her without another word.

The news that the boss's daughter had run away from her fancy boarding school swept through the Liverpool Button Company like a dose of salts. The girls couldn't stop speculating about it. Nobody could settle to work after that, not even Dinah, though she tried.

She pondered on whether Nellie might go to York to look for Mark. She could try to speak to him at his school, but perhaps it would be better not. To know his sister was missing would surely worry him.

Lunch time came and went. Richard had not returned. Dinah

propped his office door open so she'd hear his telephone when it rang. She answered it several times and Miss O'Marney did too, but it was never about Nellie. The afternoon hours dragged slowly on. Dinah walked round the workroom several times and then tried to calm her nerves by sitting at her desk and keeping the ledgers up to date. It had gone four o'clock when the phone on Richard's desk rang again. Dinah shot in to answer it.

A elderly woman's voice quavered, 'May I speak to Mr Haldane, please?'

'I'm afraid he's out at the moment. Can I take a message?'

'Oh!' The woman sounded put out. 'It's not about business. I'm . . . I'm afraid it's a personal matter. Has he gone home?'

Dinah asked eagerly, 'Is it about Nellie?'

'Oh, yes.' There was relief in the voice now.

'I don't really know where he is but I'm his wife, and we're both very worried about Nellie.'

'She's with me. Just walked in, less than an hour ago.'

'Is she all right?'

'A bit upset, but I've calmed her down and given her something to eat. She's resting on my bed. I'm Bunty Sugden, her old nanny. Will you tell her father?'

'Yes, of course, as soon as he comes in. I'm so relieved to hear she's safe with you. I expect Richard will want to come and pick her up. Does he know where to come?'

Dinah heard the pennies drop and the line go dead and knew the nanny was ringing from a phone box. She was on tenterhooks as she waited for her to ring back. Richard had sacked the nanny, and Dinah was afraid he wouldn't know where she was living now. She'd almost given up hope when the phone rang again.

'Sorry,' Bunty Sugden said, 'the money ran out and I had to get more pennies. I've got a room in Walton. Eighty-one Brunswick Street. Do you know it?'

'No, but I ought to, I used to live in Walton. Whereabouts is it?'

'Near Walton Hall Park, d'you know that? You turn down by the Horse and Hounds pub, and it's the second street on the left.'

'Right, I'll find it. Thank you very much for letting us know about Nellie.'

She put the phone down as Miss O'Marney came into the room. 'Thank goodness. Nellie's safe,' she said.

'That'll be a weight off Mr Haldane's mind.'

Dinah groaned. 'I've just thought, I should have asked Bunty if she'd rung the school to let the headmistress know. I'd better do it, and ring Mrs Banks too.'

That done, Dinah sat back and waited for Richard to return. She'd expected him back before now, but five thirty came and went and the workroom was emptying fast. Dinah was wondering if she should take the bus home when Richard came rushing in.

'It's time this place was locked up. Where's Hopper?'

'Nellie's safe. She's with her old nanny.'

'What? How did she get there?'

She recounted what Bunty Sugden had told her on the phone. She'd thought Richard would be relieved and pleased to know Nellie was safe, but his face was like thunder.

'Why the hell didn't you tell Bunty to bring Nellie home? Now we've got to go looking round the back streets of the city for her.'

Richard had calmed down a little by the time they were in the car. Miss O'Marney had found a street map so Dinah could work out exactly how to get there, but his temper was still short as he crept along Brunswick Street looking for number 81.

The houses were like many others in Walton: two sturdy Victorian terraces facing each other, with privet hedges between the pavements and the bay windows of the parlours. Number 81 was similar to but a little larger than the house in which Dinah had grown up, and the front door had been recently painted. The brass knocker shone.

'Go and knock on the door,' Richard ordered and sat back in the driving seat. Dinah did so, knowing he was watching every move she made.

Bunty Sugdon opened the door, looking older and frailer than when Dinah had met her at Ardwick House. She couldn't be much more than seventy, but myriad tiny wrinkles all over her face made her skin look like that of an old apple.

'Come in,' she invited.

Dinah looked back at Richard. 'Perhaps not this time,' she said. 'Nellie's father . . .'

'Please.' Bunty looked upset. 'I was hoping to have a word with him about Nellie. I'm worried about her; she'll be a nervous wreck if this goes on.'

'She is all right?'

'She didn't want me to telephone you, but I knew everybody would be worried.'

'She's afraid her father will be angry?'

'Yes. He's very strict – he'll be furious.'

Dinah beckoned to Richard and went inside. The hallway led to a small front room which was tightly packed with furniture. The girl had rolled herself into a small ball on a large rocking chair. She was peeping through her fingers at Dinah as she went in.

'Hello, Nellie.' Without saying a word, the child curled up tighter. Dinah went on, 'Bunty had to let us know you were here. She had no choice. Your headmistress asked the police to look for you, and Bunty would have been in big trouble if she'd let you hide here.'

Richard was close behind. 'You naughty girl,' he exploded. 'Running away from school like this.'

'Please don't be cross with her, Mr Haldane.'

'Cross with her? She needs teaching a lesson. She can't just take off from school when she feels like it. Nellie, we were all very worried about you.'

She didn't stir.

'Did you hear me, Nellie? I said we were all worried about you.'

Her voice was barely above a whisper. 'I'm sorry, Daddy. Please let me stay here with Bunty.'

'Of course you can't stay here. Get your things together. I'm taking you home now.'

'Please, Daddy, please,' she wailed, starting to cry.

'Don't be silly, Nellie. Do as I say.'

Dinah said gently, 'I think it might be better if you came home, Nellie. How much space do you have here, Bunty? Is it just this one room?' There was a single truckle bed against the wall covered with a shabby blue eiderdown. 'You see, Nellie, Bunty would like you to stay but she literally hasn't got enough room for a visitor. That's so, isn't it?'

'It is, pet,' Bunty said, clearly distressed. 'I've missed you and I'd love to have you here with me. You can come back to see me any time and spend the day with me, but I've no bed for you.'

Very slowly, Nellie was getting to her feet. Dinah put an arm round her shoulders.

'Come on, we'll talk to Daddy about this when we get home. Did you bring a case with you?'

'Just this.' Bunty gave her a brown paper bag.

'Just pyjamas and my toothbrush,' Nellie sniffed.

Richard said, 'I'm sorry she's bothered you like this, Bunty.'

'It's no bother to me, Mr Haldane. She was homesick at that school, and it's not that long since she lost her mother.'

He made for the door. 'Come along, you two.'

The old lady took Nellie in her arms and kissed her. Dinah heard her whisper, 'It was lovely to see you, pet. Do come and see me again, but next time you must let everybody know that you're coming.'

'Thank you again for phoning,' Dinah said in a low voice as they were being shown out. With one arm still round Nellie's shoulders, she led her out to the car and opened the back door. She followed her on to the back seat and pulled her close again. She could feel the child shaking.

Richard rammed the car into gear and shot off down the street. 'How did you know where to find Bunty?' he demanded. 'Has she been writing letters to you?'

Nellie sniffed. 'She sent me a card for my birthday.'

'Damn it. I might have known she'd cause trouble.'

'Richard,' Dinah said. 'You must expect Nellie to be fond of her old nanny.'

'She's fond of me too.' Nellie was tearful again.

'Yes.' Dinah was keeping her voice sympathetic. 'Of course you're fond of each other. She's always looked after you.'

'She looked after my mother too.'

That made Dinah sit up straighter. 'Did she? Then she's been part of your family for a very long time.'

'Yes.'

'That's enough of that,' Richard said sternly.

Dinah's mind suddenly filled with suspicion. Bunty must know him well and she'd have known Myra through and through. The family history too; living in the same house for eight years there'd be nothing she didn't know. Was he afraid of what she might say? He must have had some reason to suddenly send his children to boarding school and put her out.

But perhaps that was a bit fanciful. Was it just that he didn't want his children around when he brought home a new bride? She'd known him show his passion in the sitting room and hurry her upstairs. Mark was a teenager, after all, though if he and Nellie were up in the old nursery they'd see little enough.

Once home, Richard said, 'I hope you realise that you've put us all to a great deal of trouble, Nellie. I'll take you back to school tomorrow.'

She let out a wail of protest. 'I don't want to go back, Daddy.'

Richard ignored her. 'I'd better ring them now and let them know you're coming.'

Dinah said, 'Wouldn't it be wiser if we discussed this calmly first?'

He seemed quite shocked that she should intervene, but she went on, 'If Nellie is so unhappy there, is there any point in sending her back?'

'It's a good school and I've paid a term's fees in advance. She's going.'

Dinah stood up. 'I think I'll go to see how Mum is. Do you want to come with me, Nellie?' The child was up on her feet in an instant.

After she'd seen Nellie into bed, and said good night to her mother, Dinah returned to Richard.

'You're giving Nellie the impression that you don't love her and you want her out of the way,' she said. 'How d'you think that makes her feel? It isn't good for her. You should listen to what she's telling you.'

He said heatedly, 'It isn't good for her to get her own way after running away from school.'

'She says the girls are bullying her there.'

'That's probably just an excuse, but in any event it's time she learned to stand on her own feet.'

'She's scared, Richard. What if she runs away again? What would you do next time?'

'Give her a good hiding.'

Dinah felt exasperated. 'Is that how you were treated as a boy?'

He pulled a face. 'What do you suggest I do, then?'

Dinah thought he was beginning to listen at last. 'Let her stay at home and go back to her old school. She was doing all right there, wasn't she?'

Richard let out a noisy sigh.

'And why not let her visit her old nanny? Tell her she must ask permission first so we know where she's going. Or better still, bring Bunty back to live here.'

'I'm not having that old hag here.'

'I think she's rather sweet. And they're fond of each other.' He didn't answer. 'Nellie says Bunty was her mother's nanny, so she must have been working for your family for a very long time.'

'Only since Nellie was born. Before that, it was her mother's family.'

'Isn't that splitting hairs? The point is, she's living in poor circumstances considering she's been working all that time for you.'

He shouted at her then. 'I've had enough, Dinah! Stay out of this! It has nothing to do with you.'

'But it has. You disappear for hours on end and leave me to handle the problems it causes. I'd no idea where you'd gone and couldn't get hold of you. Then you complain I should have told Bunty to bring her home. If you want things done your way, you need to stay at your desk and do them.'

He let out another impatient roar. 'Drop this now.'

Dinah was determined not to. 'No, and it's no good bellowing at me. If you won't talk about these things how are you going to decide on the best course? I want to help you both. I assume you want Nellie to be happy? I'm suggesting ways to make her more content.'

He was silent and morose. This time, had she gone too far?

* * *

Dinah had reason to suspect she might have started with a baby. It didn't surprise her. Richard never tired of making love to her; it was a nightly event, if not twice nightly. She had not expected him to have so unquenchable an appetite. But he knew how to awaken her passion too.

She felt both excited and nervous about being pregnant so soon after her wedding. She wanted to slow things down. Everything in her life was changing too quickly for her. She felt she needed time to catch her breath and get used to having a husband before she had a baby as well.

Richard gave a satisfied little smile when she told him. 'A visit to Dr Jones for you,' he said, and insisted on taking her himself.

Dinah didn't know whether to be pleased or sorry when the pregnancy was confirmed. She would have welcomed a year or so to settle down with Richard first, but it was not to be.

'Soon we'll be a little family,' he said. 'I'm so pleased. Really delighted.'

Her mother was all smiles when she told her. 'How wonderful. I'm thrilled. I'd love to hold your baby in my arms.'

'You will, Mum, of course you will. You'll be here to help me look after him.'

'Him?' Faded blue eyes smiled up at her. 'Do you want a son?'

'Richard does. He's quite set on a boy.'

'I hope you get what you want, love. I hope you get everything you want in life.'

Brimming with emotion, Dinah kissed her. Poor Mum had lost what she'd wanted most, when her husband had been killed in the trenches.

In the days that followed, Dinah was delighted to see her mother's health picking up. The doctor came on a routine visit and said he was pleased with her progress. Joan Allen told her more than once that Sarah's appetite was improving. Dinah thought her more alert; she was able to read more, and she said she liked people popping in to chat to her.

'I should be spending more time with you, Mum.'

'You have a lot of other things to see to, love. I'm comfortable here with Joan. She can't do enough and Richard is very good to me.'

Dinah was pleased that her mother had taken to Richard. She didn't seem to find him like Dr Jekyll one day and Mr Hyde the next. Dinah had encouraged him to join her and Joan for a glass of sherry in Sarah's room every evening before dinner. She and Joan had made a habit of it and her mother seemed to see it as a little luxury. Sarah still preferred to have her supper up in her room with Joan. She said she found the stairs difficult when she was tired.

To Dinah's surprise, Richard had allowed Nellie to return to her old school, and she now had supper with them every evening. She was a nervous and easily upset child, who had clung to her nanny and to her brother until both had been removed from her life. At the table, Richard asked forceful questions about what Nellie was doing at school, which she answered sparingly.

Dinah thought he wasn't showing normal fatherly affection, but she'd never known her own father and had nothing to base her impression on. Nellie held herself aloof, and seemed to want as little as possible to do with Richard. Dinah felt she had to make an effort to get to know her better, and usually went up to the nursery to spend half an hour or so with her before her bedtime.

'That's a very unusual doll,' she said on one such occasion. Nellie always seemed to have it close at hand. 'It's all ribbons, very pretty.'

'She's not really a doll, Daddy said I was too old for those, she's more an ornament.'

'Have you given her a name?'

'Eugenie.'

'A pretty name too.'

'It was my mother's second name. She was Myra Eugenie, and it was her mother's name before that.'

Dinah picked Eugenie up, and suddenly saw what she was. 'These are the ribbons made by the Copthorne family business?' They were threaded through a wire frame to make a wide crinoline skirt worn by a small china doll. She wore a hat made of baby ribbons too.

'Some of them. They made lots more. My mother made Eugenie for me.'

'She's lovely.' Dinah smoothed the ribbons down. The doll was supported on a heavy wooden base and the colours were all co-ordinated. 'Your mother must have been clever with her fingers.'

'She was, and she loved the ribbons and wanted me to know all about them. Dad doesn't like them much, he'd rather have his buttons.'

'The ribbons are much prettier,' Dinah said, thinking that Nellie found comfort in her mother's gift.

Richard often had a glass of brandy after supper, and had started taking one to Sarah and keeping her company while she drank it. The first night, he poured little tots for Dinah and Joan too, and when after a sip they both found it too strong he tipped the contents from their glasses into his and drank it. Thereafter, Dinah and Joan refused the drink, though usually one or both would be there to see the same little scene re-enacted night after night.

Her mother seemed to welcome the attention, but demurred, 'You're very kind, Richard, but your brandy is like firewater. I'd rather have more sherry.'

'Brandy's good for you,' he told her. 'Just take a mouthful or two. It'll help you digest your supper and give you a good night's sleep.'

They stayed with her until her eyelids began to droop, then, as she'd usually drunk only part of her brandy, he tipped what remained into the washbasin in the corner of the room, rinsed out the glasses and took everything away on a tray.

Dinah had asked, 'Does the brandy help you sleep, Mum?'

'Yes, and I feel so much better when I don't spend half the night tossing.'

Joan encouraged Richard to bring her patient a glass of brandy every night. She didn't always drink it but it cheered her to have them all gathered in her room. Dinah was thankful that Richard kept his darker moods hidden from her mother, and Sarah continued to approve of him.

Dinah had morning sickness. After a particularly severe bout one Friday, she felt drained and listless and didn't want to eat at breakfast.

'You must eat.' Richard was in an affable mood. 'You must eat for two,' he told her. He asked Mrs Banks to pack two eggs for her to take to work. 'You can get Gertie to boil them for you when you feel better.'

He even tried to joke with Nellie, but his mood changed when he read the two letters that came in the morning post.

'Is something the matter?' Dinah asked him.

'No,' he snapped. On the way to work he looked morose and said nothing.

He went straight to his office and closed the door, but Dinah and Miss O'Marney could hear him pacing back and forth. It was clear that he was worried about something. At ten thirty he came out wearing his trilby.

As he passed her desk, Dinah asked, 'When will you be back?'

He almost looked through her. At the door he pulled up. 'I don't exactly know. After lunch.'

He'd been gone only ten minutes when the phone on his desk rang, and Dinah went to answer it. It was his trainer Bob Watchit.

'Richard's gone out,' she told him. 'He won't be back until mid-afternoon.'

'Oh.' He sounded put out. 'Tell him I'll ring again later.'

'Anything I can help with?' Dinah asked.

'No . . . no, thanks. It'll wait till he gets back.'

She put the phone down, wondering if she should have asked how the horses were. Her eyes fell on the two letters Richard had received that morning, which had been left open on his blotter. Both were from Bob Watchit's stables at Tarporley. The first was the monthly bill for stabling and feed for the two horses undergoing training. Pinned to it was a polite reminder that last month's bill had not yet been settled. The second was a handwritten note to say that Ardwick Beauty had pulled a muscle in her foreleg and Bob had withdrawn her from the handicap stakes at Haydock Park.

Dinah was shocked. This could only mean one thing: Richard was very short of cash. Surely, paying the monthly bill could not have slipped his memory? He now owed a large amount.

When he returned, she told him about Bob Watchit's call. 'He's after his money,' Richard said. 'I'm just writing out his cheque.'

Chapter Fourteen

EARLY THE NEXT morning, Dinah woke up with a jolt to find the bedroom still pitch dark and the nurse with a hand on her arm.

'What is it? What's the matter?' She felt her heart skip a beat and was wide awake in an instant.

Joan whispered, 'It's your mother. I think you should come.'

Fear was striking through her as she pushed her feet into her slippers and felt for her dressing gown. 'What time is it?'

Richard grunted irritably. 'Do you have to make all this noise?'

'It's all right.' Dinah tried to sound calmer than she felt. 'Go back to sleep. I'm just going to see Mum.'

The sickroom was in semi-darkness. 'I'm sorry, but I think she's failing,' the nurse said. 'I thought you'd want to be with her.'

'Of course. But she was better, wasn't she?' Dinah could hardly breathe. The thought that this might happen had been with her for weeks, but now the moment had arrived she felt unprepared.

The nurse said in a low but penetrating voice, 'Mrs Radcliffe, Dinah's here to sit with you.'

Her mother was lying flat, a small wasted form under the blankets. 'Di . . . nah?' Her eyes flickered, half opened and then shut again.

'Yes, I'm here, Mum.' She pulled up a chair and sank on to it, reaching for her mother's hand. 'How d'you feel?'

Dinah saw her lips move, and one word came out in a soft hiss. 'Tired.'

'Try and go back to sleep. I'll sit with you for a while.' She gave Sarah's hand a gentle squeeze and felt the frail thin hand move in return with a touch as soft as a summer breeze.

Dinah was shocked at the change in her mother since she'd said good night to her just hours before. She sat watching her, listening to her breathing. It was shallow and slow. She found herself waiting between each breath, willing Sarah to take another.

'Shall I make you a cup of tea?' Joan whispered.

'Yes, please.' She followed the nurse to the door. 'What happened to make Mum like this?'

'She was very restless earlier in the night. I rang the doctor, and he told me to give her an extra dose of her medicine and said he'd be in to see her this morning.'

'But she seemed so much better. She told me you'd taken her for a little walk round the garden yesterday. She really enjoyed the sunshine. I thought she'd continue to improve.'

Joan was biting her lip. 'It sometimes happens like this.'

'I don't want her to die!'

The nurse said quietly, 'Try to think of what life has been like for your mother. She's been ill and in pain for a long time. Perhaps she doesn't want it to go on.'

'But she was better! She said so, the doctor said so, and so did you.'

'Better than she had been, yes, but she couldn't have felt well.'

Dinah dissolved into tears and followed Joan down to the kitchen. She didn't want her mother to hear her cry. Joan watched her compassionately, and when she had wiped her eyes said gently, 'She's slipping away, Dinah. Go back and sit with her. I'll bring your tea up to you.'

Sarah hadn't moved. She hardly seemed to be breathing at all. Dinah took hold of her hand again, a lump in her throat the size of a golf ball.

'Mum, I don't want you to go. Not yet. Stay a bit longer. I want you with me. I want you to try. Say you will.'

Joan had come in with the tea. 'I don't think she can talk to you now,' she said softly. 'I'm sorry.'

'She's not dead! She can't be!'

'No, no. But I think she's losing consciousness. She's at peace now, but do talk to her. She might still be able to hear you.'

Dinah couldn't stop the tears running down her face. 'Oh, Mum, you've had a hard life. Things haven't gone well for you. Yet you did so much for me, gave me such a good childhood. I wish I could have done more for you. I do love you, Mum. Very much.'

She sat holding Sarah's hand as daylight gradually flooded the room. She knew now that Mum never would see her grandchild.

Dinah could hear the sounds of the house waking up. Richard was dressed and shaved when he came to the sickroom to see her.

'Mum's gone, Richard. She's dead.'

'Yes,' he said. 'Joan's told me.'

'I don't understand it. She was so much better yesterday. I thought she'd go on for months.'

He took Dinah's hand to pull her to her feet. 'Darling, you're so cold. I'll run a hot bath for you, and then you must get dressed and eat some breakfast.'

She clung to him. 'I couldn't eat anything.'

'You must try. You'll feel better if you do. You needn't come to work this morning.'

'Oh, God, Richard!' She struggled out of his arms. 'I'd no intention of doing that.'

'No. Well, I need to go in. I won't stay long – Saturday's a half day anyway. I'll see to the funeral arrangements; no need for you to bother about that. We'll have her cremated, yes?'

'Well . . . Poor Mum had plenty of time to think about that. She spoke once of lying in the churchyard at St Agnes's and how peaceful it would be.'

'It wouldn't. The road is busy with traffic round there – it's one of the main routes into the city.'

'The funeral must be held there. It's where she went to church and the vicar knows her. Also, it's close for all her old friends and neighbours.'

'All right.'

'I think she'd prefer to be buried rather than cremated.'

'Has she left written instructions? A will?'

Dinah shook her head. 'She had nothing but her personal belongings and nobody but me to leave them to.'

'But the churchyards are overflowing with old bones. There's no room for more, Dinah. No room for future generations. The modern thing is cremation. You'll say yes to that, won't you?'

She said nothing. Mum had only mentioned the churchyard once and the conversation had appalled Dinah at the time. She hadn't been able to think of her mother's death then. She'd wanted it to be years in the future.

Joan and Mrs Banks were being especially kind to her. They persuaded her to eat scrambled eggs, though her tears were ever present and it was a continual fight to stem the flow. Joan had rung the doctor and he came round before his morning surgery with the death certificate. To have her mother cremated meant more forms to be completed by him.

'You're doing the best thing,' he told her.

Dinah wished she was still living two doors from Aunt Enid. She went to the phone in the hall and sent a telegram to let her know what had happened. An hour or so later, Enid rang from a public phone box. Dinah could hear her sobbing on the other end of the line and that brought her own tears running down her face again. It was a long call as they tried to comfort each other.

'Tim's at a race meeting at Redcar, and I'm not expecting him back for a day or two,' Enid said. 'I'll phone him to let him know. He'll be upset too; he was fond of Sarah. I'll ask him to ring you.'

Dinah was mopping at her eyes trying to stop them flooding with tears when Nellie came through the hall and saw her.

'Joan's told me,' she whispered. 'How awful for you.' Dinah felt the girl press her body against her own in a gesture of comfort. She put her arms round Nellie and cried on her shoulder in an emotional storm, torn with grief and distress that even after such a long illness she'd felt so unprepared for her mother's death.

The days between Sarah's death and her funeral seemed to stretch on endlessly. Dinah couldn't settle to anything. She watched Joan lay her mother out; she helped to wash and dress her in a new satin nightdress that she rushed out to buy. Joan tidied the room, disposed of Sarah's medicines, packed her bags and left.

The undertakers came and put Sarah into her coffin, leaving the lid off. Dinah was in and out of the room, unable to turn her back on her mother. She took a comb to her hair, because Joan hadn't arranged it in the way her mother liked. Enid and Tim paid a formal visit to see her, bringing a single white chrysanthemum which Enid placed in Sarah's hands. She had tears in her eyes when she looked up from the coffin.

'She was a good friend to me.' There was a sob in her voice. 'We helped each other out – almost lived in each other's pockets. You and she were like family to me. The war wiped out most of our real families we had to find friends to take their place. You and she did that.'

When they were leaving, Tim kissed her cheek and squeezed her hand. 'Don't cut yourself off from us,' he told her.

'We'd both love to see you,' Enid added. 'Come down and have a cup of tea and a chat from time to time.'

Richard brought home several bunches of hothouse chrysanthemums. They were magnificent multicoloured blooms that filled Sarah's room with their sharp fresh tang. For ever after, Dinah associated the scent of chrysanthemums with her mother's death. Richard wanted to replace the flower Enid had brought with a bigger one but Dinah wouldn't let him.

'Mum would want the flower Enid brought because it was given with her love.'

'You must have a mourning outfit for the funeral.' A funeral of which he was arranging all the details without consulting her.

'I have a navy coat,' Dinah said, 'and I could wear my wedding hat.'

'You could not,' he thundered. 'It's only right and proper that you have black. You must show your grief. Take Nellie with you and buy her something suitably dark.'

Dinah was surprised. 'She won't be coming to the funeral, will she?'

'Of course. Why not?'

'She's such a nervous little thing and she hardly knew my mother.'

'Of course she did. I won't have it said that my family don't show respect for the dead. Go out and buy what's needed.'

Dinah tried to protest. 'Mum said she didn't want me to look like a miserable crow. We had plenty of time to talk about such things. She knew she was losing her fight with cancer. She said she'd accepted that she was going to die and I must too. Sooner or later everybody has to die and she was glad she'd lived long enough to see me grow up.'

'Nonsense,' Richard growled.

'Nellie will have all she needs, won't she? I take it she went to her mother's funeral?'

'Oh, yes. Yes, of course she did.'

So Dinah went to Bunney's and bought herself a neat-fitting black and white suit which she teamed with a white hat with a black band and feather, another of Carlton Hats' designs. Richard was cross when she showed it to him.

'That isn't real mourning. There's too much white – it doesn't show proper respect. What will the vicar think?'

When at last the day of the funeral came, it turned out to be a sunny morning. Richard looked hot in his bowler hat and black wool suit and waistcoat. Nellie's face was white and drained against her sombre black hat and coat.

'I wish Mark was here,' she said. 'But Dad said it wasn't worth bringing him home from school.'

Dinah held her hand. She thought it would have been kinder to let Nellie go to school as usual. She looked unhappy and uncomfortable.

'There are more people here than I expected,' Richard said. Most of them were their old neighbours from Picton Street. Dinah couldn't keep her tears at bay. It was her last goodbye to her mother.

Not so long ago Sarah had said, 'It's going to come, I'm afraid. Don't let it upset you, Dinah. You'll manage very well, I'm sure. I made Enid promise to keep an eye on you for a bit, but now you're married it's taken a weight off my shoulders. I'm sure Richard will give you a happy and comfortable life.'

Mum had been wrong about that, but nobody could have foreseen how things would turn out. Dinah stood at the church door wondering if Mum would mind being cremated. Then she got into the hired car that followed the coffin on its short final journey to the chapel of rest. After a hymn and a final address she watched the red velvet curtains part and the coffin roll away.

Dinah was unable to move. Somehow all this felt twice as awful and final as the lowering of a coffin into a grave. Richard took her arm and guided her back into the sunshine. He had arranged for a catering firm to provide sandwiches and sherry in the church hall afterwards.

'Better than asking everyone to our house,' he told her. 'We'd never get rid of them once we let them in.'

It was a stiff and formal gathering.

Tim said, 'Mum wants you to visit often. She's really going to miss your mum. She'll be lonely now she's left on her own.'

Dinah nodded her agreement. 'I will.'

After twenty minutes, Richard said, 'Come along, let's go home. I've had enough of this.'

Dinah had been fighting to control her tears all through the service and hadn't been able to eat anything. Nellie was clinging to her. They were both glad to go home.

'Cheese on toast,' Richard barked at Mrs Banks as they went in. 'Have it on the table in fifteen minutes with a pot of tea.'

He led the way to the stairs. 'Change out of those clothes, Nellie,' he said. 'We need to go to work, and we'll drop you at school on the way.'

'I couldn't work,' Dinah said. 'Not this afternoon. And I think Nellie should stay at home too. We'll be company for each other.'

'You'll feel better if you come,' he insisted.

Dinah shook her head.

'Tomorrow, then. Come down and eat something. You're pregnant, you need to eat.'

Dinah sat opposite Richard and watched him relish his cheese on toast and then call for some apple pie. She had to force her toast down, and Nellie too was toying with her food.

As soon as he'd had enough, Richard stood up and said impatiently, 'At least it's over now, and you can put it behind you. Do try and cheer up, Dinah.'

The only effect was to make her eyes flood with tears again as Richard left the room. After a few minutes, she tried to pull herself together. 'Sorry, Nellie. I can't help it today.'

'I cried when my mother died,' Nellie said. 'I was very sad about it.'

'I didn't expect it to happen just yet.' Dinah mopped at her eyes. 'She seemed a bit better.'

'I didn't expect my mum to die at all.' Nellie, too, wasn't far from tears. 'It came out of the blue for me and Mark.'

That made Dinah push back her misery. Now, at this dreadful moment, it seemed that Nellie was unbending towards her and wanted to talk about the death of her own mother. It made her heart sink. Richard had found it almost impossible to talk about Myra's suicide, but he had said she'd been mentally ill for a long time. How much did Nellie know?

'Let's go up to your old nursery,' Dinah said, taking Nellie's hand. 'Tell me what happened to your mother.'

'Me and Mark were at school, so we don't really know. Daddy doesn't want to tell us about it. Mummy didn't come down for breakfast that morning. He said she didn't feel well.'

Nellie's voice broke and Dinah could see tears on her lashes. It reminded her that it had happened only a few months ago.

'And when you came home from school that afternoon?'

'The doctor was here and a policeman, talking to Daddy.' A sob caught in her throat. Dinah put her arms round her and held her tight. The thin voice wavered on. 'They said Mummy was dead when they got her to hospital.'

'What had happened to her?'

'We don't really know. To start with, Daddy told us she was in a car crash.'

'What?' The words 'car crash' hammered at Dinah's mind. This wasn't what Richard had told her! Had he been lying? She was coming out in a cold sweat. Not another car crash! She'd been trying not to dwell on what Ivy Cummins had told her, but if it was the same . . .

Nellie's voice wavered. 'Everybody was talking about it, in the kitchen and at school. Then a boy at Mark's school gave him the newspaper.'

'Oh, my goodness!' Dinah felt her heart flip over. 'Was there a crash? Did the brakes fail on your mum's car?'

'No. It said she'd taken poison. That she'd – she'd killed herself while her mind was turned.'

'Oh, Nellie.' Dinah felt tears burning her eyes again. Her head was spinning. 'Nellie, love . . .'

For her children, what more awful death could Myra have had? And what more dreadful way was there to learn about it?

'We asked Daddy and showed him the newspaper but he wouldn't talk about it. But Mark and me . . . We both have this dreadful feeling that he killed her.'

Dinah couldn't control her gasp of horror. Here it was again, Richard being accused of another murder.

'Nellie! No, he wouldn't. Why ever would he do such a thing?'

Through her tears Nellie managed to get the words out. 'We don't think – he loved her, not any more. He was always grumpy with her – cranky. He had no patience. I heard Mrs Parr saying that she thought he wanted to be . . . rid of her. She said to Bunty that he wanted to marry a new wife, someone younger . . . Like you.'

'No, Nellie, it wasn't like that. Your father was already a widower when we first met.'

'Do you think he killed your mother?' Nellie asked, her face clouded with fear.

Dinah couldn't get her breath. Her mother! Oh, my God! The nursery was beginning to eddy round her. She had to take a grip on herself, stay calm and be careful what she said. 'No, love, my mother was very ill before she came here. You mustn't think that.'

'I saw him come out of her bedroom. Late last night when I was going down to the kitchen to get a drink of milk.'

'I wanted him to visit her, Nellie. It cheered her up. He took her a glass of sherry or brandy almost every night. Mum liked that.'

'You shouldn't have let him. I don't think he liked her.'

Dinah could feel her skin crawling. She said firmly, 'He did. It was his idea that she should come here. He found Joan to nurse her.'

'It was you he wanted.'

Dinah's teeth were chattering; she knew that was true. She hugged Nellie's thin body to her, but she couldn't get away from the awful idea that what the child was saying could be true.

The thought that Richard might have poisoned her mother was

harrowing. In a way, though, it added up. He'd been taking her brandy every night over the last few weeks though she'd said she preferred sherry. Brandy was stronger, more likely to disguise the taste of added poison.

How could she have been such a fool? She'd stood there and watched him rinse what Mum had left down the sink and wash her glass out instead of leaving it to the staff. And he'd insisted on cremating her body, so nothing could be proved now.

Mrs Cummins had accused Richard of engineering two car crashes to kill first his own parents and then Myra's. Now Nellie had accused him of poisoning both her mother and Sarah.

Nellie must have it wrong. She could have misunderstood what Mrs Parr had said. That would be kitchen gossip anyway. It was fantasy, it must be, but Dinah couldn't get the dreadful doubts out of her mind. If it wasn't true, she should surely worry about Nellie's state of mind. All right, some of the facts might lead one to wonder, but were they enough to make Nellie think her father was capable of such terrible things?

The girl pulled out of her arms and went quietly to the window. She looked pale and distressed. Dinah had to get away. She went flying downstairs and out to the garden to fling herself on to a bench. She'd been full of sympathy for Richard when he'd first told her that Myra had committed suicide. She'd put his strange behaviour and mood swings down to the distress such an event would have caused him. But to tell his children lies about it? No wonder Nellie was nervous and upset. She shouldn't be left alone so much to dwell on things like that.

It was a bright and sunny afternoon. Dinah went back up to the nursery and insisted that Nellie come for a brisk walk to Calderstones Park. They took some stale bread and fed the ducks on the lake. She felt she was on better terms now with the girl, but to settle her own mind she had to make Richard tell her how Myra had died, and, even more important, he had to talk to Nellie about it. He could not be allowed to say he found it too painful.

Dinah was waiting for Richard in the sitting room when he came home late in the afternoon. They always had a pot of tea at this time, and she had it ready to pour.

He kissed her. 'I'm sorry I wasn't more sympathetic at lunch time. I expect you've had a bad day?'

'I have.'

'It's always hard when someone close to you dies.'

'Nellie's had a bad day too, and listening to her made mine worse.'

'The answer for Nellie is to get her back to her normal routine as soon as possible.'

'It isn't, Richard. I don't think you should keep pushing her away. She's really muddled about how her mother died. She says you won't talk about it.'

'I've tried—'

'She says you told her and Mark it was a traffic accident and later they read in the paper that she'd committed suicide. And when they asked you about it, you wouldn't tell them anything.'

He was frowning. 'It was hard for me too.'

'But surely you wanted to make it easier for them?'

'I'm afraid it's not my way to talk about my problems. I find it difficult—'

'We all know that! But it's your plain duty as their father to tell them the true facts.'

The colour had drained from his face. 'I just couldn't . . .'

'Richard, they need to know. If you don't truthfully explain what happened and why, you force them to imagine it. They've talked it over together and believe it's even worse than it really is.'

She could see the alarm gathering on his face. 'What do they think?'

'That you murdered their mother.'

His shoulders sagged, and his face seemed to collapse. 'What? Oh, my God! How could they think that of me? As if I ever could.'

Chapter Fifteen

Dinah had expected an outburst of anger from Richard, that he'd rage on about how absurdly fanciful Nellie was. Instead, tears were rolling down his face; he was distraught with grief and sorrow.

Dinah put her arms round him in a gesture of comfort. 'We'd better go up to our bedroom,' she said. 'We don't want Mrs Banks coming in on us. You wouldn't like her to see you like this.'

'Poor Nellie,' he wept. 'She sees bogeymen everywhere. How could she think such things of her own father?'

Mrs Banks was rattling pans in the kitchen as they went upstairs. Dinah pulled him down to sit beside her on the bed.

He went on: 'It was a dreadful time. I was in agony. I couldn't believe Myra would do such a thing.'

'Richard, I don't know what exactly she did. How can I understand and help you if you won't talk about it?'

'You do know, and so does Nellie.' There was just a touch of irritability in his voice. 'Myra committed suicide.'

He was clinging to her; her cardigan felt damp with his tears. 'Yes, but how?'

'She poisoned herself.' Richard pulled himself upright and searched his pockets. 'A handkerchief . . . ?'

She pulled one out of his drawer and put it in his hand. She couldn't believe how quickly Richard had changed. His bombastic manner had gone, and he seemed cowed, more like a dependent child than the master of the house.

Dinah kissed his forehead. 'What with? I want you to tell me all about

Myra's death. How it happened and why.' So far she'd learned more about his first wife from other people than she had from him.

'Poor Myra was never very strong – mentally strong, I mean. She always needed a lot of support. She felt incapable of doing much on her own.'

'Did she? I understood from . . .' careful now, no mention of Mr Hopper, 'the girls at work that she did a lot with the ribbon side of the business.'

'I told her she was good at it to bolster her confidence, but when she started losing orders . . . I kept telling her it was the Depression, that business generally was going down and it wasn't her fault, but it didn't help her. She felt terribly guilty.'

'About what?'

'Ruining the business her father had built up. About the way she was bringing up Nellie. Well, you know how nervous and clinging she is, like her mother really. Myra was driven by demons.'

'I don't understand. What does that mean?'

'She felt hounded by guilt and inferiority. She was depressed most of the time.'

'You said she was mentally ill. Was that depression?'

He nodded dumbly.

'Was the doctor treating her for it?'

'Yes. He was giving her tablets. I knew she was very down, and one day she just took . . .' His voice shook with emotion.

'An overdose?'

'No, poison, I told you.'

That's what Nellie had read in the newspaper. 'What sort?'

He sprang to his feet and strode to the window, full of irritation again. 'Strychnine.'

'Goodness! Where did she get hold of that?'

Richard groaned. 'We had moles in the garden and kept a tin of strychnine to eradicate them.'

'For heaven's sake! Wasn't it kept under lock and key?'

His voice was full of regret. 'I should have been more careful with it.'

'Don't you have to sign at the chemist's for stuff like that?'

'Yes, but we'd been using it for years. Arthur Phelps signed for it three years before. We kept it in the store behind the garage with the other gardening stuff.'

'That's awfully dangerous.'

'We'd been doing it for years. The moles are in the adjoining land and keep coming back. Myra left a note, telling the children she loved them, and apologising for leaving them while they were still so young. She said she just couldn't go on any longer.'

Dinah shuddered. 'Poor Myra. What she must have gone through to reach that point. Had she ever suggested she might take her own life?'

'Yes.' He looked up. His face was wet with tears and his eyes were red. 'That's the awful thing. I did let Dr Jones know she was talking about it but nothing else. If only I'd got rid of that strychnine.' It was an agonised cry. 'But I didn't realise she knew it was there or what it was. She never mentioned how she meant to take her life, I thought it was just a vague feeling of hopelessness, and that rest and medication would sort her out. I feel I'm to blame. I let her down. I was pretty depressed myself after that, I can tell you.'

Dinah's arms tightened round him. 'You mustn't blame yourself.'

'But I do. It's given me my own demons, Dinah. That's why I couldn't talk about it to the children. I knew Nellie would be feeling bereft. To think her mother preferred to kill herself rather than stay to take care of her and Mark. She turned her back on us all. I thought it better to protect the children from that.'

Dinah was weeping with him, full of sympathy for them all. 'That you thought like that is understandable, but Nellie needs to know the truth. She'll worry about it and imagine all sorts of things unless you tell her everything.'

Dinah could see now that he'd gone through hell. No wonder he was moody and withdrawn and had made some wrong decisions. It made her feel guilty to think she'd misjudged him. She'd thought he was hiding some dark secret, when all the time he was fighting off his own worries and grief. She wanted to restore him to normality, help him and his children have a happier life.

It was later than usual when they sat down to supper. Afterwards, Dinah and Richard took Nellie up to the old nursery so that, together, they could tell her what had really happened to Myra.

By the next morning Richard had recovered and at work he disappeared into his office as usual. Dinah was still fighting her tears, and her eyes felt sore. The girls were very kind and spoke with sympathy of her loss.

In the kitchen, Gertie said, 'You'll be feeling a bit down today, so I've saved some chocolate biscuits for you to have with your mid-morning tea,' and Gilbert Hopper brought her a little posy of wild flowers for her desk.

'My grandchildren picked them,' he said. She liked Mr Hopper and got on well with him. At mid-morning she drank her tea sitting next to him at the table in the canteen. The sad story of Myra Copthorne was still very much on Dinah's mind. She knew Mr Hopper had started his working life with Copthorne Ribbons and encouraged him to talk about those long-ago days.

'I started when I was fourteen,' he told her, 'and spent most of my working life there. I was called up in the war, but when it was over Mr Copthorne said he'd be glad to have me back. They paid as well as anybody and I'd been happy there, so back I went.'

'You must have known the Copthorne family well.'

'No, only the boss. There was a son but he was killed in the war. His wife and daughter never came near the factory. The ladies didn't in those days.'

'I believe Richard's mother did.'

'So I believe, but it wasn't usual and I never knew her. I'd never heard of the Haldanes or the Liverpool Button Company until . . .' He was frowning.

'Until what?'

'Until Myra met Mr Haldane.'

'How did that come about?'

'I believe it was at a posh dinner dance. A charity do to raise money to help soldiers trying to get back on their feet in the years after the war. There was a bit of scandal, I remember, going round our factory.'

Dinah's ears went up. 'About Richard and Myra? What sort of scandal?'

'They'd hardly met each other before there was talk of them wanting to marry. Myra Copthorne was only eighteen and Mr Haldane was taking her out and about. Her parents thought he was rushing her into it, and tried to put a stop to it. They thought he was ruining Myra's reputation. They didn't like him and refused to give their consent to the marriage, and forbade her to have anything more to do with him.'

Dinah pondered for a moment. That bore out what Ivy Cummins had told her. 'But she did marry him. Did her father relent or did she wait until she was twenty-one?'

'Neither. Mr and Mrs Copthorne were killed shortly after that.'

'How awful!' Dinah had a sinking feeling in her stomach. 'How?'

'In a road accident.'

So Ivy Cummins had told the truth. 'Richard's parents died that way too.'

'Yes.'

She shivered. 'What a ghastly coincidence. It must have been a terrible shock for her.' Dinah still felt raw after losing one parent.

She was overcome with sympathy for her predecessor. She'd grown up in a fine house as heiress to a ribbon factory, only to lose her whole family while she was still young. Myra had been even younger than she'd been herself when she was married, and she'd enjoyed a more sheltered upbringing. Dinah hoped she'd been happy in the early days of her marriage, before that had ended in tragedy too.

It seemed to Dinah that Mr Hopper meant to help her fill her first morning back. He took her to the workroom and spent two hours showing her the different types of buttons. He told her in minute detail how each type was made and how the machines were controlled. A tour of the storerooms came next, and she heard about the materials they used to make the buttons. By dinner time, she felt she had a clear picture of how the business functioned.

* * *

It was a pleasant sunny afternoon, and as Richard had already gone out Dinah took her sandwiches and went out to get some fresh air. There was usually a breeze off the river, though the factory was in an area of dusty streets, railway lines and industrial buildings not far from the docks.

She walked a short distance through the smoke-blackened buildings to a recreation ground she'd often noticed as Richard had driven her to work. It was just a rectangle of grass with a couple of trees and some wooden benches along the sides. There were quite a lot of people about, mostly employees from the nearby workplaces. Some were eating sandwiches, some sunbathed on the grass, and a half-hearted game of football was being played at one end.

A girl pushing a pram came to sit down at the other end of her bench and lifted her baby out on to her knee. Dinah bit into an egg and tomato sandwich while her mind zigzagged between the loss of her mother, Richard's problems and the child she would give birth to next March. She noticed then that the infant next to her was smiling and holding a woolly pink rabbit out to her. She couldn't help but smile back.

'Hello,' she said. 'What's your name?'

'Patsy,' the girl answered for her, straightening her sun bonnet. 'Isn't she lovely?'

'She's very pretty.' Dinah was interested. 'How old is she?'

'Seven months. She's my sister's little girl. I'm looking after her while Liz is in hospital. She's just had her appendix out.'

'I'm having a baby,' Dinah volunteered.

'Lucky you. I wish I was. We've been trying for four years but no joy yet. Liz has only been married eighteen months and look what she's achieved.'

The baby gurgled happily. 'She's absolutely besotted with Patsy – we all are. I take her down to the hospital every day at three o'clock. They won't let babies in, of course, but I stand across the road with her so Liz can see her.'

Dinah reflected that many women longed for a child. Perhaps being pregnant was not such a bad thing. She'd always liked babies and to have one of her own to care for and cuddle would be very nice.

'I don't know how I'm going to give her up when Liz comes out,' the girl went on. 'It's going to be an awful wrench.'

Dinah got to her feet. 'I must get on. I hope you get your wish and have one of your own soon.'

The baby jerked up and down in her aunt's arms and waved her goodbye. The sight of the happy pair had raised Dinah's spirits. She was going to have a baby, there was no way it could be put off, and if it turned out like this one everybody would welcome it. For the first time she looked forward to holding her child in her arms.

Over the next few weeks Dinah grieved for her mother and worried about Richard. For the moment he seemed to be acting more normally. One fine Sunday afternoon, hoping Tim might be at home too, she decided she'd like to pop down and see Enid. When she told Richard, he said he'd been planning all weekend to drive over to see how Ardwick Beauty was getting on and he wanted her to go with him.

'I've seen a recently opened olde worlde tea shop where we can have cream scones and strawberry jam on the way home. You'll love the place. It's really quaint.'

It was much the same whenever she suggested going out without him. Before Sarah became really poorly, Dinah and her friend Millie used to go Scottish dancing once a week. They also belonged to a cycling club that had frequent outings on Sunday afternoons. Dinah had really enjoyed cycling long distances.

She'd sent Millie a note to tell her about her mother and Millie had written back by return saying she was sorry, and suggesting that when Dinah felt better that she should take up her old pastimes. The cycling club was planning a trip to Grange-over-Sands next Sunday; did she feel like it?

Dinah wanted to see all her old friends again. She felt she had to get back to normal, to do the things she always had, before she could get over this difficult time. She showed Millie's letter to Richard.

'Surely you don't want to go?' He looked quite upset that she should suggest a day out without him. 'I'd be lost at home all day on my own. Please don't.'

'Why don't you get a bike and come with me? There'll be a few more trips over the autumn. You might enjoy it. The club isn't just for girls – there are men and boys in it too. Tim used to come sometimes.'

'I don't think so. I'm too old for long energetic cycling trips. And besides, now you're having a baby I don't think you should take violent exercise like that.'

'The doctor said that for the time being I should carry on doing what I always have done, and he specially recommended swimming.'

'Not cycling,' Richard said. 'That couldn't possibly be good for you.'

It seemed he loved her and needed her so much he couldn't bear to be left on his own at the weekends.

'Also,' he said, 'Nellie's too young to ride long distances like that. You wouldn't want to leave her here on her own.'

'No,' Dinah said, shelving the whole idea. Having a baby and caring for Nellie meant she had to accept there were some things she couldn't do. Too much was happening to her, and the coming baby meant that even greater changes were on the horizon. It was too soon: she needed to sort out the day-to-day difficulties in her life first. She felt she was suffering from emotional overload, and would have liked to get away on her own for a few hours.

Seeing Richard reduced to tears had driven home the fact that he was in an highly emotional state too. In his case, though, the storm seemed to have blown up from nowhere. She didn't think it was because she'd told him what Nellie had said. He'd dealt brusquely with Nellie's upsets before this.

For the first time she wondered if there was some other crisis in Richard's life that she didn't know about. Something else that was pushing him to the brink. Whom did he see and what did he do every day when he left the factory? He wasn't giving away the first clue.

Heaven knows, there could be no more awful thing to confront than a spouse who had committed suicide. It would be enough to bring the strongest to their knees; Dinah knew she'd find it almost impossible to live with. But as far as she could see, Richard showed no sign of guilt or remorse for the suffering Myra must have gone through in the last months of her life.

Dinah didn't know what to make of him. She felt confused, rocking from one extreme to the other: first he was totally evil, then a husband fraught with nerves who loved her. She no longer knew which she believed.

Chapter Sixteen

'You need cheering up,' Richard told Dinah the next day. 'We'll go to the Chester Meeting. Ardwick Prince has been entered in the Delamere Hurdles. Let's go and see him run, have a day out.'

Dinah was getting over her morning sickness and as yet her pregnancy was not obvious, but when she tried on her wedding outfit its slim skirt had grown much tighter. She tried on the black and white suit she'd bought for her mother's funeral only a few weeks ago and found the same thing.

'Get yourself another smart outfit,' Richard said. 'You deserve it.'

First she made an appointment in the hairdressing salon at Bunney's to have her hair cut and styled. She went to the shop two hours before her appointment and looked through all the expensive outfits on the rails. Trying on what she thought would suit her was a pleasure there because an assistant waited on her, fetching different sizes or matching shades for her whenever she asked.

She'd never owned anything as smart as the pale green two-piece in finest wool that she finally chose. Then she bought herself new shoes, new gloves and a handbag to complement it. She had time for a snack in the restaurant before having her hair done, and then she chose her hat. It had to be a Carlton Hat and she was delighted to find they had a model she liked in pea green. It pleased her that she remembered working on the blocks for this design.

She felt she'd had a lovely day getting her outfit together. For the first time in her life, she'd not thought about the cost of what she was buying. What she liked and what suited her had been her only considerations.

When Richard received the bill, he said, 'Good gracious, I didn't think you'd be so extravagant.'

'Don't you like my new clothes?' she asked.

'Yes, of course, you look very smart.'

'I feel I've a right to be extravagant. After all, this is in lieu of wages. How many weeks have I been working in your business now?'

'But Dinah, you won't get much wear out of them. You'll soon be putting on too much weight to wear this outfit too.'

The day of the race meeting was fine if a little breezy. First thing in the morning, Richard drove her into work, but they left about eleven to go home to change. Richard was very fussy about his own appearance. He had his butter-coloured hair trimmed every three weeks by a top hairdresser.

Dinah studied him in his silk top hat and morning suit. Nothing could suit his handsome good looks better. She could see he was standing up straighter. He was a man who got a lift from expensive clothes; he thought they gave him status.

He was particular about Dinah's appearance too. 'I want to be proud of you,' he told her. 'I want other men to envy me my smart and pretty wife.'

As soon as Dinah was dressed in her new outfit and saw her reflection in the cheval mirror, she felt her spirits lift. Her old Picton Street neighbours would hardly recognise her now.

'You look like a princess.' Richard beamed at her. 'It will be a pleasure to have you on my arm. I do love you, Dinah.'

It gave a buzz to the expedition. They reached Chester to find some men in the crowd dressed as Richard was, but many more wore lounge suits and trilbies. Amongst the women, Dinah didn't feel overdressed: they were all very smart. She studied a woman with a loud laugh who was wearing an outrageously large hat and wondered if she was so rich she spent all her days seeking pleasure, or whether her everyday life had its work and difficulties like everyone else's.

Today Richard was in a jubilant mood. He picked up two racecards and gave one to her, pointing out the Delamere Hurdles, which was to be run at two fifteen. Ardwick Prince's name was in the list of runners. Underneath, together with the trainer's name and the jockey's name, was printed, *Owner, Richard Cameron Aldgrave Haldane.* She knew it gave him status in this crowd, and could see him straightening his shoulders and looking more arrogant than ever.

Her heart lurched when she saw that Tim Reece was riding Pomeroy in the same race. She read on down the card and her heart began to beat faster when she found Tim's name there again. He would also be riding Flyswitch, running at ten past four in the Manchester Hurdles.

'Let's go to the stables and see how Prince is today,' Richard said. When they found him his thick chestnut coat was being currycombed to an even greater shine. His tail hair hung in dark silken ropes, and his mane had been neatly plaited. Richard petted him, telling him he was beautiful and he mustn't let him down. He must be first past the winning post.

Bob Watchit, his trainer, came up to speak to them. Dinah had met him several times when Richard had taken her over to his stables in Tarporley, but she hardly recognised him dressed up to the nines like this. They were on affable terms. 'Come and have lunch with us,' Richard invited.

On the way to the restaurant, Bob Watchit stopped as they were about to pass the line of bookmakers' stalls.

'I want to get some bets on,' he said. Dinah heard him list three horses before saying to the bookie, 'Ardwick Prince, fifty pounds on the nose.'

Richard was next in line. 'The same, Ardwick Prince, fifty pounds on the nose.'

Dinah was taking in that the odds were sixteen to one and trying to work out what they could win. The amount seemed prodigious. She was fingering the half-crown in her pocket and wondering if Richard would be ashamed if she bet so modest an amount.

'Aren't you going to put on a bet for your bride?' the trainer asked. 'It's said to bring luck. I'll do it. Five pounds on Ardwick Prince to win. Bring us all luck, Dinah.'

She was so thrilled she laughed out loud. 'Thank you, Bob.' If the horse won, it would give her more hard cash than she'd ever owned before.

They ate in a restaurant reserved for owners and trainers at a table close to a large plate-glass window overlooking the starting line. Dinah ate lobster salad and had one glass of champagne. Another owner came over for a chat and Richard offered him a glass of champagne so they could drink to a successful day. The men finished the rest of the bottle between them.

Dinah followed them back to the paddock then to see the horses being mounted for the Delamere Hurdles.

'We've been lucky in the draw,' Richard said. 'Prince has number two.' Dinah knew that meant he'd drawn a good starting position near the rail. 'And the going is good to firm, which is what he likes. We stand a good chance here.'

At that moment, Dinah caught sight of Tim mounting his horse to take part in the race. He was wearing Horace Bellamy's silks of white polka dots on a cerise background.

Delighted, Dinah was about to rush over to have a word when Richard put a restraining hand on her arm and said, 'Come on. It's time to go up into the stand if we want to see this.'

Dinah's seat gave her a magnificent view. Below her the jockeys were already lining up. Richard couldn't sit still. His hand was covering hers and she could feel him tingling with the same fever of excitement that was burgeoning through the crowd.

'They're off!' Dinah leaped to her feet like everybody else. All twelve runners took off like rockets.

It was to be over ten furlongs and she kept her eye on the jockey in green and white silks. Ardwick Prince got away well in a bunch of three horses immediately behind the leader. They went thundering down the course until gradually the bunch thinned out and Prince began to pull away. The crowd were shouting; even Richard was screaming and waving his racecard. Coming up to the finishing line, Prince was overtaking the leader. So was Pomeroy. They were neck and neck for a few yards until Prince pulled ahead and won by half a length.

Richard wrapped his arms round Dinah in an exuberant hug, almost lifting her off her feet. He was hysterical with joy.

'He's a winner! Good old Prince, he's done it again. Third time winner this season!' He was jubilant.

He pushed through the crowd towards the winners' enclosure, towing Dinah behind him. Both jockey and horse were hot and perspiring and both were being congratulated. Cameras were clicking. Bob Watchit was there, as wildly excited as Richard.

She saw Tim on Pomeroy looking as hot and delighted as the winner. As runners-up, they were receiving plenty of attention too. She couldn't get anywhere near him before Richard wanted to take her to the bar, where he ordered more champagne to toast Prince's success.

'Richard, I shouldn't.' Dinah pulled at his sleeve.

'Don't you like champagne, Mrs Haldane?' Bob Watchit's voice was loud.

Richard's was equally loud and jocular as he announced her pregnant state. Immediately, she was borne back to a table in the restaurant and a pot of tea and some fancy cakes were ordered for her. The men decided it was time to place more bets.

'What d'you fancy, Mrs Haldane?' Bob Watchit asked.

'Flyswitch, ridden by Tim Reece.'

'He's well fancied, eight to one.'

'I think I'll go for Brunello,' Richard said and placed both bets.

'Thank you,' Dinah said. 'Can we go to the paddock to see the horses being mounted now? I'd like a word with Tim if possible.'

She had no trouble picking out Tim and Flyswitch from the other fifteen runners. He was surrounded by well-wishers, the horse's trainer and owner, and a groom leading his horse out. Tim didn't recognise her until she spoke.

'Dinah!' He was shouting down from the back of his mount. 'I was miles away, trying to concentrate on Flyswitch. You're dressed up to the nines. You must be the smartest woman here.'

'I've got a bet on you to win.'

'Wish me luck.'

'All the very best. I'll be shouting for you.'

The horses were making their way to the starting line. The Manchester Hurdles was run twice round the course, to make two and a half miles.

'Better get back to our seats,' Richard said. 'We'll see nothing down here.'

'I do hope he wins,' Dinah said. She knew that for Tim winning was everything. But Richard wasn't listening.

Once again, everybody was gripped by anticipation, excitement and hope. A hush fell on the crowd as the horses lined up to start. One jockey was having difficulty controlling his mount. They were ready at last, but he set off seconds before he should have done. Back they all had to come and now all were restless and on edge.

They got away the second time and came thundering down the course in one large group, but Flyswitch seemed to be boxed in in the middle. By the time they came round for the second time, the field was strung out. Dinah was on her feet. It was not so easy to see Tim when everybody was jumping about.

Yes, there he was, with five horses ahead of him, but he was going full out now and beginning to gain on them. Could he win? Could he really do it? It was going to be touch and go.

'Come on Flyswitch,' she yelled. 'Come on Tim.'

He was streaking ahead and passed the finishing line three lengths ahead of the second horse. Dinah flopped back in her seat exhausted but delighted. She was exultant.

They went to the winners' enclosure again but couldn't get close to Flyswitch. Dinah could see Tim had a smile that was splitting his face and showing every tooth he had. She knew he was feeling on top of the world.

'You've won again.' Richard was pleased. 'And I haven't done badly: I backed Brunello each way and he came in third. Give me your tickets and I'll collect your winnings for you.'

Dinah stood behind him, mentally adding up what she thought she would receive. Eighty-five pounds on Ardwick Prince and forty-five pounds on Flyswitch. In Picton Street that would be considered riches. An amount that would be impossible to save on their wages, and on which a family could eat three good meals a day for a year or more.

She knew Richard had won a prodigious amount, one she could hardly envisage. She'd asked him once if he had another source of income and he'd said no. Tim had told her that the owners often spent more on their horses than they earned in prize money. The prize for the winner of the Delamere Hurdles had been stated on the racecard as £3,000 and then Richard had bet on him and won a lot more. This must be where he earned enough for his luxury lifestyle.

She could understand and share the attraction racing had for Richard. She too had had an exciting and glamorous day. She wished she'd had more time to talk to Tim, she'd have loved to hear how he was getting on, but at least he'd won his race.

'What are you going to spend your winnings on?' she asked, when Richard came back stuffing notes into his wallet.

'I've no big plans. It'll go on the horses and general living expenses.'

'Did I really win one hundred and thirty pounds?' She found it almost unbelievable.

'You did.' He smiled and took her arm.

Dinah didn't move. 'Aren't you going to give it to me? You did collect it?'

'Oh, I'll look after your winnings for the time being. It would be so easy to have your handbag snatched in this crowd.' He made it sound a sensible precaution.

'I think I'd like spend some of it on driving lessons,' she said happily. 'You wouldn't mind, would you?' It seemed only sensible to say that while Richard was in such a good mood.

At home, Dinah and Richard were changing back into their everyday clothes in the bedroom.

'I'm delighted with Prince.' Richard had already told her that three times. 'Bob Watchit suggests we enter him for the Willmington Handicap at Haydock Park next month. Prince is on top form now.'

'He's done marvellously well for you. For me too, of course.' The mention of Bob Watchit's name had jogged Dinah's memory. 'Wasn't it kind of Bob to put a bet on for me? I can't believe I've come by so much money so easily.'

Richard had tossed his bulging wallet on the bed.

'Can I have my winnings?' she asked.

He seemed at a loss. 'Dinah, I think it would be better if I looked after them for you.'

She froze. They were both staring at his wallet. 'We're safely home now.'

'Yes, but it's quite a large sum. What if I give you ten pounds now and pay the rest into a bank account for you?'

Dinah was gripped by a wave of anger. 'Absolutely not!' she stormed. 'I'm not a child and I'm perfectly capable of looking after my own money. I want it now.'

'Do be reasonable, dear. I'm only trying to do what's best for you.'

'Reasonable? It's up to me to decide what's best. You don't want to give it to me, do you? I call that unreasonable behaviour. That is legally my money. If it's going into a bank account, I want to put it there myself.'

A red tide was running up his cheeks. She could see he was reluctant to hand the money over. 'You've won a small fortune today yourself, and yet you don't want to hand over what is my due. I can't believe it. You're a real Dr Jekyll and Mr Hyde. One minute you're loving and giving and the next you're horrible and mean. Well, I'm not putting up with it. I want my money now. All of it. This minute.'

For the first time ever, she'd stood up to him; not allowed him to force his wishes on her. And miraculously, it seemed, she'd got the upper hand.

'And I'm going to learn to drive,' she finished. 'You can't stop me now.'

Without a word, he tossed notes to the value of her winnings on to the bed and strode out of the room, slamming the door behind him.

Dinah gathered up the money and hugged it to her. She'd never owned such a large sum before. She'd open a bank account in her own name; it would be her nest egg for doing things Richard didn't approve of. She'd start with driving lessons. She'd love to be able to drive, and if she was careful with it, and could win a little more, she might be able to buy herself a car.

She wandered round the room, opening her drawers, trying to decide where she'd keep it for the time being. She came across the beaded evening bag her mother had treasured but never used. She put the money in that and then tucked it among her nightdresses.

She closed the drawer and lay down on the bed to think. Why had he wanted to keep her money? He'd won so much himself, it couldn't be that he needed hers as well. Why was he doing his best to keep her short of ready cash? Why was he so against her having money of her own?

She knew why, of course. If she had money of her own he couldn't control what she did and what she spent it on. It would prevent him from dominating her completely.

Chapter Seventeen

In the days that followed, Dinah found it difficult to be loving towards Richard. He'd taken a turn for the worse; more often than not now he was gripped by anger. She'd noticed he talked to himself from time to time but these days he often seemed to wander round the house muttering to himself, and she could hear the rage in his voice.

'Are you worried about something?' she'd asked. 'Is something wrong?'

'No,' he'd snapped at her.

On Friday morning, Richard was in a foul temper from the moment he got out of bed. He said very little on the drive in to work and within fifteen minutes of arriving he was telling Miss O'Marney off for a typing error in the letters he'd dictated the day before.

Dinah watched him storm out of his office and crash the workroom door open. Both she and the secretary kept their eyes down on their work as they heard him raging at Mr Hopper. Then he came back at the double, slammed into his office to pick up his trilby and was on his way out again.

'Are you going to be away for long?' Dinah asked. 'It's pay day, isn't it? I'll need to get money from the bank to make up the wages.'

He held out his hand for the ledger she was working in. 'How much does it come to this week?'

'I haven't finished working it out yet.'

He was agitated, his face crimson. 'I've just sacked three girls,' he barked. 'They work a week in hand, don't they? You'd better add that in.'

Dinah was shocked. 'Why?' She saw Miss O'Marney's mouth drop open. 'Which three?' she demanded angrily.

'We haven't enough work. They're just standing about chatting. I'm not paying them for that.' He spun on his heel.

'When will you be back?'

'Straight after lunch.'

When the outer door slammed shut, Dinah leaped to her feet and went to the workroom. The place was in an uproar and three young girls were in tears. A white-faced Mr Hopper was trying to comfort them. He'd switched off all the machines because nobody was tending them.

'I'm getting married next Saturday,' one of the girls wailed. 'He said I could have a week's holiday, and now he's sacked me without notice. What am I going to do?'

'I'm so sorry.' Dinah put an arm round the girl's shoulders. She didn't know how to cope with this.

'They're all entitled to a week's notice,' Mr Hopper said. 'Mr Haldane knows that. If he wants them to leave tonight, he'll have to pay a week's wages in lieu.'

Dinah returned to her desk and sank down feeling beaten. Why the snap decision? What on earth had possessed Richard to do such a thing? Why wasn't he trying harder to get more work for his business? It didn't make sense.

He'd lost his temper, of course. If he'd stopped to think, he'd know it was better to give notice. He'd get an extra week's work out of each of them that way.

Mr Hopper came in. 'Can you have a word with Mr Haldane about this?'

'I doubt if it would do much good,' she said.

'Please try. Nora's mother is ill and her father's on the dole. She's the only one taking a wage into the house.'

Dinah sighed. She understood what a shortage of money meant. Her mother had been a good manager, but even so they'd found it hard. 'All right, I'll do my best.'

It was nearly two o'clock when Richard returned. Dinah had done all she could towards making up the wages, including writing out the envelopes.

'Please sign this cheque, Richard,' she said. 'The bank closes at three, and if I don't get there before that we won't be able to pay anyone.'

He signed the cheque without even glancing at the amount, though usually he made a great show of checking her figures. She was back with the cash within an hour and began tucking the required amount into each envelope.

Richard usually handed out the money himself and got his employees to sign for it, but today he asked Dinah to do it. When she came back to his office she carefully closed the door so that Miss O'Marney wouldn't hear what was being said. 'I've handed out the wage envelopes, apart from the three girls you've sacked. Do you want to reconsider—'

'No, certainly not. Why should I?'

'You didn't give it much thought.'

'I gave it plenty of thought, Dinah. It's just that I didn't discuss it with you, and I saw no reason to do that.'

'It means you'll only have fifteen people working here.'

He snapped, 'I can count up to fifteen too.'

'Then the business is failing?'

'Of course it's bloody failing,' he bellowed.

'Don't shout,' she said, 'or everybody will know how things stand. Is it a question of finding more work for the factory? Why don't you let me see your books? Perhaps—'

'No need for you to worry your head about money.'

'Then you have some other source of income?'

'How many times do I have to tell you that I haven't?'

'So we need to get more orders. What are you doing about that?'

'I'm doing my best. Surely you can see that?'

'I can see it worries you.'

'Of course it worries me.'

'Why don't we sit down and talk about it, and try to find —'

'You wouldn't understand, and I know nobody who would.'

'Mr Hopper understands how everything works.'

'He'd be no help.'

'Why don't you try us? What harm could it do?'

Richard's eyes rolled up to the ceiling, and Dinah lost her patience. 'Well, if you have to sack three machine operators, I can't see how you can afford to keep racehorses.'

He looked totally taken aback. 'Don't speak to me like that! Don't interfere, and don't pretend you know more than I do. You'll only upset me.'

'I'm trying to help you. Is it beneath your dignity to accept help from me?'

'I'm going out,' he said, reaching for his trilby. 'I don't know when I'll be back.'

Dinah flounced back to her desk in the adjoining office. Richard was acting like a spoiled child. She'd seen what money problems had done to her mother and Aunt Enid. If Richard wouldn't let her help, there was nothing she could do.

There could only be one explanation: he was spending more than he earned. If she were in his shoes she'd be ashamed of being such a spendthrift, on such luxuries as racehorses, cars, boarding school fees and housekeepers.

Dinah could see now that Richard wasn't in control of his business. Was this why Myra had tried to take over the day-to-day running of it? Dinah felt he belittled both her and Myra, but that was his attitude to everybody.

She felt she could achieve more than making up the wages. Once it had been her ambition to go out and get orders for Mr McKay's beautiful hats. Now Richard was desperate to get orders to make beautiful ribbons and she didn't think it would be beyond her. But he wouldn't even discuss it. Dinah wanted the business to be profitable again, so the girls could keep their jobs.

Having cut his wages bill, Richard no longer appeared worried by lack of money. He began talking about a race meeting at Doncaster and how much he was looking forward to it. Ardwick Prince had been entered for the Doncaster Cup, which was a step up for him into top class racing, and Richard was thrilled.

Then, a few days later, Bob Watchit telephoned to say that Ardwick Beauty had been given a clean bill of health and he proposed taking both her and Prince to Doncaster for the three-day meeting. He'd entered Beauty in a race on the second day, and Prince would compete for the Doncaster Cup on the Saturday, the last day of the meeting. Richard called Dinah into his office to tell her the news.

'We'll go to Doncaster on Thursday.' He was enthusiastic. 'We'll have two nights away to see them run and make a little holiday of it. After all, we had a very short honeymoon.'

'Can we afford it?'

'Of course we can. We can't miss a chance like this.'

Dinah was worried about the cost but thought it would make a welcome break in routine. 'What about Nellie?'

'She'll be all right here with Mrs Banks,' he said. 'We'll go and enjoy ourselves.' Richard's mind seemed to be exclusively on his horses when they were about to race.

'Is that wise? We'll be away for three days.'

'She'll be at school all day, and Mrs Banks will have only her to worry about in the evenings. She'll be fine.'

As the date of the race meeting approached, Richard seemed to grow more stressed. He every day rang his trainer to enquire how his horses were doing in practice.

'They've got to win,' he told Dinah. 'It would make my day if Prince could win the Doncaster Cup.'

The evening before they were due to leave, Dinah packed a case for each of them and took them down to the hall. On Thursday morning Dinah was first at the breakfast table, wearing her smart pale green outfit, and was surprised not to find Nellie there. In a few minutes Richard joined her.

'Where's Nellie this morning?' he asked when Mrs Banks brought in their eggs and bacon. 'Have you called her?'

'Yes, sir. She says she's coming, but I don't think she's very well.'

'What's the matter with her now?' he barked.

'I heard her get up in the night.'

A white-faced Nellie appeared behind her, still in her pyjamas and dressing gown.

'You're going to be late for school,' Richard told her. Nellie made her own way to school, a penny bus ride away.

'Daddy, I was sick in the night. I don't want to go. I don't feel well.'

'What d'you mean, sick?'

'I sicked up all that fat meat you made me eat for supper last night.'

'There was nothing the matter with that pork. It wouldn't make you sick. You'd better sit down now and eat your breakfast.'

'I couldn't eat anything. I still feel sick.'

Dinah could see tears welling up in her eyes. She said, 'Would it be better to let her stay at home this morning? Mrs Banks could keep an eye on her. Perhaps, Nellie, if you feel better by lunch time, you could go in for the afternoon session.'

'Don't interfere, Dinah,' Richard snapped. 'This has nothing to do with you. Nellie, get yourself dressed quickly and we'll drop you off at the school gates.'

They all heard the telephone ring in the hall then, and Mrs Banks went to answer it.

'Go on, Nellie. Get yourself ready for school. You'll be perfectly all right.'

Mrs Banks came back. 'It's for you, Mrs Haldane,' she said.

'For me?' This was unusual. Dinah hurried out, half expecting it to be Aunt Enid or Tim. She felt guilty because she'd not made more effort to keep in touch with them. She didn't at first realise who was speaking.

'Bunty Sugden,' the caller repeated. 'Nellie's nanny.'

'Oh!' Dinah turned to see if Richard had followed her, but his voice was still sounding from the dining room.

'I'm worried about Nellie,' Bunty said. 'She needs help.'

Dinah knew Richard would be furious if he knew she was having a conversation like this with the nanny. And what could Bunty possibly mean? At that moment, Nellie slammed the dining room door and ran past Dinah to the stairs with tears streaming down her face.

Dinah swallowed hard and asked, 'What sort of help?'

'She's looking for support. She came here yesterday, did she tell you?'

Dinah had a sinking feeling in her stomach. 'No.'

'She came to see me. I told her to tell you, but I was afraid she wouldn't.'

'I've tried to talk to her.' Dinah was afraid Nellie had not found what she was looking for when she ran away from school. 'I thought she was accepting me, but . . . Why are you worried about her?'

'It's her nerves. I'm afraid her father will have the same effect on her as he had on her mother. He turned her into a nervous wreck.'

Dinah felt at a loss. 'I'd like to help her, but I don't know how.'

'Can you come and see me? I need to talk about it.'

'Yes. I don't know when I'll be able to, but yes.' Since the disastrous conversation with Ivy Cummins, Dinah had stopped looking for more information about Richard's past. But Bunty was right about Nellie's needing help.

'If you give me your phone number, I'll let you know when I can come.'

'I haven't got a phone.'

'No, I'm sorry, I forgot. I'll just come when I can, then?'

'Yes please. As soon as possible.'

Dinah put the phone down just in time. Richard was at the dining room door, bellowing, 'Dinah, come and finish your breakfast. It's time for us to be off.'

She was glad to pour herself another cup of tea.

'Who was that?' he demanded, glowering at her, but fortunately he didn't wait for an answer. 'I don't want your friends ringing up here all the time. At this hour of the morning, too, when most of us don't have time to stand about and chat.'

Nellie, now in her school uniform, came back looking sullen and tearful. 'Are you all right?' Dinah asked her.

'Of course she's all right. Come along, both of you, let's go.'

Dinah felt she should be doing more to help Nellie, but had no idea what. She said, 'Are you sure, Richard? She doesn't look well.'

His face went crimson, and she knew he was angry with her. He tightened his grip on the steering wheel, but kept quiet until he'd put Nellie out at the school gates. Then he said, 'You're being very argumentative, Dinah. You're getting on my nerves. Perhaps it would be better if I went to Doncaster by myself? And as you're so keen to concern yourself with Nellie's welfare, you can stay at home and do it.'

When he parked at the office to check the post, he took her suitcase out of the car and dumped it on the pavement in front of her. Dinah knew she was being punished.

'Nellie needs to be disciplined,' he said. 'You're too keen to interfere when I try to do it. I hope this will teach you not to.'

Dinah was shocked. Here she was dressed up in her best. 'I was looking forward to seeing Ardwick Prince win the Doncaster Cup,' she said. He half smiled, looking almost pleased she was disappointed.

She would have enjoyed the race meeting, but this would give her three days without Richard and she found herself looking forward to that. Also, she'd be able to visit Bunty Sugden without his knowing.

Richard kissed her goodbye, but it was a cold quick peck on the cheek. She knew his mind was already on his horses.

Tim had travelled to Doncaster with the horses on Wednesday evening. They got them safely into the stables although one restive horse called Tarquin was misbehaving as usual. Pomeroy was calm enough and Flyswitch always travelled well. The stable boys were with them to do the routine mucking out and feeding, and to be with them while they were away from home and lodged in racecourse stables. Digby liked to give his stable stars plenty of time to settle down before they went out on the racetrack.

But for the jockeys there was no such luxury. Tim had tossed and turned on his narrow hostel bed. He felt wound up, as he always did on race days. All the jockeys had raw nerves whether they admitted it or not. They all had to win to stay in the game.

This year, the Doncaster meeting would last three days and Tim was booked to ride in twelve races. He was expected to win a goodly proportion of them and knew he'd disappoint Digby and several owners if he didn't.

On Thursday Tim had four rides. On Fast Approach in the one-thirty he came second. On Tarquin in the three-thirty he won by a neck.

In the four-five he made a hash of riding Dido and came in ninth. Robbie Forbes was listed to ride Bonnatella at five fifteen but he didn't make the weight. Tim was switched at the last moment and felt he'd revived his fortunes by romping home on her. Robbie was generous enough to say Tim should be proud of himself.

On Friday morning, Tim got out of his hostel bed with even more of a jerk than usual. Everybody was on edge and the horses picked up on it and became even more excitable. Tim no longer ate breakfast. He would miss any meal if he didn't feel too hungry. He was growing taller, and although he was quite skinny he was getting heavier and could not afford to keep piling on the pounds. Robbie Forbes, like most other jockeys, had tea and a cigarette for breakfast, and he didn't drink much tea before a race. Tea could weigh heavy too.

A horse could soon lose condition without exercise, and Flyswitch was the star who had to be kept in prime condition. Tim had ridden him round the course a couple of times last night, and he saddled him up and did the same this morning. Just a leisurely canter to stretch his legs; nothing that could tire him.

When he brought him back to the stable, Tim saw Richard Haldane's horses being brought in by their trainer and his stable boys. He already knew from the racecard that Ardwick Beauty would be racing against him and Pomeroy in the two-fifteen today. He was grooming Flyswitch when he saw Richard Haldane come striding in with his nose in the air, waving a silver-headed cane as though he owned every horse in this stable.

Tim watched the group round the Ardwick horses, expecting Dinah to join them at any moment. Richard was giving the impression he thought he was God and everything in the world revolved round him. As though this race meeting was being held for his benefit, to give his horses the chance to win and prove he owned the very best animals.

Tim had smartened Flyswitch up and moved on to Pomeroy but he could hear Haldane's lordly voice taking his leave of his trainer and jockey. As he passed him on his way out of the stable, Tim called, 'Good morning. Is Dinah here with you?'

'No,' Richard said shortly. 'She's stayed at home this time.'

'Oh!' Tim was disappointed. 'Why?'

Richard looked through him as though he'd ceased to exist. 'Her wish.'

That reminded Tim that Dinah was having a baby. 'I hope she's keeping well?'

'She's very well.'

Tim found it hard to believe Dinah didn't want to come. Hadn't she told him she loved race days? And that Richard bought her lobster and champagne when she came? He was sure she'd have been here given half a chance.

Richard gave Pomeroy's flank a condescending pat. 'In good form, is he?'

'Excellent.' Tim smiled. He wanted to take Haldane down a peg. Let him know that it wasn't going to be a walkover for his horses. 'Pommy's really picked up these last few weeks. He won by six lengths at Chester.'

Richard sauntered out. He had a way of making Tim feel small. Tim smouldered with dislike and resentment but he'd get his own back on the racecourse. He wouldn't let Haldane's horses win, not if he could help it.

He could hear the bookies shouting the odds, and found Pomeroy and Ardwick Beauty were now joint favourites for the two-fifteen. That made him more determined than ever.

Tim stopped Digby when the trainer tried to talk him into a winning mindset.

'Don't waste time on me,' he told him. 'I'm going to win if it kills me. Help me get Pommy fired up, would you?' Digby just laughed.

As they lined up to start, Ardwick Beauty kicked up her heels and made a fuss. Her jockey had trouble keeping control, but she'd drawn a better position in the line-up than Pomeroy.

Pommy was a good starter and got away well as usual, but Beauty was close to the rail and holding her position. It was a ten furlong race. Tim had Pommy forging ahead, and Beauty was sticking to them. Soon they'd left the rest of the field behind. The going was firm, which was what Pommy liked. To be swept down the field at forty miles an hour over moving muscles was a tremendous thrill that Tim never tired of. Only when they'd covered eight furlongs did he touch Pommy with his whip to signal to him that he must go flat out for the winning post. Digby didn't believe in whipping his horses. He said they put heart and soul into their racing, and wanted to win as much as their jockeys did.

Tim could see that Beauty was getting plenty of whip as they powered down the final furlong of the home straight. They were neck and neck.

'Come on, Pommy,' Tim urged through his teeth, giving him another light flick with his whip. Could they do it? 'Come on, now.' He felt the horse pulling ahead, to cross the finishing line half a length ahead of Beauty.

The crowd went mad, cheering and shouting. Tim was delighted. That was one in the eye for Richard Haldane. Later, when he saw him in the winners' enclosure, his face was a mask of fury and hate. Coming in second was not good enough for him.

Tim was not so pleased with the other rides he had that day. To come in third on Pepperton was considered reasonable, but on Saucy Sue and Rombola he trailed in the field.

On the day of the Doncaster Cup there was a feverish atmosphere in the stables. Tim would be riding Flyswitch in that.

First, he had to ride Ormorod in the one-thirty and was first past the post which gave him a real lift. Robbie Forbes again failed to make the weight for the two-fifteen and he had to ride Loggerheads for him, and came in sixth in a field of ten. Nothing to be proud of. Digby slapped him on the back and said he doubted Robbie would have done much better.

Then, with his heart in his mouth, Tim waited for the big race of the day. He took a surreptitious glance at Ardwick Prince as they were saddling up. He was a strong-looking grey, but Flyswitch was keen and ready to go, as though he'd been kept waiting too long for his turn. He had great zest and energy and did everything right. Tim knew he was enjoying himself. Soon he was showing a clean pair of heels to the rest of the field, including Ardwick Prince.

When Tim realised he would win he was euphoric, and positively romped over the finishing line. He'd done what he'd set out to do.

Flyswitch positively loved all the fuss being made of him, as did Tim.

Prince came in fourth. Tim made a point of looking out for Richard Haldane. His face was grey and he looked stricken. He didn't wait to see the last race. Tim saw him heading for the car park.

He couldn't stop smiling. He'd won an important race. Horace Bellamy, Flyswitch's owner, had thumped him on the back in congratulation. There had been champagne all round to toast his success. Tim knew he'd won big prize money for Mr Bellamy, who would share it with Llewellyn Digby and give Tim himself a handsome bonus. He was beginning to feel quite rich on the bonuses he'd earned.

'If you and he can keep it up, we could have a strong contender for the Grand National.' Bellamy thumped him on the back again.

Tim had long had an ambition to race in the Grand National. To imagine being entered was as far as he could go: to dream of winning the National seemed hopelessly over-ambitious.

He would be competing against many famous horses and jockeys, all with more experience. He was twenty-one now and jockeys had to be that age to enter. The horse had to be over five years and next year Flyswitch too would be old enough, so it might just be possible to try. If they could get him into peak form.

Chapter Eighteen

As soon as Richard set off for Doncaster, Dinah told the staff he'd be away for two nights and saw the relief on their faces. She was worried about what Bunty wanted to tell her and decided to see her straight away. Feeling somewhat over-dressed in her pale green race meeting outfit, she removed her Carlton Hat and told Miss O'Marney she was going out and might or might not be back that day.

She took the bus to Walton and walked briskly when she got off. As she turned into Brunswick Street she saw an old lady with a shopping bag walking slowly ahead of her, and thinking it looked like Bunty she quickened her step and caught her up. One glimpse of those bright cheeks criss-crossed with tiny wrinkles told Dinah she was right.

'Bunty,' she said, and the old lady stopped and changed her shopping bag to the other hand. Her face lit up.

'Thank you for coming so quickly. There's so much I want to tell you.'

'Let me carry that bag for you. Go on.'

'I'm worried that Nellie hasn't been sent back to that boarding school.'

Dinah had expected her to be pleased. 'I persuaded her father to let her stay at home. She's gone back to her old school. It's what she wanted.'

'Yes, I know, but . . . Well, I don't trust him to treat her kindly.'

Dinah was silent.

'She'd be safer if she didn't live with him. How is she?'

'Not so well this morning. A tummy bug, I think: she vomited in the night. Her father insisted she went to school this morning.'

'Oh dear. I promised Myra I'd look after her, but now I don't live in I can't do anything. Nellie needs someone to lean on, someone to look after her.'

'She misses you, and Mark too.'

'I know she does. After she came to see me again yesterday I thought I ought to ring you.'

'You don't mind her coming?'

'Of course not, it made my day. We went for a walk, but it worries me that she doesn't tell you or her father that she visits me. He won't like it.'

'Shall I tell him?'

'I'd prefer that he did know, she is his daughter, but . . . I'm afraid he'd forbid her to come, you know what he's like. I don't want that.'

'He'll go spare if he thinks we're keeping something from him. I'll try and persuade Nellie that she must tell him, and be on hand to smooth it over.'

'Thank you. Here we are. This is where I live . . . but of course you've been before, haven't you? Ruby and her husband were kind enough to take me in at short notice. Richard threw me out, you know? Ruby was the housemaid at Ardwick House before she married, so she knew what he was like. They've sub-rented the parlour to me.'

'Goodness!' Dinah said. 'I wish I'd known. I wanted to find somebody who would tell me about Richard when he was young.' But that was before she'd found Ivy.

Bunty put a key in the lock. 'Come in. I'll make a pot of tea and we can have a chat.' She led Dinah into the front room.

Dinah settled back in the rocking chair in which Nellie had been curled up on her previous visit. Bunty poked the fire and balanced the kettle on the hot coals.

'I was Nellie's mother's nanny. In fact, I was her uncle's nanny for three years before Myra was born.'

'Then you've known the family for a long time.'

'You could say I've spent my working life with them.' Bunty was unpacking her shopping bag on the table: a small loaf, a jar of plum jam and a box of matches. She unwrapped three eggs from a screw of paper and put them in a bowl. 'Nellie's a troubled child. I'm sure she's frightened of her father.'

'Many people are, but she gives her imagination full play. She told me she thinks he killed her mother.'

Bunty straightened up and looked Dinah in the eye. 'I'm afraid she might be right.'

'What?' Dinah felt her stomach turn over. 'She can't be! Surely it's all in her mind?' But she could see Bunty didn't think so.

'That's why she's frightened of him. I am too,' Bunty said. 'I hope you'll forgive me for saying bad things about your husband.'

Dinah felt a trickle of horror run down her spine. Yes, Bunty would be able to tell her her a great deal about Nellie and her family, and perhaps what she said would be more reliable than Ivy Cummins's account. She seemed a gentle caring person, not a bitter woman out for revenge. 'I want you to tell me all you know, whether it's good or bad. You must know Richard well.'

Bunty was weighing her words carefully. 'Yes. It's twelve years since I first saw Richard Haldane and I've never liked him. He was a young man of twenty-five then, very handsome, and didn't he know it. He fancied Myra, and set out to spin a web of fantastic stories to her about how wealthy he was, and the wonderful life he could give her. He was determined to marry her, there was no doubt about that. He swept her off her feet, and she thought she'd fallen madly in love with him.

'She was eighteen and a very pretty girl then, full of fun and life. She had a lot of friends and was invited to all the houses nearby for tennis parties and the like. She was a good player. There were several decent young men interested in her, but she chose Richard Haldane.

'Her family didn't like him and Mr Copthorne showed him the door. He forbade Myra to have anything to do with him. He was her first real boyfriend. Her mother was a social butterfly, always gadding out somewhere to lunch or tea, or arranging some dinner party at home. I was closer to Myra than anyone and she confided in me. She told me she was in love with Richard. Myra was pretty headstrong as a girl – until she married Richard, that is. He soon knocked that out of her.'

'But how did they come to marry if she was forbidden to see him?' Dinah hugged her knees and waited with a sense of foreboding. Richard would be furious if he could see her now, raking over his past life. That he didn't want her to know anything about it only made her more curious. Surely, most new husbands expect their wives to be interested in their past history? Bunty put a cup of tea into her hand and came to sit down on the other side of the fire.

'Her parents were killed in a car crash. It was a terrible shock to us all. Devastating. It changed everything.'

Dinah's mouth was dry. 'Do you know Ivy Cummins?'

Bunty was nodding. 'Yes, Richard's cook. I met her and Ruby when I went to live at Ardwick House.'

'Ivy told me she thought Richard had tampered with Mr Copthorne's brakes. That he wanted to kill him because he'd refused to let Myra marry him. But it seemed so fantastic . . .'

'At the time I believed it was an accident, but his parents died in a car crash too, and as time went on there were other things . . . well, now I'm certain Ivy was right.'

Dinah could no longer think straight. How could she believe Richard was capable of murder? But she could see Bunty was in deadly earnest, and she was clearly a well-balanced woman.

'There's nothing Richard doesn't know about cars.'

Dinah knew that was true, but even so . . . yet Bunty was giving her the same story as Ivy. Could she count that as confirmation?

'Richard was determined to marry Myra.'

'But he could have eloped with her. Gone to Gretna Green. Lived in sin. He didn't have to kill her parents to get her.'

'But this way gave him control of the Copthorne fortune at the same time. He got Myra and he didn't have to wait to get her money.'

Dinah felt her head swim. She was beginning to feel sick. 'No, Bunty, this is too far-fetched. I can't believe it. It must have been an accident.'

Bunty was shaking her head. 'It was no accident. I'm quite quite sure of that now.'

Dinah could feel herself shaking. That Bunty was confirming what Ivy had told her was unnerving.

'Tell me about Myra,' she said. 'What happened to her after her parents were killed?'

'She was heartbroken. For her, it was the end of normal life as she'd known it. A nightmare.'

'She was left all alone in charge of a big house? I mean, just with you?'

'There were other servants at Barnstone Grove. But Richard didn't leave her alone. He was coming round to the house every day. At the time, I thought he was comforting her, helping her through her grief.'

'If she loved him, it surely would have been a comfort to her.'

'That's what I thought at the time. Myra told me he'd said he wanted to marry her and take care of her for the rest of her life. To be honest, although her parents hadn't approved of him, and I didn't like him much, I thought it was probably the best thing for her.

'Myra was very young and quite shy. She'd been brought up in a house where women were only supposed to do the flowers and entertain the guests. She'd learned to perform on the piano and play tennis, but she'd never been near the factory.

'We knew nothing about the ribbon business. Mr Copthorne had a works manager and an accountant who came to dinner at the house once or twice a year, so Myra knew them socially. When her father died, they continued to run the business for her until she was twenty-one. It continued to be profitable. I suppose they would have been happy to carry on doing that, but Myra had married Richard by then and he wanted to control it. As he had a business of his own, everybody assumed he'd know how to run it at a profit.'

'But he didn't, did he?' Knowing what she did of Richard, Dinah could see how vulnerable Myra had become. 'Didn't she have other relatives to look after her?'

Bunty took out a handkerchief and blew her nose. She looked distressed.

'Her grandfather was still alive – her mother's father – but he was over eighty, crippled with arthritis and in a nursing home. The family visited him but apart from that they'd had little contact. Myra's brother and uncle were killed in the trenches. She took Richard to meet her grandfather, and she told me the old man was in favour of the marriage. He thought she needed somebody to look after her.'

'But her fortune too? Wasn't there a solicitor looking after her interests?'

'Yes. She didn't take control of the property and business until she was twenty-one, but she was paid a generous living allowance until then. She was married from Barnstone Grove and then the solicitor agreed for it to be put on the market. I moved to Ardwick House with her, and the other servants were dismissed when the house was sold.' Bunty was frowning. 'Richard needed me to look after Mark. Myra didn't know of his existence until after they were married.'

That made Dinah catch her breath. 'Typical.'

'He told us that the child was the son of a cousin who'd been killed in the war and his mother had died of TB. As his only relative, Richard said he thought it was his duty to bring him up. He impressed on me that Mark and Nellie were to be brought up as brother and sister. For the sake of the little boy.'

'I'm sure they believe they are.' Dinah was aghast. 'Richard referred to them as brother and sister to me. But why? If the story was true, what difference would it make to Mark?'

'Very little providing he's been told the truth from an early age.'

'Yes, but now it will. He's grown up believing Myra to be his mother.'

'Exactly, but Richard can never admit he's done anything wrong. He has to hide anything like that. Do you know who Mark really is?'

'Ivy Cummins told me he was Richard's illegitimate son, but I didn't believe her.'

'Let me get Ruby in. She'll tell you the same thing.' Bunty opened the door of her room and called her friend. When Ruby appeared in the doorway, Bunty said, 'Come and sit down, dear. This is Dinah, Richard's new wife.'

Ruby was plump, middle-aged and wearing a cross-over floral print overall and carpet slippers.

'Hello,' Dinah said, smiling at her. 'I've seen photographs of you.'

'Surely he didn't show you old family photographs?'

'No, I found them.'

'Is he nasty to you? He was to Myra and the rest of us.'

'Ruby,' Bunty said, 'tell her that it's true: that Mark is Richard's son by Esther Phelps, and he let us know we'd be in big trouble if we talked about it to anyone.'

'He threatened us kitchen staff with the sack,' Ruby said.

'Myra swore us to secrecy too, when she discovered the truth. I can't remember who told her, but I suppose it doesn't matter now. She was afraid of upsetting him. She was beginning to find him difficult to live with.'

Dinah trembled. Hadn't she herself gone out of her way not to upset him? But she mustn't think of that now.

'It came as a big shock to Myra to find Richard already had a son.'

'It must have done.'

'He had a nursemaid looking after him,' Bunty went on, 'but she was sacked because Myra wanted me there. He told her a whole lot of lies about the fighting on the Somme, how he'd led his men into battle and earned a medal for his bravery. He bragged about his exploits; he had all sorts of stories about how he'd saved lives. He even went to a photographer and had his picture taken in his brother's uniform.'

'Poor Mrs Haldane believed everything he told her. She thought he'd been a hero,' Ruby said.

Dinah caught her breath. She'd heard all that and believed it too. Suddenly she was seeing Richard in a new light.

'And all through the war,' Ruby's lips were twisting with disapproval, 'the gardeners were telling us in the house that Arthur Phelps was hiding him. We knew Mr Haldane had been called up as a private, and that he'd run away so he couldn't be sent to France to fight.

'Then when Myra started to work in Richard's factory, she heard the gossip about her husband, but she didn't believe it. There was a photograph of him in his study, showing he was an officer like his brothers.'

Dinah felt as though she'd been kicked in the stomach. 'He told me the same story,' she whispered. 'Showed me the same picture. I believed him too.'

'I was afraid,' Bunty said, 'that he might have done. His stories aren't true.'

'Lies, all lies,' Ruby confirmed. 'I'm hungry. It's dinner time.'

Bunty sighed, 'Yes, I am too. I'll boil us each an egg and make some toast.'

'No.' Dinah knew she was too emphatic. 'Not for me, thank you. I'm not at all hungry.'

'But it's nearly two o'clock.'

'It's kind of you, but I have some sandwiches.' The last thing Dinah felt like was food, but she took her lunch box out of her bag and opened it up on the table. Mrs Banks cut their sandwiches to a dainty size, wrapped them in damask napkins and packed them in a tin. 'Richard went off to Doncaster without his share,' she said. 'Please help me eat them.'

'They look lovely.' Ruby was impressed. 'Ham and tomato? The Haldanes always ate well. I'll put the kettle on the gas, Bunty, it'll be quicker.'

Dinah ate only one sandwich and found it hard to swallow. She had to wash it down with tea. She could hardly get the words out. 'Tell me about the Copthorne business. Did Richard ruin it?'

'I only know what Myra told me,' Bunty said. 'But I know he has a very high opinion of his own capabilities and wanted to take control. I think he'd expected Myra to receive her inheritance as soon as she was married, but her father's will was specific: she had to wait until she reached her twenty-first birthday. As soon as she did, he sacked the senior staff because he believed he could make the business more profitable, but it soon began to lose money.

'He was taking Myra to work every day, thinking she knew more about running the ribbon side of it than she did. She felt he blamed her for the losses, and he told her she must make it profitable again. It really upset her to see the business her father had built up going downhill so fast. Eventually, he had to stop operating.'

'But Myra had money, didn't she? From the sale of her old home?'

'Yes, and a big investment income too. But Richard took it and spent it on himself. He bought racehorses and lived the millionaire life, while

Myra hardly went out. She'd become pregnant, and was in need of support. She couldn't stand up to him. She was afraid he no longer loved her. She had been a lovely bright girl, but he turned her into a frail little thing who spent all her time playing with baby Nellie and crying over what had happened to her.'

Dinah felt sick. But there was worse to come.

'Little by little Myra learned that many of the things he'd told her, and she'd believed, were not true. He gave her one shock after another. She was frightened of him, and eventually she realised that marrying him had been a mistake. A mistake her parents had tried to stop her making.'

Dinah was horrified. Myra's story was so similar to her own.

'He's an evil man,' Ruby said. 'We're all sure he killed his own parents and then Mr Haldane's. They were lovely people. His mother couldn't do enough for him.'

'That's why I'm so worried about Nellie,' Bunty said. 'I'm worried about you too. It's hard to know who he'll turn against next.'

'Surely he wouldn't turn against his own child?'

'He turned against Myra and I thought he loved her.'

'They were like lovebirds when they were first married,' Ruby confirmed.

'But he didn't kill her. It was suicide, wasn't it?'

'Yes,' Ruby said softly. 'But we believe he drove her to it.'

Dinah felt ready to faint. If he'd turned against Myra he could turn against her. 'Surely you went to the police this time?'

'I tried,' Bunty said. 'Like you, they didn't believe what I told them could be true. They started asking me which king was currently on the throne, and the name of our prime minister. I couldn't remember. I said it was Stanley Baldwin but I was wrong. I knew they thought I was losing my marbles. I gather that when they questioned Richard about it he burst into tears and acted very distressed. They believed him, not me.'

Dinah felt her flesh creep. She didn't want to hear any more. But she knew she'd regret it if she didn't find out all she could while she had the chance.

'At least it wasn't another car crash.' She was reliving the terror she had felt on her honeymoon when Richard had driven so recklessly down the side of that mountain.

'It was worse than that.' She could see the horror in Bunty's faded eyes and dreaded what was coming. 'I can't believe how long it took me to realise what he was doing. Richard dominated her completely. He undermined her confidence slowly and steadily; over the last years he kept her a virtual prisoner in the house. I thought she was ill. He asked the doctor to visit her and medicine was prescribed for her.

'I should have done more to help her, taken her out to the shops or thc park, but she didn't want to go out by then. She gave up all her own interests and her friends when she married. The only thing she did was work in his factory. He discouraged her from making friends with the girls there, saying they were not her class. Her life was empty except for me and the children and I felt powerless to help her.'

Dinah was icy cold. That was happening to her too. Richard had cut her off from her friends. She realised how very much alone she'd become.

She made herself ask, 'You think Richard drove her to take her own life?'

'Yes. The doctor told me Myra was mentally ill. She seemed to have no will of her own and did exactly what Richard told her to do. I think he made her write the suicide note. That he stood over her and dictated what he wanted her to write. Then he gave her poison and stood over her while she swallowed it.'

Dinah couldn't get her breath. 'That's too fantastic, he couldn't have . . .' She swallowed hard, tried to move the lump in her throat. 'He told me she'd found strychnine in the garden store and helped herself to it.'

Bunty's face showed how troubled she was. 'He kept a large tin of strychnine to kill the moles in the garden. At her inquest, he told the coroner he didn't think Myra knew it was there.'

'Wouldn't she have done? She'd lived there for a long time – she must have seen the molehills.'

'I wouldn't put it past Richard to suggest suicide to her and show her the tin.'

'Oh, heavens!' Dinah felt transfixed with horror. 'Did she ever threaten to take her life?'

Bunty slowly shook her head. 'No. The trouble is,' she said, 'I can see him doing the same to Nellie. She's a nervous little thing just like her mother. I'm telling you all this so you'll recognise what he's up to and be able to stop him.'

Dinah felt shaky. She feared for herself as well as for Nellie. She could see now what she was up against.

Bunty's gentle voice went on. 'I was too slow to realise what he was doing to Myra, but you're brighter than I am, and now you've been warned you'll be able to stop him hurting Nellie.'

Dinah covered her face with her hands and lay back in the chair. Bunty was very wrong about her. She had no idea what to do. Her mind went blank; she was helpless. She was being totally swamped by a torrent of panic.

'No, Bunty, I'm no stronger than you.' Her head felt as though it would burst with the awful facts she'd had spelled out to her. She hadn't believed Ivy and thought Nellie's imagination had run riot. But she had to believe Bunty. She was overwhelmed by what Richard had done.

'For him to be in love with Myra,' she whispered, 'and then kill her parents. It's hard to believe any man could be so heartless. He must have known how she'd grieve for them.'

Bunty looked very old and gentle. 'I've come to believe he doesn't know how others feel. He sees nobody's point of view but his own. What he wants is all that matters.'

'But he loved Myra enough to marry her.'

'Yes, he did. Richard wanted her and her money and set out to take control of both. And when he'd bullied her into submission and spent her money, he grew tired of her. I think he's never really loved anyone but himself.'

Dinah sat stock still. Bunty was right. He'd wanted power over her and done his best to get it. 'When Nellie ran away from school and you came with him to collect her, I was afraid for you, but you're stronger than Myra, and you know now what happened to her.'

Dinah felt sick. She had grave pointers now to what she could expect of Richard. 'I'll have to go.' Hurriedly, she stood up and reached for her coat. She couldn't stand any more.

Bunty said, 'Take good care of yourself. And look after Nellie for me.'

CHAPTER NINETEEN

DINAH RAN DOWN the street. Her head was whirling and she was too frightened to think. Thank goodness Richard wouldn't be home tonight. She needed time to straighten herself out. She must calm down and sort things out in her head.

She did the same things as when she'd fled from Ivy. She went to Walton Hall Park and sat down on the same cold seat, but things were ten times worse than she'd thought then. Ivy had been full of bitterness and the desire to take revenge. Bunty was wise and gentle; all she wanted was to protect Nellie. Dinah must not ignore her warning.

She was shivering. She felt as though she had a block of ice inside her, yet the sun was shining from a clear blue sky. She could not forgive Richard again, not ever. Not after what Bunty had told her. But she had to do something. Have some plan in her mind, otherwise she would end up as Myra had.

She felt a terrible urge to run away, get far away from Richard and Ardwick House while she still could. She had to find herself a safe place. But where could she go? Her mother was dead and her old home sold up. She could go to Enid. Yes, of course she could. Enid would take her in and protect her. She'd been suspicious of Richard from the start.

Enid had only two bedrooms and Tim still slept in his when he had time off, but they'd willingly make room for her. She'd have to go. She'd never be able to go to bed with Richard, let him make love to her, and not show the revulsion she now felt for him. And once he saw that, it would be the end for her. After all, if he'd killed five people already and got away with it, he'd hardly be bothered about making it six.

Fortunately she had money to take with her. Hadn't she won a small fortune at Chester? She'd go home now and pack her things, pick up her money and be gone before Richard returned. She had to. She couldn't face him.

The suitcase she'd packed to go to Doncaster was still at the factory, but that was full of her race going finery. Such fancy clothes wouldn't be any good for life in Picton Street. She could pick it up tomorrow morning. Now, she wanted to pack her everyday clothes and go straight round to see Enid. Her mind made up, she got to her feet and hurried to the bus stop.

Just to see Ardwick House as she walked up the gravel drive was scary. She let herself in. All was silent; there was no sign of Mrs Banks. Dinah crept upstairs to the room she shared with Richard and started throwing the clothes she wanted to take with her on the bed.

She had to find more suitcases. She went along to the boxroom and found several, so no problem. They were dusty, heavy, and old-fashioned but they'd do; she had a lot to take. She'd pack the hundred and thirty pounds she'd won at Chester races in with her clothes. She'd never owned such a sum before, and it would stand her in good stead now.

She opened her underwear drawer to look for it, but the beaded evening bag was not under her nightdresses.

Could she have put it in the drawer with her stockings and slips? She tipped all the contents out on the carpet. It wasn't here either.

Richard had wanted to keep her money himself, or at least stop her having it. She sifted through everything again as calmly as she could, but it had gone. Did Richard know where she'd put it? He must have taken it: there was no other explanation.

She pushed a suitcase on to the floor, threw herself on the bed and had a little weep. What a fool she'd been not to take the money straight to the bank. She'd known he wanted to take it from her and now she knew why he'd never paid her any wages. Without cash, it would be much harder to escape from him.

Could she go to Enid and throw herself on her mercy without any money? Enid was short of money; she was struggling to support herself.

Oh, God! Dinah pulled herself up short. She was pregnant, and wouldn't be able to work for much longer. And then there'd be another mouth for Enid to feed, and a baby to think of. Lack of money altered everything, as it always had.

She felt half paralysed with fear as she realised that without money she was as much as a prisoner here as Myra had been. If she couldn't pay her own way, she would be a burden on someone else. She'd have to rethink her plans.

What an utter fool she'd been. Hadn't Enid tried to warn her? Richard tried to dominate everybody and most let him. She'd let him do it to her. He seemed to enjoy the power it gave him; there was something sadistic about him. She'd let Richard talk her into doing exactly what he wanted. He was controlling her: she was a marionette and he was pulling all the strings. He'd changed her.

Why had she let him do it? She'd known all along that he was a very strange man. She'd known he was hiding things from her. He was turning her into another victim and she was letting him do it.

Slowly Dinah began putting all her clothes back neatly into their drawers. She returned the suitcases to the boxroom, and was surprised to find she felt empty and devoid of energy. It was nearly four o'clock; she was pregnant and had eaten only one dainty sandwich since breakfast. She went downstairs to the kitchen, where Mrs Banks was baking cakes.

'I've not had much lunch,' she said, 'and I'd like something to eat now. Something savoury.'

'There's some soup I could warm up. Would that do with a slice of toast?'

'Yes, that would be just the thing. Thank you.'

Mrs Banks headed towards the stove. 'Would Nellie like some too? She was sent home from school this morning because she wasn't well. She says she feels better but she's eaten nothing yet.'

Nellie! Dinah had forgotten all about Nellie! What had she been thinking about? She couldn't take Nellie away from her father! And neither could she turn her back on her and leave her to Richard's tender mercies. Whether she had money or not, there had never been any possibility of her finding refuge with Enid.

* * *

Dinah felt better with food in her stomach, and probably Nellie did too because she became quite chatty. The school holidays were about to start. Next week, her school would break up and Mark would be home on Thursday. 'I'm looking forward to that,' she said. 'It seems ages since I saw him.'

Dinah told Mrs Banks to make supper half an hour later than usual, and went up to the old nursery to keep Nellie company. The jigsaw puzzle was still unfinished on the table and together they tried to fit more pieces in.

It left Dinah's mind free to think about what she must do. She would have to fight Richard, stand up to him; there was no other way. She would have to behave as she always had but keep her wits about her and never ever let him talk her into things she didn't want to do.

She would have to go to bed with him every night, and let him make love to her. If he'd married Myra for her money, the only reason Richard could possibly have had for marrying her was that he wanted her in bed with him. He called it love and making love, but Dinah could no longer think of it like that. He certainly had a voracious appetite for it and she knew she'd have to submit without showing any sign of revulsion. She had already found out that just to show reluctance or lack of enthusiasm could make him angry. She knew he'd be incandescent with rage if she let him see her true feelings, and punish her by being especially rough.

He was a very good actor and she would have to learn to be one too. She would have to put all her worries out of her mind and pretend nothing had changed. That would be very hard.

Ever since she'd heard that Myra had been poisoned with strychnine she'd been thinking about her mother. Richard had been taking her glasses of brandy every night and been careful to wash away any she hadn't drunk. She remembered how he had finished her glass and Joan's that first night; he had never once finished Sarah's. And he'd wanted her to be cremated. Why had she not been suspicious? With hindsight, she should have been.

Had she brought Mum here only to have Richard poison her?

Knowing what she did of him now, Dinah could quite believe he'd got tired of having Mum in his house and had taken steps to get rid of her. Perhaps that had always been his plan. He'd been quick to cut off any refuge she might have in mind.

That she'd been happy to bring her here would be on her conscience for the rest of her life. She might still have her mother if she'd left her with Enid and the neighbours in Picton Street.

Dinah sat up with a jerk. What was the matter with her? She should go to the police and tell them all she knew. It was the only safe way; she couldn't fight this on her own. This was murder, serial murder.

But hang on, hadn't Bunty tried that, and they hadn't believed her? Dinah would be telling them the same facts, so how could she expect to be believed? It was altogether too fantastic a tale. And she had no proof at all.

Richard had persuaded her to have her mother cremated so he'd never be brought to book for her murder – if in fact he had poisoned her. Dinah couldn't know for sure; it was all supposition. And once Myra had been persuaded to write her suicide note, there was nothing to say she'd written it under duress. As for the car accidents, they were now so long ago that any wrong doing would be impossible to prove. Why would they believe her?

And if the police were to question Richard about it, he'd find out how suspicious she was of him. A moment later her heart was hammering in her chest and she was struggling to get her breath.

Richard must never know she was wise to him. She must carry on and pretend nothing had changed or, if Bunty was right, he might turn against her and try to kill her.

It was a relief to know she would be alone all night and be able to relax. After tormenting herself for hours trying to make up her mind what she should do, she didn't think she'd be able to sleep, but she was away the moment her head touched the pillow. She woke up at six in the morning with a clear head, but was afraid all the decisions she'd made yesterday wouldn't be enough to keep her safe from Richard.

He saw himself as all powerful both at the factory and at home, and most other people, including Dinah, as being his to use and abuse at will. Dinah knew she needed to find some way of exerting power over him, but how?

She was still worrying about whether he'd poisoned her mother. She guessed the police would have removed the large tin of strychnine from the garden store after Myra had died. If Richard had indeed gone on to poison her mother with it, he'd have had to keep some back, probably in a smaller unmarked tin or bottle.

She couldn't rest. With Richard out of the way now was a good time to look through his wardrobe and drawers. If she found such a thing, it would be proof he could have poisoned Mum. She went through all his possessions methodically, making sure she left them looking exactly as she'd found them.

Almost immediately she found her mother's beaded purse in the top drawer of his little bedside chest. He'd made no attempt to hide it and she knew without opening it that the money was gone. It was too flat to contain one hundred and thirty pounds. She felt a rush of anger, Richard had wanted her money, and despite the fight she'd put up he'd taken it back. Stolen it. Her knees wouldn't support her weight; they felt like bits of putty. She was frightened as well as angry; it was an indication of the lengths to which Richard would go to get his own way.

How could she and Richard have a happy marriage when he treated her as though he owned her, body and soul? He expected to dominate her completely, but she expected a husband to treat her as a partner. She was happy to give way to him on some things, but for this relationship to be normal she needed to have a little money she could call her own. She took her mother's beaded bag and replaced it in her drawer. She gave up looking for strychnine. She had other things to think about now.

Money was very important to Richard: he needed vast amounts of it to buy status. Perhaps he'd be less likely to dominate her if she could make money from the factory when he couldn't. Dare she confront him with the purse and ask for her money back? Accuse him of stealing it? She was afraid she was too much of a coward for that.

But she was going to have to stand her ground and fight him. It was going to be a war of nerves for her. She must push him hard enough to let him feel her confidence and strength but not so hard that he'd lash out and retaliate.

Dinah got up and had breakfast, and then ran upstairs to see Nellie. 'I'm all right to go to school,' she said. 'I feel fine this morning.'

Mr Hopper opened up the factory at eight o'clock, but for Nellie there was no hurry to get up for school. Dinah rushed for the bus, glad she'd have a whole day at work without Richard. She meant to take a long hard look at the ribbon business to see if she could make some money from that. For some time now, she'd had in mind that she would ask Mr McKay if he'd give her an order to supply Carlton Hats.

If she could get a few orders, start the business up again, it would make her more important to Richard and give her a stronger hand. It was the best she could come up with.

When Dinah reached the factory, she found the workforce in buoyant spirits. The girls knew Richard would not be in today and were laughing together in the cloakroom. They greeted her cheerily, and she knew they were all on her side. Mr Hopper was wheeling a trolley load of materials that would be used today into the button room.

'Good morning,' she said. 'Did I tell you that I would like to start up the ribbon business again?'

'Well, you said you were interested. But it's some time since we made any ribbon.'

'You said you'd tell me how it was done.'

'I'll never forget how the machines work, but I'm not sure where we bought all the materials or who gave us the orders.'

'Did you find the old records?'

'I had a quick look round for them,' he said. 'They used to be in that cupboard there, but we cleared it out to make more room for the current button records.'

'I think they could have been moved down to the cellar. I have the keys.' She'd kept those she'd taken in her handbag, knowing she'd want to use them again because there were two more cupboards she hadn't yet opened.

* * *

'This place smells horrible,' she said. But now she'd heard from Ivy Cummins that Richard had hidden down here during the Great War, she couldn't resist peering further into the rooms and passages opening off it. 'Have you explored any further?'

Mr Hopper had a fit of coughing. 'No. They only put the electric light on the stairs and here at the bottom for the cupboards. There're some old machines somewhere. It does stink. It's the damp, and because there's no ventilation.'

Dinah slid the key into one of the cupboards she'd not opened on her earlier visit. It was packed tight with old files with pink covers.

'These are what we want,' Mr Hopper said. 'Copthorne's always used pink covers. But they go back to the early years of the century. What we need are the most recent.'

Dinah unlocked the other cupboard and that too was stacked with old files and ledgers. Mr Hopper found a thinner file dated 1930 and flicked through it.

'Yes, here are the names and addresses of the companies who bought from Copthorne's, with copies of the invoices, giving the exact width, colour and type of ribbon, together with the amounts they bought and the sums they paid.'

Dinah's spirits soared. 'That will be very useful.' When she'd studied it, she'd know where to aim her sales drive.

Mr Hopper was licking his finger and turning over the pages of a battered ledger. 'This gives the names of the companies that supplied us with thread, all the different types and the prices they charged. We bought most of it from Dawstone's on the Dock Road.'

'Excellent.' Dinah felt victorious as she locked up the cupboards. They took their finds upstairs to the room where the ribbon-making machines were and pored over them together.

'I remember this royal blue petersham for Carlton Hats.' Gilbert Hopper stabbed his finger at the bill and sounded quite excited. 'That machine there is still set to seven-eighths of an inch and in the cupboard there's half a reel of the thread that was left over. Do you remember the hats it went on?'

'No.' She shook her head. 'The date on this is June 1931. I hadn't started working there then. Let's see if I can make a bit of ribbon.'

'Anybody can do it.' He slid the reel into the machine, and showed her how to thread it up. 'We just switch it on and there you are.' The machine was noisy but the ribbon was growing before her eyes.

She laughed. 'Excellent. I'll need this sort of thing as a sample.'

'We used to have lots of samples all put neatly together. Now where would they be?' A minute or two later he found a small attaché case and from it drew out a leather-bound book with samples mounted on each page. 'This shows all the sizes, types and colours we used to make.'

'But what about now? Could you still make them?'

'Ye – es.' He stopped the machine and scratched his head. 'It's a long time since I did it; I need to think. Yes, each weave has a number that has to be set on this dial, like so. This should now make a smooth satin ribbon.' He set the machine to work again.

'Marvellous!'

'Well, really you need a different thread for satin hair ribbons.' Mr Hopper led her to the storeroom next door and showed her the half-used reels of the different types of thread. 'There's another old account book here, though there're only a few entries in it. It's for 1932. That was the last year we made any ribbon.'

'Do you know why we stopped?'

'Mr Hopper sighed. 'Myra wasn't getting enough orders.'

'But it wasn't a separate business with a separate workforce and premises. Even with just a few orders, it could have carried on, brought in a little pocket money for Myra.'

'It was a bigger business than the buttons once. Until old Mr Copthorne died. Some of his best customers stayed with Myra, and continued to buy from her for a few years. But she wasn't well and she knew she was losing orders. She blamed herself. I think she felt she was letting her dad down. It was his business, you see.'

'She must have felt terrible.'

'She did, poor girl. I don't think Mr Haldane was all that interested in carrying on.'

'He's interested now – he went to Carlton Hats in March asking for another order. We need more work here, any sort of work.'

And she was going to have to get it. 'I'm very pleased with these samples. I can match them to the invoices and find the price we charged customers.'

'Yes, but that was two or more years ago. Would Mr Haldane want to charge the same price?'

Dinah sucked her lip. 'I don't know.'

'You could ask the thread manufacturers for an up-to-date price list first. Our wages haven't gone up. Then you and Mr Haldane would be able to work out a profitable price to charge.'

But would Richard feel she was showing him up by doing something he'd failed to do? Dare she go ahead without involving him?

There were times when he'd treated her like a brainless idiot. He'd told her too often that she wasn't capable of this and wouldn't be able to cope with that. It wasn't just her, of course; he treated everybody that way. It made him feel superior to run others down. Richard thought he was capable of doing anything, but he couldn't be more wrong.

She wanted to do it. She'd fancied getting orders for hats, and ribbons couldn't be so very different. Richard had relied on his first wife to do it for him, hadn't he, so why not her?

Mum had brought her up to stand on her own feet. Many times, Sarah had said to her, 'Go ahead and see. You won't know what you can do if you don't try. I've surprised myself at what I can do, and so will you.'

All the years she'd been growing up, all the families in Picton Street, including hers, would have grovelled for any means of making a few pence. She could see that with the present workforce, money could be earned with these ribbon machines.

It was the only way she could think of to strengthen her position. If she could earn money, Richard would want to keep her doing it. She'd prove her worth.

'Mr Hopper,' she said, 'will you arrange to have this room thoroughly cleaned? And I suppose the ribbon machines will need to be serviced.'

'I can do that. I always have.'

'Thank you. I'm going to see if I can find work for them.'

He hesitated. 'Is that what Mr Haldane wants?'

'It's what I want.' Dinah quaked as she said it. 'If he asks, you can tell him I ordered it.' A second later, she had a crisis of confidence. Should she have put her neck out like this? She comforted herself with the thought that if she failed to persuade Mr McKay to give her an order, Richard need be none the wiser.

Chapter Twenty

SHE WENT TO her desk in Miss O'Marney's office and gave it more thought, deliberating on whether it would be better just to walk in on Mr McKay or whether she should telephone and tell him what she wanted and make an appointment. The appointment would be more professional, but she didn't want him to say no without seeing her. He had, after all, said no to Richard.

Mr McKay knew all there was to know about company accounts. If she took the button factory figures for 1918 with her, and the rapport she'd once had with him was still there, she might ask him to explain them.

She decided she'd walk in on him and that she should go as soon as possible. Today was Friday. Tomorrow morning Mr McKay would be thinking of his weekend; by Monday, Richard would be back. It made sense to go straight away.

She'd go home and change into her pale green outfit and its matching Carlton Hat. She wanted Mr McKay to see that she'd advanced from being an apprentice to being a customer. She picked up Myra's sample case and caught the bus home, and then returned to Carlton Hats.

She told herself she mustn't be nervous, not of her old boss. But as she went in through the front door instead of the back entrance she'd used as an employee, she kept her fingers crossed. She reached his office door without meeting anybody and tapped on it as she always used to.

She heard him call 'Come in' in the friendly way he had. No employee of Richard's had easy access to him like this. She took a deep breath and pushed the door open.

'Good morning, Mr McKay,' she said. 'Can you spare me a few minutes?'

'Good gracious, if it isn't Dinah Radcliffe.' He smiled a welcome. 'Don't tell me you want to come back to work already?'

'No. I'm Mrs Haldane now.'

'Oh dear, yes, I'm sorry. Your smart hat should have reminded me. Come and have a seat. What can I do for you?'

'I know Richard came to see you a few months ago, asking for an order to supply you with ribbon.'

'He did, but he didn't get it. Now he's sent you with a sob story to try again.'

'No, Mr McKay, he hasn't. He doesn't know I'm here. Yes, I've come to ask for an order to supply some of your ribbons. I'm having our machines serviced and we still have the workers, but they haven't enough work to keep them busy. I know we can supply your needs.'

'Young lady, your husband let me down. D'you know, when I started Copthorne's were my sole supplier? Their work was top class and they always delivered on time. That is, until Arthur Copthorne and his wife were killed. I went on ordering from them, but suddenly, without warning, everything stopped. When I tried to ring their office the phone was dead. I eventually heard that a certain Richard Haldane who made buttons had taken the company over and closed it down. Then one day his wife comes and introduces herself as Myra Haldane, daughter of Arthur Copthorne. I'd never seen her before, but Arthur used to come in from time to time for a chat and he'd mention her.

'I felt sorry for her losing her parents like that and I'd liked her father, so I gave her some business. Things were all right for a time. There were little hiccups, colours and sizes wrong, and delays too. I expected the same service as I'd had from her father, but I wasn't getting it.'

'You'll get the best from me,' Dinah said. 'I'll make sure you do.'

'Then in spring 1932 I gave Myra a big order for ribbons for my new collection, but time went on and it wasn't delivered. When I rang up about it, I was told she was ill, but they were working on it. It still didn't come, so I rang again and spoke to your husband. He was none too polite, damn rude in fact. I told him what to do with his ribbon and found another firm to make what I wanted in a hurry. I couldn't believe it when he came in again this year asking for another order. I thought it was a bit hard-faced.'

Dinah was taken aback to find he had such a definite complaint. She felt she had to plead. 'I'll see to it myself, Mr McKay, and I won't let you down.'

He looked at her and shook his head. 'I thought I could make a good milliner of you, but you didn't finish your apprenticeship. That was letting me down, and yourself as well.'

'I'm sorry. Yes, I suppose it was. I didn't see it that way at the time.'

'To marry the handsome Mr Haldane was a big temptation, eh? And he wanted a wife to send out asking for work from the likes of me?'

'No he didn't. It was my idea to come, honest. The workers are scared they'll be sacked if no more work comes in. Any order you give us will have our best attention, I promise.'

Mr McKay was deep in thought. She hoped he was weighing things up and would give her an order. Instead, he asked, 'What happened to the Copthorne business?'

She shook her head. 'I wish I knew. Did it go bankrupt?'

'I don't think so. I would have said it was as sound as a bell before Arthur died. Ask your husband, he'll know.'

There was an awkward pause until Dinah said, 'What was Myra like?'

He laughed. 'A pretty young girl. Not much older than you when she was coming here.'

'Was all the ribbon side of Richard's business handled by her?'

'Dear girl, how would I know? She used to come in from time to time and we'd chat over a cup of tea, but we didn't discuss how our businesses were run, or our respective spouses, only what I wanted her to provide.'

'Yes, of course.'

'All right, young lady. I'll give you a small order to see how you get on.'

'Thank you, thank you! I so hoped you would.'

'If anything goes wrong and you can't deliver on the agreed date, I want to know straight away.'

'I understand. I'll do that, I promise.'

He pulled some designs from the racks above his head. 'This is what we're going to make for spring. I want petersham ribbons in pale colours.' He took some swatches of felt from his drawer. 'I want you to match these colours for me.' He showed her pink, green, blue and cream.

Success was giving her a beaming smile. 'How wide and how much of each?'

'I'll fill up an order form for you. You'll need all the sizes written down, they've got to be exact.'

She smiled. 'I know that.'

He sighed. 'Oh well, you always seemed to know what you were about. I hope you still do.'

'I've done my homework. You can rely on me.'

'I'm banking on it, don't forget. Look, I'm sure you'd rather have a cup of tea with your friends from the workroom than with me. Did you hear the bell ring? It's their dinner break; they'll be in the canteen by now.'

'I'd love to do that.' She stood up. 'Thanks again, Mr McKay. I'm very grateful.'

'Come back for the order form before you leave. By the way, there's a firm called Barnes Brothers down on the Dock Road. They've been making bowler hats for years but they're branching out now and making trilbies as well. If you want more work, I'd try there.'

'Oh, thank you. You're the tops, Mr McKay. I won't forget this.'

'Young lady, I must be a daft old fool to do this for you.'

Dinah almost skipped to the canteen. She'd brought with her the sandwiches Mrs Banks had made, and really enjoyed eating them and chatting with Millie Hunt and her old colleagues.

'Have I missed you,' Millie told her. 'We used to have a good time, you and me. I didn't think you'd cut yourself off like this.'

'I'm sorry, I didn't intend to, Millie. It's just that Richard wants me to spend my time with him.'

'I suppose you've much more exciting things to do now?'

'No, not really.'

'Well, why not come dancing with us? You used to love that.'

'There's a hop at St Stephen's church hall next week,' Jenny Brown said. 'With Tommy Dayton's band. That was your favourite, wasn't it?'

'I'm a staid married woman now,' Dinah said. 'Richard would have a fit if I told him I was going dancing.'

'What about the pictures then?' Millie asked. 'He wouldn't object to that, would he?'

Dinah knew he probably would. But she mustn't allow him to isolate her as he had Myra. This seemed another way she could avoid his control.

'Not with an old friend like you,' she said. 'It's ages since I went to the pictures.'

'Jenny and I thought of going to the Odeon in town, tomorrow. It's Shirley Temple in *Bright Eyes*. Are you on?'

'Yes. Yes, I'd like to. Can I bring my stepdaughter? It would be right up her street.'

'Course you can.'

'I'll tell you what, how about meeting me in Bunney's café earlier and I'll stand you tea and fancy cakes first.'

'Marvellous,' Millie chortled.

'You don't know how lucky you are,' they all assured her. 'Married to a rich man.'

Had she been alone with Millie, Dinah knew she'd have been tempted to confide in her. She felt she'd never needed a friend more.

When she went back to Mr McKay's office for the order he'd promised her, she took out the old button accounts and asked him to explain what the figures meant. He was good at teaching his apprentices and after ten minutes with him she had a fair grasp of what the figures showed.

'Clever of you, young lady, to bring an out-of-date annual report.

Right not to embarrass your husband by letting us all know how much his business earns.'

Carlton Hats had always been a friendly place to work, it had given her an easy and comfortable life. Given her time over again, Dinah knew she wouldn't have turned her back on it in such a hurry.

Now that she had her order form she intended to go straight down to the Dock Road and look for the thread manufacturer. They might not have the colours she needed in stock and she wanted to start the job as soon as possible. She had to have the ribbon made in plenty of time if she were to get more work from Mr McKay.

Mr Hopper had recommended the best company to approach and she found their office without any trouble. The manager treated her like royalty. Dinah knew that in these hard times he'd be glad of any business he could get, but he still asked for prompt settlement of their bill. He showed her samples of their standard threads and thought they could match the cream and the pink felt. He took her through their workrooms and gave her samples to take back. Dinah was feeling her lack of experience and wished she'd brought Mr Hopper with her. She said she'd ring him to confirm it was the quality they needed.

She was very pleased with the progress she was making as she caught a bus to take her back to the button factory. As soon as she sat down, she saw a sign on a building they were passing which read: *Barnes Brothers, High Class Hatters*. She scrambled to her feet, pushed a penny at the conductor and walked back from the next stop. She'd tasted success today and was keen to try to further her luck right away.

She was shown into an office shared by two managers. She said her bit and displayed her samples and found they'd previously bought from Copthorne Ribbons. She didn't get an order right away, they said they would like to think about it, but she went away hopeful.

Mr Hopper said the quality of the sample thread was exactly what they needed and Dinah rang Dawstone's to confirm the purchase and ask them to go ahead and order the same quality in blue and green.

* * *

Dinah thought Saturday was turning out to be another successful day. The order from Barnes Brothers came in the morning post, just as Mr Hopper was taking delivery of the cream and pink thread she'd ordered. She put the bill on Richard's desk and got Mr Hopper to thread up the machines and set them to work.

Watching the ribbons being woven gave Dinah great satisfaction and she felt it brought a new feeling of hope to the factory. Mr Hopper said, 'I'll move a girl in from the button room to tend the machines, and I'll keep an eye on things.'

They closed at twelve thirty on Saturdays. Dinah went home to lunch feeling exhausted but pleased with what she'd managed to do. She was dreading Richard's return this evening and knowing now what he'd been hiding from her she was scared. But she was looking forward to seeing her friends again before she had to face him. She scribbled a note telling him she was taking Nellie to the pictures and didn't know what time they'd be back. It would be better, she wrote, if he didn't wait supper for them.

Nellie was delighted at the prospect of seeing Shirley Temple. They met at four o'clock in Bunney's, and Dinah had a jolly time with her old friends, urging them to eat as many cream cakes as they could. Nellie laughed and joined in more than Dinah had expected. They were in good time for first house at the Odeon and they all enjoyed the Shirley Temple film. It was still early when they came out, and a lovely balmy evening.

Millie said, 'How about a stroll down to the Pier Head? There's usually a chippy van down at the bus terminus in the evenings.' There were not many people about at that time and they linked arms and stepped out four abreast.

Dinah insisted on treating them to a fish supper and they ate it on a bench overlooking the river. By the time they had finished it was half past nine and Jenny was suggesting they go to a dance.

'Not us,' Dinah said. 'It's time we went home.'

'We've had a great time,' Millie said. 'Thanks ever so.'

'We'll have to do it again,' Dinah told them as she and Nellie went for their bus. She'd learned a great deal that had shocked her since

Richard had gone away, and without him life had seemed more normal. But now he'd be back and she began to worry about what sort of mood he'd be in.

She used her key to let them in and stood listening. The atmosphere seemed heavy and threatening. Then she heard Richard's angry voice and her heart sank. He was ranting on, though she couldn't make sense of what he said. He spoke to himself quite a lot and was often angry, but she didn't know if he was alone or whether Mrs Banks was with him.

'Get yourself a glass of milk and go up to your room,' she said softly to Nellie. 'I'll be up to say good night later.'

At that instant Richard came storming out of his study and cut off Nellie's escape.

Dinah forced a smile and said cheerily, 'Hello, Richard. Back safe and sound?'

'Where the hell have you been?' he demanded furiously. 'You know I want you here when I come home.'

Dinah had no idea how to turn off his ill temper, but she knew she mustn't let him see how much it frightened her.

'Well, we're here now, and I left you a note so you wouldn't be worried.'

'Worried? I left you here to look after things and you ignore me and my needs and go haring off to the cinema.'

Nellie was hanging on to her hand, but displayed a new-found confidence. 'It was a lovely film, Daddy.'

'Dinah, you know I think Nellie's too young to have her head filled with all that film nonsense.'

'I knew you'd say that.' Dinah managed another smile. Never again must she quake and look like a victim. That was where she'd been going wrong. 'It was a Shirley Temple film, Richard. Not too old for her at all.'

'*Bright Eyes*,' Nellie added. 'It was lovely. Shirley Temple's a real moppet, very sweet.'

Dinah had to laugh. 'She heard Millie say that.'

'The school sent me home again on Thursday. I was sick on the floor in morning prayers. Miss Clarke said if I feel sick I should stay at home.'

'So, you're too ill to go to school but not too ill to go to the pictures? You shouldn't have taken her, Dinah. You're to do what I tell you and not take matters into your own hands as soon as I turn my back.'

'I went to school yesterday, Daddy, and felt all right.'

Dinah held her breath. Nellie was telling him he'd misjudged matters.

'And I went to see Bunty. She said I must tell you before I go again and so did Dinah, so you mustn't tell her off.'

'Bunty! You're not to go there again. Do you hear me?'

'Get yourself a drink of milk, Nellie, and go on up to your room,' Dinah repeated, giving her a little push. She hoped to have her safely out of the way before Richard exploded.

Nellie didn't need telling twice, 'Good night,' she said and shot off to the kitchen.

'That child needs discipline. Give her an inch and she takes a mile. She's not to go near that woman again.'

Dinah took a deep breath. She had to make Richard see reason on this.

'It would be wrong to stop her, Richard. For all Nellie's life Bunty has looked after her. They're fond of each other; Nellie needs her. She represents stability in Nellie's life. Why prise them apart?'

Was he going to blow up at her? He looked taken aback. Encouraged, she went on, 'To separate them would do Nellie more harm than good. Bunty phoned me; she was worried because Nellie had been to see her without you knowing. She predicted you'd be angry and forbid her to visit again. She wanted you to know. Richard, Nellie hasn't got over Myra's death yet. You should be trying to help her.'

'I have tried, but don't forget I was bereaved too.'

To Dinah that sounded outrageous. She made herself say, 'You found your own way to overcome your grief. You took up with me.'

Richard looked upset, almost tearful. 'I have tried with Nellie, but I can't get through to her. What more can I do?'

'You could bring Bunty back to live here. She worked for your family for years. You owe her something, don't you?'

He shook his head. 'I'm not having her back here. Mrs Banks is a far better cook.'

'I didn't mean get rid of Mrs Banks,' she choked. The trouble was, she didn't know how to handle Richard when he was like this.

'You'd fill this house with women if you could.' He was glowering at her. 'All right, if it means so much to Nellie, she can visit her once in a while.'

Dinah smiled. Had she won that round? Had she done the right thing by refusing to lose her temper or show her terror? She wasn't sure, but it had cost her dear. She was quaking. Arguing with him like this was scary. 'Good. It's the right thing, Richard. They'll comfort each other.'

She went into the sitting room and curled up on the sofa, trying to appear more at ease than she felt. She'd hoped that by ignoring his taunts and appearing to be in a good mood she'd calm his anger, but it wasn't working.

'Come on then, tell me about Doncaster. I've been dying to know how you got on. Did you win?'

'No,' he burst out. 'It was utter and total disaster. Neither horse won anything. I'm thinking of looking for another trainer. Bob Watchit should be able to do better than this for me. What d'you think?'

Dinah sat up straighter. Richard had never asked her opinion on anything before. She had to build on the victory she'd achieved so far.

'I think a better idea would be to sell the horses. They only upset you when they don't win. Their upkeep costs too much. It's a waste of money.'

'You stupid fool!' he screamed. Dinah's heart jolted into her throat. 'You know nothing about horses!' He picked up a vase of roses and hurled them at the grate. The vase shattered. Dinah felt the water splash over her legs.

She jerked to her feet, as angry as he was. 'You're right, I don't know anything about horses, but you did ask. And I do know what they do to you. You don't want to ride them, and you certainly don't want to muck them out. What obsesses you is seeing which one can run the fastest.' She was heading for the door with as much dignity as she could muster.

'Come back here, I've not finished yet. I want to talk to you.'

'Richard, we're both too angry to talk sensibly. Leave it till morning, we can talk then.' Dinah wanted to fly for the stairs to get away from him, but she made herself walk slowly. There was another crash followed by more splintering of glass, then silence.

Dinah had a long slow bath locked in the bathroom and didn't hear him come upstairs. Eventually, she got out, put on her nightdress, and crept warily into their bedroom. The curtains were not drawn and moonlight was streaming in. Richard was curled up, a motionless log on his side of the bed.

She hoped he'd stay like that as she slid under the bedclothes on her side as quietly and gently as she could. She didn't think he was asleep and half expected every moment that he'd heave himself over on top of her. She lay awake for a long time dreading that, and worrying about how he'd be the next day.

Dinah was late waking up the next morning and found the sun streaming into their bedroom. She could hear Nellie's voice drifting up from the bottom of the stairs. Richard didn't appear to have moved in the night; his back was towards her.

'Morning, Richard.' She was still trying to sound cheerful. 'We've overslept, I think.'

He neither moved nor answered. She got out of bed and went to the bathroom. He still hadn't moved when she came back and began to dress.

'Aren't you going to get up? It's a lovely morning.'

He grunted.

'Didn't you sleep well? Come down for breakfast in your dressing grown. Mrs Banks is frying the bacon, and it smells delicious.'

He sat up. 'Of course I didn't sleep well. You didn't expect me to sleep well, did you, after you'd been so damn difficult last night?'

'I'm sorry, I didn't mean to upset you. It's the last thing I want —'

'Of course you upset me.' He was roaring with fury, 'I'm away for two nights and when I come back you're not here. I wanted to be welcomed home and have a nice supper with my family. Whatever made you go out?'

'Aren't I entitled to a bit of pleasure? I met Millie Hunt and she suggested I go to the pictures with her and Jenny. It was like old times.'

'Those times have gone. You're my wife now and I don't want you mixing with girls like that.'

'They're my friends. I'm fond of them.'

'And I particularly don't want Nellie to know them. You're always arguing about Nellie. All that fuss about keeping her off school . . .'

'She needed to be kept off school.'

'There you go again. Don't interfere between me and my daughter, I won't have it.' Richard's handsome face was twisting with fury. He was always like this if she questioned his decisions. 'You're turning her against me.'

'No, Richard.' Dinah was as gentle as she knew how. 'I'm trying to turn her into a normal happy girl. She spends too much time on her own. I haven't seen Millie for a long time and I enjoyed myself. Nellie enjoyed herself, too. She opened up and chattered twenty to the dozen. We all need to get out and about, meet friends and have a bit of fun. You do it – you've just had three days' racing.'

'I didn't enjoy it.'

She was glad she hadn't gone with him. 'Because you didn't win,' she said. 'Why don't we go out to dinner one evening next week? You used to enjoy that. Or we could go to the theatre.'

'Yes.'

'I really want to go and see Aunt Enid this afternoon. I feel I've been neglecting her.'

Richard's whole attitude suddenly changed. He looked woebegone. 'Stay with me,' he pleaded. 'I don't want you to go out and leave me.'

For the first time, Dinah realised he had no friends. Acquaintances yes, his trainer for one, but no real friends.

'I'm sorry,' he said tearfully. 'I know I'm a bit crotchety sometimes. I do try to please you. I didn't insist on Nellie going back to boarding school, did I? I want things between you and me to be better. You know, as they were in the first weeks after we were married. I do love you, Dinah. Please don't fight me. I want us to be happy together.'

Dinah almost burst into tears herself. 'I don't want to fight either.'

She didn't know whether he really meant what he said or whether it was another act to win her over and regain power over her.

'Let's have a quiet afternoon at home together.'

'Yes.' Perhaps a quiet day together would help. They had tea in the garden and he was calm and even affable towards Nellie. Dinah felt a little better, but she didn't know where she was with him. He'd allowed her a few small victories but it was impossible to have a normal relationship with him. She knew she was still treading on eggshells.

CHAPTER TWENTY-ONE

ON MONDAY MORNING, Richard seemed subdued until he shouted at Mrs Banks that his bacon was half raw. 'You should know by now that I like it crisp.'

She took it back to the kitchen to grill it for a little longer, and when it was returned Richard complained it was as hard as nails.

When they reached the outer office, Richard carried on through to his. Dinah told Miss O'Marney she looked quite tanned, and was hearing about her summer weekend on the beach at Ainsdale, when Richard snatched open his office door. His face was crimson with fury. He was holding out the Dawstone's bill for the thread between his finger and thumb.

'What d'you think you're doing?' he demanded. 'You've no business to go putting in orders like this.'

Miss O'Marney cleared her throat. She was always embarrassed by Richard's displays of anger. She picked up her handbag and went out without saying a word, closing the office door quietly behind her.

Dinah told him about the order from Carlton Hats. Yesterday, by the time Richard had calmed down she'd not had the energy to do so. She'd expected a pat on the back, certainly not this.

'We can start making ribbon again,' she said. 'I thought you'd be pleased. I know you wanted the work, because you went looking for it yourself.'

He looked shocked. 'McKay gave you an order? What exactly?'

She took it from her desk drawer and handed it to him. He read it with a face like thunder, then sneered, 'What did you have to do to get this?'

That made her cross. 'Just ask for it.'

'Of course, he knows you. That gives you a great advantage. But you don't know anybody else, and it's hardly worth the trouble of starting up those machines for a job of this size.'

'It's cost nothing to get this far. I asked Mr Hopper to service them and get the room cleaned. Things are getting desperate in the button room, and we need more work to keep the girls busy. I had to buy that thread to do the job. I'd like you to write a cheque now to settle the bill.'

He was turning impatiently away. 'It can wait till the end of the month. I settle all the bills then. They know me, they know how I operate.'

Dinah picked up the other order she'd achieved and followed him into his office, closing the door quietly behind her.

'Richard, you've done no business with this company for years. They gave me to understand they'd treat us as a new account. They want settlement quickly.'

'Don't they trust me to pay?' Anger was bubbling out of him. 'I see no reason—'

'I need to order more thread from them. Barnes Brothers has given us a big order.'

He stood staring down at her, astonished. 'You've got another order?' He snatched it from her.

'All black this time, best quality silk, in several different widths.'

'Bowler hats,' he said through clenched teeth. 'Well, I suppose when a pretty girl like you asks for an order, you're more likely to get it than a man.'

Dinah ignored that. She should have expected he'd still try to put her down. 'Right, if you'll write out the cheque, I'll take it down and give them another order for this thread.'

He said in an off-hand manner, 'No need to waste your time. You could put it in the post.'

'I want them to get to know me, Richard. We don't want any hold-ups in our thread supplies. At Carlton Hats, Mr McKay knows everybody he deals with.'

She stood over him while he wrote it out.

'Right, then you'd better carry on, see if you can get more orders. I'm sure you'll be able to get this factory working overtime for me before long.'

She knew he was pleased, but he couldn't stop being objectionable. Dinah was glad the matter had come up while they were at the factory with people all round. She wouldn't have dared stick her neck out like this if they were alone at home.

With the cheque in her hand, she said, 'There are conditions this time. I'm not even going to try unless you pay me. I want to go on the payroll and have a regular wage. And I believe salesmen also receive a percentage of the new business they bring in.'

He was astounded now. She was glad she'd found the courage to say it; he clearly hadn't expected her to.

'Hang on, Dinah. This is a family business and you share my standard of living. In addition you have your account at Bunney's. You can have everything you want already.'

'I want to stand on my own feet. Your way makes me feel beholden to you.'

'A wife is beholden to her husband.'

She could see his jaws tightening. Dinah took a grip on her nerves and looked him straight in the eye.

'Not a working wife. Not entirely.' It seemed there was a narrow line between standing up for what she wanted and making him furious. It was almost impossible to do one without the other.

She could feel herself shaking. 'So, it's up to you.' For her this was a war of nerves. 'If you want more orders and to get more profit from this business you'll have to pay me. Otherwise I'll play around as I have been, doing jobs that Miss O'Marney did before I came and could very well do again.'

She saw the crimson tide run up his neck and into his face again. 'Dinah,' he barked. 'I will not have you making demands on me. I will not be dictated to by you or anybody else.'

'Suit yourself,' she said quietly and went back to her desk, shutting the door between them.

She was quaking. It had taken a lot of nerve to try to force Richard to pay her a normal wage and it looked as though she'd failed. She could hear him furiously muttering to himself and slamming about his office. Her head was reeling. She couldn't settle to do anything at her desk while he was giving vent to such an audible tirade.

She thought a cup of tea might help and went to the kitchen. The big brown enamel teapot was kept under a cosy on the stove and Mr Hopper was filling a mug for himself. Dinah pushed another mug alongside it and he poured for her too.

'I'm fed up,' she said.

He led her into the ribbon room, where one row of machines was spinning and carding Mr McKay's ribbon. Three-quarters of the machines still stood idle, but even so, the machines that were working were making too much of a clatter for the girl tending them to hear what they said. Dinah told him of her dispute with Richard.

'You can't stop now,' Mr Hopper protested. 'I've been lifted up all weekend because of this, and the girls too. They could see this place closing if they didn't get enough work to keep them busy.'

'I've told Richard I'm not doing it unless I'm paid,' Dinah told him, still upset by the fight she'd had to put up. 'That shouldn't be too much to ask, should it?'

'No. You've got to stick up for yourself, I see that. Myra should have done it. He's a strange one is Mr Haldane.'

Dinah sighed. He was more than strange, he was impossible. 'Did he have any friends in the old days?'

'Not that I know of, but I don't move in the same social circles.'

'There must have been people coming in, salesmen, business contacts, manufacturers of threads and the materials to make buttons.'

Hopper thought for a moment. 'Well, he and Myra were quite friendly with one of the women who worked here, a machine operator. She worked on that row of machines there. Olive something, her name was. Yes, Olive Jennings, but that's going back five or six years.'

Dinah couldn't see Richard being friendly with an employee; he had too much pride and thought his workers belonged to a class beneath him. 'What was Olive Jennings like?'

'She was getting on a bit, used to mother the younger ones, Myra included. She was good for her.'

But she couldn't have been Myra's friend. Richard would have put a stop to it.

'Olive was the sort to jolly you along, all outgoing and chatty.'

'What happened to her?'

He shrugged. 'She just moved on.'

Dinah sat sipping her tea and wondering where Richard went and what he did in the hours he was missing every day. Was that likely to have anything to do with this woman?

The door crashed open and an angry Richard jerked to a halt in front of the table. 'All right, Dinah,' he said through clenched teeth. 'Have it your way. Come back to my office and we'll talk about what you want.' He spun on his heel and whirled out again. Dinah scurried behind him, wondering what to expect.

'You win,' he said. 'You can put your name on the payroll, but I don't like the way you've gone about it. It's underhand. I'd call it blackmail.'

Dinah set out her terms, asking for a modest salary and percentage. 'You'd have to pay that if you hired a salesman.'

He was still agitated. 'All right.' He took a directory from the drawer of his desk and pushed it over to her. 'This, in case you don't know, is the local trade directory. You'll probably find it useful.'

'Thank you.'

He reached for his hat and went out, slamming the door. Dinah felt enclosed in a bubble of relief. She'd been afraid she'd pressed him too hard, but she'd won.

The following morning, Dinah visited four more businesses that had ordered ribbon from Copthorne's in the past, but none showed any interest in doing it again. Somewhat disheartened, and finding herself not far from Walton, she decided she'd give up for the day and go to see Enid. She bought a chocolate cake as a gift, knowing how few treats Enid was able to afford, and knocked on the door. Enid's face lit up with smiles when she saw her on the step.

'Come in. It's lovely to see you.' Tears were stinging Dinah's eyes. Enid looked achingly familiar, a steadfast rock to rely on, and she was reminded of her mother. Enid gave her a welcoming hug before ushering her into the front room.

'Tim's here. Well, he's out getting a bit of shopping at the moment. He's been off sick for the last few days.'

'What's the matter?' Dinah couldn't imagine Tim Reece as anything but fighting fit.

Enid groaned. 'He had a fall at Haydock Park. Dislocated his shoulder and sprained his wrist. It happens to all jockeys from time to time. He's lucky he wasn't badly hurt, but of course he can't ride until he gets the strength back in his wrist.'

'Poor old Tim.' Dinah knew only too well what it meant if he couldn't work.

Enid had the kettle on and the chocolate cake out on a plate in no time. 'How are you?'

'I'm fine.'

'You look a bit peaky. I suppose losing your mum hasn't been easy for you.'

'No,' Dinah said, 'and the first few months of pregnancy haven't been easy either.' But that wasn't the half of it. She was on the point of saying more when Tim came home with his left wrist all strapped up. He dropped the shopping bag and threw his good arm round Dinah, planting a hearty kiss on her cheek.

It was lovely to see Tim again with his brown hair tousled as always. 'You've grown,' she told him. 'You're taller than me now.'

'Don't I know it.' He was grinning at her. 'I thought I'd have finished growing and be OK by now, but I'm piling on the pounds.'

'You're painfully thin,' his mother protested.

'Yes, you are,' Dinah agreed. He was reed slim.

'Don't you nag me too.'

'I'm sure he's making himself ill by not eating,' his mother went on. 'Dinah's brought us a chocolate cake. You'll have a slice of that?'

'I'll have a cup of tea and just a sliver.' He cut a paper-thin slice and then cut that in half.

'That's barely six crumbs.' Enid was derisory.

'Mum wants me to stuff myself,' he said. 'But she knows I can't, not if I'm to carry on being a jockey.'

'Is it that bad?'

'Yes, and Mum's always cooking, filling the house with delicious smells to tempt me, then piling up my plate.'

Dinah found it comforting to be back in Picton Street with them. She showed them her ribbon samples and told them what she'd been doing. She stayed longer than she'd intended.

'I wish you didn't have to go,' Tim said when she stood up.

'It's five o'clock. Richard will wonder where I am.'

'I'll see you to the bus stop.'

As they walked down the street, Dinah asked, 'How long will you be off sick?'

'I'm going back next week, but just to help where I can. Digby's very good to me: he'll pay me a wage to keep me going. He understands the problem.'

'Aunt Enid never did want you to be a jockey, did she?'

'She's afraid I'll maim myself for life or even get killed. It's a job I love, but I won't be able to carry on much longer. I'm growing too heavy to get the rides.'

Dinah realised that she was not the only one with difficulties. 'What will you do?'

'Digby says I've done wonders with Flyswitch, that I've really brought him on, and if only I can do that with other horses I could become a trainer.'

'Wouldn't you like that? You'd be good at it.'

'Yes, training horses would be the next best thing to riding them. But it takes a lot of money to set up a stable and take on staff, and I don't know whether I've got the business sense to run one. Good trainers sometimes go bankrupt, especially in times like these. One did in Southport last year, and Digby took over four of his horses.'

They were walking up the street that ran into County Road when Dinah saw the bus she wanted to catch go past in the line of traffic. 'Oh, Lord, I've missed it.'

'Does it matter?'

Dinah knew Richard would be home before her now, and he'd want to know where she'd been. They reached the bus stop in time to see the bus she'd wanted held up by traffic lights three hundred yards away.

'They only run every half-hour,' she groaned. She felt hot and tired.

County Road was a long dusty thoroughfare, not very busy at this time of the day because the small shops that lined it had mostly closed. Near the bus stop was a greengrocer's; the blinds were down and the fruit and vegetables usually on display outside had been taken in. The wooden staging had been left in place ready for tomorrow.

'We can perch on that while we wait,' Tim said, leading her to it. 'It's in the shade too.' He settled himself beside her and took her hand in his. 'What's the matter, Dinah?' He was sympathetic. 'I know something is. You aren't as happy as you try to make out.'

Dinah was biting her lip.

'Is it Richard?' he asked.

She could feel tears stinging her eyes again. She blinked furiously; she mustn't cry now. 'How did you know?'

'I can see it. I could the day we came to visit your mum.'

'It shows that much?'

'Only to me. I've been worried about you. Mum has too. Richard Haldane isn't popular with the racing crowd. He's got a terrible temper.'

'Don't I know it!' Dinah couldn't hold her worries back any longer. She told him how she'd known Richard was hiding something, how she'd delved into his past, and suddenly the secrets she'd unearthed were flooding out.

'He murdered his parents.'

'What?' He was grinning at her; he thought she was joking.

'And the parents of his first wife. Ivy his cook told me.'

'That's four people! Dinah, how can that be true?'

'I didn't believe it at first, but Bunty the nanny confirmed it. And there's worse. Nellie's mother committed suicide and they think either he drove her to it, or he poisoned her. And on top of that, I've got an awful suspicion that he might have poisoned my mother too.'

'Aunt Sarah?' He was aghast.

'I feel a bag of nerves.'

Tim put his arm round her shoulders and pulled her closer. 'I can see you're scared, but Dinah, it can't possibly be true. How could he murder all those people and get away with it? It's very unlikely.'

'It's what people who lived with him are telling me. Servants living in the house at the time. I didn't believe it either, not at first, but now . . .'

'What proof do they have?'

'None.'

'There you are then, it's just gossip. Nobody likes Richard; he's always trying to get the better of people. They say he's half crazy.'

'I wish I could be sure one way or the other. About the murders.'

'I can feel you shaking. You're scared stiff of him. Let me take you back home now. You'd be safe with Mum.'

'No, Tim. She doesn't have the space.'

'She'll make space for you. You've got to get out, Dinah, before he turns on you. If he doesn't do that he'll drive you down. I wish I had a place of my own so I could give you a refuge, but I know Mum will. She'll be glad to take you in.'

'He might be an innocent man. And anyway, I don't think he'll hurt me. He says he loves me.'

She saw Tim wince at that. 'Do you love him?'

'I don't know.' She felt hopeless and helpless.

'It's only a couple of months since you married him. You were in love with him then.' There was pain in his voice. 'You told me you were.'

Dinah sniffed into her hanky. 'Sometimes I think I do, but then he flies into a rage and he's quite nasty. That spoils any feelings I have for him.'

He pulled her closer. 'You can't go on like this. You've got to leave him.'

'I'm having his baby, Tim. And there's Nellie and Mark, I can't just abandon them.' There was a lot she had to explain. 'I think I'm beginning to get the upper hand. If I can do that, I'll be able to handle him.'

'Handle a murderer? You? Heavens, Dinah, you're crazy to stay with him. But you've got guts. Has he ever hit you?'

'No. I'm not scared of that – he never would. He storms at everybody round him, frightens us, torments us, but what he does is not physical.'

'You're his wife, he says he loves you, yet he treats you like that? He must be mad.'

When she saw the next bus coming, she got to her feet. 'Sorry. I've pushed my worries on you now, but I had to talk to someone.'

'I wish there was more I could do. I still think you should leave him. Let me tell Mum?'

'No, Tim. No.'

'She'll want to help you.'

'Just to talk about it to you has helped.'

'If things get any worse, you must let me know. Or just run to Mum. She'll be glad to take you in.'

'I'll be all right.'

'Keep in touch, promise? There's a phone at the stables. If you don't, I'll be coming round to check on you.'

'I will, I promise.'

He kissed her cheek. 'You really have got guts.'

Dinah climbed on the bus and sank on to a seat. She felt better now she'd confided in Tim. She'd find the strength to keep her end up in front of Richard. She expected to find him in the garden on this hot evening, but as she let herself in the front door he came rushing to meet her.

'Where have you been till now? I've been worried stiff.' He was agitated.

She said as calmly as she could, 'I had a terrible day. I went to four different companies trying to drum up more orders but had no luck at all. They didn't want to know.'

'I told you it wasn't easy. Give it up. There's no need to let those fools brush you off as though you're an idiot.'

'It wasn't meant as a personal insult,' she said, 'so there's no need for me to take it that way. It's just that they don't want our ribbons. I'll have another go tomorrow.'

He seemed surprised. 'Will you?'

'Then I went to Walton to see Aunt Enid. I don't want her to feel I'm ignoring her, I told you I felt guilty about not going, didn't I?'

'Yes.'

'Tim was there.' She told him about Tim's injuries. 'It quite bucked me up to see them. I must go more often. Have I got time for a bath before supper? I feel so hot and sticky.'

Dinah didn't hurry. She lay back in the bathwater and thought of Tim. Seeing his concern for her and confiding in him had changed everything for her.

Of course she didn't love Richard. How could she, now? Perhaps it had been infatuation from the start. He was wily; he knew how to charm people into believing he loved them. She was sure now he had set out to trap her. She'd believed he loved her and she'd certainly believed she was in love with him. She couldn't trust him with anything. He told lies, he'd stolen her winnings, he could twist the truth to serve whatever purpose he had in mind. And that was before she took into consideration the murders he was said to have committed, and that he had no self-control when it came to money, no business sense and no common sense.

No milk of human kindness either. How could she love somebody who would put an old lady like Bunty out of his house, when she had lived there and worked for him for years? Dinah thought he had done that to get the nanny out of the way before his new wife arrived. He'd been afraid Bunty would tell her things he didn't want her to know. He thought only of his own ends. She didn't love him and couldn't even respect him.

Dinah had to admit now that she was frightened of him. What a silly fool she'd been to get herself in a mess like this. She wished now she'd listened to Enid, who had pleaded with her to take her time and be careful.

Tim was worth ten of Richard She could at least rely on him to do his best for her and trust him to tell the truth.

Dinah shuddered, feeling tears sting her eyes. But no, she mustn't give in to self-pity even though the future looked grim. She got out of the bath and reached for a towel. What could she do about it?

She must stay alert, not let him pull any more wool over her eyes. She couldn't see any way out of this hole but she'd dug it for herself. She didn't dare mention the word divorce to Richard.

Chapter Twenty-Two

THAT WEEK, THE schools broke up for the summer holidays, and when Dinah and Richard returned from work on Thursday Mark was in the garden with Nellie. It was another hot day, and they were drinking lemonade under the trees.

Richard sent Nellie to the kitchen to ask Mrs Banks for a tray of tea, and threw himself on to a chair. 'You got home all right then,' he said to Mark. He'd not suggested meeting him at the station.

'I took a taxi,' Mark told them. 'They make us bring most of our stuff home and I had a lot.'

Boarding school had changed Mark. He'd grown, and now looked a confident young man. Dinah could see Richard eyeing him approvingly.

'Where's your school report?'

'I put it on your desk.'

'Go and fetch it, there's a good lad. I want to see how you've done.'

Mark shot off and brought it back to his father. 'You're doing well,' Richard told him.

'I came top of the form in the end of term exams.'

'It's a very good report, both in the classroom and on the sports field. I'm proud of you.'

'Can I see it, Dad?' Mark read his teachers' comments hungrily.

His father watched him for a moment. 'Have you made up your mind what you want to do when you leave school?'

'Not yet, Dad.'

'You must know what you're good at, what you fancy doing.' Richard sounded impatient now. 'Would you like to train as a doctor? Or perhaps a lawyer?'

Mark handed his report to Dinah and said with a smile, 'You used to say you wanted me to take over the family business.'

Nellie came back with the loaded tea tray and put it on the table. 'Can I pour out?'

'What a pity, Nellie,' her father said, 'you didn't stay at that excellent school I found for you. They'd have turned you into a fine young lady.'

'Nellie's already a fine young lady,' Dinah murmured, helping herself to a biscuit.

The next morning, Dinah drew back their bedroom curtains before beginning to dress. 'It's going to be another hot day. Are you planning to take us all somewhere nice?' In Picton Street, everybody dreamed of taking a trip to the seaside in the summer.

'No, I'm happy at home.' Richard took a clean shirt from his wardrobe.

'What about the children? Don't they need a holiday from time to time?'

'I used to rent a chalet at Abersoch for a couple of months every summer. The nanny used to take the children away.'

'But this year? Now they don't have a nanny?'

She saw him pull a face. 'Mark's away at boarding school all year. To come home for a change should be holiday enough.'

'What about Nellie?'

'She's had her chance and turned it down. They're old enough to take themselves to the park or the swimming baths. You could take them into town and buy them new bathing suits and shoes. They always seem to need new shoes, and Mark's brought home another list of things the school thinks he needs.'

Both children came down for breakfast before Richard and Dinah left for work. Dinah suggested that one day she could take them on a ferry trip downriver to New Brighton, but Mark said he and Nellie were thinking of doing that today on their own.

Dinah was not sorry. At work she was planning a campaign to get more orders for ribbons, and at home she was still searching for any trace of strychnine that might still be here. And all the time her mind was struggling with doubts and worries about Richard.

He drove her home from work that afternoon and left his car at the front steps. They found Mrs Banks in the kitchen boiling the kettle for the tea they always had at this time of day.

'Did the children go to New Brighton?' Dinah asked.

'Yes. They said they'd had a lovely time. I gave them a packed lunch to eat on the sands. They came back an hour or so ago. Nellie's gone round to play with her friend Alice and Mark's out in the garden.'

'I told you,' Richard said, 'they could look after themselves. We'll have our tea in the garden today. We ought to make the most of this hot spell.'

'I'll bring it out,' Mrs Banks said.

Richard went upstairs to change and Dinah went out alone, to the garden furniture they left under the trees all summer. She sat back and closed her eyes, trying to relax. But she could hear voices and turned to see who they belonged to. Mark and Arthur Phelps were sitting side by side in deck chairs in the shade cast by the garage. Arthur was leaning towards Mark and they were deep in conversation.

Dinah pulled herself upright in her chair as she remembered that Ivy had said Mark was the son of Arthur's dead wife Esther.

'Here we are.' Mrs Banks placed the tray she'd brought out on the table beside Dinah. It bore a large teapot covered with a cosy and three cups and saucers. Richard had walked out behind her and chose to sit in a chair that faced the garage. Dinah poured their tea, fearful he'd be upset by the interest Arthur was showing in the lad.

When she'd asked Arthur about Richard's family he'd kept his mouth shut, but did Richard trust him to treat Mark the same way? She pushed a brimming cup across the table and held out the plate. 'Would you like a biscuit?'

Richard didn't reply. All his attention was on Arthur Phelps and she could see the storm clouds gathering on his face.

Richard had told her Myra was Mark's mother, though Bunty had said he'd told Myra a very different story when he'd married her. Had Richard seen that untruth as a harmless cover-up when Mark was a baby? A cover-up to hide an unforgivable lapse on his own part? But Mark was now in his teens and had been brought up to believe Myra was his mother, so the truth had become a secret that Richard would want kept hidden.

Suddenly Richard leaped to his feet. 'Mark,' he called, and waved imperiously. 'We're home. Come and tell us what sort of day you've had.'

Dinah twitched her chair round to look. She saw Mark give a cheery wave back, but continue to listen intently to what Arthur was telling him.

'Come and have tea with us, Mark.' Richard was getting impatient. Dinah took it that he was afraid Arthur would say more than he wanted him to. Was he worried about the effect the shattering news would have on his son? Or was it was his own loss of face he cared about.

'Pour a cup of tea for him,' Richard spat at her, then raised his voice an octave. 'Your tea's getting cold, Mark.'

The boy was getting slowly to his feet and saying goodbye. He smiled at them as he came across the grass.

'Hello, Dad,' he said, nodding at Dinah and pulling a chair round to join them. 'Arthur's been telling me such a sad tale about his wife. They didn't have an easy life.'

'What's that he's given you?' Richard barked.

'It's a model of Lord Kitchener riding a horse.' He held it up. 'Arthur thought I might like it. He thinks it's bronze. It belonged to his wife.'

Dinah saw Richard's lips tighten, and knew he'd found that ominous.

Later in the evening, Dinah went upstairs to the bathroom to wash her hands and face. Richard was in the habit of having a drink in the sitting room before supper, and although Dinah drank no alcohol these days, he liked her there with him. She was glad her pregnancy gave her a good excuse to say no to the glasses of sherry and brandy he handed out. She couldn't banish her suspicion that he might have kept some of the strychnine that had poisoned Myra to use on others. Dinah feared for herself now.

As the original tin of strychnine had been kept in the gardening store, she'd already gone very carefully through the countless tins and packets of preparations used to combat garden pests like slugs and aphids. She'd done the same thing with the tins of oil, grease and polish on the dusty shelves in the garage. She didn't find what she was looking for, but she couldn't be entirely sure it wasn't there.

It occurred to Dinah now that one place she hadn't yet looked for any strychnine Richard might have saved was in the bathroom cabinet. She opened up its two doors. The shelves and drawers inside were filled with half-used bottles of medicine and jars and tubs of pills. She recognised aspirin but started opening others. The trouble was she didn't know what strychnine looked like and wasn't sure she'd recognise it if she saw it. She almost jumped out of her skin when Richard came quietly up behind her.

'What on earth are you looking for?'

There was a familiar bark of anger in his voice. Was he afraid she'd find something he wanted to keep hidden? She couldn't be sure, but she couldn't be sure of anything about Richard any more.

As she searched for a reply her gaze settled on a tin of talcum powder. 'I thought I'd turn out some of the things my mother used,' she said. She'd been using the talc. Its scent reminded her of Mum and was a sort of comfort.

'Joan threw out all her stuff, surely?'

'Not quite all,' was the best she could manage as she stuffed half-used tubes of ointment back into a drawer.

'You could throw most of that stuff out too.'

She followed him down to the sitting room and he poured himself a glass of sherry. Mrs Banks came in bringing a jug of home-made lemonade and some glasses.

'Is Nellie home yet?' she asked. 'She usually takes Arthur's supper over for me.'

Mark was reading in the window seat. 'Not yet,' he said. 'I'll do that tonight.'

Dinah couldn't help but notice Richard didn't like that. 'Be back in time for your own supper, Mark; we don't want to be kept waiting,' he said sternly, gulping all the sherry in his glass and turning to refill it.

Nellie came dashing in to help herself to lemonade. Her cheeks were pink, her eyes sparkled and her blonde hair was windblown. 'Alice has got a new puppy.' She was excited. 'It nearly got away, and we had to chase it.'

'I was wondering where you'd got to,' her father said. 'I want you back earlier than this. Before you drink that, go upstairs, wash your hands and tidy yourself up.'

When they'd finished eating, the children headed out into the garden again. Dinah followed. The heat of the day was going. 'The scent of the roses is heavenly tonight,' she said, 'I think I'll pick a few to take indoors.'

'I'm going to see Arthur,' Richard said, and strode purposefully towards his flat. Dinah got a pair of secateurs from the kitchen and was cutting a few of the best blooms when she heard Richard's voice shouting angrily at Arthur. She was on her way back to the kitchen when he overtook her, saying, 'He doesn't feel at all well. I think I'll ring Dr Jones and ask him to call and see him in the morning.'

When she took the vase of flowers to the sitting room, he was using the telephone in the hall to do it and later on she removed Arthur's plate from the top of the phone book with much of his dinner still on it.

The next morning Dr Jones rang Richard when Dinah happened to be in his office. 'Is he all right?' Richard asked. 'He seemed a bit down.'

When he'd put the phone down, he said, 'According to the doctor, Arthur says he wants to go into a home, but Dr Jones told him he was better off in his own flat with all the help he's getting now. He's left him a tonic. He says he's all right really, but his arthritis is bothering him and he's got a weak heart.'

Dinah wondered if Arthur was now scared of Richard too and wanted to move further away from him; certainly Richard would want him to stay here where he could control him. Arthur knew too much, and it sounded as though they'd fallen out last night.

That evening after supper, they were listening to the nine o'clock news on the wireless, when it was announced that Adolf Hitler had become the German leader and henceforth he'd be known as their

Führer. 'The Nazis are becoming more powerful,' Richard said. 'It makes me nervous. There was an article in today's paper suggesting that Germany is rearming for war. I do hope it's just a rumour.'

Dinah was doing her best to get new orders to keep the ribbon machines working. The next day she went to see Mr McKay again.

'You did well young lady,' he told her. 'I couldn't fault the ribbon you supplied and you delivered it early.' He gave her another, larger order. 'Keep it up,' he said. 'You're doing fine.'

But what really pleased her was that using Myra's old records she'd targeted four companies making baby clothes and two had responded with orders for narrow pink, blue, and white satin ribbon. Dinah left the factory early, called in at Dawstone's to order the thread she'd need, and then made her way to a driving school she'd seen advertised and booked her first lesson for the following week.

She went home on the bus. She knew she'd had a successful day and ought to feel jubilant, but inside she was still quivering with nerves. She couldn't banish Myra's awful death from her mind, or the fear that her mother might have been poisoned too. It was still only mid-afternoon when she got home and it was another lovely sunny day. She took a book out into the garden. She meant to try to switch off for an hour or so before Richard came home.

She'd hardly settled under the trees when she saw Mark cycle past to the garage. He was an athletic lad, who had a sensible side to his nature. On the way over to the house, he called, 'Dinah, would you like a glass of lemonade?'

'Yes please.'

Five minutes later he was back with a jug and two glasses. He looked hot and tired and threw himself on to another chair.

'How's Arthur today? Is he feeling better?'

'I don't know.' Dinah felt guilty that she hadn't asked Mrs Banks.

'He's usually outside in nice weather. I'll pop over and see him now, before Dad comes home. He doesn't like me talking to him.' So even Mark had noticed that. 'He was telling me he used to grow orchids. He knows everything there is to know about gardening.'

Dinah watched him finish off his lemonade and push himself out of the chair. She opened the book she'd brought but had hardly read a paragraph before Mark came hurtling back to her. He was calling out before he reached her.

'He's dead, Dinah! At least I think he is. He's flat on the floor, fallen off his chair. What can we do?'

She came out in a cold sweat. Her book fell to the grass as she leaped to her feet. 'I'll go and phone the doctor and ask him to come.'

Mark followed her at a distance, and listened white-faced from the front door as she spoke on the phone. It was the doctor's wife who answered.

Dinah could hear fear crackling in her voice as she tried to pass on to Mark what she'd been told.

'It seems Dr Jones is out on a visit, but his wife's expecting him back soon. She'll get him to come here as soon as he gets home.'

'But that might be ages.' That was exactly what Dinah had thought. 'What if he isn't really dead? What if . . .'

She could see Mark trembling. For heaven's sake, he was only fifteen. Dinah pulled herself together. 'Go and sit under the trees again. Pour yourself another glass of lemonade. I'll go and see if there's anything I can do.'

She headed towards the garage. Perhaps Mark was mistaken, perhaps Arthur wasn't dead. Perhaps he needed help. She had to pull herself up the steep stone steps to the flat above. The front door was standing open. She'd never been inside before, and had to force herself over the threshold.

She was in a small living room that was stiflingly hot. She caught her breath as she saw his body in a twisted heap on the floor. She crept nearer. Yes, he was dead. There was no doubt, though the only other dead person she'd seen was her own mother.

Arthur's face was distorted in a terrible grimace and there was froth round his lips. It looked as though he'd been writhing in agony.

Dinah took a step backwards, feeling sick. There was a tumbler on the table with some sediment left at the bottom, and beside it a small tin half full of a white gritty powder. Its label was half torn off, and she had to bend her head to read it – Epsom Salts. But was it? What did Epsom Salts look like?

She could feel the perspiration coming out on her forehead. Was this the strychnine she'd been looking for? Was this another death by strychnine poisoning? If it was, it was surely proof that some of the large tin meant to keep moles under control had been kept after Myra was poisoned.

She took a deep breath. Did Richard have anything to do with this? Some time ago, she'd thought he was being kind to Arthur by providing help so he could remain here in his own home. But had he wanted to keep him here for less altruistic reasons? Perhaps he no longer trusted Arthur to keep his secrets. Perhaps he had fallen out with him and knew Arthur wanted revenge?

But now Arthur was suddenly dead. If Richard had helped him die, then he'd have had the poison available when her mother died.

Dinah felt her skin crawl with horror. She rushed out of the flat and skidded down the stone steps.

CHAPTER TWENTY-THREE

DINAH SHOT ACROSS the grass in a state of panic. Nellie had come home and was standing with Mark under the trees. He had his arm round her shoulders and they were both watching her.

'He's dead.' She knew she sounded a little wild. 'There's nothing we can do but wait for the doctor.'

Bile was hot and bitter in her throat, and she was afraid she was going to throw up. She ran on into the house and up to the bathroom. She bolted herself in and began empty retching over the lavatory. How long did it take her to realise she wasn't going to be sick? She filled the washbasin with cold water and splashed her face with it, over and over.

If that powder was strychnine, she must make sure the police knew about it. If Richard was responsible for all these deaths, he must not be allowed to get away with this one too. Wasn't this what she'd been afraid of, that he could go on to kill others?

Her mind went back to the night before last when she'd seen Richard watching Arthur talk to Mark. Hadn't he tried to separate them? Hadn't she believed then he was afraid of what Arthur might be telling Mark? It had made him agitated.

Nellie was banging on the bathroom door. 'Dinah? Are you all right? The doctor's here.'

So soon! 'Isn't your father home yet?'

'No.'

'All right, I'll be right down.'

Hurriedly she dried her face and ran down after Nellie. Dr Jones was in the hall listening to what Mark had to tell him.

'I'm sorry to hear this, Mrs Haldane. Your husband was fond of Arthur.'

'Shall I take you over to his flat to see him?'

'Are you sure? I mean, I could go alone. I don't want you upset, not in your present condition.'

'I'm quite all right,' she said as briskly as she could. She had to be if she was to make sure this death wasn't glossed over as being of natural causes. 'I've already been over to see if there was anything I could do for Arthur.'

'Right then.' The doctor picked up his black bag. Dinah felt her nerves were barely under control as she walked back across the grass with him.

'I saw him only yesterday,' he said. 'I knew his heart was weak.'

Had Richard deliberately called him out yesterday, knowing it would make it seem like a natural death? Dinah had to speak up now.

'Mark had a long talk with him the day before and Arthur didn't mention that he felt ill. He was reminiscing. Recently he's been sitting outside enjoying the good weather.'

'He was eighty-seven, and with his underlying heart condition, Mrs Haldane, I knew he might go at any moment.'

Dinah felt hot with suspicion, while it seemed Dr Jones had already made up his mind that this was a natural death. They went into Arthur's cramped living room.

'There's something that bothers me,' she said, knowing she would have to make a fuss to have her worries taken seriously. 'It looks as though Arthur swallowed a dose of this powder just before he died. Do you think it could have hastened his death?'

'Not Epsom Salts.' The doctor picked up the tin and sniffed at it. 'He's had this a long time – the tin's very old. They're usually sold in crystal form, aren't they?' He paused to think. 'But . . . Now you mention it, it doesn't look as though he had an easy death.'

Dinah was twisting at the neckline of her dress. 'That's what I thought.' The voice didn't sound like hers. 'Is that powder really Epsom Salts?'

He sniffed at it again.

'Don't forget Richard's first wife died of strychnine poisoning.' She felt as though she was betraying him. He would see that as unforgivable.

'Did she?' The doctor was alarmed. 'Was it . . .'

'It was thought to be suicide. They kept strychnine here for killing moles in the garden.'

The doctor looked at her sharply, his eyes shocked behind their heavy-rimmed spectacles. 'And Arthur was his gardener? It does look as though he might have been having convulsions.'

Dinah caught her breath. 'Is that what happens? In strychnine poisoning?'

He was deliberating. 'Perhaps I'll ask the police to take a look before we touch anything else.'

'Yes.' Dinah was relieved she'd made her point.

'I need to lock up the flat.'

She found Arthur's front door key on the mantelpiece and watched the doctor lock up and put the key in his pocket. 'How long ago was it that Mr Haldane's first wife . . .'

'Shortly before Christmas.'

'I see. I don't know your family,' he said. 'I've only recently begun attending them.'

Dinah shivered. 'I've only recently married into it.'

Mark was waiting outside, wanting to hear the outcome. Nellie was twenty yards behind him. They followed the doctor back to his Morris Eight while he told them as gently as he could that he thought Arthur might have hastened his own death.

Dr Jones had been gone only a few minutes when Richard came home. The children tore after his car as he drove past them to the garage. They were were agitated and upset, words bubbling out to tell him what had happened.

He came striding over to Dinah, who had collapsed on one of the chairs under the trees. She could see he was incandescent with fury.

'You should have waited. You had no business to call out the doctor. You should have left this to me.'

'Where were you? You should have been here,' she said, but he was already striding into the house. The children came to sit with her. Nellie was holding her hand when they saw Richard come out again and rush over to Arthur's flat. He raced up the steps and let himself in.

'He must have spare keys,' Mark said, aghast.

'He shouldn't go in, should he?' Nellie sounded horrified.

Dinah was consumed with terrible suspicion. She felt ready to swear now that Richard had poisoned Arthur. Over the next hour, he ranted and raved at everybody and everything, but Dinah felt it was aimed particularly at her.

The children were subdued and she was frightened but it didn't stop her saying, 'I hope you didn't touch anything in there.' That had brought another tirade of rage down on her head.

Two policemen had arrived after what had seemed a long wait, a sergeant and a constable.

'Leave this to me,' Richard instructed his family, going outside to the police car. 'I will handle this.'

They watched from the front door. It seemed the policemen wanted to view the body on their own but they were not able to prevent Richard from accompanying them.

'This is my private property,' he'd bellowed. 'I decide who goes in, not you. Kindly come this way.'

But then he had to bring the policemen to his study, where he was unable to stop them speaking alone to Mark who had discovered the body and Dinah who had seen it and called out the doctor. He fumed and fretted in the hall.

Dinah learned that Richard had made no secret of entering the flat after the doctor had locked it up and that the white powder and the dregs in the tumbler had been removed for analysis. If it proved to be anything sinister then an inquest would take place. In the meantime the body was to stay where it was, and Richard had been forced to give up his spare key. He said to Dinah, 'They think it might be suicide.'

None of them wanted to eat but at seven o'clock on the dot, their usual supper time, Richard led the way to the dining room. Tonight it was steak and chips, Richard's favourite, but even his appetite was ruined.

In her mind's eye, Dinah could still see Arthur's body twisted on the floor and the awful grimace on his face. She was dreading hearing that the white powder was strychnine, and that his death was the second suicide on these premises by poisoning within a year. She could feel herself coming out in a cold sweat. The coincidence was too great, especially with the car accidents that had happened before. How could she not suspect it to be murder? How long would it take the police to suspect that too?

Dinah was also dreading bedtime. She cringed when she thought of Richard kissing and fondling her. She didn't think she could even touch him.

She went to bed early, leaving him in his study. She couldn't sleep, but she pretended to be sleeping when he finally came upstairs. He switched on all the lights and banged about opening cupboards and drawers, making it impossible for anyone to stay asleep. She gave what she hoped sounded like a drowsy grunt, turned over and pulled herself to the edge of the bed, away from him. The bed springs sank as he got in and she waited for his strong arm to pull her back towards him. Instead he gave a soft snore. She could smell alcohol on his breath. She need not have worried; he didn't want to make love tonight. The evening's events had put even Richard off sex.

Sleep evaded Dinah. She was still seeing Arthur's twisted body writhing on the sisal matting of his living room floor. His death had been truly terrible. Not only had he died alone, but it looked as though he'd died in agony. She was sure the white powder must be strychnine, which made it all the more likely that Richard had hurried her own mother's death in the same way.

No it didn't. She listened to a nearby church clock striking midnight and thought about it. Mum's death had been very different. She'd died peacefully, just slipping quietly away. Hadn't the doctor said strychnine poisoning would cause an agonising death with convulsions? She'd ask him about that again next time she saw him, but she was almost sure she'd been tormenting herself for nothing. And suspecting Richard of a most heinous crime when he was innocent. The more she thought about it, the more certain she became that he'd not hastened her mother's death with strychnine. What was the matter with her? She'd been telling herself she was in love with him until recently. Was she or wasn't she?

Richard's temper became more volatile over the days that followed. He often walked about muttering to himself and didn't seem to care that he was seen doing it at work.

Dinah did her best not to upset him. She explained that she wanted to concentrate on getting more orders to keep his factory busy, and he'd agreed that she should hand back the payroll work to Miss O'Marney.

It helped that she was out and about quite a lot and Richard no longer expected her to be always at her desk. She worked hard, and slowly but surely she was succeeding in getting orders. More of the ribbon machines were in use now and she'd started looking for button orders too. Now that she was being paid, she'd booked a twice weekly driving lesson.

After the first one, she wondered whether she'd done the right thing. She didn't feel she had any talent for it. But after the second she thought she might master it in time.

'You should have left it until after you've had the baby,' Richard told her. 'It won't be long before you're too big to get behind the wheel of a car. Anyway, I'm not sure it's safe for you to be doing it now.'

Mark had returned to school before the inquest was held. Richard told Dinah she didn't need to go either.

'I'd like to,' she said. 'I think I could spare an hour; I'll slip in if I can.'

It meant she had to find her own way there on the bus, but Dinah thought it was a good thing for her not to rely on Richard. She hoped she wasn't imagining it, but it had occurred to her that his attitude was changing; that he was beginning to accept that he couldn't dominate her as he had Myra. She put it down to the work she was finding for the factory. He still wouldn't tell her how much profit it was making, but she knew it must have increased. The atmosphere amongst the girls was changing too, since they no longer expected to be sacked at the end of every week. They could see there was work for them to do.

The day of the inquest was cold and wet. Dinah was late getting to the hall where it was being held and found there were very few people there. She could see Richard sitting on the front row, but she slipped into a seat at the back.

Dr Jones was giving evidence. He told them that Arthur was terminally ill with heart disease and frequently breathless and in pain. He was low in spirits and rather depressed. He'd been retired from his gardening job for over twenty years but his employer Mr Richard Haldane had allowed him to stay in his flat and had provided the help he needed to live there. Now he could no longer potter round the garden, he was bored and lonely, and he felt he was a burden on Mr Haldane.

The summing up made the legal position very clear. Arthur was in possession of strychnine which he'd used to eliminate moles from the garden in which he was employed, and he'd self-administered a large dose of the poison to end a life he no longer found tolerable.

The coroner came out strongly on the need for greater care to be taken with dangerous substances. It was the fact that Arthur had signed the register at the chemist's shop some years earlier and that his circumstances had changed that prevented any further suspicion from falling on Richard.

So there had indeed been two cases of suicide by strychnine poisoning on the premises in a short space of time. And Dinah couldn't be certain that Richard had had nothing to do with it.

She told herself she must not allow her imagination to run away with her. The legal position was that Arthur had not been murdered. It looked as though she'd frightened herself unnecessarily over the old gardener's death.

When everybody stood up to leave, Richard saw her. 'You came after all?' He looked pale and stressed. He'd been frightened too.

'Yes. I wanted to know the verdict,' she said.

'It was what was expected.' He sounded testy. 'And I could have told you.'

She didn't trust him to tell her the truth, but she couldn't say that.

It was lunch time. 'How about taking me out to lunch?' she suggested. 'I fancy one of those long hotel lunches that you often have. We could both do with a chance to talk this over, couldn't we?'

'I'm too busy today,' he said brusquely. 'I want to go out to Tarporley to check on the horses. Anyway, it'll all be in the *Echo* tonight.' He was looking into her eyes. 'I didn't murder him, Dinah, if that's what you thought.'

That took her breath away. She didn't know what to say, but she felt a chill of foreboding run down her spine. He knew what she was thinking: that she suspected him of murder, and probably more than one. Her stomach was churning. He'd been cleared of any involvement, but the inquest had left him very stressed. Was it just that he was clever enough to stay ahead of the police? How she wished she could trust him.

'Come on, I'll take you back to the factory. We'll share Mr Banks's sandwiches.'

Richard went out shortly after they'd eaten and left Dinah wondering just how much time he did spend with his horses. She'd arranged to have a driving lesson at three o'clock that afternoon, and her instructor came to collect her. When she went outside his Morris Cowley was parked at the kerb and he was sitting in the passenger seat. He had a lot of grey hair with a fresh schoolboy complexion. His dark eyes darted everywhere and missed nothing.

'Good afternoon Mr Poole,' she said, getting nervously in to the driving seat. Dinah didn't feel all that confident, but after her last lesson, Mr Poole had congratulated her on her double declutching, so she must be making progress. She tried to remember everything he'd told her and managed to move off smoothly.

It took every ounce of her concentration. She drove exactly to his directions and was not really aware of what part of the city she was in. He tended to take her out to the quieter suburban streets though he'd promised that her last couple of lessons would be in Liverpool's busy shopping area.

'If you'd learned to drive last year you wouldn't have had to take the test,' he explained to her. 'But since last March, everybody who starts to learn is going to have to, to get a licence. Still, another few lessons and you'll be fine, I'm sure.'

Mr Poole made Dinah practise emergency stops, back into side streets and turn the car round. Then he directed her through some traffic lights and into a busier road, and said, 'I want you to reverse behind this stationary car and park at the kerb. You were fine on that last time. Let's see if you remember what I told you.'

Dinah was half aware that the car was a Riley of the same type as Richard's, but she'd backed the Cowley into position, run it forward to straighten up the wheels and put on the handbrake before she looked up and found herself staring at the number plate. The car ahead of her was Richard's!

'Where are we?' she gasped.

'Not far from Crosby.'

She'd parked in front of a newsagent's in a parade of small suburban shops, the sort where the proprietor lived in the flat above. Next to it was a café with gold lettering on the plate glass window telling her it was called the Olive Grove. Richard's car was parked outside, but what was he doing there? He'd eaten his share of their sandwiches today and told her he was going to Tarporley this afternoon.

She looked again at the café. Its gauzy curtains were looped up and she could see large potted plants inside that screened off the interior. There was a price list displayed on the door, showing that afternoon tea cost one shilling and threepence. It didn't look the sort of place Richard would patronise.

An elderly man with a shopping bag walked past the car and went further along to a grocery shop. Two plump ladies pushed open the café door and went inside.

'What's the name of this road?' she asked.

Mr Poole was looking at her rather strangely. 'Erm, Longmoor Road. Why?'

She shook her head. 'Nothing.' She didn't want to explain; she needed time to think this out. 'Which way now?'

She didn't know how she got through the rest of her lesson. On the way back to the factory she went to pieces and drove quite badly, but when she'd calmed down and was safely back at her desk, she felt she'd made something of a breakthrough. How many times had she wondered where Richard went to almost every day? She'd imagined he was living it up in expensive restaurants, but it seemed he might be at that café in Longmoor Road.

When he returned just before closing time, she asked, 'How are the horses?'

'Very well,' he said with a smile. 'Bob Watchit has entered Prince in the Melling Chase at Aintree next month. That's the main race of the meeting.'

Dinah was holding her breath. That was very convincing. She almost told him she didn't believe him and why, but before she could he said, 'Bob says Prince is on top form. If he wins, he'll school him hard over the jumps all winter and try him in the Grand National next March.' March was when her baby was due; she'd have other things on her mind then.

'Come on, Dinah, are you ready to go home?'

She followed him out to his car, knowing he'd deliberately lied to her and knowing too she needed to question everything he told her in future. Her knees didn't feel strong enough to support her. He was her husband, he said he loved her, but she couldn't trust him to tell the truth about anything.

What was she going to do?

Chapter Twenty-Four

BACK IN THE office the next morning she looked for Longmoor Road on her street map. She'd been driving round Liverpool with Mr Poole with no real idea where she was going. She needed to be more on her guard with Richard. If Mr Poole didn't take her along the same route on her next lesson, she'd wait until Richard went out and then take the bus to the Olive Grove and see if his car was parked outside again. If it wasn't she'd go in and have a cup of tea. If it was . . . well, what she did would depend on how strong she felt. It would give Richard a shock to see her there.

But perhaps he went to several different cafés? He might have friends he didn't tell her about. As always with Richard she was full of doubts. There was so much she suspected but didn't know. It left her feeling shaky; she must try to find out more, get to the bottom of all this.

Richard was in a good mood that evening. 'How are you getting on with your driving lessons?'

'Fine,' she told him. 'I'm really enjoying them, but Mr Poole thinks I need somebody to take me out to practise.'

At the time that had sounded like a stumbling block to Dinah. She was afraid Richard would feel it was beneath him, and that even if he agreed to do it he'd lose patience with her and end up in a bad temper.

'What about now?' he said.

Dinah felt she had to show she was keen to have his help. She was quaking as she walked to the garage beside him and climbed into the driving seat of his Riley.

He started by pointing to each instrument in turn and explaining its use as though she'd never had a lesson before, but in a way she was glad of it, as it refreshed her memory and his car was a little different from the Cowley. He knew as much about driving as Mr Poole, and on the ten-mile drive round the suburbs she managed to follow his instructions sufficiently well to earn his praise.

'You could have taught me yourself,' she said, as she returned the car to the garage.

'Of course I could, but I thought it would take you much longer to learn than it has. You're doing quite well. Once you've got your licence it would be more convenient for you to drive yourself when you go out calling on factories. It would save you a lot of time and it would be less tiring, especially while you're pregnant.'

'There's nothing I'd like more.' She gurgled with delight. She'd been wondering if she dare suggest it to him, and was thrilled he'd brought it up himself. 'Could I use one of these cars?'

He seemed to consider it. 'They're old-fashioned now and not easy to drive. Cars are improving all the time. It might be better if I got you a new one, something small.'

'Marvellous.' Dinah was pleased as well as surprised, but since he'd taken her winnings she couldn't afford to buy one herself. For a moment she considered confronting him with the theft, but was too scared of his reaction even in his present good humour. 'Will you? I'd be absolutely thrilled if you would.' Ever since Tim had suggested she learn to drive, it had been her ambition to have a little car of her own.

'You're working hard and bringing in business. You deserve it.'

Dinah felt up on cloud nine.

During her next driving lesson with Mr Poole, she was directed past the same parade of shops twice. Both times she saw Richard's car parked outside. It couldn't just be that he went in there for a bite of lunch: he was staying on into the afternoon.

Later on in the lesson, Mr Poole made her practise the emergency stop. She was so quick he was thrown against the dashboard.

'Excellent,' he told her. 'And the brakes on this car are excellent too.'

Dinah had been having second thoughts about Richard's offer of a car of her own. She was afraid he might tamper with the brakes, as Ivy Cummins maintained he had on his father's car. She'd already made up her mind to discuss the subject with Mr Poole, and now he'd given her a lead in.

'Is there any way a driver can test whether the brakes on his car are working efficiently?'

'You've just done it,' he said. 'You choose a level road without traffic and do an emergency stop. Just stamp on the brakes as hard as you can. That will jerk it to an abrupt halt.'

'What if it doesn't? I'm a bit nervous about car brakes. My husband has relatives who were killed because the brakes on their cars failed.'

'Not recently?'

'No, just after the war.'

'There used to be accidents like that but it wouldn't happen with a modern car. In 1932, it was laid down by law that cars must have two independent braking systems, and they won't both fail at the same time.'

'But if my car failed to stop when I did an emergency thing, what should I do then?'

'Yank on the handbrake as hard as you can. That'll do it, Mrs Haldane. You don't need to worry about it.'

Richard took her out to practise again, and said, 'I read an article about the Austin Seven this morning. It sounds the sort of car that would suit you.'

'That's not a new design, is it?' Dinah was thinking about its brakes.

'No, it came out about ten years ago, but they've improved it since then and it's still a good little car.'

'It sounds just the thing. I'd like to read that article.'

When they got home, he shuffled through the magazines on the sitting room table. 'This is it.' He turned to the right page.

Dinah took the magazine over to the window, wanting to know about the car's brakes. She read that it had two independent braking systems and was one of the first cars to have brakes on all four wheels. It was described as the most popular car in Britain because it was one of the cheapest.

'It sounds great.' She smiled at him. The front wheel brakes worked on a series of levers and cables, and there were brake drums at the back, which the writer of the article didn't think were very efficient. Still,

Dinah thought she'd manage, as millions of other drivers clearly did. She was really looking forward to owning one.

She went to bed that night feeling on better terms with Richard than she had been for some time. His lovemaking was more passionate than it had been recently, but although she did her best to respond she simply couldn't. She told him it was her advancing pregnancy that was putting her off.

Richard went to sleep almost immediately but she lay awake beside him, wandering if it been a mistake to learn to drive. Ivy and Bunty had told her that Richard had already killed four people by tampering with the brakes on their cars. If that was the truth, he might well do the same to her, independent braking systems or not. There was little he didn't know about how cars worked.

She knew she was becoming more nervous. Slowly but surely, fear was playing on her mind until she could believe Richard capable of heinous crimes. She didn't feel safe when she was near him.

During another driving lesson, Dinah was instructed to go past the Olive Grove café once more and saw Richard's Riley parked outside yet again. This time she'd half expected it and therefore it didn't shake her up. None the less, it proved there was something he was keeping secret from her and that really bothered her. Why did he feel he had to hide part of his life from her? And what was it he was hiding? Could it be another woman? But if so, why had he married her? It didn't make sense, but then what Richard did rarely did make sense.

Surely any husband would want to introduce a new wife to his friends? He'd want her to share in his activities and pleasures, wouldn't he? But Richard didn't even want her to know he visited this place regularly. He'd never once spoken of it, and that made her uneasy.

Life went on as he dictated it should, but Dinah felt she must keep up with the friends and interests she'd had before she'd married him. She'd asked Tim not to telephone her because it would infuriate Richard, but she rang Tim from Richard's office almost every day around lunch time when she knew he'd be free to talk. Now she had greater contact with him she could visit Enid when she knew he had time off. Tim became a lifeline she clung on to. She confided her difficulties to him and felt stronger because she could talk about them, but his advice was always the same: get away while she could; Richard was dangerous.

Now the schools had gone back after the summer holidays, she made a point of doing something with Nellie at the weekends. She often went with her to Bunty's, encouraging Nellie to take small gifts with her: a few eggs or half a pound of butter from the larder, with a piece of cake or apple pie. Today, they had cut her a few flowers and a cabbage from their vegetable plot. Dinah was aware how little Bunty had and knew she'd be grateful for anything.

It was fine but blustery day, and rather than sit in Bunty's room Dinah suggested they go to the park. Now that she had entered her fourth month of pregnancy, Dinah felt she should be getting a layette together, and she asked Bunty what she would recommend.

'I don't think you'll need to buy very much at all. Deary me, no. If you get George Weeks to go up in the loft, he'll find cots and push-chairs, several prams, and high chairs too. Everything you're likely to need.'

'Is my pram up there, Bunty?'

'Yes, Nellie love, and I asked him to take the old rocking horse up when you said you were too old to play on it, so that's there too.'

'It'll all come in handy.'

'Dinah, the prams might seem a bit old-fashioned to you, but we only kept things that were in good condition. There's all sorts of clothes stored in the nursery cupboards, from first size for babies through to toddlers and bigger. The Haldane babies always had so many clothes they couldn't wear them all.'

'And there are baby toys in the cupboards too,' Nellie added.

Dinah had told Nellie that she would soon have a baby half-brother or sister and she'd asked excitedly whether Bunty would come back to Ardwick House to look after it. Bunty herself had asked the same thing.

Dinah was making a point of dropping in on Enid almost every week and having a cup of tea with her. When Enid showed her some white wool and a book of knitting and crocheting patterns that she'd bought, and asked her what she'd find most useful for the baby, Dinah invited her to Ardwick House one afternoon to look through the baby clothes and equipment in the nursery.

George Weeks had already been up in the loft and brought down the cots and prams that were stored there. 'I'll oil the springs and wheels for you,' he said, 'and with a bit of a polish they'll be fine.'

Nellie helped Mrs Banks with the polishing, and as they'd found two full-size cots Dinah let Nellie choose the one they should use. It was big and had mahogany rails. Dinah really liked the basketwork crib with its hood and rockers. It was odd to think that as a baby Richard might have slept in it.

When Enid arrived they started opening the nursery cupboards and getting the baby things out. Nellie came home from school in time to help. They found dozens of first-size nightdresses, some flannel and some cotton. There were flannel binders and napkins galore, both terry towelling and gauze.

They came across a long christening robe and several other long robes, some hand-embroidered, as well as smocks and short dresses in white, blue and pink. Nellie amused herself sorting the boys' clothes from the girls' and putting on one side anything that might be used for either.

The woollen garments had perhaps suffered most from the passing years: gossamer shawls and matinee jackets that had been beautiful but were now yellowing with age.

Enid and Dinah sorted out what needed to be washed again, and returned to the cupboards those items they didn't think would be used.

'I wouldn't buy much of anything else,' Enid advised. 'I'll start crocheting a shawl and Gladys is working on a matinee coat. Wait until the baby's born and then decide whether you need anything else.'

'I've already knitted a pair of bootees,' Nellie said. 'I'd like to try a bonnet. Mrs Banks said she'd show me how.'

'Lovely to see all these baby things,' Enid said. 'It takes me back.'

'This pram is enormous. It'll be very heavy to push around.'

'Dinah, it's just the thing to put in the garden so baby can have daytime naps in the fresh air.'

'You're right, and I'll have the pushchair,' Dinah said. 'Come down to the sitting room for a cup of tea.'

'Mrs Banks has made a sponge cake,' Nellie added. 'We're having that with chocolate biscuits.'

Enid was fascinated by the grand piano. 'I've seen them before, of course, though mostly in pictures or on concert platforms, but I've never played one.'

'Go ahead,' Dinah said. 'I play it sometimes, but I don't practise enough.'

'You never did,' Enid laughed as she pulled out the stool. Dinah lifted the lid and propped it open as Richard did for her.

'It's a very elegant piano.' Enid began to play and the room was filled with the tranquil sounds of Beethoven's Moonlight Sonata. In the middle of it, Richard came in and stood listening. He seemed both surprised and impressed.

'How did you learn to play like that?' he asked.

'My mother taught me. I play a lot, but not on a piano like this.'

'It was my mother's. She was very proud of it.'

'Enid teaches the piano,' Dinah said. 'I told you, she taught me.'

'It's a lovely instrument, but I'm afraid it's much in need of tuning now.' Enid smiled. 'I hope you don't mind me telling you.'

Richard looked at Enid with new respect.

Mr Poole told Dinah that he considered her to be a competent driver and wouldn't need any more lessons. Dinah was triumphant. 'What about that car you promised me?' she asked Richard.

'We could go to the garage tomorrow and order it.'

'It's as easy as that?'

He paused and rubbed his face with both his hands. 'Perhaps I should sell those old cars. It would make room in the garage for a new one.'

Dinah waited. Did he need to sell them to pay for the new Austin Seven? What had he done with her hundred and thirty pounds?

'Yes, I will,' he said. 'The Daimler belonged to my father. What's the point of having it standing there?'

'None at all.' Dinah was pleased. It seemed he was beginning to act more reasonably.

Ten days later, Richard drove her to the garage to pick up her new car. She had decided on the saloon model in dark red and black and it sparkled all over. Dinah felt thrilled with it as she drove it home. She wanted to be delighted that Richard was making an effort to stay on good terms not only with her but with everybody else. She wanted to be hopeful that all would be well, but she could not quite rid herself of the burden of black suspicion that for him it was all an act. She couldn't put the other life Richard must have at the Olive Grove out of her mind.

Now that she had her own car and Richard expected her to be out and about seeking orders, Dinah couldn't keep away from the Olive Grove.

She'd found there was a large factory some half a mile away from it that made uniforms for transport staff working not only for the railways but also for bus and tram companies. Before calling on the management with her button samples she drove along Longmoor Road. Richard's car was parked in its usual place, and it was still there when she returned.

Today, they were expecting her to call at the factory again with brochures and figures in order to discuss likely costs. She hoped to be asked to quote for the specialised buttons they needed, but she was still at her desk when Richard came out with his hat on.

'I'm just going out too,' she said, picking up her briefcase and walking out with him. 'I'm hoping to get an order from Teddington's.' He smiled, his mind on his own affairs. 'What are you going to do today?'

'I've got some people I want to see too.' He'd reached his car. 'See you later.'

Dinah got into her Austin Seven. Moments later, Richard overtook her and she made all haste to follow him. He was making no effort to hide the fact that he was heading towards Crosby and the Olive Grove, though he knew she would be going in the same direction. He wasn't being careful, so she decided he didn't suspect she knew where he was probably going.

She had to concentrate hard once she arrived at Teddington's. She was ushered into the manager's office and offered coffee, and when the time came to discuss buttons two more managers were sent for and faced her across the desk. She'd gone through the costings three times with Mr Hopper, so she felt reasonably confident when she talked about prices.

She was delighted when they asked for firm quotations for three of their own designs of brass-faced buttons. Taken together it was the largest first order she'd yet achieved. After nearly two hours at Teddington's, she motored down Longmoor Road and saw the blue Riley outside the Olive Grove.

So Richard had been here all that time. What on earth was he up to? She'd seen from her street map that there was a public library down here, and she had in mind to ask to inspect the electoral roll in order to see if she could find out who lived at 74 Longmoor Road. She found the library had just closed for lunch and wouldn't open again for an hour and a half. She went back to her car feeling frustrated, not wanting to waste all that time.

Her success at Teddington's had given her confidence, and she decided she felt strong enough to go in and face him. It would knock him sideways to see her marching in as bold as brass, when he thought he'd kept the Olive Grove a deep secret. She left her car where it was and walked back.

Yes, his car was still here. He would be inside tucking into a hot meal. How was she going to play this? She'd say it had surprised her to see his car outside; she certainly had been surprised the first time. She'd tell him she was hungry and thought she'd join him and give him the good news about her visit to Teddington's. As she walked past the window she tried to peep inside; she could see only that the place was busy. It made her hesitate. Don't get cold feet now, she told herself. Unless she went in, she'd never know why Richard was drawn here all the time.

She was met by hot savoury scents as soon as she opened the door. A bell above it clanged loudly, drowning out the buzz of conversation for a moment or two. She let her gaze travel from table to table as she searched for Richard. Then she gasped, unable to believe it. He wasn't here!

There was a small unmanned counter opposite the entrance with a door behind that. On the counter was a display of cakes and pastries under glass domes together with a cash register. Propped against the side of the latter was the incoming midday post. The top envelope was addressed to Mrs Olive Jennings, Proprietor of the Olive Grove Tea Rooms.

A pretty young waitress came out of a rear door with two plates of chicken salad which she served to customers at a nearby table. She came over to Dinah, smiling at her.

'For one? There's a vacant table at the back.'

The girl took a menu from the counter and led her over to the empty table. Dinah sat down feeling half dazed. So the proprietor was Mrs Olive Jennings. The name meant nothing to her, but had she heard it before? She wasn't sure.

The waitress looked the sort of girl Richard would take an interest in. Dinah followed her quick precise movements as she went from table to table collecting used plates. She was in her early twenties with dark curly hair, but was she also the proprietor? The kitchen door swung open and again came her ready smile.

'Are you ready to order?'

Dinah stabbed her finger at the menu. 'I'd like a soufflé omelette, please.' What on earth was a soufflé omelette?

'It comes with a side salad and bread and butter, yes?'

'Yes, please, and a pot of tea.' Once it would have given her great pleasure to come to a café and do this, but today her nerves were jangling.

The girl was off at the double and Dinah tried to collect her wits. Her table was in the back corner of the room, a good place from which to survey the customers. Apart from a couple of pensioners, they were all women, mostly middle-aged and middle-class. Not at all the sort of place where she'd imagined Richard would eat his lunch. She didn't have to wait long for the soufflé omelette. It was huge, and as light as a feather. The egg white had been whipped to a froth before it had gone into the pan. The meal was nicely served.

But where was Richard? It couldn't be him working in the kitchen; he never set foot in theirs at home except to complain. Anyway, the heaped plates were coming out too quickly and efficiently to be Richard's work.

Dinah only realised she was close to the wall cutting off the stairs when some few minutes later she heard footsteps clattering down. She heard Richard's voice and froze, holding her breath. It still had its whine of complaint. He came through the door behind the counter; she was glad her table was in a dark corner and out of his line of vision.

A customer was settling her bill and the young waitress was behind the counter taking the money. Richard spoke to her and Dinah thought he called her Rosanna, but she rang up the cash register at that moment and she wasn't sure.

Another woman had come downstairs with him. Dinah could see her now, tearing open one of the envelopes she'd spotted against the till, so she presumed it was Mrs Olive Jennings. She was about Richard's age or even older, and of a matronly build. She said goodbye to him and came weaving though the tables towards Dinah, making her stomach churn, but she was going to the kitchen. The door swung shut behind her.

Dinah had already decided the family lived upstairs, for she'd seen net curtains at the upper windows. Richard had been up to their living quarters. He was still behind the counter talking to the waitress. Impossible to hear anything he said against the hum of customers' conversations. Did he sound amorous? Hardly; she was letting her imagination running wild. She'd not suspected him of having another woman before. After all, he'd been impatient to get her, and he had a prodigious appetite for making love to her.

The waitress was collecting dirty plates again and Dinah heard the bell clang as Richard went out. She drained her teacup, relieved now that she'd not made a scene.

She'd give him five minutes to drive off and then be glad to go. What good had it done her? None at all; it had frightened the living daylights out of her and raised more questions than it had answered. She was glad to get back to the safety of her own Austin Seven.

Chapter Twenty-Five

DINAH HAD HEARD from Tim about the growing excitement in the stables as a big race day drew near, and she felt much the same was happening at Ardwick House. The October meeting at Aintree was getting closer and Richard couldn't stop talking about Prince. He was convinced that he had an excellent chance of winning and was always on the phone to Bob Watchit, wanting to know what the horse was achieving at practice.

On race days Dinah had to admit she felt a quickening of her own heart. She was taking care not to upset Richard; she hadn't forgotten what had happened before the Doncaster meeting and didn't want him to tell her she must stay at home.

The day came. At breakfast Richard was talking twenty to the dozen about his horses and was so full of anticipation he could hardly eat his eggs and bacon. Mrs Banks brought in some fresh toast and paused to ask after Ardwick Prince. 'George the gardener has put a bet on for me, half a crown each way. He's put five shillings on for himself.'

Richard smiled. 'We're very hopeful he'll win.'

'Dad, can I come with you?' Nellie asked.

'No,' he said impatiently. 'You're too young. They wouldn't let you in the owners' bar. If you're a good girl I'll take you when you're eighteen.'

Dinah was now driving herself to work, but this morning she went in with Richard as she always used to, because they only intended to spend two hours or so at the factory. Richard couldn't settle and did nothing but read the racing pages in the paper. Dinah felt she accomplished little herself. His restless mood had infected her.

As Aintree was only up the road, Richard had decided they would have lunch at home before going, but he was impatient and took Dinah home to change earlier than he'd intended. Although the housekeeper was setting out their meal on the dining table, he said, 'I've changed my mind, Mrs Banks. We'll have a light lunch when we get to the racecourse.'

Dinah could see the housekeeper wasn't pleased. She'd gone to some trouble and Richard seemed to be turning up his nose at it.

'More of a treat,' he said to Dinah.

She smiled at Mrs Banks. 'The pie looks delicious. Perhaps, Richard, we should have it tonight for supper?'

'We'll need a hot dinner by then. Don't forget you have to eat for two.'

Dinah changed into her pale green outfit, which still fitted, but only just. However, the coat was loose and she felt comfortable and smart in it.

Richard was very much on edge as he drove to Aintree, but when they arrived he discovered Ardwick Prince was favourite to win the Melling Chase and that really cheered him up. Dinah followed him to the owners' bar where he ordered smoked salmon sandwiches. She enjoyed them, but thought she might have preferred Mrs Banks's ham and veal pie. She sipped orange juice and listened to Richard praising his horse and his acquaintances detailing their hopes and expectations for the afternoon.

From the racecard, Dinah discovered there were to be fourteen runners in the main race, one of which was Flyswitch, ridden by Tim Reece. She had a feeling of foreboding. At Doncaster, Flyswitch and Ardwick Prince had raced against each other and Flyswitch had won. If Tim managed to win again, Richard would take it harder than if one of the other horses did.

Richard was so keyed up he could no longer sit still. 'Let's go to the stables and see Prince,' he said. He strode out so quickly through the crowd that she had difficulty keeping up with him. As they passed the ring, they heard the bookies shouting the latest odds. Flyswitch and Ardwick Prince were now joint favourites. It made the lines round Richard's mouth harden.

Dinah linked her hand through his arm and he patted it absent-mindedly. She knew she mustn't show any sign of support for Tim. If she did, Richard would count it as disloyalty to him. She didn't want him to take against Tim; already she felt he barely tolerated him.

'The fences look as high as houses from here,' she said.

'I believe they build them even higher for the Grand National.'

She felt a shiver of anxiety for Tim. She was keeping a close look-out for him, but trying not to look as though she was. Richard swept her into the stable yard. Two rows of horse boxes faced each other, and from many a horse's head looked out over the half-height stable door.

'Now where's Prince?' Richard looked round. 'Oh, there he is. Being a grcy he stands out.'

Dinah was being towed towards him when she saw Tim not much further along the row. He seemed to be whispering words of encouragement to Flyswitch and patting his neck.

Dinah was very surprised when Richard gave her a little push in Tim's direction and said, 'Why don't you have a word with your friend?'

She needed no persuasion: she'd been wondering if it would upset him if she went to say hello to Tim. When she greeted him, Tim turned away from the horse and gave her a little hug. 'Lovely to see you, Dinah. How are you?'

'Fine. Looking forward to seeing you race. How are you?'

'My stomach's full of butterflies. Always is before a big race.'

'I'll keep my fingers crossed.' She smiled. 'You know I wish you all the luck in the world.'

Only then did she realise that Richard had followed her and was on the other side of Flyswitch. At that moment, Patrick Skillen, one of Digby's grooms, shot the bolt on the lower half of the stable door and led Flyswitch forward.

'How is he?' Richard made the horse pause and was patting his shoulder. 'Still in good fettle?'

'On top form,' Tim said. 'He stiffens up a bit if he's kept waiting, so a turn round the yard helps.' He turned back to Dinah. 'Mum and I were talking about you only yesterday. She's got half Picton Street knitting for you.'

Suddenly, Flyswitch gave a snort of distress and reared up on his hind legs. Panic-stricken, Dinah jumped back from his flailing front hooves, her heart in her mouth. She saw Tim leap the other way, towards the horse.

'All right, Fly, what's the matter then? What scared you? Come on, old boy, you're all right.' He was hanging on to the horse's bridle. 'There's nothing to worry about.'

Patrick was trying to comfort him on the other side, grooms and stable boys nearby all looking on. Digby came over at the double. 'What happened?'

'I don't know,' Tim said.

'Something must have frightened him.'

'But Flyswitch is usually so placid. This isn't like him.'

Patrick was almost incoherent with shock. 'It was that man. He put the frighteners on him.'

'Come on, Fly. There's nothing to be scared of.'

'What's this on the ground?' Dinah asked, bending to pick up what she thought was a small strip of sponge. 'Was he frightened of this? Yuck, it's slippery.'

'My God!' Digby snatched it from her. 'Somebody's tried to nobble him! It's the oldest trick in the book. Stuff a bit of sponge up one of a horse's nostrils and the poor animal can't fill his lungs with air. He'd have been starved of oxygen and never have won another race. Who's been close enough to do this?'

'If he hadn't reared up, the rotter would've got away with it,' Patrick exclaimed.

Dinah had already missed Richard. It was as though he'd melted into thin air.

'Richard Haldane,' Tim gasped. He looked apologetically at Dinah. 'He was here a minute ago.'

'It was him,' the groom said. 'He took the bridle from me and asked for a curry comb. He said there was muck in his mane.'

Dinah felt all eyes turn on her, and she knew a blush was spreading up her cheeks. Richard was desperate to have Prince win, and this seemed exactly the sort of thing he would do. But to do it here, with all these people watching? He'd taken a huge risk, but then Richard was a risk-taker. This time it hadn't come off: he'd been seen. More people were crowding closer. Dinah turned on her heel.

'That's Haldane's wife,' she heard somebody say. 'Are you sure she wasn't deliberately distracting you?'

'No,' Tim's voice said firmly. 'She wouldn't.'

Dinah had to push her way through the crowd, and wondered where in this sea of people she'd ever find Richard again. She felt disorientated and wandered around aimlessly until it occurred to her that the owners' and trainers' bar was the most likely place for him to go.

She'd guessed right. Richard was there with a double whisky in his hand, his cheeks flushed and his manner agitated. He took her arm and led her to a seat in a quieter part of the bar. 'What were they saying?'

Dinah gave it to him straight. 'That you tried to nobble Flyswitch by stuffing something up his nose so he couldn't breathe properly.'

'How ridiculous! As if I would.' Richard's handsome amber eyes stared aggressively into hers.

'The groom said he saw you do it.'

'Nonsense, he couldn't have done.'

Dinah was angry. 'It was a stupid thing to do. In such a public place, too – of course you were seen. You think you can do anything and get away with it, but you can't.'

He was taken aback at her outburst. 'There was nothing to see, I tell you. I did nothing to that horse.'

Dinah knew he was lying. 'You used me. You pushed me towards Tim. You meant me to distract him and I did.'

It seemed Richard was trying to brazen it out, but he was more agitated than ever, up on his feet and pacing back and forth to the window. The bar had emptied; it was almost time for the first race.

'D'you want to go down to the paddock to see the horses being saddled up?' Dinah asked.

'What's the point? I haven't a horse running in this race.'

'Then let's go to our seats and watch it.'

Richard downed the last of his whisky and led the way. They were only just in time. All round them spectators had binoculars clamped to their eyes, and others were waving their racecards and roaring encouragement. Richard sat still, and Dinah shivered. For once the magic of the race didn't touch them.

'Ardwick Prince will win,' he insisted irritably. 'Everybody else thinks so too, otherwise why would he be favourite? Why would I need to nobble another horse?'

'Only you know that.'

'We'll go home,' he said. 'It's no fun today.'

'You go if you want to,' she returned. 'But now I'm here, I'll stay and see the big race. Don't worry about me. I can come home on the bus.'

Richard didn't go. He followed her to the ring where he placed a bet on Prince and Dinah put much smaller ones on both Prince and Flyswitch. They saw other races which left them cold, had afternoon tea in the restaurant and then went down to the paddock to see Prince being saddled up. Everywhere they went, Dinah could see people eyeing Richard and whispering behind their racecards to their companions. Bob Watchit seemed to be avoiding them, but Richard patted Prince and told his jockey he had every chance of winning. The horse was prancing round and and it was taking all the strength of his groom to hold him.

'He's rearing to win,' Richard said with great confidence. Dinah made no effort to speak to Tim again. He and Flyswitch were surrounded by well-wishers and stable staff.

By the time they took their seats, Richard had cheered up, and Dinah felt a tingle of anticipation. There was a false start, which kept everybody on tenterhooks, and then the horses were thundering down the course.

Richard screamed himself hoarse in his efforts to urge Prince over the jumps, but his good mood started to evaporate as other horses drew ahead. Flyswitch ran a perfect race and was first past the winning post. The crowd cheered and roared their approval. A horse called Tintangel took second place and Prince came in third.

'Not good enough,' his owner snarled.

'He's won a place,' Dinah said. 'He can't win every race he's put in for. Let's go to the winners' enclosure. You should congratulate Bob and the stable staff.'

'No, let's collect our winnings, such as they are, and go home. I think I might change his trainer. Bob Watchit should be able to get more out of him than this. He's a good horse.'

Dinah was considering going alone to the winners' enclosure, but by the time they'd queued for their winnings the cheering and clapping from there was dying down and the crowd dispersing. She went home with Richard.

'That was a disappointment,' he said. 'A miserable day's racing.'

Dinah didn't agree. She'd won on Flyswitch and was thrilled for Tim, but Richard sulked silently all the way home.

Dinah used her key to let them in the front door. They were met in the hall by an agitated Mrs Banks.

'Mr Haldane, the butcher didn't deliver the weekend order today. I rang him when it didn't come and he said his bills hadn't been paid these last few weeks and that he'd make no more deliveries until they were.'

Dinah saw Richard's face drop. 'Damn,' he said. 'I must have overlooked them.'

Dinah knew the cause was more likely to be shortage of funds, though, as usual, at the racecourse he'd been spending as if he'd come into a fortune.

'I'll get my car out and run down now,' she said. 'I'll pay him and pick up the order.'

'He'll have closed twenty minutes ago,' Mrs Banks told her.

'Oh! It'll have to be the veal and ham pie then,' Dinah said. 'A good job we didn't eat it at lunch time.'

'I didn't think you'd be back in time, so I asked George to go down on his bike and buy something. He knows a lad who sells rabbits and he got two for me. Sixpence each they were. I paid out of my own pocket.'

'Thank you. I'm very grateful,' Dinah said, feeling in her purse for a shilling. 'Let me pay you back now lest I forget. It was good of you to think of that.'

'Mr Haldane said he wanted a hot supper, not the pie and salad. One of the rabbits looked much older than the other, so I'm making rabbit pie with that and I'll roast the other for Sunday lunch.'

Richard liked beef for Sunday lunch. 'That'll make a nice change,' Dinah told the housekeeper.

Richard was fuming and snapped rudely, 'I don't eat rabbits. They're vermin. We'll have to change our butcher.'

'Mr Edwards is one of the best in Woolton.' Mrs Banks's chin had gone up. 'He has lovely meat, but every butcher expects to be paid.'

Richard's face was crimson. 'I'll not have you speak to me like that!'

'Well, Mr Haldane,' she said with as much dignity as she could, 'I can't stand any more of your bad tempers. I've had enough. I do my best but you're never satisfied. I'm not staying here to be insulted. You'll have to change your housekeeper as well as your butcher. I'll leave tomorrow morning.'

'Go now, this minute,' Richard spat out. 'Get yourself packed and go.'

'No.' Dinah felt she had to step in. 'Tomorrow will be more than soon enough. I'm so sorry you feel like this, Mrs Banks.'

'And I'm owed a week's wages. I'd be grateful if you would see to that, Mrs Haldane.'

'Yes, of course,' she said. 'I'll make sure you get what you're owed.'

'And I'd like a reference too, please.'

'Yes.' Dinah caught sight of a horrified Nellie sitting on the stairs. 'Yes, of course.'

'Mr Edwards sent several reminders about his bills. He left them with me when he delivered the meat and I put them on your desk, Mr Haldane.'

Richard turned to Dinah and said brusquely, 'I shall go out for my supper tonight.' He marched out, slamming the front door behind him.

'Oh, dear!' Dinah had known he was short of money, but not that he was so short he couldn't pay the household bills. And how ridiculous that he'd spent so freely all afternoon on luxuries and gone out for supper again tonight. He had no idea what thrift was, and that was another cause for worry.

Nellie came running down to her. 'What's happened? Didn't Daddy's horse win?'

'Prince came in third. Tim won on Flyswitch.'

'He wouldn't like that,' Nellie said. 'He wanted the prize money.'

'Yes.' He'd wanted it badly. Dinah had thought, by getting more work for the factory, she was making his business more profitable. Well, of course she was, but the income she brought in was not enough to support a lifestyle that included racehorses.

Richard had been in a foul temper ever since he'd failed to nobble Flyswitch. She was glad he hadn't got away with it: that was downright cheating, and cruel as well. She knew he'd be infuriated by Mrs Banks finding out he was short of ready cash, but it was all his own fault.

She and Nellie ate their supper at the kitchen table with Mrs Banks that night. 'The rabbit pie is delicious,' Dinah told her. 'I do wish you'd stay. Won't you think it over?'

'After Mr Haldane told me to pack and get out straight away? Certainly not.'

'He'll have changed his mind by now,' Dinah said.

She was reading in bed when Richard came home. He was banging about and throwing his racecourse finery on the chair when usually he hung it up straight away.

'Where did you go?' she asked.

'Out to get a decent meal.'

She wanted to ask if he'd been to the Olive Grove, but was afraid it would cause another outburst of rage. Instead she asked, 'And did you get one?'

'It was reasonable.'

'The rabbit pie was delicious. Mrs Banks is a good cook.'

He stopped undressing. 'You'd better tell her she can stay. It would save us the trouble of looking for someone else.'

'It's too late for that now. I've already asked her and she refused point blank. She's packed and says she's going to stay with her daughter.'

Richard shrugged. 'Then we'll have to find another cook.'

Dinah laid down her book. 'I've been thinking about that. Why don't we ask Bunty to come back?'

'That old hag? No, she's nearly eighty, and can't do much work any more.'

'She'd do a bit, and it would mean there'd be somebody here when Nellie's off school.'

'Nellie's old enough to take care of herself.'

'But what about the school holidays?'

'I don't like Bunty. Never did.'

'Nellie likes her. They're fond of each other, and as she worked for you for years don't you owe her something? You did the right thing by Arthur Phelps – why not her?'

'She didn't work for me for very long. She was with the Copthornes for much longer. Dinah, you could do a bit of cooking, couldn't you?'

'I thought you wanted me to work in the business?'

'Well, I did.'

'Now I'm going after orders and having a bit of success, I'm more use to you there, aren't I?' Dinah couldn't believe he'd risk losing the orders she'd fought to get.

Richard got into bed beside her and switched off his bedside lamp. 'Then I'll go to the labour exchange tomorrow and hire another cook-general,' he said.

Chapter Twenty-Six

After they'd had supper the following evening, Richard was reading his newspaper in the sitting room when the phone rang. Dinah answered it as she went through the hall, helping Nellie to clear the dining table. It was Bob Watchit. He enquired how she was keeping and then asked to talk to Richard. She called to him.

'I'll take it in my study,' he said as he swept past her. He didn't quite close the door, and as he was soon shouting Dinah was in no doubt as to the problem. It was shortage of money again.

'I know I'm occasionally a little late paying and I do apologise. With the pressure of my business, I have a lot on my mind, and I'm afraid I overlooked it. But I'll put a cheque in the post to you tonight.'

Nellie was on the way back to the dining room with her empty tray but stopped to listen, her eyes wide with surprise. She whispered, 'Has Daddy lost all his money?'

Richard continued to argue and was clearly reaching dizzy heights of frustration. Both she and Nellie jumped when they heard the phone slammed violently back on its hook. Dinah pulled Nellie towards the dining table and loaded the rest of the dirty dishes on to her tray. She'd known yesterday that the racing fraternity had turned against Richard. All the time she washed up, Dinah could hear him muttering furiously to himself and striding round the house banging doors.

He was like a bear with a sore head all through that weekend. On Monday morning, Dinah dropped Nellie at the school gates and drove on to work. Richard had not yet got there.

Miss O'Marney was opening the morning's mail and sorting it into two piles: matters that she and Dinah could cope with, and those that Richard, as manager, would want to know about. She put the latter on his desk together with an envelope marked *Private and personal.* Dinah had seen it and knew it was from Bob Watchit.

She was at her desk making appointments for visits she wanted to make later in the day when Richard stormed through their office and slumped at his desk. Within minutes, he was shouting for her. Dinah went in and shut the door carefully behind her.

His face was crimson, 'Just look at this, I always knew the man was useless.' He pushed the letter towards her. She sat down and read:

Dear Mr Haldane,
I was sorry to hear that you are not satisfied with the training we give to your horses. I assure you we do our best to bring every horse in our care to its full potential. I felt we were doing well with both Prince and Beauty and they were beginning to achieve success.

I think it would now suit us both if you found another trainer and removed your horses from my stable.

I attach copies of my stabling bills for the months of July, August, September and October and I would ask for prompt settlement and certainly before you remove your horses.

Dinah was appalled. 'You can't be so hard up you can't pay your regular monthly outgoings? First the butcher's bill, now this?'

'Don't pretend to be stupid. You know I can't.' He leaped up from his chair and crashed over to the window to thump on the sill. 'I can't. I just can't.'

'Richard, I knew you had cash flow problems, but with average care you could have prevented it from reaching this stage.'

'How?'

'Have you never heard of thrift? Everybody else has to live within their income; why can't you?'

He snorted. 'That's all right for the likes of you. The poor are brought up to be careful with the pennies.'

'And you've never had to? You've always had unlimited wealth to draw on? Hard luck, Richard, but it's all gone now. You've spent it on luxuries.'

'I've bought you a car. I gave your mother a home, and paid for her nurse.'

'Yes.' Dinah hardened her heart.

'You won money at Aintree.'

'So did you.'

'Less than I'd expected.'

'But you carried on spending like . . .'

'I want you to lend me what you won.' She felt her mouth fall open, and rocked back in her chair. 'I need it, Dinah. I've got to pay Bob Watchit off. He never did much for the horses. I need to find a better trainer.'

Dinah dropped her chair back on its four feet. 'No,' she said. 'No, you need to sell your horses. You can't afford them. Until you do, you'll have no money for anything else.'

'You've got to help me.'

He was no longer the all-powerful bombastic millionaire. Gone was the handsome face that made women's heads turn; now it was twisting with fury. And was that hatred she saw there too? It made her shiver, but she knew she had to stand firm on this.

'We've got to eat. I'll settle the household bills and apologise for your oversight.' But of course, he wouldn't pay them next week or the week after that. It would happen all over again. 'But only on condition that you leave all the ordering to me. I'll continue to pay the household bills from my wages until I get this business earning what it should. D'you agree to that?'

Richard looked beaten. He'd slumped down at his desk again and was supporting his head on his hands. 'Yes.'

She hadn't expected a crisis to blow up like this and didn't feel ready to deal with it. When Richard was gripped with fury she couldn't cut through it and make him listen. She had to say what was on her mind now, ready or not.

With all the authority she could muster, she said, 'Owning racehorses is a hobby you can't afford any longer. You've spent what you inherited from your own family. You've also run through the Copthorne fortune belonging to your first wife, and what have you got to show for it? Two racehorses that are running you into debt.

'Yes, you love racing. We all do. It's great fun, but it's taken your energy away from the business. You've taken no interest in that for years.'

'Buttons and ribbons.' His tone was derisory. 'I never did have much interest in them.'

'That's no reason to let the business run down. It used to make a good profit; you could have lived well on what it earned. Perhaps you still could.'

He lifted his eyes to hers. 'Could I?'

'Yes, but only if you get rid of those horses. You've got to sell them, Richard. There's no other way.'

She watched his expression change. 'There must be.' He was mutinous now. 'I'll not sell them.'

Dinah got to her feet. 'I'm going out.'

She needed to get away from him. She rushed through her office, picking up her handbag from her desk, and went out to her car. The cash position was even worse than she'd imagined.

In the following days Dinah did the cooking, helped by Nellie. Then Richard found a new cook-general and she moved in. Martha Foggerty seemed a jolly person and was Dinah's idea of what a cook should look like: she was as round as a barrel and had cheeks like dumplings.

She was not as light on her feet as Mrs Banks had been and not nearly so time-conscious. On weekday mornings, when he had got himself dressed and down to the dining room, nothing annoyed Richard more than having to wait for his breakfast to come to the table. He tried to hustle her.

'Mrs Foggerty will be all right once she's found her feet,' Dinah told him. 'She doesn't know what you like or even where things are kept.'

'I don't like her cooking much. The food's cold by the time I get it on my plate, and I like Yorkshire pudding with my roast beef on Sundays.'

'That's what she gave us.'

'Proper Yorkshire pudding, not those little things like fairy cakes. And the beef was tough. You didn't order the right cut.'

'It was what we usually have, sirloin. Just give Mrs Foggerty a chance. You did say her pastry was good.'

'We can't live on pastry alone.'

Dinah sighed. 'Don't keep losing your temper with her. You make her nervous and put her off.' But Richard couldn't control his temper any more than he could control his spending.

Dinah came home from work on Friday afternoon to find two suitcases waiting in the hall and Mrs Foggerty with her hat already pinned in place.

'I'm going, Mrs Haldane. I'm sorry to walk out on you but I wouldn't be happy here. I can't put up with your husband. He's always firing off about something.'

'I'm sure with time . . .'

'No, I've made up my mind. I'd like to be paid off, please.'

Dinah did so. Mrs Foggerty had lasted only one week.

When Richard came home, Dinah was in the kitchen cooking the vegetables and warming up a stew Mrs Foggerty had prepared for them. He was a little later than usual and stood in the doorway watching her for a moment. 'Why are you doing this?' he asked.

'Mrs Foggerty has gone.'

'Gone! For God's sake, why?'

Nellie came dancing back from setting the dining table. 'She thinks you don't like her, Dad.'

'Like her? She was here to work. Why do I have to like her? I hope you didn't pay her, Dinah.'

'I did,' Dinah was mashing potatoes, 'for the time she'd worked.'

'You shouldn't have! No wonder we're short of money, wasting it on the likes of her. Damn and blast, she walked out on us. She's the one breaking her agreement. We don't have to pay her for that.'

Nellie edged past him to pick up her ribbon doll, which she'd left on the kitchen table. 'She didn't think she'd be happy here, Daddy.'

'Surely she didn't expect us to make her happy?' he shouted. 'Don't be so ridiculous.'

Nellie cuddled Eugenie and patted her back realistically. It brought a further burst of irritation from her father.

'I do wish you'd stop playing with that stupid toy. Grow up, can't you? You're nearly nine years old, not a baby of four.'

Nellie edged it back on to the table, looking guilty. She would have scampered away except that he caught hold of her wrist and held it in a vice-like grip. 'How many times do I have to tell you? It's time you gave up childish things.'

Dinah could see Nellie's face crumpling in distress, and to distract him she asked, 'Richard, are you ready to eat?'

'No, I'm bloody not. How can I eat when you're both churning me up like this?' In a further burst of rage, he picked up Eugenie and hurled her at the pan rack. She bounced off the fish kettle with a gong-like boom and crashed to the floor in smithereens. Nellie let out a scream as she rushed to her.

'What did you do that for?' she cried.

'I should have done it long ago and got rid of the damn thing.'

'You've broken Eugenie.' Nellie was belligerent now, her face was streaming with tears. 'I hate you, hate you, hate you. You're the most hateful person in the world. Everybody hates you.' She opened her mouth and wailed with all the force of her lungs.

'You little bitch!' Richard roared and gave her a swipe across the cheek.

'Richard!' Dinah was aghast. 'Stop that!'

'Shut up, Nellie, can't you? You're howling like a banshee and it's getting on my nerves.'

'Nellie's mother made that doll for her before she died.' Dinah couldn't help but raise her voice. 'Her last gift and you deliberately broke it! How could you be so cruel?'

With a ferocious look in their direction Richard headed for the stairs. Nellie was gathering up the broken pieces. Dinah put her arms round her and tried to pull her away. 'Nellie, I'm afraid you'll cut yourself.'

'He did it on purpose,' she sobbed. 'He always hated Eugenie because Mummy made her for me.'

That caught in Dinah's throat. Did Richard feel guilty that he'd treated Myra so badly? Was that why he couldn't stand the sight of the doll?

'I might be able to mend her for you.'

'Can you glue all these little bits together?'

'No, that's not practical. We'll go out tomorrow afternoon and see if we can buy another doll like this. If so, you'll hardly know the difference.'

Dinah put the crinoline skirt up on a shelf, together with a couple of the larger pieces of the doll, then swept up the bits.

'I want us to eat supper now,' she said gently. 'Everything's ready. You can help me dish up, and while you put it on the table I'll run upstairs and tell your dad.'

Richard had calmed down and surprised her by joining them at the dining table. They were all a bit subdued.

'Don't you think,' Dinah broke the long silence, 'that it would be a good idea to ask Bunty to come back?' She saw Nellie perk up and concentrate on what they were saying.

'She's too old and too slow.' Richard was repeating his earlier objections. 'She's got no energy left.'

'At least we know she'll stay,' Dinah said. 'Mrs Parr does the heavy work in the house and she'll do a lot towards preparing the meals in the mornings.'

'Oh yes, Daddy, please. I'd like that and I think Bunty would too.'

'Well . . .' He was reluctant to please them. 'Oh, all right, do what you want. I suppose she's better than nobody.'

'Thank you!' Nellie was all smiles.

Dinah smiled too. 'Let's put these dishes in the sink, Nellie, then go round and ask her if she'll come back.'

'I know she will.' Nellie was eager. 'It's what she wants. I know it is.'

The drive gave Dinah time to wonder if she was doing the right thing. After all, Bunty was over seventy and Richard was not easy to live with.

'I'm used to him, love,' Bunty said when they asked her. 'I don't let him faze me. Anyway, he never comes near the nursery.'

Dinah loaded the back seat of her car with some of Bunty's

belongings, boxes she'd never unpacked containing books and pictures she'd had no room to put out.

'In the morning I'll ask Mrs Parr to get your room ready for you, and I'll fetch you on my way home from work in the afternoon.'

'Lovely.' Bunty was beaming with pleasure and Nellie was delighted at the prospect.

On the way home, Dinah said, 'Oh, Nellie, I forgot – I was going to take you out to buy a replacement for Eugenie tomorrow.'

'I'd rather you fetched Bunty home.' Nellie gave an excited little giggle.

'We'll get a doll another day, or perhaps I'll find time to look round myself while I'm in town.'

Later that night, after Nellie had gone to bed, Dinah took the remains of Eugenie down from the kitchen shelf to study the fragments. One of the larger pieces was from the doll's shoulders and the name of the maker was clearly marked. Good: she knew now what to ask for. She thought she'd probably find it in one of the large Liverpool department stores.

It had occurred to Dinah that there was plenty of room under the crinoline skirt to hide something for Nellie to find when she was grown up. Myra might have wanted to leave her something: a diary perhaps or some Copthorne keepsake. She'd surely realise Nellie would have countless questions she'd want answered.

The ribbon skirt had been fashioned over what appeared to be a lampshade frame, which had been fitted to a solid wooden base so it would stand firmly. Eugenie had been more an ornament than a doll. She could see there was no diary inside. Dinah smiled. She longed to know more about Myra, her life and her problems, but to imagine finding her diary full of intimate details had been a fantasy.

But hang on – she shook it. There *was* something inside. Richard was in his study, but might come out at any moment. She took the skirt to the little room where his mother had done her sewing and closed the door quietly. As she eased a soft satin pouch through the small hole that had fitted round the doll's waist, her heart began to beat faster. She untied the gathering cord and a pearl necklace, some earrings and three rings dropped into her hand. A beautiful diamond ring, a rather old-fashioned emerald ring and one set with tiny gems all round it given to show eternal love. Expensive rings and very pretty they were.

Dinah felt tears prickling her eyes: it was the emotional impact of coming face to face with Myra's jewellery. She'd have worn it and must have valued it. Perhaps it had been her mother's and she wanted to hand it on to Nellie? It told her one thing loud and clear: Myra hadn't trusted Richard to give it to their daughter. Did she expect him to sell her jewellery? Or possibly give it to someone else?

Dinah's own diamond engagement ring glinted up at her. It too was a beautiful and expensive ring. Soon she'd have a child to whom she might want to give it. She must take more care of it than she had been doing. Richard had helped himself to her winnings when she'd left them unattended in a drawer, and he was more pressed for cash now. How Myra must have resented the way he'd ruined the Copthorne Ribbons business and run through her family's fortune.

Dinah deliberated whether she should give Nellie the jewellery she'd found or keep it for her until she was older. No, she decided, she'd buy another doll tomorrow, put the jewellery back where she'd found it and fix the ornament securely together. That was what Myra had decided and Nellie would be unlikely to bring it down where her father could break it again. Dinah could tell Nellie about the jewellery later if she wanted to, perhaps on her twenty-first birthday, but she had plenty of time to make up her mind about that.

At lunch time the next day, she went out and bought an exact copy of the broken doll, so that she'd be able to make a perfect copy of Eugenie for Nellie.

On the way home from work that afternoon she collected Bunty, but found herself wondering again if she was doing the right thing. Bunty was happy to come but in her shabby navy nanny's coat and felt hat she looked a frail old lady. Dinah felt she was making herself responsible for yet another person. Bunty might well need protecting from Richard: he made no secret of his dislike for her. Still, Nellie was overjoyed to have her back.

CHAPTER TWENTY-SEVEN

DINAH COULD NO longer understand why she'd been so attracted to Richard in their early days. She'd felt total fascination and they'd shared an instant rapport. But all that had disappeared when she'd got to know him better. She'd had to fight against his domineering ways and volcanic temper.

Yes, she was frightened of him when he ranted and raved, but she'd had to learn not to let him see that. She'd had to push fear behind her; she'd had to help herself and take control from Richard where she could. She'd had to use her wits to survive. Even with support from Tim, it was very wearing.

Over the following weeks, Dinah knew Richard was finding it difficult to get another trainer for his horses. He'd tried all those with stables in Lancashire and Cheshire that would be within reasonable reach. Several told him their stables were full and they couldn't take on any more horses.

She knew from Tim that he'd even asked Llewellyn Digby to take over Beauty and Prince. Only when he refused did Richard understand that no one in the racing world wanted to do business with him. Bob Watchit kept sending him bills.

'I thought he was a friend,' Richard complained to Dinah. 'He keeps asking if I have a date when I'm going to take my horses away, and he makes no effort to enter them in races any more.'

'To do that and take them to racecourses would mean he has to lay out more money.'

'I know that.'

'Well then . . .'

'But how do I know he's providing the exercise they need? If he isn't, they'll be losing form.'

'Pay his bills,' Dinah advised, making Richard snort with disgust.

He did find a young lad just setting up as a trainer near Southport willing to take them, but the facilities he had for his horses were not good. Richard thought Prince and Beauty deserved better, but it was either that or send them further afield.

'There are plenty of top class trainers around Newmarket, who hopefully won't have heard of this ridiculous vendetta the northern trainers have against me.'

But the distance meant he'd see less of them and the cost would be greater. Richard was trying to make up his mind.

'Sell them,' Dinah insisted. 'If you don't you'll be up to your neck in debt in a year or two.'

The racing journals were still being delivered and Dinah looked through them to see if it would be possible to sell his horses by advertising them for sale. Yes, he could, and there was even one advert seeking to buy racehorses. But her eye was caught by another possibility. She took the journal in to Richard. 'Have you thought of putting Beauty into a seller race? Here, look, there's to be one at Aintree in a fortnight.'

He read out, ' "A seller race over hurdles for fillies of three and four years of age. The winner to be offered for sale by auction immediately after the race." '

Dinah knew that would appeal to him. Beauty might win or she might not. She might be sold or she might not. Richard would find it easier to say yes to that than putting her up for sale in the normal way. He was a risk-taker and to him risks were a bit of fun.

'You're turning into a very bossy woman,' he told her.

'But you know I'm right.'

He told her later that he'd talked to Bob Watchit and Beauty was entered in the sellers' race. Richard grumbled continually that she was pushing him into doing something he didn't want to do.

'I'm not taking you with me on the day,' he told her. 'You'd give me no peace.'

'You'll get top price for her if she wins,' Dinah assured him. 'And even if she doesn't, I've heard that sometimes offers are made for the other horses too.'

When the day of Beauty's sellers' race came round Richard was more than edgy. It was to be run at three in the afternoon. Usually, when one of his horses was racing, Richard went to the course in time to enjoy a full day's racing.

Dinah spent the morning seeing two clients who had previously put in small orders. They were pleased with the service they'd received and each had given her a repeat order, not large ones but it was all business. She went back to the factory meaning to eat her sandwiches with Miss O'Marney, but Richard was still sitting at his desk.

'Aren't you going?' She was afraid he'd changed his mind and didn't mean to sell Beauty. If she won and received bids at auction, he had to be there to agree the price and sign her over.

'Of course I'm going.' He glowered at her. 'That's what you want, isn't it?'

Dinah tried to smile. 'I told Bunty not to make sandwiches for you. I thought you'd go to Aintree and have a nice lunch there.'

'No.'

'I'll share mine with you if you like. They'll keep you going until you get there.'

'What's in them?'

'Bloater paste with lettuce and tomato.'

'No thanks.' Richard wasn't even reading the racing pages. 'Get Gertie to bring me tea and biscuits, will you?'

Dinah went to the kitchen and made a pot of tea for two and added a plate of biscuits. Perhaps he was ashamed to go to the bar or restaurant at Aintree. He'd know he'd meet his racing acquaintances who would all have heard how he tried to nobble Flyswitch. Mixing with the leaders of industry and the aristocracy had made him feel he was as rich and powerful as they were, but now he'd feel they were looking down on him for cheating.

She took the tea tray into his office and sat down with him, opening up her sandwiches. She munched on the first one.

'They're really good, Richard,' she said. 'Try one.'

He did. It went down rapidly without comment, then he put out his hand and took another.

'We ought to think about hiring an accountant,' she said.

He shot her a look of black hate and said through straight lips, 'I do the accounts.'

'Yes, for the button side of the business.' She smiled. 'But I've been keeping the books for the ribbons. I've written everything down but I don't know even the basics about double-entry bookkeeping. We need to keep clear and proper accounts to know where we are.'

'Get an accounts clerk. We don't want any hireling to take control of our accounting.'

'I was thinking perhaps we do.'

'No. If you can't manage them, I'll take the ribbon figures back.'

'No thank you, Richard.'

She was building up the business, which was giving her real confidence, and she hoped sapping his since he'd failed to do it. She'd cut Richard out of the ribbon side of the business and wanted to keep him out.

'You left all the ribbon work to Myra, so I'm sure you're happy to leave it to me, now I'm increasing the income.'

He didn't answer.

'I'm so pleased I've been able to turn the business round. Thrilled in fact, and I know you must be too.'

He glowered at her and his body slumped lower over his desk. Without putting it into words, he was telling her quite clearly that he didn't like her crowing about her success. He couldn't say so, of course; it would make him look a fool.

'I might as well go,' he said, pulling himself to his feet. She understood he'd had enough of talk like this. He had none of the feverish excitement he usually had on race days.

'I'll keep my fingers crossed that Beauty wins,' she told him but he didn't reply. He slammed Miss O'Marney's door as he went out.

She went to find Mr Hopper. He was happy now to take orders from her, and sometimes even asked for her advice. She'd managed to get two new orders for buttons as well, and the button room was busy turning them out. 'It's getting that we could do with more help,' Mr Hopper said. 'It's a shame Mr Haldane sacked those girls a few weeks ago.'

'Did they find other jobs?' Dinah asked. 'If not, do they want to come back?'

He asked around and found that two had new jobs and the third didn't want to return. At least the news made Dinah feel better about the sackings. She would take on a qualified accountant, one with a bit of experience. She meant to make this business grow.

She told Mr Hopper about her two repeat orders. He took the news with more enthusiasm than Richard had shown, laughing, rubbing his hands together and congratulating her. Then he swept her into the ribbon room to see the latest satin weave for Woolworth's threepenny and sixpenny stores.

'This is the ribbon that's to be sold by the yard for children's hair?' Dinah was particularly pleased about this order, because Copthorne Ribbons hadn't sold to Woolworth's before.

'Yes. Beautiful stuff.' Mr Hopper stroked it. 'Who could resist buying a yard or two of this to put bows in their daughter's hair?'

Dinah thought Nellie would like them. 'If you've got any off-cuts I'll take them home. Nellie does sometimes wear an Alice band or tie her hair back in bunches.'

'We've got some bits you can take now.' He went to lift them off one of the machines. In that instant, Dinah knew where she'd heard the name Olive Jennings before. He'd told her she used to work on that row of machines.

'D'you remember telling me once that Richard had been friendly with a machine operator called Olive Jennings?' she asked.

'That was years ago, but isn't it great to have all these machines in use again? Olive Jennings, yes. She was friendly with the boss.'

'When did she leave?'

He sighed. 'I don't know – ages ago.'

'How long did she work here?'

'Several years.'

'What can you remember about her?'

He was looking at her as though she'd lost her marbles. 'Nothing much. She was a good-looking girl – well, hardly a girl any more. She had a daughter.'

'Really?' Could that be Rosanna? 'I don't suppose you remember her name?'

'To be honest, I don't remember ever hearing it.'

'No matter.' Dinah could go back to the old wages books and check.

'Why d'you want to know about her?' he asked.

'Just curious. Do you know what she did afterwards?'

'Sorry, no. I'm not much help on this, am I?'

Dinah went back to her desk with the old wages ledgers and found Olive Jennings had left in May 1923. From the personnel files for that period, she found she'd been born in 1880 which made her forty-three at the time and fifty-four now, so she was a lot older than Richard. Sixteen years older to be exact. She was said to be single and there was no mention of a child.

Rosanna might be her daughter and might not. She might be Richard's daughter and might not. Probably not; Richard would have been very young when she was born. Clearly he'd had a long relationship with Olive Jennings though she didn't seem the sort of woman who would attract him. But Rosanna did.

Dinah didn't understand how they fitted into Richard's life. Should she feel resentful that he had friends he'd never mentioned? Jealous? No, nothing like that. She'd given up on Richard; there was no way now she could find happiness with him.

What she wanted was to get away from him, divorce him. But she didn't know anyone who had been divorced. And there was a stigma attached. A divorced woman was thought by many to be a fallen woman. But she was coming round to accepting that she'd have to do it, to have any sort of life.

Dinah was anxious to know whether Beauty had won, but she worked on until six that afternoon because she knew Richard would be unlikely to get home before then. When she did get home, he wasn't there.

Bunty and Nellie were cooking supper. Nellie seemed more settled now that Bunty was living with them again. For the first few days she was there, Dinah had made a point of going to the kitchen just before supper time.

'For goodness' sake, I don't need help,' Bunty had told her. 'I've been cooking and serving up meals here for years. Anyway, I'm teaching Nellie to cook.'

Nellie had been delighted to have Eugenie back looking very little different. 'I'd keep her upstairs,' Dinah advised, 'out of your father's way.'

'Don't worry, I will,' she'd said, and later Dinah had seen the doll on the dressing table in Nellie's bedroom.

She grew more anxious as she waited for Richard to come. The time dragged, and supper time came. She'd begun to wonder if they should start eating without him when she saw his car go round the house and head towards the garage. She shot out of the back door to meet him. 'How did it go?'

She knew from his face he was still in a black mood. 'Beauty won,' he told her. 'And Beauty sold. That's what you wanted, isn't it?'

'Did she make a good price?'

He shrugged. 'She was a good filly.'

'Have you paid what you owe to Bob Watchit?'

'Do you think he'd let me get away without doing that?' he asked irritably. 'He's found me a buyer for Prince.'

'Oh! That's good, isn't it?'

'It's bloody awful.'

'They have to go, Richard. You know you can't afford them.'

'The business is picking up now. I think we could afford one horse. I think I'll keep Prince.'

'You'd still have to find a new trainer. And don't you need to build up capital in the business?'

He was looking at her with eyes that were black with hate. Dinah had never seen him look at her like that before. An icy shiver ran down her spine.

The next day was Saturday and all morning Richard was in a mood of almost manic high spirits which frightened Dinah more than his rage.

They drove home separately to a lunch of toad in the hole cooked by Bunty, which Richard ate with gusto.

He'd always had huge mood swings. Dinah knew all too well he could change in minutes from an excited and happy man to one gripped with volcanic rage. When it was spent, he'd simmer with anger for days and then flop down in deep misery. Recently, he'd been having more melancholy moods and they'd been lasting longer. On several occasions, Dinah had found him sunk in the depths of despair with all his aggression spent. At such times she knew she'd be safe for a while, but his moods of despair threw a blanket of misery over everything, and with the misery came fear.

The telephone rang in the hall when he'd almost cleared his plate. 'See who that is, Nellie,' he said.

'It's for you, Daddy,' she called.

As usual, Richard went to the phone in his study. Dinah knew there were things in his life he didn't want her to know about, so he meant to keep his phone calls private. But today he was shouting, all his good humour gone.

'Who was it?' Dinah whispered to Nellie as they collected the dirty plates.

'I don't know. It was a woman. She just asked for him.'

Bunty was bringing in the next course. 'Don't start eating until he comes back,' Dinah reminded Nellie. 'It always annoys him if we do.'

His voice rose and rose, fury in every note. 'Something's upsetting him.' Nellie said sadly. 'We do our best not to, but then somebody else does. He'll be very cross now.'

Dinah got up and went out to the hall. He was really riled now. He hadn't closed the door of his study properly, and she heard him scream, 'I haven't touched Rosanna. As if I would.' There was a moment's silence. Dinah's mind was churning. She knew whom he was angry with. Olive Jennings was complaining about something he'd done. So that relationship had its difficulties too. She heard him crash the receiver down and a second later he flung his door wide open. She knew he was taken aback to see her so close.

'What are you doing here? Eavesdropping?'

'No, no,' she said quickly. It took her a moment to get on top of her nerves. 'No need to eavesdrop, Richard, not when you shout at the top of your voice.'

'How would you like it if I followed you everywhere? If I watched every movement you made?'

Dinah cringed back. 'What would be the point? I'm not hiding anything.'

'So you think I am? You're spying on me.'

She knew she was making things worse. She turned to go, but he grabbed hold of her wrist and spun her violently back to face him.

'What dark secrets d'you think I have?' He lowered his face to within inches of hers. 'Come on, tell me.'

Pain shot down her side. Dinah knew this was a moment to keep her mouth shut, but she was afraid the name Olive Jennings was written in her eyes. The woman must be in the forefront of his mind.

To find mental strength was one thing, but to find physical strength to face him was even harder. He was twelve stone to her eight, almost six feet to her five foot six. He had the strength of a man in his prime while she was five months pregnant.

She was terrified, expecting him to subject her to more pain. 'Leave me alone,' she ground out. 'You're bullying me.'

He pushed Dinah as hard as he could and made her stagger backwards. She fell against Nellie, who'd come to see what was going on, and felt her arms go round her and help to keep her upright. Bunty's voice rang across the hall, as though scolding a naughty child.

'Mr Haldane, that wasn't kind. You really must learn to control your temper.'

In the silence that followed he muttered through clenched teeth, 'Sorry, Dinah.'

'Now all of you,' Bunty went on. 'Sit up at the table and eat your pudding. I've made a rhubarb fool for you, Mr Haldane. You've always been fond of that.'

Richard obediently led the way back to the dining room. To Dinah, it seemed miraculous that frail old Bunty could still assume the authority to correct him to such good effect. She returned to the kitchen, leaving them to eat in silence.

As they were putting their spoons down, Richard got to his feet and said stiffly, 'I won't stay for coffee. I'm going out.'

Dinah nodded. 'When will you be back?'

'Maybe not until late.'

'But you'll want supper here?'

'Oh, I don't know.'

They heard him drive round the house fast enough to make the gravel spurt up in the air.

Chapter Twenty-Eight

DINAH FELT SHATTERED. She was unable to do anything that afternoon but mull over what had happened. She ached down one side where Richard had twisted her round and it worried her that he'd begun to use his physical strength against both her and Nellie. His behaviour had ratcheted up another notch in the tension that had been simmering for some time. Things were worsening.

She wanted to talk to Tim, but she couldn't do that from home in case Richard returned unexpectedly. Almost from the beginning, she'd been careful to play down how much Tim meant to her because she'd been afraid Richard would think he was her lover. He was her friend and the only support she had, and she didn't want Richard to know how special Tim had become to her.

But she knew what Tim would say. He kept telling her to get get out while she could. 'If you suspect him of murdering five people, do you honestly think you've any hope of preventing him making it six?'

She'd promised him she'd go straight to Enid if things got worse, and she should be thinking seriously about it now. How much longer would she and Bunty be able to keep things under control?

She no longer knew what had given her the idea she could stand up to him. Too much of that seemed as dangerous as allowing him to knock her into submission. She had really no idea how to stay safe. And worse, since she'd made herself responsible for them, how to keep Nellie and Bunty safe.

Dinah knew where she'd gone wrong. She'd made herself more important to him by bringing in orders and improving the profitability of his business, but she hadn't understood the effect that would have on him. He didn't like it. It was showing up his failures and nobody could stand much of that.

Neither had she taken into account that Richard could be upset and thrown off balance by events in his life that she had no part in. Things were definitely going wrong between him and Olive Jennings, and racing had turned sour for him too.

She knew Richard was being pushed to his limit and she must be more careful. She must put not only her fear of him out of her mind but also his aggression. Any retaliation could land her in big trouble.

Before supper she heard his car go round to the garage and felt another shaft of anxiety. She didn't know whether she was ready to cope with another argument. She dreaded that he might use physical force again, but came in acting as though nothing had happened. He seemed quiet, almost subdued, as he ate his supper. Neither she nor Nellie dared ask where he'd been or what he'd done all afternoon.

In the sitting room later, he threw himself silently on the sofa and lapsed into a state of brooding misery, gazing vacantly into space. Dinah left him and went up to the nursery to be with Nellie and Bunty. She was afraid Richard was cracking up.

On Sunday Richard remained subdued, but he went over to the garage after breakfast. It was a chilly overcast day and he kept the doors closed. Dinah walked round the garden getting more and more stressed. She didn't like him being close to her car when she couldn't see what he was doing. He'd been right when he'd accused her of being suspicious of him. She couldn't get out of her mind the vision of him tinkering with the brakes of her car.

It was fear and suspicion that made her creep in through the side door. She had to see what he was doing. She almost collapsed with relief to find he had the bonnet of his own car open, not hers, and then she'd had to struggle to appear normal.

'Is there a problem with your car?' she asked.

'I'm just topping up the oil.' He seemed much as usual.

Dinah knew she was on tenterhooks and told herself she was looking for trouble where there was none. Nobody ate much at Sunday lunch and nobody spoke much either, and afterwards Richard went up to their bedroom. Dinah tried to read the Sunday paper but she couldn't stop wondering what he was doing Everything was making her uneasy now. She knew she shouldn't follow him up; hadn't he complained that she was spying on him? But she couldn't keep away.

His good mood was gone and he snapped at her, 'Aren't I allowed to have a bath in peace? Playing about with cars is dirty work.' He was dressing again and took a new sports jacket from his wardrobe. 'I'm going out.'

'Where to?' She knew it must be the Olive Grove, but she didn't dare say its name.

He stared at her, his face working with anger. 'Get off my back. It's none of your bloody business where I go, d'you hear?'

His virulence shocked her. If she'd betrayed her knowledge of the Olive Grove his reaction couldn't have been more violent. 'You've been nothing but trouble since I married you. I wish I hadn't.'

Dinah's heart was pounding like a sledgehammer, but she made herself say the word.

'Does that mean you want a divorce?'

'Don't be so damned stupid. We can't. We've only been married six months.' He pushed past her and rushed for the stairs as though he needed to put as much distance between them as he could. 'Don't you know the law requires us to be married for two years before we can think of that?'

Dinah stood stock still. She didn't! Her mouth had gone dry. She hadn't realised there would be conditions like that attached to getting a divorce. She was well and truly trapped.

Moments later she heard his car zoom round the house as though it was on a race track. She had to go out, get away from his house. She'd go to see Enid. She felt a growing need to talk over what was happening to her. She knew Tim wouldn't be there: he was at a race meeting in Yorkshire with the team. Digby had given him the weekend off and a fellow jockey who came from Hull had invited him to spend it there with him before the Tuesday meeting at Beverley. Perhaps the time had come to confide in his mother. Dinah felt she needed help. Things were getting beyond her.

As she got out of her car in Picton Street, Enid came out of her door with Flo, each carrying a large bundle of cloth tied up with string.

They rested their parcels on the bonnet of the car to throw their arms round Dinah in welcome. Flo hadn't seen the Austin before. 'I didn't know you had this! How marvellous.'

'I told you,' Enid protested.

'Are you going out?' Dinah was disappointed.

'No, love, we're going round to Gladys's. It's her birthday and this is her present. We bought a lot of curtains in a church bazaar and cut them down to fit her windows. Enough for her whole house as well as a draught excluder.'

'Come with us. She'd love to see you.'

Gladys immediately invited her in. Dinah had a jolly afternoon with her old friends and it made her feel almost normal again, but she had no chance to talk to Enid on her own.

She went home and knew when she put her car in the garage that Richard wasn't yet back. After taking just one step inside the house, she felt the atmosphere of nervous fear wrap itself round her. It brought her difficulties thundering back to the forefront of her mind. Bunty had made the usual light Sunday night supper and she and Nellie were about to eat. Dinah sat down with them and toyed with the food on her plate.

There must be some way she could escape from Richard. Yes, of course there was. She could rent a house in Walton now she was earning a wage; in Picton Street if possible, if not close by. It would take a bit to furnish it since she'd given away all her mother's household goods, but she had a little money. There would be room enough to take Bunty and Nellie so that they could be safe too. She could even put Mark up during his school holidays if he wanted to come.

For a few moments she thought it might all be possible, but one stumbling block remained. Richard was not only her husband but the owner of the business that employed her. She would have to get his agreement to her plan, or he could sack her and she'd find herself without any income to pay the rent.

And the other difficulty was that she was pregnant. Would it be possible for her to work through her pregnancy and on into the future?

Bunty would want to take care of the baby, she knew, but would that be too much to expect at her age? Probably yes, and she definitely couldn't expect her to keep house as well, but more help could be found in Picton Street.

She'd have to get Richard's agreement first, there was no way round that, and she was afraid he was unlikely to give it. Unless he did, she had no other way out of this loveless marriage.

Dinah felt exhausted and went to bed before Richard came home. When he did come, she felt she'd been asleep for hours. It was a stormy night and rain was hurtling against the window panes. He was putting on all the bedroom lights and making no effort to be quiet. Suddenly the smell of burning was acrid in her nose. She stifled a sigh and squinted at the alarm clock. It was gone two in the morning.

'Have you been to a bonfire?' she asked.

He stood stock still, coldly furious, eyes glowering down at her. 'No I haven't,' he barked.

She knew that was a lie. 'You smell of fire, you've made the whole room stink of it and you have burn marks on your jacket.' He opened the window wide. 'And you've singed your sleeve quite badly.'

'What?' He thrust his right arm behind his back.

'Is that a burn on your hand too? It looks sore.'

He was shrugging out of his jacket, let it fall to the floor.

'What a pity. It was a smart jacket and new on today, wasn't it? There's a black mark on your trousers, too.'

He took a clean pillowcase from the drawer where they were kept and stuffed his clothes into it. His shirt followed.

'Throw them out. Get rid of them,' he said, as he banged out to the bathroom leaving all the lights on.

She heard the geyser roar into action and couldn't believe he was going to have a bath at this time of night. What sort of fire had it been? He'd been very near to it, nearer than one would go to a bonfire. He was taking a long time in the bathroom. Dinah had composed herself for sleep by the time he came back.

'Wake up,' he said as he threw back the bedclothes and got in beside her. He'd used her talcum powder liberally and smelled clean and scented now. 'You know what I want.'

Recently, Dinah had found that he wanted sex less often, and she'd hoped that now he'd said he wished he'd never married her he wouldn't want it at all. But she'd never dared to refuse him. If she caused his temper to erupt there'd be no sleep for either of them for hours.

She didn't say no now, though she no longer made any effort to pretend she enjoyed it. He was seething with anger and he was rough, tugging at her nightdress and flinging her over on to her back.

'Come on,' he grated. 'It's like making love to a dead body.'

Dinah shivered with revulsion. She hadn't been able to think of it as making love for a long time. 'Don't expect me to be eager,' she said. 'I'm pregnant.' Her bump was growing and she was conscious of his weight pressing down on it uncomfortably.

'Oh, for goodness' sake! I hate you when you're like this. Why can't you try to be a better wife?'

'I have, Richard, in the past. I've tried very hard. It's got me nowhere.'

He grunted and tossed over to his side of the bed, pulling all the bedclothes with him. Dinah pulled some of them back.

'Now that you've thoroughly woken me up,' she said, 'there's something I want to suggest.' He ignored her but she knew he was listening. 'You said we can't get a divorce yet, but we don't have to continue living together, do we?' She outlined her idea about renting a home for herself in Picton Street so they could live apart, and how it would depend on her keeping her job in the business.

He sat up with a jerk. 'It's not up to you to make decisions like that. Don't you dare do any such thing! If you leave my house, you'll not set foot in my factory again. I married you to get a woman in bed beside me.'

At least that was honest. He made it quite obvious.

'I thought you'd be better than this in bed. You're hopeless.'

Dinah swallowed hard. 'You said you loved me.'

'All women like to hear that. You're just a girl from the slums – there's nothing special about you to love. Of course, you're good-looking, but so are plenty of others.'

That took her breath away.

'You've got too big for your boots,' he raved on. 'Deciding on this and then that. I'll have no more of it – you'll do what I tell you. You'll stay here until I decide otherwise. D'you hear?'

Dinah was not far from tears. This was too raw for her. 'I loved you,' she told him. 'I thought you wanted us to be happy together. I didn't think you were like this.'

Before Dinah was properly awake in the morning she knew Richard was up and getting dressed. It was dark, and she could hear rain hurtling against the window.

She yawned. 'You're up early. After a late night, too.'

'I've got things to do,' he told her.

Dinah knew if she asked what was so urgent he wouldn't tell her. She slid out of bed, padded to the bathroom and had a quick bath. When she came back Richard had gone, and she could hear him talking to Bunty downstairs. Still feeling drowsy, she dressed and followed him down. There was nobody in the dining room, but at his place there were toast crumbs on his plate and dregs in his teacup. Bunty was in the kitchen, still in her dressing gown.

'An early start this morning,' she said. 'Mr Haldane took me by surprise. Where's he off to in such a hurry? He wouldn't wait for the porridge to be ready or anything.'

'I've no idea. He said nothing to me.' Nellie came down in her school uniform to ask the same question.

As Richard had gone, Dinah fetched the crockery from the dining room where the table was always set the night before, and sat down at the kitchen table so they could have breakfast together. But breakfast wasn't the time for friendly chatter.

'Come on, Nellie, we must get going or you'll be late for school.' Dinah pushed her sandwiches into her bag and collected her umbrella from the stand by the front door, then cut through the kitchen to the back door which was a shorter way to the garage.

'It's stopped raining,' Nellie said, hoisting her school bag on to her shoulder.

'Almost,' Dinah said. She could feel drizzle in the air as they hurried to the garage, but it wasn't worth putting up her umbrella.

She opened one garage door while Nellie saw to the other. They'd done it so often in the mornings that they'd got it down to a fine art. It gave Dinah pleasure to see her car standing ready; she'd grown very fond of it. She tossed her things on to the back seat and Nellie did the same with her books, then Dinah eased herself into the driving seat. She knew that in another couple of months she'd find it a tight fit behind the steering wheel.

As she routinely did, she started the engine and let the car roll forward a few yards so Nellie could close the garage doors behind her.

She waited for Nellie to get in beside her, and off they went crunching over the gravel. There were a couple of tight turns as the drive wound round the house and as always she gave a farewell toot on the horn as she passed the kitchen door. Bunty waved from the window where she was washing up.

One more bend and Dinah could see the drive before her. George the gardener was coming to work on his bike wearing yellow waterproofs, and pedalling hard up the incline. Behind him the drive sloped down to the large ornamental iron gates on to the road.

It surprised her to see the gates standing wide open. Richard was very fussy about always keeping them closed, so why? A reason suddenly burned into her mind, and she put her foot on the brake, but the car didn't stop. Oh Lord, she was right!

She did the emergency stop she'd practised in her driving lessons, ramming her right foot down as hard as she could, but that had no effect either. Dinah heard Nellie scream as she yanked on the handbrake with all the strength she could muster. It didn't slow the car one iota.

Panic exploded in her head. Richard was trying to kill her and Nellie, as he'd killed his parents. He'd disconnected her brakes, he must have done. Hadn't Mr Poole told her that all cars had dual braking systems these days, and it was impossible for them both to fail at the same time?

Nellie was yelling, 'Stop, Dinah, stop, for heaven's sake!'

The gates were getting closer with every second and she knew that if she went through and turned towards town as she always did, she would soon be in heavy traffic. She must not go through the gates! They'd be likely to be killed and to kill other road users if she did. But what else could she do? She could hardly breathe. Disaster was closing in on her.

'Hang on,' she yelled at Nellie, as she swung on the steering wheel to make the car turn right. It bounced off the drive down a couple of feet of rockery to squelch on to the lawn. It was rocking dangerously on two wheels, first to one side and then the other. It was almost impossible to control.

'Make it stop,' Nellie was crying. 'Can't you make it stop?'

Dinah felt clamped in cold fear, unable to think.

'Do something,' Nellie wailed with terror in her voice. 'Do something!'

Miraculously, it came to Dinah then. She reached for the ignition key and turned it off. She must turn the car back towards the house because the land rose in that direction. She was fighting with the steering wheel to do that when she caught one agonising glimpse of the stone sundial, but it was too late. The front of the car clipped it.

The next moment they were airborne, and she was hanging on to the steering wheel for dear life. The car turned over and righted itself and then turned over again. She was flung painfully against the roof, banging her head and hurting her arm, then back in her seat and forward against the steering wheel. It cut into her abdomen, knocking the air out of her lungs. She was upside down again and her right leg had twisted. Nellie was slumped heavily against her, pinning her in an impossible position.

Inertia was keeping the Austin on the move. Dinah knew it was sliding into the rose hedge. She felt disorientated, her breakfast was coming back into her mouth and everything was going black.

Chapter Twenty-Nine

It was Nellie's screams that brought her round. Dinah was aware they were upside down and she was hurting all over.

'All right, little one, let's get you out.' George had the car door open and was pulling at Nellie. The weight on top of Dinah lifted and she was able to breathe again. Nellie was still sobbing, but more quietly.

'Your turn, missis.' George was talking to her. 'Are you all right?'

'Get me the right way up,' she groaned, 'and I might be.'

'Push yourself round, can you?'

She couldn't move. 'My foot's jammed somehow.'

George always did seem slow. She could hear him breathing heavily, but he seemed to have kept his wits about him. 'Your shoe's wedged itself between the pedals.'

He reached in and she felt him release it, but it involved a painful wrench on her leg. It made her scream and she still couldn't budge.

'OK, I can see the problem now. Your leg's caught too.'

She could feel him pulling at it. She turned, altering her own position, and suddenly she almost fell out of the wreckage into his arms. He lowered her to lie on the waterlogged grass. Her teeth were chattering with cold and shock, but she was relieved to have stopped the car and be lying flat and free of the wreckage.

An instant later, she was conscious of the most awful pain in her belly. It took a moment before she could gasp out, 'Is Nellie all right?'

'She's making more noise than you, but there's more blood and grazes on you. I'll get Bunty to ring for an ambulance.'

'No, ring for the police.' She had to get them here before Richard could right whatever he'd done to the brakes of her car.

She heard Bunty's voice, full of concern. 'My goodness me, look what you've done to your car, turned it over! Such a noise it made! Whatever happened?'

Dinah knew what she had to do. It was a huge effort to lift her head from the ground.

'Richard tampered with my brakes. Bunty, I've got to get the police here as fast . . .' The pain in her abdomen was building again. 'As fast as I can.'

'I'll phone for an ambulance.'

'No, no.' Dinah clutched on to her skirt, the pain receding again. 'The police first. I've got to talk to them.'

'You need a doctor, and so does Nellie.'

Dinah made one last effort. It was making her head spin. 'Richard tried to kill us. He did something to the brakes so they wouldn't work but he'll know how to right them and he will if he gets half a chance.'

'Don't worry about that.'

'The proof is here in my car now. You must get the police here before he comes home.'

The pain was building again. Her head was thumping and because she'd been jolted this way and that she ached in every bone.

'Please. You must get the proof. Or he'll do what he did after his parents' accident.' Bunty's worried face was swathed in mist as she looked down at her, and the mist was getting thicker and blotting everything out . . .

Dinah woke up alone in a narrow bed, the searing pain in her abdomen doubling her up. It was building and getting stronger, until she had to clench her teeth. She gasped in agony, and then the pain was fading. Relieved, she took a deep breath. The air smelled strongly of antiseptic. Was she in hospital? She must be, but had Bunty managed to get the police to look at her car?

A nurse in a flowing headdress was pushing a dressing trolley past her bed. She glanced at Dinah and stopped.

'Hello, you've come round then. How d'you feel?'

'Not too good. Could I have a drink of water, please? I'm thirsty.'

'Well, we don't want you to drink now. You'll be going down to theatre soon.'

'What for? Where am I?'

'In the Casualty department of the Liverpool Royal.'

'Is Bunty here?'

'Who?'

'Did somebody come in with me?'

'No, but Sister has rung your husband to tell him you're here. He shouldn't be long.'

Dinah shuddered. He was the last person she wanted to see. She couldn't bear this. She wanted him to stay as far away as possible, both from her and from her car. She was cringing, dreading the tightening grip of the pain she knew was coming.

'I'm having a pain,' she gasped. 'It's cutting right through me.'

'We'll get you something for that.' The nurse patted her bandaged hand. 'I'll see if the doctor's free. He said he wanted to talk to you.'

Minutes later she returned to pull floral blue curtains round Dinah's bed. With her was a handsome young man in a white coat.

'Mrs Haldane, I'm Dr Pierce. Tell me about these pains you're having.'

Dinah was in the grip of another one and couldn't speak for a few moments. 'They're strong, they come and go. What's the matter with me?'

'Labour pains. You were in a car crash—'

'Yes, I know about that.'

'We're worried about your baby. We haven't been able to hear the foetal heart since you came in, and you're losing a lot of blood. I'm going to examine you now, but I'm afraid we may not be able to save the baby.'

It sounded stark. 'But you will try?'

'Yes, we'll do all we can, but it may be impossible.'

Dinah hadn't been very pleased to find herself pregnant so quickly, particularly as it tied her even more tightly to Richard, but since that day in the park when she'd talked to the young aunt she'd begun to think differently. A baby would bring compensations.

The examination was over quickly. It brought home to Dinah how much blood she was losing. It was everywhere.

'You're eighteen weeks pregnant, yes?'

'Yes.'

'Mrs Haldane, it isn't possible for this pregnancy to continue. That there's no foetal heart sounds means your baby was killed in the crash. We can't delay any longer – we have to stop the bleeding as a matter of urgency. To let it continue would put your life in danger.'

'What are you going to do?'

'Take you down to theatre for a dilatation and curettage.'

Dinah felt another pain coming.

'You're in labour now. Nature is trying to do the job for you, but unfortunately it can't repair any tears. I've already asked for the theatre to be prepared. You'll be going down quite soon.'

'What about the policemen?' the nurse asked quietly.

'Oh, yes. I've told them she isn't well enough—'

'I am,' Dinah insisted. 'I am. I want to speak to them. I have to.'

'We'll let them in for two minutes then.'

Dinah lay back and tried to be patient. The nurse was whisking in and out and putting operating gown, thick socks and turban on to her bed. She brought in two men who looked ill at ease.

'Mrs Haldane, we're sorry to disturb you at a time like this. It's about the accident you've just had.'

'It was no accident.' Dinah was making an effort to be strong. 'My husband tampered with the brakes so they didn't work. It's not the first time he's done this. Ask Bunty . . .'

'She's spoken to us, and also an Ivy Cummins.'

'He knows everything there is to know about cars,' Dinah gasped. 'Please don't let him anywhere near my car until it's been properly examined.'

'We've sent a low loader to get it, and it'll be taken to a police garage. Don't you worry about that.'

'That's good. What about Nellie, the little girl who was with me? Is she all right?'

'She was taken to the children's hospital in Myrtle Street.'

'How is she?'

'We understand she's not seriously hurt.'

Dinah felt she could relax now. The nurse was shooing the policemen out and coming back to dress her in her theatre garb. The last thing she felt was a prick in her arm. 'Your pre-op,' the nurse explained. 'It'll take away the pain.'

The electric lights were on when Dinah came round and blue dusk showed at the windows. She felt heavy-eyed and her left arm was heavy too. She couldn't move it and it felt sore.

She lifted her head to see that her arm had been splinted. There was a needle in it and rubber tubing was leading up to a bottle of fluid on a stand above her. Moving her neck had given her a jolt of pain, enough to make her keep it still. More gingerly, she moved to squint up at the label on the bottle. It was labelled dextrose and saline. She felt her forehead. There was a lump there under a dressing and it was sore. So was her right hand, which was heavily bandaged.

It was all coming back to her now. She felt her abdomen and found it soft and flabby. With a pang of regret she knew she'd lost her baby. Yes, she'd become an expectant mother before she'd had time to settle into being a wife, and when she'd wanted to escape from Richard that fact had chained her to him more than anything else. There had been times when she'd resented her unborn child, but now it was gone she grieved for it. She was sure that Myra had gained comfort from baby Nellie, and it would have been the same for her.

She was in a different part of the hospital now, in one of a long row of beds. The patient in the next one was attracting the attention of a nurse, who came to Dinah's bedside.

'How do you feel?'

'I'm all right, thanks.' She had a nasty taste in her mouth as well as a cloying dryness. 'But I'd like a drink.'

The nurse fetched a feeder and supported her head so she could drink from the spout. Dinah had never needed a drink more and she gulped at it.

'Not too much at once,' the nurse murmured. 'It could make you sick. Just sips now to clean your mouth. You're getting all the fluid you need from this drip. Do you have any pain?'

'A little, yes.' She was aching all over.

'I'll get you something for it.' She whirled away to return a few moments later with some pills, which she helped Dinah to swallow.

'It's all over now,' she said. 'All you have to do is get your strength back.'

Dinah flopped back against her pillows. She couldn't see that her problems were over; they might have multiplied. Now she had accused Richard, her world would have to change completely. Right now, everything was hanging in the balance. Would Richard be charged with attempted murder? Or would he get away with it yet again?

Dinah had a restless night despite the medication she was given. The ward was in semi-darkness with the night nurse sitting at a desk lit by a green glow. All round her other women tossed and turned and slept. Some snored, some groaned and some called to the nurse. Dinah was worried sick about what Richard would do to her if he wasn't convicted of attempting to murder her and Nellie. The worst possible outcome would be for him to be free and presumed innocent as he had been in the past. She couldn't go on living with him after this: she'd be terrified of what he'd do next. He really must hate her.

She found it impossible to get comfortable with the needle in her arm and the nurse coming at intervals to replace the emptying bottle with a full one. She was glad to see the sky getting light; she could hope now for news of what was happening.

At breakfast time she was offered porridge and tea, and later in the morning the nurses made her more comfortable, re-dressing some of her cuts and grazes and taking out the needle in her arm.

Sister decided she should be moved to a side ward because the police were coming back to interview her. The nurses trundled an empty bed into the big ward, and pushed her and the bed she was in into a small bleak room between the ward kitchen and the office. Dinah fell asleep hoping the police would come soon. They might be able to settle her mind. She was woken up when a nurse she hadn't seen before announced that she had a visitor and a flustered Bunty was shown in.

'Dinah love, how are you?'

'I've lost the baby.'

'I know, they told me. I was afraid you'd been seriously hurt, maimed for life, Nellie too.'

'Have you seen her?'

'Yes. It was a shock for her, poor girl, but she's broken no bones, just cuts and bruises. Thank goodness you're going to be all right too.' She kissed her. 'I've been so worried about you both. You do look as though you've been in the wars.'

'Just cuts and grazes.'

'Bruises, too. But when I saw your car turned upside down on the lawn . . . Glory me, I feared much worse.'

'Have the police taken it away?'

'I don't know. I rang them and they sent a policeman round. He listened to what I had to say and wrote it all down. I told him that Ivy and Ruby could tell him more about the earlier deaths and gave him their addresses.'

'Good,' Dinah said. 'I knew you must have because two policemen came to see me last night, but I wasn't able to ask them anything.'

'Well, love, I was in a real dither when the ambulances took you and Nellie away. And then this policeman came and stayed for ages asking question after question. When he went, George and me had to sit down and have a cup of tea. He saw it all happen, you see.

'Then I thought I ought to let Mr Haldane know what had happened, so I rang his business. His secretary told me he already knew; that before he'd arrived the hospital had rung to tell him that you'd had an accident and were in Casualty, and he should go in to see you.'

Dinah groaned.

'Miss O'Marney told me she gave him the message as soon as he came in and he shot off out again. She assumed he'd gone to the hospital.'

'I don't think he came here.'

'No, because later on two plainclothes policemen called in, asking to speak to Mr Haldane. They said they were looking for him.'

Dinah's heart sank. 'Did Miss O'Marney tell him I turned the car over in the garden? He'd surely expect me to drive out on to the road.'

Bunty looked apologetic. 'I don't know exactly what was said, do I?'

'I don't suppose it matters. All he'd have to do is retrace the route we take to work and he'd find the wreckage. I'm afraid he'll want to fix the brakes so they appear normal by the time the police examine them. To do it in the privacy of his own grounds would suit him very well.'

'Don't you fret about it, love.'

'I can't help it.'

'I should have waited and watched to see what happened, shouldn't I? But with you and Nellie taken to hospital I was too scared to stay in the house by myself. I was afraid Richard would come back.'

'Of course. I would have been afraid in your place. Where did you go?'

'Round to see Ruby. I stayed with her last night. They've rented out the room I had to someone else, so it's only for a night or two, just till I see how things are going.'

'You did the best thing.'

'George was there when I left. He'd be able to say that Mr Haldane had done something to the wreck.'

'Perhaps . . .' Richard could very easily send him away. It had been a wet morning; there wouldn't be much work he could do.

'The police told George they'd send someone to take the car away and he was not to touch anything in that part of the garden. Not to go near it or try to repair the damage to the grass or anything.'

'It might already have gone. The police might have everything under control,' Dinah said. It was just that she didn't know. 'Will you go round and tell Enid I'm in hospital? She'll be expecting me to call round today or tomorrow.'

'Yes.'

'Picton Street, number nineteen.'

'That's not far from Ruby's.'

'You've managed marvellously well, Bunty. Done everything that was needed. I'm very grateful.'

Dinah wished she knew what was happening and whether the police had spoken to Richard. She wouldn't be able to relax until she knew he was no longer free. They were all terrified of him now.

It was four o'clock when Miss O'Marney came in. 'So sorry to hear you of your accident. Everybody sends their best wishes and we hope you'll be back at work soon. Mr Hopper sent you this bunch of chrysanthemums – he went down to his allotment in his dinner hour to get them. And these books are from me. I enjoyed them so I hope you will. They may help you pass the time while you're in here.'

'You're all very kind.' Dinah pushed her face into the flowers to hide the tears welling up in her eyes. Yet again she was on an emotional knife edge and couldn't hold them back.

'And I've brought some of the mail too. It seems awful to bother you with business mail when you're ill in hospital, but Mr Haldane hasn't been in so there's nobody to say what's to be done.'

'Let me read them.' Dinah spread them out in front of her. 'Two new orders for ribbons – this is great news. Write letters tomorrow thanking them and say we'll give them prompt attention. Ask Mr Hopper to organise the threads we'll need, and he can deal with these others as he thinks fit.'

When she was leaving Dinah picked up the chrysanthemums again. 'Please thank Mr Hopper for these. They're lovely.'

'Better than those you can buy. He gets prizes for his chrysanths,' Miss O'Marney said.

They were wrapped in newspaper. Mr Hopper always brought a local paper to work and left it on the kitchen table, and she had often read snippets while she drank cups of tea.

A heading caught her eye: WOMAN DIES IN TEA ROOM FIRE.

Holding her breath, Dinah unwrapped the sheet from the stems and smoothed it out on her counterpane so she could read on.

The Olive Grove, a popular tea room in Longmoor Road, Crosby, caught fire late last night. The flames spread rapidly and adjoining flats and shops had to be evacuated. Several people, including Mrs Olive Jennings, proprietor of the Olive Grove, were taken to hospital suffering from smoke inhalation. Rosanna

Jennings, 20, daughter of the proprietor, who was asleep on the top floor of the premises at the time, died from her injuries.

Dinah felt sticky with sweat. Her heart was pounding as she read the whole thing through again. Richard hadn't wanted to admit it, but she knew he'd been close to a fire. He'd come home at two in the morning yesterday stinking of it. He'd also been keen to get rid of the clothes he'd been wearing. At the time, she'd thought it seemed suspicious, though she'd had no idea what he could be guilty of.

Poor Rosanna. Had he known she was dead when he came home? He'd certainly wanted to wash every trace of fire off himself. Had he lit it? Deliberately? And – the most chilling thought of all – had he killed Rosanna?

Dinah straightened the crumpled paper out more carefully to find the date. Yes, it was yesterday's paper. She felt sick.

Chapter Thirty

TIM HAD ENJOYED his stay in Hull with Eddie Spellow. When they returned to Digby's stables in Birkdale on Tuesday night, Tim was given the message that his mother had tried to ring him. There was no indication of why, and since he'd seen her only the day before setting off for Yorkshire with Eddie he was not unduly concerned. He went to bed, deciding he'd pop round to see her the next day.

He exercised Flyswitch and did his share of the morning chores. It was three o'clock when he rode his motor bike to Picton Street.

'I've been that worried,' his mother told him. 'Bunty came round yesterday and told me Dinah had turned her car over and is in hospital.'

Tim gripped the arms of his chair. 'Is she badly hurt? How is she?'

He felt weak at the knees as his mother told him about it. 'Nellie was with her. They're both shaken up but no bones broken. Cuts and bruises, that sort of thing. But Dinah's lost the baby.'

Richard Haldane's baby. 'Poor Dinah. Is she upset?'

'Most expectant mothers would be.'

'Where did she crash? Why did it happen?' He'd been dreading something like this since the day she'd confided her fears about Richard to him. 'Are the police involved?'

'Yes. Bunty said Dinah thought Richard had tampered with the brakes of her car and caused the accident. Did you know she thought he'd killed his parents that way?'

'Oh, my God! I told her to take care.'

'You should have told her to get right away from Richard Haldane.' His mother was cross.

'I did. I told her to come here. I told her you'd look after her, but she wouldn't listen to me. Dinah knew what he was like, but she thought she could handle him. Have the police examined the brakes of her car?'

'Bunty doesn't know. She was scared of being alone in the house with him, and went to stay with a friend who used to work for the Haldanes years ago. The police have been to interview her.'

'But does Dinah know what the police found when they examined her brakes?'

'She didn't last night. She didn't even know whether they'd looked at them or whether her car was still in the middle of their lawn. I went to see her but they only let me stay five minutes. Nobody seems to know anything about it, and, worse, they don't know where Richard Haldane has got to. He's disappeared. As far as Dinah knows, Miss O'Marney was the last person to see him.'

Tim was blaming himself. He should have done more to help. 'Poor Dinah, pinned down in hospital and not knowing what's happening. She'll be out of her mind.'

'Yes. She was worried stiff when I saw her. She's been told she'll be in hospital for a week or more but Nellie will be coming out in a few days. Bunty says she'll take her home and look after her, but she'd like to know whether Mr Haldane will be there too or not.'

Tim made up his mind. 'Will they let me in to see Dinah if I go there now?'

'You could try. They said I had to leave because it was supper time.'

He got to his feet. 'I'll call at Ardwick House first. At least I'll be able to see if her car is still there.' He remembered Dinah telling him Richard had lived on the premises during the war years without his family knowing he was there. He'd been hidden in the flat above the garage. 'I might have a look round and see if he's there.'

He put on his wet oilskins again and went out to his motor bike. The cold November rain was coming down in sheets, blowing in his face and trickling down his neck inside his shirt. He had goggles, but it was difficult to see where he was going when he wore them. The ornate iron gates of Ardwick House stood open. He chugged into the drive and stopped halfway up.

There was no car on the lawn now, but the lopsided sundial, deep tracks of more than one vehicle, and grass churned to mud showed him where Dinah had crashed. The sight made him shudder. His mother had told him she'd turned the car upside down; it sounded as though she'd been lucky to get out relatively unhurt. The rose hedge he'd admired when he came last time was partially uprooted now. But all the tracks headed back towards the gate and he was sure the wreckage of her car had gone that way.

He looked at the house. It looked gaunt and unwelcoming, and no smoke came from the chimneys. He started his bike again and rode up to the front steps. With the engine switched off the only sound was the rain lashing down and the wind howling through the tall trees. He rang the doorbell twice and then tried to push against the door, but it was locked solid. He went round the back to the kitchen window, where he could see cups and saucers on the draining board. He rapped hard on the glass and banged on the back door, calling out, 'Is there anyone at home?' Then he laughed to himself, wondering what he'd say to Richard Haldane if he should answer.

But he didn't, and it was the sort of house to give anybody the creeps. He went on round. He remembered the steps going down to the cellars, with the door and windows below ground level. The stone steps were slippery with wet leaves and soil, and the windows were shuttered so he couldn't see in. He knocked on that door too to no effect.

He almost headed back to his bike, but then remembered about the garage which stood well back behind the house. Dinah had taken him there and he'd admired it then, but today in the driving rain everything looked drab. It had had modern garage doors fitted on the side facing the house, but when he tried them they were locked. The flat above, originally meant no doubt for the groom, would be quite a pleasant place to live.

Tim continued round the building. There was another road here behind the garden wall, which had another wide gate set into it. A much less ornate gate than that at the front, it was heavily chained and padlocked. It was easy to see this had once been the front of the stable block. There was a high doorway with an arched top for the horses, which had been filled in at some time and stuccoed over.

On each side of the building was a locked door and three smallish windows. The first looked into what seemed to be a garden store: Tim could see lawn mowers, hedge cutters and bags of fertilisers, with shelves for smaller items.

To get close enough to look inside the other windows, Tim had to step on the soggy soil of a border set with chrysanthemums. He thought they'd originally let light into store or tack rooms, but now the inside partitions had been removed to make a large open garage space. The glass hadn't been cleaned for some time and it was darker inside so he couldn't see very much, but what he did see made him leap back in surprise, ruining two chrysanthemum blooms.

He strained his eyes into the darkness and thought he could see Richard's blue Riley, but there was something else. He moved to the next window for a better view, regardless now of the well-being of the flowers because he thought he could see tubing coming from the rear of the car and feeding through the front window. He also thought he could see somebody inside the car who wasn't moving.

He jumped backwards on to the path and the movement caused another rivulet of cold rain to run down his back. He said out loud, 'Oh, my God!'

He felt desperate. He had to get inside. He absolutely had to, even if he had to break a window. The first window he'd looked through was open a fraction at the top, so he climbed on the sill and pushed and pulled at the upper sash until his fingers were sore. It had not moved in years and was stiff, but eventually he eased it down enough to climb inside.

The effort left him panting, and he was shaking as he crept towards the car. It was Richard Haldane he could see inside, lolling back in the passenger seat looking for all the world as though he'd fallen asleep. He was as handsome as ever, with healthy pink cheeks and rosy lips.

Tim swallowed hard. What should he do now? He rapped on the window as hard as he could. Richard didn't move. He was dead, of course he was dead. He'd gassed himself with carbon monoxide.

The only noise was of rain lashing against the windows. He put his hand on the car bonnet; it was cold. The engine had stopped when it had run out of petrol.

'Oh, my God,' he said again. His knees felt as though they were giving way under him. There was nothing he could do. Better if he didn't touch anything.

There was an inner door with the key in the lock. He turned it and found himself in the garden store. He grazed his knee on the lawn mower and upset a garden fork before he reached the outer door. The key was in the lock here too. It was a relief to be outside again gulping great mouthfuls of wet cold air into his lungs.

He tried to run down to his motor bike but he felt stiff and clumsy. Once riding it he felt better, but he was going in circles because he was a stranger to this district and didn't know where to find a police station. He had to head towards Picton Street and home. He knew where to find one there.

Tim was kept in the police station for over an hour. He was made to go through his story more than once so that an officer could write it down. He was then asked to sign it as a statement.

After that he went straight to the hospital to see Dinah. When he asked to see her, he was told by a starchy sister that he'd be allowed in this once but in future visiting hours must be respected.

He followed her directions down the corridor and found the door of the side ward half open. Peeping round it, he saw Dinah lying back against her pillows looking washed out and woebegone.

'Hello,' he said and saw her face light up. She struggled to sit up.

'Tim! I'm glad you've come.'

He bounded to her bed and kissed her cheek. 'I told you to take care and you didn't,' he told her. Pulling a chair forward he sat down.

'I'm all right.'

He was studying her face. 'You've got a few bruises.' There was a black and yellow one on her forehead as well as several healing grazes.

'I've survived.' She tried to smile. 'And I've got good news to tell you.

It's official, Richard did tamper with my brakes, so that's proof he tried to kill me and Nellie. And he did kill our unborn child. You wouldn't think a father would want to harm—'

'Dinah.' Tim felt for her hand. That too was bruised and cut.

She was agitated. 'He'll not get away with it this time. Knowing what I do now makes me certain he contrived those accidents for his parents and for Myra's parents. I was never quite sure and felt I had to give him the benefit of the doubt. He's a serial murderer. I feel sick when I think about what he's done. Do you think they'll hang him?'

'Dinah.' He squeezed her hand and saw her wince. 'Sorry, sorry. Listen, I must tell you. I went to your house before coming here. Mum said you didn't know whether the police had got as far as taking your car away.'

'It's not an hour since a policeman came in to tell me. It made me feel so much better.'

Tim was afraid he was about to upset her again. 'I have more to tell you, and I don't know how you'll feel about it.'

'You saw Richard there? You need to tell the police; they're looking for him.'

'I have. They were going to come in to tell you, but I offered to do it. I thought it would be better coming from someone you knew.'

She was looking at him now wide-eyed with horror. 'You saw him?'

'Yes.'

'He's dead?'

He moved nearer to sit on the bed and put his arms round her. 'Yes. He was in his car in the garage. He killed himself by carbon monoxide poisoning.'

She buried her face in his pullover and he held her, rocking her gently as one would a child.

'A terrible shock for you,' he said gently. Finding Richard had been a nasty shock for him. 'But you won't have to worry about a trial.'

She lifted her face and he was surprised to see it wet with tears.

'You're sorry?'

Tim had been struggling for control since he'd left Ardwick House.

To see Dinah in tears brought his own gushing down his cheeks, hot and blinding. His arms tightened round her as he tried to wipe his face on his sleeve.

Between her sobs Dinah said, 'I don't really know what I feel. I'm raw all through, physically and mentally.'

'This year has been an emotional roller coaster for you,' he said.

She nodded. 'It's been awful.'

He found his handkerchief and dried his face, then as she didn't have one he gave it to her. 'What this does is draw a line under Richard Haldane more quickly than if he were charged and sent for trial. That would have dragged on and on.' And then there would probably have been the horror of a hanging.

She was wiping her eyes. 'To think of him being dead in his garage for days. How long exactly, do they think?'

Tim shook his head. 'The police will be able to tell you that later. They looked over the premises on Monday afternoon. Richard was last seen on Monday morning and it's now late Wednesday afternoon. At some stage he must have gone home and found the police had taken your car. That would have told him he'd be unlikely to get away with it this time, and made him decide suicide was the best way out for him.'

'It's all awful. Is he still there in the garage?'

'I doubt it. I heard somebody being detailed to collect his body and take it to the morgue.'

'To think of him there isn't any better.'

'It's what he wanted, Dinah. He arranged his end like this.' He gave her another hug and kissed her cheek. 'You must try to forget him. You're his widow, not his wife. Whatever you felt for him, you're free of him now.'

'I don't feel free,' she said quietly. 'There are a hundred strings knotting me to him.'

'You mustn't worry about them, love. I'll help you cut them.'

Tim felt Dinah had been returned to him and this time he didn't mean to let another man take her. It had been a year of huge changes for her, and the next one was going to bring big changes for him.

* * *

When Dinah was well enough to go home from hospital, Enid came to collect her in a taxi. Bunty had lit a good fire in the sitting room and she and Nellie were there to welcome her.

Enid stayed for tea and they all made a fuss of Nellie. They were concerned about her, as now both her parents had committed suicide. It was an immense tragedy for a young girl to come to terms with, though Dinah thought Nellie was in better spirits than she had been back in early summer when she and Richard had first been married. Things would be easier for them all now he was no longer with them.

Dinah felt only relief, but she was afraid Nellie might grieve. It had been a horrific end for her father. Nellie needed new activities in her life, and as she said she'd like to learn to play the piano Enid offered to teach her. She opened up the grand piano and gave her a short first lesson there and then.

'I'll arrange for a piano tuner to come round,' she told Dinah. 'It's a lovely instrument and it should be kept in good condition. You can practise on it, Nellie, and if you come to my house after school on Mondays I'll teach you to play it.'

The police informed Dinah that Richard's body would now be released and she should make arrangements to bury him. There was a church just a hundred yards down the road from Ardwick House, so she called in to see the vicar. He told her he'd known the older members of the Haldane family but Richard had not been a churchgoer, and as he'd committed suicide he didn't think a burial in hallowed ground was appropriate.

Dinah asked Enid for advice and together they arranged for Richard to be cremated.

'You don't have to be there at the time,' Enid told her. 'Not unless you want to.'

'I don't want to exactly,' Dinah said. 'But I think I should. I'll probably be the only person who will go. It'll be a sort of end of my connection with Richard.'

She couldn't make up her mind what would be appropriate for her to wear. Richard would want her to wear deepest black, but she had no intention of doing that. She had a lot of smart clothes and didn't mean to buy any more. She considered the outfit she'd worn at her mother's funeral, but that was light and summery and the weather was cold now. In the end she decided on the heavy red coat and tam that she often wore for work.

Tim offered to go with her. Everything inside the chapel at the crematorium reminded Dinah of the time she'd come here with her mother's coffin, though for Sarah there'd been a church service first. The same organ music was being played.

Today they were greeted by a cleric who introduced himself, but she didn't catch his name. There were only the three of them in the building. He said a brief prayer asking for forgiveness for Richard's soul. Dinah felt tense and held Tim's arm in a fierce grip. It took only a few brief moments before the curtains closed behind Richard's coffin and it was all over.

'He wouldn't have liked that,' she said as Tim led her out. 'His choice would have been to have all the pomp and ceremony of a state funeral.'

'I can feel you shivering,' Tim said when they emerged into the open air. 'I'm taking you to a café. You need a hot lunch, and then the sooner you get back to normal everyday life the better.'

But Dinah felt frozen for most of the afternoon and spent a lot of time turning things over in her mind.

She knew she had to make a completely different life for herself and for the little family she'd acquired. She wanted more of Tim in it, but she wasn't sure how he felt about that. It wasn't so long since she'd pushed him away to marry Richard. She'd turned to him for support since and he'd given it, but did he see her merely as an old friend who needed help? She was afraid she couldn't put the clock back now.

Then there was Bunty. 'From now on, we'll all eat together,' she told her. 'There's to be no more pushing you out to eat by yourself. We all need a more social life. I'll book seats for us at the theatre next week, and we must invite our friends round for meals. Christmas is coming and we'll have a party here on Boxing Day.'

'Mark will be home for the holidays in another month.' Nellie was enthusiastic. 'Can we go to the pantomime?'

'Yes. You find out what pantomime they're putting on at the Empire this year and I'll book seats. We're going to enjoy ourselves from now on.'

But Dinah went to bed that night feeling drained and lacking in energy. She knew she'd still have to face Richard's inquest before very long.

Chapter Thirty-One

DINAH CALLED IN to see Enid at least once a week. When Enid told her Tim would have a day off the following Sunday, she invited them both for lunch and they spent most of the day with her. Tim suggested a trip to the cinema later in the week.

Dinah felt she'd got her life moving again when she visited Carlton Hats. Mr McKay was pleased to see her and gave her another order. Millie and Jenny hugged her and said they were sorry to hear of Richard's death. Millie was engaged now, and Dinah asked her to bring her fiancé round to her house. Millie seemed pleased and excited at the prospect of coming to see it.

Dinah threw herself into preparations for Christmas and didn't stay off work for long. She was glad to go back to where she had more company and there was plenty to occupy her. But whether at home or at work, everything reminded her of Richard. She found it impossible to put him out of her mind.

She cancelled his racing newspapers and magazines and cleared out his study and his office to move her own things in. Mr Hopper was invited to take over her old desk near Miss O'Marney's, and she gave orders that in future the doors were not to be closed to the other workers.

From time to time more facts about the fire at the Olive Grove Tea Rooms appeared in the newspapers. Mr Hopper was very interested because he'd known Olive Jennings, and now it appeared others in the factory remembered her too. There had been a lot of gossip about Richard and Olive Jennings. She was said to be Richard's long-term mistress, and that really set the tongues buzzing in the workroom. But they all said they didn't believe it. Why would he want Olive Jennings when he had a pretty young wife like Dinah?

One morning, the post brought a letter informing Dinah that the date of Richard's inquest had been set. Dinah was asked to be present as she would be required to give evidence. She showed the letter to Tim. 'As I found the body,' he said, 'I've had one too.'

But a week later they each received another letter postponing the inquest as the police needed to make further inquiries. Two officers came to interview Dinah again but she could tell them little more. George Weeks said he'd been asked to make a statement, since he'd seen Dinah turn her car upside down.

She thought Tim had been premature in saying that the difficulties Richard had caused were over. Her Austin Seven was a complete write-off and she was taking the bus to work. Richard's Riley was still in the garage, but she felt queasy about using it because he'd died in it. She told herself she was being silly and asked George to get a can of petrol. Tim came round to start the engine for her, and it caught immediately. Tim smiled.

'No problem,' he said.

'There shouldn't be. Richard spent hours tinkering about trying to get the best from it.'

'Come on then, let's take it for a spin.'

'Where to?'

'Anywhere, just to try it. What about going to see Mum?'

Dinah knew why, of course. He didn't want her to put off driving it any longer. Once she'd tried it, he thought she'd be able to banish the ghost. She needed a car in order to do her job efficiently. She was nervous to start with, but once she was used to driving it she found it a much better car than her Austin.

Dinah searched through Richard's study and his office for a will, and when she failed to find one she consulted Arnold Acton, the solicitor retained by the business to look after its legal affairs. He asked her to come to his office. She found him a plump, kindly man with a large paunch crossed by a gold watch chain.

'Richard Haldane? Deceased, you say? May I offer my sympathy,

Mrs Haldane.' He was frowning. 'I've had little to do with him.'

Dinah pushed the documents she'd found in Richard's desk in front of him. 'But the business has been paying you a retainer for legal advice for years.'

'He hasn't required my services for a long time.'

'That's Richard all over,' Dinah told him. 'He liked to do things his own way.'

Mr Acton found his file on the button company. 'It was Mr Haldane senior who set up the retainer. I see I was appointed executor in his will and acted as such in 1920 when he died.'

'It's Richard's will I'm looking for now,' Dinah said. 'I can't find any trace of one amongst his things.'

'I don't appear to have written one for him. Just to make sure, I'll send a clerk to look in our will archives; we keep a great number of them there. And she might as well bring up the deeds of Ardwick House and his factory building. We'll need to arrange for them and his business to be valued. Would you like a cup of coffee while we wait?'

The coffee came and Mr Acton chatted to her about Richard's children until the clerk returned.

'There's no will, sir, but I found deeds to three properties and he owned two businesses.'

'Oh! Did you know that, Mrs Haldane?'

'Would that be Copthorne Ribbons and the Liverpool Button Company?'

Mr Acton was studying the documents. 'No, Copthorne Ribbons was taken over by the Button Company. These deeds are for a property in Longmoor Road, Crosby and the business carried on there, the Olive Grove Tea Rooms. Did you know of this?'

Dinah sat up straighter in her chair. 'Yes, but I didn't know Richard owned it. Gosh!' Richard must have bought it for Olive Jennings!

Mr Acton's finger came up, signalling that he'd remembered something. 'These are the premises that went on fire recently and a woman lost her life.'

'Yes, Rosanna Jennings. I think Richard must have bought the business for her mother, Olive Jennings. He didn't talk about them, so I don't know anything more.'

'Did the fire badly damage the building, d'you know?'

Dinah had driven past when she'd been out seeking further orders for her ribbons. 'Yes, especially the flat upstairs. It's all boarded up.'

'So business can no longer be carried on there. I've read in the papers that the blaze was due to arson, and that gives any insurance company a legal right to refuse to honour the policy.'

'Oh, dear.'

'Yes. Well, I think we must accept that Richard died intestate. A pity – it'll take longer to settle his affairs and means the state decides who benefits. Right, I'll apply for letters of administration on your behalf. There's nothing more I can do until we have those. But you could start by listing what he owned: bank accounts, shares, his cars. Everything.'

'How will his estate be divided?' Dinah asked. 'What decision is the state likely to take?'

'It's fairly complicated, and depends how much he leaves. There're you and two dependent children, you say?'

Dinah nodded. 'And a long-serving nanny who deserves a legacy.'

'Without a will she'll get nothing. Roughly speaking, you'll get half and the other half will be divided between his children.'

'Oh!' Dinah smiled. If Richard had troubled to make a will she doubted she'd have got so much.

'I can help you administer the estate, but you need to think about how you want it done. The best thing for the children is to have their share given in cash and securities, and put into a trust until they're of age. Do you want to keep any part of his estate, his house perhaps? Or would you prefer to see everything sold and have cash too?'

'I'd like to sell the house. It's a creepy place and too big to manage without household help. But his button and ribbon business, I think I'd like to keep that. I know how it's run and it would give us an income. I'll need to provide a home for the children and then there are their school fees.'

'You can charge school fees to their trust fund, once I've set it up, don't worry about that,' Mr Acton said.

He went on to explain that although she could carry on running the business, she could not draw from Richard's personal bank accounts, nor could she sell Ardwick Prince even though Bob Watchit had a purchaser for him.

'In the meantime, will you need money for living expenses?'

'No,' Dinah told him. She worked in the business and was earning enough salary to cover their day-to-day living.

'Count yourself fortunate that you have that, my dear,' he said.

Tim knew he couldn't put it off any longer. The time had come for him to make some big decisions. He'd been letting things drag on for months, but soon it would be Christmas. And the new year was the time for making resolutions and starting new things.

While it was Dinah's way to confide her worries and talk them through, his was to keep quiet and hope they'd go away. He'd known for some time that this one wasn't going to go away.

For as long as he could remember it had been his ambition to ride in the Grand National, and knowing how much it meant to him Digby had promised that he'd give him the chance. It would be a one and only chance, because he was losing his fight to keep his weight down. It wasn't that he was getting fat, far from it, but he was growing taller.

His mother said he'd held his growth in check by not eating what she called proper meals, and that had given him a few more years to learn the skills a jockey needed, but now, like many others, he had to accept that it was impossible to carry on. Although his father had been a jockey, he'd joined the army and been killed at a young age, so nobody knew whether he'd had this problem too. All Tim knew was that he was not one of the few riders naturally tiny enough to stay in the game.

He told himself it wasn't as though he was likely to win the Grand National. Competing in it was one thing, but actually winning? He knew many horses would fall at one or other of the fences and not complete the course.

He'd tell Digby that he'd made up his mind to opt out. He owed him that, and it would make it impossible to backtrack and change his mind.

Tim felt heavy-hearted. He didn't want to give up his morning rides and the pleasure that working with horses gave him.

Later that morning he saw his boss checking equipment in the tack room. He was by himself, so Tim went in to have a word. Digby smiled and said, 'Flyswitch was in top form this morning, wasn't he? I clocked him over the mile at one minute fifty-two.'

Tim was stiff and unusually formal. 'Mr Digby, I think it's time I faced facts. Since the meeting at Beverly I've not won much.'

'You did well there, Tim. The owners were pleased.'

He went on quickly. 'I've had fewer rides since, and those I have had . . . Well, I got nowhere on Saucy Sue the other day. I was half a pound over her weight.'

'Flyswitch can still do it for you,' Digby said. 'I thought you were desperate to have a crack at the Grand National?'

'I was. I know you're willing to let me try because I've had a winning streak with Fly.'

'He responds better to you than to any other jockey.'

'Even so, better for me to give up now while I'm still near the top.'

Tim knew plenty of jockeys who hadn't given up when they should have done. They rode at less important meetings, in less important races, and they won fewer times and earned less. Ill health overtook them because of prolonged dieting, and that meant they lost strength and had more accidents. Tim knew what it felt like to be dehydrated, and Digby had already asked a doctor to prescribe water tablets for him.

'Flyswitch will be an outsider in the National, and with me up he might be carrying more weight than he has to. Anyway, you know it would take a minor miracle to get him past the post first.'

Digby was staring at him. 'You really mean to give up, then?'

Tim groaned. 'I don't want to, but Flyswitch might stand a better chance with Eddie Spellow as his jockey. I won't be much good to you from now on. I think it's time I went.'

'Have you something lined up? Are you going to try your hand at training?'

'You know I can't afford that.'

'What are you going to do, Tim?' Digby's gaze was kindly.

'I don't know. I've nothing on the cards. I'll have to think about it.'

'You don't have to leave straight away, not unless you want to. Stay on for a month or two, teach the new apprentices to ride,' Digby told him. 'Give yourself time.'

On his next day off, Tim went home knowing Dinah would be there. His mother had made a Victoria sponge cake to have with their tea.

'You can cut me another slice of that, Mum,' he told her. 'I'm giving up the horses. I've told Digby.'

He watched his mother's smile broaden. 'You're giving up being a jockey? You've given your notice? Oh, Tim! I'm so glad, truly glad.' Enid was delighted.

Dinah looked as though she didn't believe it. 'You're giving up jockeying? It's been your life blood.'

Enid was cutting him a bigger wedge of cake. 'I'm made up you've seen sense at last. Thrilled to bits that you're giving up before you get maimed.'

'What are you going to do now?' Dinah asked quietly. 'It means a complete change of career, doesn't it?'

Tim knew she'd guessed how much it was costing him to walk away from racing. 'Digby's giving me a couple of months to look round,' he told her.

Dinah had agreed to go to the pictures with him that evening. They went out to the Riley together and he got in the passenger seat. 'I'd love to be able to drive,' he said. 'It seems all wrong for me to be driven round by you. I wish you'd teach me.'

'Of course I will. Everybody should be able to drive.' Her brown eyes were sparkling like stars; he found her enthusiasm attractive. 'D'you want to start now? We've got time before the film starts.'

'Yes please.'

'Right. I know of some waste land where I used to practise,' she said. 'There are roads of a sort.' When they got there, they found the tracks were deeply rutted and unmade. 'At least it's been dry so they aren't muddy.'

He'd been keen to have a go at driving a car for a long time. He sat in the driver's seat while Dinah explained the controls.

'You're used to riding a motorbike,' she said, 'so it's just a matter of getting used to a car.' He thought that was encouraging, though he didn't seem to be doing all that well.

It was getting dark when another learner driver arrived. Dinah said, 'You've made a good start, but you'd learn faster from the man who taught me.'

Tim stopped the car near the hedge, out of the way of other vehicles. 'Driving lessons?' he said. 'I hoped by asking you I'd avoid that expense. I need another job first.'

Dinah slid across the gear lever when she saw him getting out. As he got into the passenger seat she said, 'I can't believe you want to give up being a jockey.'

'The truth is I have no choice. I'm getting too big and heavy.'

She shook her head. 'But horses have been your life.'

'There are more important things than horses.'

'Such as what?'

'People. You.'

That made her spin round to look at him. In the half-light he looked serious. 'Me?'

'Yes. You know how I feel about you.'

'Well, I don't, not really. You were there when I needed you, but so was your mother. I was afraid you felt sorry for me. I know we were friends, but . . .'

His fingers brushed her cheek. 'I love you, Dinah.'

Tears were prickling her eyes, but they were tears of joy. She'd been in an over-emotional state for the last few months. She'd felt unsure of Tim – unsure of everything, come to that.

He was pushing her curtain of dark hair back from her face. 'Dinah, love, what's the matter?' She knew he'd seen her tears. 'Come on.' He took her in his arms and gave her a comforting hug.

'I'm so happy,' she choked. 'I love you too.'

He held her closer.

'What a silly fool I was to get myself mixed up with a man like

Richard when I could have had you. What a mess I've made of my life.'

'That's nearly sorted now. Richard saw to that.'

'You've put up with a lot from me. I turned my back on you but you were my source of strength. I don't think I'd have survived the last six months without you.'

'Course you would. You're a natural survivor. I've been trying to tell you for a long time how much you mean to me.'

'Have you? I know you tried when I'd first met Richard, but I was infatuated by then.'

'Yes.' He smiled, and there was a tenderness about him. 'All Picton Street thought you were making a marriage in a million and you were a very lucky girl. I couldn't compete with that. And even when I knew what Richard was like, well, I couldn't, could I? You were married to him. And after he . . . Well, you'd had a traumatic time. I was afraid it was too soon and you'd shy away from me again.'

'I can't believe you'd want me, not after I've been with him.'

'Dinah, I've never stopped wanting you. That you were married and I couldn't have you only made me want you more.'

His lips found hers, sending shivers of ecstasy down her spine. Richard had not been able to do that for her from the day they were married.

It had gone from dusk to pitch dark without her noticing. 'It's too late to go to the pictures tonight,' she said. 'What about going out for a meal instead? We've never done that, but you can eat now.'

Tim laughed. 'I'm full of cake. I don't think I could do justice to a full meal.'

'Your stomach must have shrunk, you've been under-eating for so long. All right, come home with me. I told Bunty I wouldn't be in for supper so she and Nellie will have had theirs. But I'm hungry. How about poached eggs on toast?'

'That would hit the button,' he said.

Dinah left her car by the front door. 'So I can run you home later,' she told him. There was no light in the kitchen; Bunty and Nellie had already gone upstairs. She ran up to say she was home and had brought Tim with her.

They ate in the kitchen because the Aga made it always cosy. Afterwards, she took their tea to the sitting room but it was decidedly chilly there. Mrs Parr had laid the fire in readiness, but it had not been lit that day.

'It's too late to light it now and too cold to sit in there.' She took him back to the warmth of the Aga, and they pulled two kitchen chairs together and sat half supported against the table with their arms round each other.

'I love you, Tim.' When things had gone wrong, she'd found out who cared about her.

It was gone midnight when he said, 'It's time I went home. Don't you come out again, I'll walk. It'll clear my head.'

'It's too far to walk. It's a long way and it's late.' Dinah thought of all those nights when she'd gone to bed with Richard and tried not to show her true feelings. With Tim, it would be so very different.

'Don't go,' she said. 'Stay with me tonight.'

Tim was used to getting up very early in the morning and he woke up at his usual time. He didn't know where he was at first, and then when he saw Dinah fast asleep beside him with her dark hair spread over the pillow he felt acutely embarrassed.

'Wake up,' he urged. 'Wake up.'

She smiled lazily up at him.

'I should never have stayed,' he said.

'Yes you should.' Dinah's arms went round him. 'I love you.'

'I love you but I've got to go.' He peeled her arms away. 'Mum would have a fit if she found out I'd spent the night with you. She's very strong about things like that. Anyway, I'm expected at work.'

Dinah got out of bed. 'I'll run you home.'

'Thanks. I'll collect my motor bike from the back yard and get straight off.'

'No breakfast?'

'Absolutely no breakfast. No time.' It wasn't yet light.

In the car, he said, 'You'll have to marry me now so I can make an honest woman of you. But you said you would when you were ten.'

'I said it again last night,' Dinah told him. 'Don't you remember asking me?'

'Yes, and I intend to hold you to it this time.'

Dinah flashed him a smile. 'You went to sleep before me, and it gave me time to think. If you're giving up your job with Digby, how d'you feel about a career in ribbon and button making? The factory is expanding, and I'm going to need more help.'

'Gosh!'

'Think about it.'

'I don't need to. Dinah, I'd love that.'

'Good. Next time you're off, we ought to think long and hard about what we're going to do in the future.'

Chapter Thirty-Two

Dinah and Tim spent three evenings talking over their plans and decided that Tim should start work at the Liverpool Button Company as soon as it re-opened in the New Year. Dinah took him in to see the factory and meet the staff. She asked Mr Hopper to teach him all he could about the business, just as he'd taught her.

'I'm glad you'll have somebody to help you,' Mr Hopper said. 'I'm sixty-seven, well over retirement age, you know. I won't be able to go on much longer.'

'Don't go yet, please,' Dinah implored him.

'It'll take me at least six months if not a year to get a grasp on all this,' Tim told him. 'It all looks very different from what I'm used to.'

'The way things are going,' Dinah said, 'there'll be plenty of work for both of you.'

She took Tim into her office and said, 'I'm going to order a new desk for you, and if I push mine a bit further that way, there'll be room to put it there.'

'I'm going to share the boss's office?'

'Tim, I'm out a lot of the time. I'm going to need you to run this place when I'm not here.'

'You're giving me a real opportunity, d'you know? I was afraid I'd be going back behind the counter in a newsagent's.'

Dinah knew Enid understood how things were between her and Tim when she said, 'You shouldn't let him stay overnight with you. It's dangerous, Dinah. What if you started another baby?'

'I'm wiser now about such things,' she said.

'Your mother would shoot him if she knew. Probably shoot me, too.

She made me promise to look after you. I've talked to Tim, but all he says is you're going to get married.'

'We are.'

'Then I'd love to help you arrange things. Fairly soon and in church, don't you think? Would you want a big show?'

'No,' Dinah said. 'A quiet wedding. But not so quiet as last time. I'd like to invite all our friends.'

Christmas came and Dinah kept open house. She invited not only Tim and Enid but several other neighbours from Picton Street. Some of the girls from Carlton Hats came as well as Mr Hopper and his wife, and Miss O'Marney. Dinah was generous to Nellie and Mark and she thought they all enjoyed it.

'Best Christmas ever,' Mark told her. He seemed a normal healthy lad and said he was happy at boarding school. The only problem for Dinah was that both his school fees and Nellie's were due. Mr Acton suggested she borrow money from the business to pay them. 'We can straighten everything out once Richard's estate is settled,' he said.

St Agnes's church served the Picton Street community and Enid booked it with the vicar for their wedding, together with the church hall next door for their reception.

'I didn't have to ask Mum twice,' Tim said to Dinah. 'She thinks the sooner the better.' Dinah was seeing much more of Tim, both at Ardwick House and in the factory. He was learning the ins and outs of the button trade quickly and becoming enthusiastic about it. He seemed to get on with everybody. Even Nellie and Bunty had taken to him.

Dinah was enjoying life again and finding it much easier, but Richard's inquest hung over her like a black cloud and she knew she wouldn't be completely free of him until it had been held.

A new date in the middle of February was fixed for the inquest. Dinah was keen to get it over and done with.

'I'll take you,' Tim told her. 'We'll go together.' They found that a connection with the death of Rosanna Jennings was officially assumed and both inquests would be held on the same day in St George's Hall. Rosanna's was scheduled first.

'I want to know what's said at Rosanna's inquest,' Dinah told Tim.

'So will half Liverpool,' he said.

More details of the Olive Grove Tea Rooms case were leaking out and articles were appearing in the national papers. Dinah cringed as she read them. Bunty's curiosity had been whipped up like many others', and she wanted to be there too.

When the day came, Dinah and Bunty dropped Nellie at school before going to Walton to collect Enid and Tim. They reached St George's Hall in plenty of time and were surprised at the number of people who were coming in.

Dinah had no trouble picking out Olive Jennings. She'd lost weight since she'd last seen her and was wearing deepest mourning, with a thick black veil hiding her face. She kept pushing a white handkerchief up behind it and was obviously distressed. Dinah felt sorry for her.

Arnold Acton nodded a greeting to Dinah across the court. He was talking to a group of other men she took to be more solicitors. The coroner started promptly, telling them they were here to inquire into the circumstances of Rosanna Jennings's death.

'She was the adult daughter of Olive Jennings, who is the proprietor of the Olive Grove Tea Rooms in Crosby. Neither was married and they lived together on the premises in a flat above the tea shop.

'On the evening of Sunday the fourth of November, the flat caught fire, and two fire engines from the Crosby fire station attended.'

A uniformed fire officer was called to give evidence and asked to give the cause of the fire.

'Arson,' he said. 'No doubt about that.' A stunned ripple ran round the court. Dinah heard Tim's soft gasp at the word.

The fire officer cleared his throat and told them the blaze had been started in three different places.

'Burning coals had been removed from the grate and scattered over the seats of two fireside chairs. A paraffin heater had been turned over and the fuel spilled on the carpet. The room was well alight when we arrived on the scene.'

Dinah remembered the acrid smell of burning on Richard's clothes that night and felt ready to faint with horror. First murder, now arson –

with Richard she always had to consider the most awful acts.

Tim felt for her hand and whispered. 'For goodness' sake! Was there no limit to what Richard would do? This is horrific.'

Mrs Jennings was called to the stand. The clerk of the court said, 'On that evening you had a visitor. Please tell us about him.'

'It was Richard Haldane.'

'Richard Cameron Aldgrave Haldane of Ardwick House, Woolton,' he repeated. 'And what is your relationship to him?'

'He set me up in the business some twelve years ago.'

'I'm having difficulty hearing you, Mrs Jennings,' the coroner said. 'Could I ask you please to speak up, and if you wouldn't mind to lift your veil as well.'

With one sweep of her hand she tossed it defiantly back. Dinah was shocked at the change in her. Her eyes were red and puffy, but they showed determination. Her mouth was twisting with the same need for revenge against Richard that Dinah had seen in Ivy Cummins.

'Tell us, if you will, how long you have known him and the circumstances of your original meeting.'

'Yes.' She hesitated a moment. 'I first met him about fifteen years ago when I got a job as a machine operator with the Liverpool Button Company, a manufacturing business he owned. He pursued me, begging for sexual favours. He wouldn't leave me alone.'

Dinah shuddered. She could certainly believe that.

'Mr Haldane was a married man, wasn't he? You were not married, but you had a daughter. Rosanna was five years of age at that time. He made you his mistress and bought the tea rooms to provide a home and an income for you both. He visited you often and you were on good terms with him and continued as his mistress. He watched your daughter Rosanna grow up. Tell us what happened then, Mrs Jennings.'

There was a long pause. Mrs Jennings blew her nose and mopped at her face. 'When Rosanna was about eighteen, Richard started paying her attention.'

'Sexual attention, you mean? Instead of you?'

'Both of us. I didn't like it and took him to task. He promised to stop but he didn't.'

'What did Rosanna think of this?'

'She was in love with him and thought he loved her.'

Dinah covered her face with her hands. Hadn't she been in exactly the same position?

'I complained to him again and he tried to persuade me that he was in love with her. He said he wanted to marry her. She wanted it too, so I agreed. We thought he was a rich man.'

'But he was not free to marry her at that point, was he?'

'His wife was poorly. He said he didn't think she'd last much longer, and she didn't.' Dinah heard several gasps of horror from the body of the court that any man could be so heartless.

Mrs Jennings went on, 'When Myra Haldane died in December 1933, I pressed him to marry Rosanna as he'd promised.'

'But he wouldn't?'

'He always had some reason why it had to be put off for another month or so. But he continued to call on us wanting meals and sexual favours at all hours, and about that time we discovered he'd frittered away his fortune. He said his business wasn't making money in the Depression and he asked me for money. He said we were now earning enough from the café to start repaying him, although he'd never mentioned any need for us to repay him up till then.'

'Did you give him money, Mrs Jennings?'

'I refused, but he went straight down to the till and emptied it. I had to give him money when he asked for it.'

Dinah could feel her anger boiling up. He was taking money from them as well as from her.

'Then Rosanna found she was with child and begged him to keep his promise. He told her he would and talked about it as though it would happen soon, but the weeks went on and it didn't. Things were strained between us by this time, but I didn't say too much because I still hoped he'd marry Rosanna.'

'And at this time, were you still his mistress, Mrs Jennings?'

'No. That had ended when I agreed he should marry Rosanna.'

'But he kept coming round to the Olive Grove to see her? She had taken your place in his affections?'

'Yes.' Her voice was stony. 'Then we heard he'd remarried without telling us. We talked it over a lot, Rosanna and I, but we didn't know whether it was true or not.'

There was a longish pause while she mopped at her face, until the solicitor prompted her. 'What did you do then, Mrs Jennings?'

'I telephoned his business and asked to speak to Mrs Haldane, because I knew his first wife had worked there. I was hoping to be told she had died.' Her voice shook. 'But the woman told me Mrs Haldane was out at that moment but was expected back within the hour. She asked me to leave my name and phone number so Mrs Haldane could ring me back. I put the phone down when I knew it was true that he had remarried.'

'And what did Rosanna think of that?'

'I couldn't bring myself to tell her. She was upset enough as it was. I was waiting for a better time to break it to her but it never came.'

Dinah felt for Tim's hand. She could imagine Mrs Jennings's agony.

'Let us now return to the evening of November the fourth last year. Tell us in your own words what happened.'

Haltingly, with many pauses to mop at her eyes, she told them that Richard Haldane had arrived between six and seven o'clock that evening. 'He asked for dinner but I told him I had nothing ready. The café doesn't open for business on Sundays; it caters mainly for people working in the surrounding offices. I and my daughter had spent the day cleaning and cooking. On Sundays we cook meats, bake, and prepare food to be eaten in the café in the following week.

'Rosanna was fretting. She wanted to take him up to the flat on her own and pin him down to a date. She still thought . . . hoped it would be possible. I couldn't leave my baking at that point so Rosanna made a pot of tea and they went upstairs.

'I didn't leave them for long. I was up and down the stairs, trying to keep up with what was going on. He was trying to persuade her that it would be quite all right to leave things as they were and he would look after her. Well, I'd been in that position myself and knew exactly what Rosanna could expect.

'Then I had to go down to the kitchen as my farmhouse fruit cakes were due to come out of the oven. I make six each week, and some were ready but some needed a few minutes more. I was busying myself with the boiled hams when I heard them shouting. I ran up again to find Rosanna in tears. He'd told her that he couldn't marry her because he had married someone else. "Stop fussing about it," he was shouting. "I can't marry you, and that's the top and bottom of it."'

Dinah felt for them. She understood Richard's ways only too well.

Mrs Jennings went on, 'It was a terrible way to treat a young girl and I told him so. But I'd half expected something like this and had had time to think of an alternative to marriage for Rosanna.

'I wanted him to take us to a solicitor and make over the business and the shop premises to her. I told her she must insist on it. Everything was in his name, but we had taken over the café twelve years ago when it only opened for afternoon teas. We've more than doubled the turnover by our hard work and by opening for morning coffee and lunches as well. I didn't trust him; I wanted what I'd built up to be in my own name. Well, mine or Rosanna's.

'He seemed to be agreeing to my plan when I had to go downstairs again and see to the roast pork. We serve it cold in the café but on Sunday nights I do a few vegetables and cut off a few slices while it's hot for our dinner. All had gone quiet upstairs so I thought things had settled down.

'Then Richard Haldane came down, seeming very much on edge. "You smell of smoke," I told him, and he said the chimney was smoking and he'd been making up the fire for Rosanna. She was tired and wanted to rest.

'He turned to leave and I said, "Aren't you staying to have dinner with us?" But he said no, he'd go to the Blossoms, an hotel near the river which he liked. I was determined to get something out of him for Rosanna and her baby and he said he'd make the arrangements. He was very restless and seemed glad to escape. I suppose I spent another fifteen or twenty minutes making the meal and tidying up the kitchen.

'Then the smell of smoke seemed stronger and I ran up to the flat. When I opened the door I found the living room ablaze. The extra air made the flames leap higher, and the place was full of smoke. I shouted to Rosanna but all I could hear was the crackle of the flames. Then I saw her lying on the sofa. The smoke was making me cough and choke and I thought she'd been overcome by it. I dragged her out and across the landing and almost fell downstairs with her. I got on my feet to go to the telephone on the shop counter but I could see my neighbour hammering on the door. I unlocked it and let him in, and he told me he'd already phoned for a fire engine. When he saw Rosanna, he picked up the phone and called for an ambulance for her.

'Together we carried her out to the street, and that's when we noticed she had a silk stocking tied tight round her neck.'

'It was her own stocking, wasn't it, Mrs Jennings?'

'Yes. She'd washed out two pairs in the bathroom and hung them there to dry.'

'Thank you, Mrs Jennings, you can step down now.'

She said with a sudden burst of anger, 'He killed her. He strangled her and started a fire in the room to cover it up, and then he kept me talking downstairs to give it time to catch hold.'

'You have my sympathy, Mrs Jennings. Take your time, but please leave the stand. I now want to ask Mr Hubert McArthur, a forensic pathologist, to give his evidence.'

Dinah's heart bled for Olive Jennings.

Mr McArthur held himself erect as befitted a man asked by a court to give his professional opinion. He spoke slowly and clearly. 'At the time of her death, Rosanna Jennings was a healthy young woman of twenty years. I found her to be about fourteen weeks pregnant. The fire did not cause Rosanna's death. There was no trace of smoke in her lungs. She had stopped breathing before the fire had been lit.'

The atmosphere in the court room was electrifying. He stood down in complete silence.

George Weeks was called to the stand. He told them that he was employed by Mr Haldane as a gardener, and that Mr Haldane had given him a pillowcase stuffed with his own clothes and told him to put it out for the bin men to take away. He'd examined the clothes, which were almost new, and decided to keep them himself. Mr Haldane was much taller than he was and his wife had been able to turn up the cuffs so the burns didn't show very much. He'd handed them over to the police when he'd heard about the fire.

Then the coroner told them gravely that the only possible verdict was deliberate murder.

'The evidence, as we've heard, points to the late Mr Richard Haldane as the person responsible. Court will now break for lunch and will resume at two o'clock to examine the circumstances of Mr Haldane's death.'

They all streamed out feeling shocked by Olive Jennings's evidence.

'That was horrific.' Bunty winced. 'I knew Richard was evil, but that . . .'

'Truly wicked, what he did,' Enid agreed.

'If I'd realised just how dangerous he was, I would have done anything to take you away from him.' Tim shuddered. 'What risks you took.'

It had snowed slightly earlier in the morning and it was now turning to muddy slush under the wheels of the traffic. The air was bitingly cold. Dinah was taking great gulps of it into her lungs.

'Now I know what occupied the other half of Richard's life,' she breathed. She still felt half dazed by it. 'If I'd known what he was capable of I'd have been terrified. Just hearing about it brought me out in a cold sweat.'

Tim took her hand. 'We'd better have something to eat.'

'There's the buffet in Lime Street Station,' Enid said. 'We've only got an hour and that's the nearest, just across the road.'

He hesitated. 'We could get a hot meal in the Kardomah café.'

'I've got a stew for us for tonight,' Bunty told him. 'All we need is a snack to put us on.'

They went to the station buffet. Dinah didn't feel she could eat anything, but she asked for a cup of tea and a cheese roll. She'd last seen pretty Rosanna Jennings whisking between the café tables, and she couldn't get over the fact that she'd been murdered by the man they'd both once thought they were in love with.

She still didn't feel herself when they all returned to St George's Hall.

Mr Acton was waiting for her and drew her aside for a quiet word on her own. Mostly it was about Richard's estate.

'No need to be nervous here, Mrs Haldane,' he told her. 'When you're called to give evidence just take your time and recount the facts as they happened.'

Richard's inquest opened. Dinah shivered as facts were read out about his business and about his marriages that were only too familiar.

Ivy Cummins was the first to be called to the stand to answer questions about his past life. She made as much of the facts surrounding the deaths of his parents and parents-in-law as she could.

Dinah was called next. She was nervous as she made her way to the stand and almost tripped. Mr Acton smiled encouragingly as she gave her name and was asked about her relationship to Richard, and how long she'd been his wife.

'I'd like you to think back to the night of the fourth of November and describe what happened when your husband came home.'

'It was two o'clock in the morning.' Dinah found herself floundering as she told of how he'd smelled of burning and had taken a bath. 'He washed his hair too and came to bed with it still damp.' She described his frame of mind as agitated and excitable.

'The next morning, Mrs Haldane. Tell us in your own words what happened when you tried to drive your car.'

Dinah had recounted the tale many times. First at the hospital and then several times over to different police officers; she'd gone through it again to her colleagues at the factory and her friends, so many times that the recollection no longer made her shiver. She talked of her injuries and Nellie's injuries and the panic she'd felt when she realised she couldn't stop the car.

'And I lost my baby,' she said. 'I was twenty weeks pregnant at the time.'

She wasn't asked about the worry and confusion she'd felt afterwards, not knowing whether the police had proof that Richard had tampered with the brakes or even where he was or what he was doing. It had been a very bad time.

She was glad to stand down and let George Weeks take her place. She heard him say that he'd witnessed her accident and had called both an ambulance and the police. He'd been told by them not to go near the crash site.

'Did you see your employer again that day?' he was asked.

'Yes. It was a wet morning so I was working in the greenhouse, though there wasn't much needing to be done there. He came home by the back gate within an hour or so of the accident. A policeman had remained on the premises; I saw Mr Haldane go down to talk to him and view the wreckage. He came back and told me I might as well go home as it was too wet to work outside.'

Then it was Tim's turn to describe how he'd found Richard's body. A forensic doctor was called, who told them that although no note of intention had been found, the cause of death was self-administered carbon monoxide poisoning.

The coroner summed up by reminding the court of Richard Haldane's connection to the subject of the previous inquest, Rosanna Jennings. 'Having killed her,' he went on, 'we must assume that he tampered with the brakes on his wife's car in an attempt on her life, and that of his daughter Fenella Haldane, who was eight years old at the time. His actions resulted in the death of his unborn child.

'I would hope that Mr Haldane repented of his murderous acts and that his purpose in taking his own life was not just to avoid the retribution that would undoubtedly have followed if he were still alive.'

His verdict was suicide.

Dinah drove home because she was the only one who could, but she hardly felt in control of the car. Her head was swimming, she'd been sitting still with her muscles clenched for hours and now she felt stiff all over.

'It's over now,' Tim comforted her. 'We can all forget Richard.'

Enid was in a hurry to get home: she had a pupil coming for a piano lesson. Bunty was in a hurry too. She had a meal to prepare and she didn't want Nellie to come home from school to an empty house.

The winter's dusk was drawing in as Dinah drove through the gates of Ardwick House. Nellie had reached the top of the drive and turned to wave when she heard the car. Dinah hooted as she passed her and drove the last thirty yards to the kitchen door to drop Bunty. Nellie was running after them, her yellow hair bouncing, her school velour squashed under her arm. Dinah went on to the garage and Tim got out to open the doors for her. When she got out of the car he put an arm round her waist and pulled her close.

'Come on, you'll feel better once you're indoors.' His breath felt warm against her cheek. They ran together to the kitchen door. Dinah felt the warmth wrap itself round her. Bunty was pouring water into the teapot and Nellie was getting out biscuits.

Dinah began to relax once she had a cup of hot tea in her hand. 'Guess what Mr Acton told me? He's advertised this house for sale and a property developer wants to buy it.'

'Is it going to be knocked down?' Bunty asked.

'Yes. It seems the garden is a very good shape to put a road down the middle and build a row of smaller houses on each side. It's very good news because the developer will give us a good price for it.'

'But where will we live?' Nellie wanted to know.

'We'll have a good look round and find somewhere nice. Not too far from here because you'll want to stay at your school.'

'A smaller house?'

'A more convenient house. I'd like no more than two floors.'

'So would I,' Bunty said feelingly.

'I'd like a modern house with central heating,' Dinah said. 'And we'll need at least four bedrooms.'

'Will you be able to run to that?' Bunty asked.

'Probably not, but we'll be able to get a mortgage,' Tim said.

Dinah sighed. 'I felt so sorry for Olive Jennings,' she told them. 'She suffered more at Richard's hands than I did. She lost her daughter, her home and her livelihood. So I asked Mr Acton to arrange to have the deeds of the Olive Grove made over to her, as well as a thousand pounds from my share. It might be possible for her to have the place repaired and be able to carry on her business again. It seemed the least I could do.'

'What did he say?' Tim asked.

'That I was very generous and that he'd do that.'

Two weeks later, while Dinah was at work, Arnold Acton telephoned her and said that Richard's estate had been settled and all that remained for him to do was to distribute the funds.

'The sale of the house and of Ardwick Beauty are going through now, and I contacted Mrs Jennings. She was almost overwhelmed by your generosity and will be writing to thank you.'

'You're a rich widow now,' Bunty said. 'You deserve to be after what you've gone through.'

'She'll be a wife again before very long,' Tim said.

CHAPTER THIRTY-THREE

Early March 1935

DINAH WAS FEELING heady with anticipation as she changed into her new floaty dress of apricot silk and pinned the tiny Carlton Hat of net and flowers on her head.

'You look gorgeous,' Tim told her.

'You look pretty good yourself,' Dinah told him. He was now two inches taller than she was, and with his broader shoulders he carried his new grey suit well. He'd even had his brown hair neatly trimmed for this special occasion.

It was mid-afternoon and they were to be married in St Agnes's church at four o'clock. Both had attended services and Sunday school there as children.

Dinah had changed her mind about having a quiet wedding. She'd told Mr Hopper to close the factory early and invited all the workers to the ceremony and the reception that was to follow. In addition, her friends from Carlton Hats and Tim's friends from the racing world were all coming.

Nellie's eyes were sparkling. She was to be the only bridesmaid and was wearing a frilly dress just one shade paler than Dinah's. Mark was home for his Easter holidays, and as Tim had passed the new voluntary driving test he drove him and Bunty to the church first and then returned for Dinah and Nellie.

When they arrived at the church they found all Picton Street had turned out to see them tie the knot. Once inside, Dinah was touched by the solemnity of the occasion and suddenly found herself struggling with a tide of emotion. This time she was making a real marriage. She concentrated hard on the ceremony. This time she meant to savour it all.

Tim took her hand and said, 'I Timothy take thee Dinah to my wedded wife, to have and to hold from this day forward . . . to love and to cherish till death us do part.'

She met his gaze and could see he was feeling emotional too, but knew without a doubt it was a promise he would keep.

They signed the register. As they moved slowly down the aisle together Dinah felt wrapped up in the love and good wishes of the congregation. They walked across to the church hall with their friends streaming behind them. Everybody was in high spirits. A magnificent buffet meal was set out and a dance band had been hired for later in the evening. Mark danced with his little sister and both seemed happy at last. There was a real party atmosphere and it roared on until after midnight when Tim drove Dinah home to bed.

They were very late getting up the next morning for the egg and bacon breakfast Bunty cooked for them. They had decided not to go away just yet; they would take a holiday in the summer. Tim wanted to find his feet at work first, and Dinah needed time to look round for a house that would suit them all. Furthermore, today was Grand National day and neither of them wanted to miss that.

Even as early as this Dinah could feel a tingle of anticipation and knew Tim could too. It was the biggest day in the racing calendar not only for Liverpudlian racegoers, but for all England. Tim went out into the garden; he was taking an unusual interest in the weather.

'It's fine with a light wind, but cool,' he said with satisfaction. 'Just what the horses need. They'll be in a frenzy of nerves at Rivington Lodge this morning.'

'Are you missing it, Tim?'

'I'm not racing so my nerves are steady, and we're going to have all the fun of being there and seeing it, aren't we?'

By way of a wedding present, Llewellyn Digby had invited them to be his guests for the day. As arranged, he came to collect them in his car. For the first time ever, Digby had a horse entered for the big race and seemed almost intoxicated with enthusiasm and hope. 'If Flyswitch can do it, I'll ask nothing more in this life,' he told them.

At the entrance to the course, the flags were fluttering in the breeze on their poles and the biggest crowd that Aintree had ever seen was pouring in. Dinah could feel the tension in the air. They headed straight to the stable to see how the horses had coped with the short journey.

'Fine,' they were assured. As the stable star, Flyswitch had his own horse box and his groom travelled with him. He hadn't forgotten Tim and nuzzled at his pocket for a sugar lump. Tim went round greeting the other horses from the stable who would run in the earlier races. They all remembered him and so did the grooms and stable boys, who made much of him. He had a chat with Eddie Spellow, who had a ride on Pomeroy today as well as the big one on Flyswitch.

Digby took them to the bar for a glass of champagne and then to have a lobster lunch in the restaurant reserved for owners and trainers. It was familiar ground to Dinah but Tim laughed and said, 'I'd heard there was luxury up here, but though I came lots of times I saw nothing but the stables and the weighing room.'

'And the winning post,' Digby said. He left them then, as he wanted to talk to the owners of the horses he trained. Dinah knew her way around, and they placed bets on Flyswitch and on Pomeroy, Dido and Saucy Sue, who were to run in the earlier races. They viewed the fences; seeing them close to, Dinah thought they seemed impossibly high and felt a shiver of anxiety for the horses.

The wireless was broadcasting news of the course, listing the horses and their form. Flyswitch was not much fancied.

'An outsider can win this,' Tim assured her. 'And sometimes does.'

All the attention was on the famous and more experienced horses and jockeys. Golden Miller had won last year and was hot favourite to win again.

Digby had provided them with excellent seats. The afternoon sped by. They shouted encouragement to Pomeroy and were ecstatic when he won easily. Saucy Sue came third in her race and they visited the winners' enclosure to add their congratulations. As the time for the Grand National drew closer, Dinah could feel the tension mounting in the crowd. They went to the paddock to see the horses being mounted and Tim had a few words of encouragement for Flyswitch and Eddie Spellow.

Dinah was afraid he was hankering for Eddie's chance to win. 'It could have been you up on Flyswitch's back now,' she said. 'I know how much you've given up, and how much it meant to you.'

'I've been very lucky.' Tim shook his head and smiled. 'I really enjoyed my time as a jockey but I've got so much to replace it. I've got you and what looks like being a rosy future.'

They had to push through the crowd to get back to their seats so as not to miss the start of the National. They barely made it before the horses were off. Digby was already there waving his racecard and telling them he was having a punt on Golden Miller. All round them the crowd was going mad.

A broadcast commentary was being relayed through the stadium so the crowd could follow the race even when the horses were not in view. Dinah was watching and listening for any mention of Flyswitch. She thought Tim was holding his breath. Golden Miller had started well and was leading the field, the crowd cheering him on, but after successfully clearing Valentine's he raced up to the next fence and at the last moment refused to jump. Dinah watched with horror as the jockey was tossed over his head. The crowd howled with anguish, but Digby bounced in his seat with pleasure.

'Why?' Dinah asked him. 'You've lost your bet.'

'The strongest competitor is out of the running. Come on, Flyswitch,' Digby shouted. 'Come on.'

The horses were starting on the second circuit of the course, and they could see Flyswitch trapped in the middle of the leading group, against the rail with no way forward.

'Come on, Eddie,' Tim said between his teeth, 'you've got to get out of there.'

At every fence horses were falling and Dinah's heart was in her mouth until she saw or heard mention of Flyswitch again. A horse by the name of Reynoldstown was being mentioned more and more. He was leading the group when they went out of view, but they knew he was maintaining his lead. The crowd were screaming for him. Reynoldstown passed the post first. He was said to have run a faultless race. Flyswitch didn't get a place.

'Never mind.' Digby was philosophical. 'At least he finished the course.'

Tim's cheeks were scarlet. 'Perhaps he'll win next year. He's got a rosy future in front of him.'

Dinah felt exhilarated, on top of the world. Tim was looking at her with love in his eyes. 'Like us,' she smiled.